THE PERK

The Perk

Mark Gimenez

sphere

SPHERE

First published in Great Britain in 2008 by Sphere

Copyright © Mark Gimenez 2008

The moral right of the author has been asserted.

A CIP catalogue record for this book
is available from the British Library.

Hardback ISBN 978-1-84744-071-6
C Format ISBN 978-1-84744-070-9

Typeset in Bembo by Hewer Text UK Ltd, Edinburgh
Printed and bound in Great Britain by Clays Ltd, St Ives plc

Sphere
An imprint of
Little, Brown Book Group
100 Victoria Embankment
London EC4Y 0DY

An Hachette Livre UK Company

www.littlebrown.co.uk

For Sandra Trujillo-Garcia,
who fought for all her students every day.

Acknowledgements

Special thanks to:

In London: David Shelley for his brilliant editing, Sean Garrehy for another fantastic cover, and everyone else at Sphere/Little Brown for another terrific publishing job.

In New York: Larry Kirshbaum and Susanna Einstein at LJK Literary Management.

In Dallas: Archana Ganaraj, M.D., a skilled and compassionate breast cancer surgeon, Barbara Hautanen for the Spanish translations, and Clay Gimenez for his research.

In Fredericksburg: To all my friends there, who spoke so openly about their lives and their town – you know who you are and you know why I'm not mentioning you by name. It's a small town.

Justice?—You get justice in the next world, in this world you have the law.

From *A Frolic of His Own* by William Gaddis

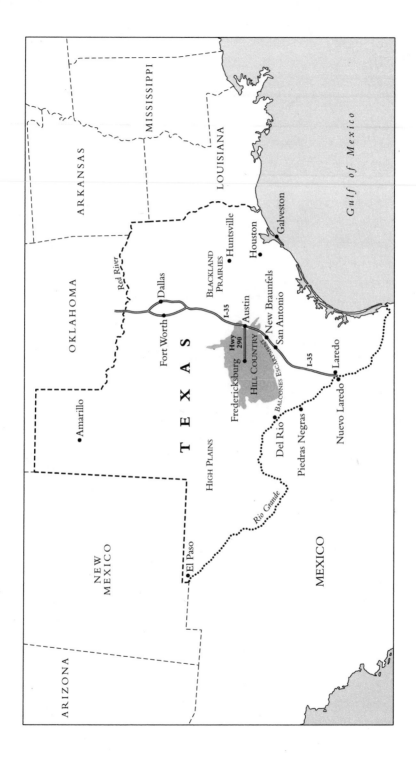

Prologue

She was posing outside the limo with a dozen other girls, like illegal Mexicans waiting for work on L.A. street corners.

Sixth Street was packed with perks.

He had come back to Texas for the Austin Film Festival—okay, it's not exactly Cannes or even Sundance, but there were always plenty of gorgeous Texas girls willing to play groupie-for-a-day to a famous movie star. Jesus, they came out of the woodwork, especially in a college town like Austin, incredibly beautiful coeds thinking that if they laid a movie star they might become a star, too.

Of course, all they become is laid.

But he viewed groupies the same way he viewed private jets, personal trainers, Swedish masseuses, and chauffeured limousines like the one he was riding in tonight: perks of the trade. He was twenty-nine, he was remarkably handsome, and his last film had grossed $250 million domestic. He got a lot of perks.

And he had just spotted his next one—blonde, beautiful, and built like a Playmate.

It was New Year's Eve and she was wearing a white blouse so sheer a blind man could see she wasn't wearing a bra, a butt-hugging black miniskirt, and black stiletto heels; she was swinging a little black purse like a hypnotist swinging a pocket watch in front of her subject—and he was mesmerized by her. He lowered the blacked-out window and pointed at her like he was picking out a prime cut at the meat market. She damn near dove into the limo through the open window.

It was that easy.

He snorted another line of the white powder and chased it with a shot of whiskey while she settled back into the plush leather seat across from him and looked around the limo like a kid at Disneyland. You couldn't slap the smile off her face. She said, "I always wanted to ride in a limo."

"Honey, you're gonna get to do more than just ride."

She said, "I'm Heidi Fay," as if he would actually remember her name tomorrow. "I'm gonna be a big star one day."

"Sure you are, sweetie. You go to UT?"

"Uh, yeah."

He patted the seat next to him and she bounced over. He dove into her breasts and slid his hand up her smooth inner thigh until he touched a bit of heaven on earth. She scooted away from his hand and said, "Can I have something to drink?"

Playing hard to get, was she? Well, he had the cure for that. He removed his hand from under her skirt and raised up; she was holding out a cell phone.

"No one will believe this is happening to me."

The thought that she had just taken his photo never entered his intoxicated mind because his brain's diminished capacity could focus on only one thing now.

"Oh, it's about to happen to you, honey."

He turned to the bar and retrieved the whiskey bottle. He turned back and saw she was still fiddling with her cell phone.

"You don't want to call anyone."

He took the phone out of her hand and tossed it onto the seat across from them. Then he filled the shot glass and held it out to her. She said, "I mean, like Coke."

"Darlin', you don't drink my kind of coke. Bottoms up."

She downed the whiskey and almost gagged. He refilled her glass, twice to make sure. Then he lined out some more cocaine on the little mirror and held the straw out to her.

"Oh, I don't do drugs," she said.

He thought, *Yeah, and you're a virgin, too.* He said, "Then you don't really want to be a star, do you?" He gestured outside with the straw. "Maybe I'll make one of those girls a star."

She stared out the window like a kid leaving home for the first time, then took a deep breath and the straw, bent over, and snorted the coke. She straightened up and sneezed. Twice. Hell, maybe she really was a first-timer. Maybe she was a virgin. That got him more excited, so he nudged her head down for two more long lines. When she came back up, her blue eyes were so dilated they looked black. He unbuttoned her blouse without objection—now that was more like it—and buried his face in her soft breasts. He leaned into her, and they fell back onto the seat. He reached up her skirt and pulled her thong down, then unzipped himself and pushed into her.

He lasted almost a full minute.

He pushed himself off her and drank whiskey from the bottle. She struggled up, fell onto the floorboard, then crawled onto the seat across from him. She worked herself into a sitting position.

She was a sight: her blouse hanging open and her bare breasts staring back at him like twin sisters, her skirt up around her waist like a tutu, and her black lace thong wrapped around her ankle. But she still smiled pretty-please and said in a slurred speech, "Can you get me an audition in Hollywood?"

They all asked the same question. But before he could give her his stock reply—"Honey, that *was* your audition"—her eyes rolled back in her head and she fell over like a stunt girl acting as if she'd been shot dead.

"Aw, shit."

He looked at her lying there passed out and shook his head. *What the hell was he going to do with her now?* He couldn't just

3

open the door and roll her out onto the Sixth Street sidewalk crowded with agents, writers, managers, groupies, panhandlers, drunk college kids, and cops. And he couldn't very well throw an unconscious coed over his shoulder and haul her right through the front door of the five-star Driskill Hotel in downtown Austin, waving at fans and walking through a gauntlet of paparazzi on the way up to the Cattle Baron's Suite—that wouldn't sit well with the studio brass, not to mention his pregnant wife. And he couldn't just leave her to sleep it off; what if the cops found her in his limo? That would make *Entertainment Tonight* for sure. And besides, he needed the limo, much like a professional bass fisherman needed his lures: the night was young and the fish were biting.

He'd take her home. That's what he'd do. He *could* haul her right into her apartment without fanfare or embarrassing photos. College coed, he figured she lived near the UT campus. So he grabbed her purse and searched inside for her student ID. He found it, stared at it, shook his head to clear his vision, and stared at it again. He felt as if some part of him had died.

Heidi wasn't a college coed. Her student ID wasn't from the University of Texas. She wasn't twenty-one or twenty or even nineteen. Heidi Fay wasn't her real name—it was Heidi Fay Geisel. *And Heidi Fay Geisel was a fucking sixteen-year-old high school junior!*

He then did what he always did in stressful personal situations: he freaked. So he snorted another line and downed another shot, which calmed him down and allowed his mind to work. Sort of. And he came up with a plan. The same plan.

They would take Heidi home.

But she didn't live in Austin. So he climbed over her and crawled up front and handed her ID to Rudy, who consulted the map in the limo's glove compartment and located her home-town—some burg seventy miles west of Austin. Thirty minutes later, they were carefully driving the speed limit down a dark highway so as not to get pulled over by some Barney Fife looking for his fifteen minutes of fame: PODUNK COUNTY SHERIFF ARRESTS MOVIE STAR WITH UNDER-AGE GIRL IN LIMO.

I don't think so.

He called up to Rudy for the fifth time: "We there yet? How much longer?" Rudy just shook his shaved head and shrugged his broad shoulders. Rudy Jaramillo had been his driver and bodyguard since *A Hard Night*, his first $100-million-gross film. Driver/bodyguards were perks of the trade, too.

It was now past midnight, and it had started to rain. Flashes of distant lightning illuminated the night sky outside and the nearly naked Heidi inside. She had a great body . . . an unconscious great body . . . a sixteen-year-old body.

Shit.

He gazed out at the dark Texas landscape and sighed. The night was ruined and he was bored, a condition he could not tolerate for any extended period of time. So he pulled out his cell phone and was surprised to get a signal. He dialed his manager back in L.A.; it was two hours earlier out west, not that he hadn't called Billy at three A.M. when the urge hit him. Billy answered on the third ring.

"How's Texas, my boy?"

Billy always called him "my boy," which sort of pissed him off. He said, "Playing cowboy for the local yokels."

"And you're so good at it."

"I'm an actor, Billy." He took a deep breath and then said, "What's the word?"

Billy sighed into the phone. "Clooney."

His blood pressure spiked. "*Clooney?* Are you shittin' me? He's what, forty-fucking-years old?"

"Actually, forty-two."

"*Forty-two?* That's way too old to be the sexiest man alive! I'm the sexiest man alive!"

"Yes, of course you are, my boy. You are indeed. Absolutely! It's just not fair. Not fair at all."

He immediately decided it was his manager's fault; Clooney had a better manager—that's why he had won! So when he returned to L.A. he would fire Billy and hire a better manager. Maybe Clooney's manager. At least a manager who didn't call him "my boy."

After his blood pressure had returned to normal, his attention returned to the phone at his ear; his soon-to-be-ex-manager had launched into a long discourse about the unfairness of it all, like the judging at the Olympic figure skating competition— *the figure skating competition?*—but he was already thinking of names of potential new managers.

When Billy finished, he disconnected then called his pregnant wife to find out how much of his money she had spent that day on baby stuff. She was due in one month. He could barely bring himself to look at her naked; she looked like a beached whale. Heidi did not.

Thank God for perks.

He leaned his head back and closed his eyes.

"We're here."

He struggled to open his eyes. "Where?"

Rudy said, "The girl's home."

He glanced at Heidi. She was still sleeping it off.

"What time is it?"

"Almost one."

He had fallen asleep. He was still groggy. He put his face against the wet window as they slowed and entered a small rural town; they pulled up to a red light. The light changed and just as they eased through the intersection a flash of lightning off to his right lit up a huge ship looming large overhead like it was about to ram the frigging limo. He ducked back into the seat.

"*Shit!*"

But another lightning flash showed it was just a goddamn building with a second story shaped like the bow of a goddamn boat—*what's that, some kind of fucking joke?*

The limo moved forward at a slow crawl; no doubt Rudy,

with his record and an unconscious minor female in the back, was wary of local law enforcement. They drove down a deserted Main Street—the street sign read *Hauptstrasse*—and under a big banner that read WELCOME-WILLKOMMEN-BIENVENIDOS and a canopy of Christmas lights strung over the street. He stared out the window, expecting to see the typical small Texas town Main Street lined with convenience stores, fast-food joints, a liquor store, a VFW Hall, a used-car lot, and maybe a Piggly-Wiggly. But instead he saw a motel fashioned like a Bavarian chalet, a German brewery, and Old World-style buildings outlined in twinkling lights with second-story balconies and colorful awnings shading art galleries and quaint shops selling antiques and boutiques selling fashionable clothes and stores selling handmade crafts, quilts, and jewelry, and . . . *a Hawaiian shirt shop?*

Buildings shaped like boats and cowboys wearing Hawaiian shirts—*where the hell am I?*

Even on a stormy night, it was like he was looking at a postcard and not from anyplace in the Texas he knew. Christ, he was glad his wife wasn't with him, and not just because of Heidi lying there; because this was exactly the colorful picture-perfect Christmas-card kind of small town that his wife would "ooh" and "aah" over as being so quaint and cute and cuddly that she'd want to buy the whole damn place—*with his money!*

Red, black, and yellow German flags flapped in the dark night, colorful umbrellas at outdoor restaurants sported names like *Spaten* and *Franziskaner* and *Weissbier*, and signs with *Ausländer Biergarten, Vereins Kirche, Alte Fritz, Der Lindenbaum, Der Küchen Laden, Der* this, and *Der* that hung on buildings up and down this Main Street.

Where the hell were they, back in Berlin for the European premiere of his last film?

He closed his eyes and rubbed his face and tried to shake his head clear of the whiskey and coke, and when he opened his eyes, he finally spotted a name he recognized, reassurance he

7

was still in Texas: Dairy Queen. Man, he could use a DQ Dude and an Oreo Blizzard right about now, but it was closed. The entire town was closed, not a living soul in sight. This was one of those small Texas towns that rolled up the sidewalks at sunset, just like the one he had never grown up in.

Few people outside his parents knew it—and those who did had signed a confidentiality agreement—but his real name was Theodore Biederman, the only son of a vascular surgeon in Houston. He was a city boy; he had attended a private prep school and then the University of Texas at Austin where he had parlayed his chiseled jaw line, curly blond hair, and deep blue eyes into a string of local television commercials, one of which had caught the attention of a Hollywood talent scout.

Austin, Texas, had been a hot spot for talent scouts ever since Matthew McConaughey and Renée Zellweger were discovered there. Hollywood came calling, and Theodore Biederman couldn't get the hell out of Texas fast enough. He wanted to be a star and Texas didn't have stars, except for football players, which he had never been. (He didn't like physical pain, notwithstanding his Hollywood image as an action-hero.) Of course, he always wore jeans and cowboy boots on TV, smoked big cigars, and played Texan on Leno and Letterman, a good ol' boy made good in Hollywood—"Aw, heck, Dave, I ain't nuthin' but a country boy like to swim nekkid in the creek down on the ranch"—even though he didn't own a ranch, didn't want to own a ranch, and had never even set foot on a fucking ranch.

But he always said "Yes, ma'am" and "No, ma'am" in public and he tossed in a few Spanish words—"*Muy bonita, señorita*"— just to sound authentically Texan and even a "golly" every now and then to sound down-home, and damned if it didn't work. It was all about image, and he had image. Part of which required that he return to Austin every year for the fucking film festival to prove he was still a Texan at heart. Yeah, right. *Get me back to L.A.!*

He leaned forward now and gave Heidi a shake.

"Wake up, princess. You're home."

Nothing.

"Come on, wake up."

He pushed her hard, and she rolled off the seat and onto the floorboard. Cutting through the fog of whiskey and cocaine in his mind was a sharp sense of fear. He slid down the seat to his knees and gently slapped her cheeks. She felt cold to the touch.

"Jesus!"

Rudy turned back. "What's wrong?"

"Pull over!"

The limo slowed to a stop in front of a park where colorful Christmas decorations lit up the dark night. Rudy got out and came around back. He opened the door and leaned in. He wiped the rain from his face and looked at the girl; his eyes got wide.

"Shit!"

He jumped in and pushed on her chest and blew in her mouth and pushed on her chest again. After a few minutes, he was breathing hard. Heidi wasn't breathing at all. Rudy sat back and stared at her then turned to him and said, "She's dead, man."

He slumped against the seat. "She said she was a college coed . . . she said she wanted to be a star . . . she said . . ."

Rudy said, "Boss, what she said ain't gonna mean jack to the law. She's a minor and she's dead 'cause of your coke. That's all that's gonna matter to the cops."

He had now broken out in a full-body sweat. His heart was beating against his chest wall so hard he was sure he was having a heart attack. He felt Rudy's dark eyes boring into him.

"What do you wanna do, boss?"

At that moment, in a split-second, his mind played out alternate endings to this horror movie he was suddenly starring in, as real as if he were sitting in on a test screening. The first ending had his character taking Heidi to the nearest hospital and telling the doctors in the ER that she had drunk whiskey—*his whiskey!*—

9

and she had snorted cocaine—*his cocaine!*—and they had had sex—*was sixteen still jail bait in Texas?*—and then she had passed out. The doctors would try desperately to bring her back to life—they would inject her heart with epinephrine; they would perform CPR until their arms were numb; they would hit her with the defibrillator so many times he could smell her soft flesh burning—but there would be no medical miracles that night. They would finally look up from her lifeless body lying there on the gurney, slowly turn to the camera, and say to him, "She's dead."

He knew all this because he had played an action-hero ER doctor/CIA operative in *Doc Op* ($175 million domestic gross). And he knew the next scene in this script: the local police would arrive at the hospital. And then the national media. And reporters and cameras and scandal: MOVIE STAR GIVES WHISKEY AND COCAINE TO 16-YEAR-OLD HIGH SCHOOL JUNIOR; GIRL ODs. And maybe worse: indictment . . . trial . . . conviction . . . prison. His rich celebrity life would be ruined. His career would be over. His fame and fortune would be gone. Along with the perks. When the credits to this ending began rolling across his mind's eye—arresting officer, district attorney, judge, jury—he immediately chose the alternate ending to this movie.

"Let's dump her and get the hell outta here!"

Rudy ran back up front, climbed into the driver's seat, turned the wheel hard, and made a U-turn in the wide street. He glanced out the window just as a bolt of lightning lit up the dark sky and the building they were turning in front of— Gillespie County Courthouse—and he felt a sudden chill. Rudy accelerated out of town. When they reached a desolate stretch of road, Rudy pulled the limo over and came back again. Together, they buttoned Heidi's blouse and slid her thong back on. He put his arms under her to lift her out, but Rudy stopped short.

"Did you use a rubber?"

10

"What?"

"With her—did you wear a rubber?"

"No. You think she's got AIDS?"

"No, man, she's got your DNA . . . inside her. Like on those *CSI* shows."

Panic gripped his cloudy mind. He glanced around and grabbed a bar towel. He stuck it inside her thong and wiped. Rudy was shaking his wet bald head.

"It don't all come out."

He sat back and tried to think clearly. After a moment, he looked up at Rudy and smiled. "They've got my DNA, but they don't got me. No one saw us together . . . they'll never tie me to her . . . they'll never be able to match that DNA to me . . . and I'm sure as hell never coming back to this fucking place."

Satisfied with that story resolution, he picked up Heidi's black high heels and started to push the first one on her foot, but Rudy held his hand out.

"Give 'em to me . . . and that towel. I'll toss them out on the way back to Austin, into that river we drove over."

"Why?"

"'Cause they can get your fingerprints off that smooth leather and they might be able to trace fibers back to that towel and this limo."

"Really?"

Rudy was again shaking his head. "Man, don't you ever watch TV?"

Rudy stepped outside and checked the road for cars; then he leaned back in and grabbed Heidi's legs, and together they lifted her out of the limo. The rain hit her face, and her mascara started running down her cheeks like she was crying black tears. They bent down and gently placed her on the wet ground. They stood straight and stared at each other as if waiting for the other to say a prayer over her like they always do in those western movies; but neither said anything, so Rudy shrugged and gave Heidi a little nudge with his boot. She rolled down into a shallow ditch under a road sign that read: FREDERICKSBURG, TEXAS, POP. 8,911.

FOUR YEARS, SIX MONTHS, AND FOUR DAYS LATER

Chapter 1

She died on her thirty-seventh birthday.

But not without a fight. Mastectomy. Chemotherapy. Radiation. More chemotherapy. But the cancer would not be denied. It took her breasts, her lymph nodes, her hair, and her life. An unrelenting, unthinking, uncaring, unfeeling disease—the doctors called it "invasive ductal carcinoma"—had killed his wife and their mother. Beck wiped his eyes.

"Daddy, you okay?"

He glanced back at Meggie in the rearview mirror. Only five, she knew her mother had gone to be with Jesus, but she thought it would be like a vacation, and when it was over her mother would come home. She didn't know it would be forever.

"Yes, baby."

"I gotta pee."

"Bad?"

"Way."

Beck steered the big SUV off the interstate at the next exit and pulled into a gas station. It wasn't one of the modern ones at a brightly lit convenience store with pay-at-the-pumps outside and inside young employees in colorful striped shirts serving

15

gourmet coffee with sparkling restrooms that smelled of pine-sol; it was an ancient stand-alone station with manual pumps and an old man with greasy hands slouched behind a dirty desk and holding out a key chained to a hubcap that allowed access to a single restroom around the side of the concrete bunker-like structure, a restroom that likely hadn't been cleaned in years, if ever.

Welcome to Texas.

The hubcap banged against the steel door as Beck tried to insert the key into the rusty lock. He finally succeeded, worked the lock until it released, and gave the door a firm kick to pry it open. He felt around for a switch and turned on the light, one dim exposed bulb hanging from acoustical tiles long dis-colored from a leaky roof. Beck stepped inside and checked the dingy space for rats, roaches, spiders, scorpions, snakes, and other creatures of the dark; he found none, stepped out, and looked down at Meggie. Her knees were tight, her legs were bent, and she was bouncing slightly; a pained expression had captured her face.

"I gotta go."

"It's okay. Go ahead."

"*By myself?*"

"You need help?"

"*Duh.* Mommy showed me how to pee in a filthy restroom, but I can't do it by myself."

"Oh."

Beck followed her inside and shut the door, but not before checking on her ten-year-old brother locked in the black Navigator twenty feet away. Luke's ears were still covered with head-phones and his eyes still glued to the Gameboy. Beck turned back to Meggie; she was pinching her nose.

"It stinks."

Stale urine, mold, and the July heat had combined to create an overwhelming odor; he pulled the door halfway open and let in fresh air and the sound of eighteen-wheelers whining past

16

on the interstate. Meggie held her arms out and said, "Help me up."

"Onto the seat?"

"Unh-huh."

"You don't sit?"

"No way. I squat. Mommy showed me."

Beck lifted her up so she could stand on the seat. She was heavier than she looked.

"Don't let go," she said.

Embarrassed, Beck averted his eyes as she pushed her shorts and underwear down to her ankles, then squatted, holding onto his arms for stability. She closed her eyes and inhaled deeply and exhaled slowly, as if she were doing a relaxation exercise.

She peed.

He gazed at her innocent face and saw Annie. It was an amazing thing, how a man and a woman could create two children, each a clone of one parent. Luke was Beck's clone, tall for his age and rangy, brown curly hair and dark penetrating eyes, athletic and intense; Meggie was Annie's, the same creamy complexion, the same black hair, the same blue eyes, an unusual combination that had always struck him. And she possessed the same gentle spirit.

"TP, please," she said.

Beck held her with his right hand and with his left hand he pulled a length of yellowed toilet paper from the roll in the holder attached to the wall. Meggie wadded it up and reached down. Then she pulled her underwear and shorts back up in one motion as she stood. She grinned as he lifted her down.

"That's how Mommy and I do it."

Meggie still spoke of her mother in the present tense, as if she were still alive.

"Does she . . . did she squat, too?"

"Unh-huh, but she doesn't stand on the seat."

Beck tried to picture his wife squatting over a public toilet, but that wasn't the Annie he knew.

17

"She never told me."

"It's our secret," Meggie said.

Beck pulled the door fully open and held it there for Meggie.

"Did you and Mom have other secrets?"

Meggie walked under his arm and out the door and said, "Lots."

They had married twelve years before, when he was thirty and five years out of Notre Dame Law School, and Annie Parker was twenty-five and a new lawyer. They had met at a law school mixer after a football game. As a former Notre Dame quarterback and then a lawyer at a big Chicago firm that hired a dozen Notre Dame law grads each year, Beck Hardin had returned for every home game and received invitations to every law school function. He had walked into the crowded room and his eyes were instantly drawn to her across a hundred other human beings and lawyers.

He never looked at another woman.

Annie hired on with another Chicago firm, and they became a two-lawyer family. He tried cases; she wrote wills and trusts. Then Luke came along, and Annie opted out of the law for full-time motherhood. Her choice. Five years later, Meggie was born. They moved to a sprawling home with a big yard in a safe suburb with good schools. Beck took the train into the city each morning and back out each evening. He always worked late, and he often worked weekends. He billed three thousand hours a year, every year. He made partner, and he made great money.

Annie made their lives great. She was a soccer mom, a tee ball mom, and a room mom. She drove the kids to school, to baseball practice, and to piano lessons. She gave birthday parties, helped with homework, and went on class outings. She shopped, she cooked, and she ran the household. She was there when he left each morning and there when he returned each night. They had great kids, a great home, a great marriage, and a great life. The Hardins were the perfect family. Everyone said so.

A routine mammogram changed everything.

Now Annie was gone, born and buried in Chicago, and her family was moving to Texas. In the six months since Annie had died, Beck had tried to be a father, mother, and lawyer; he had failed at all three. He couldn't get the kids to school each morning and fed and to bed each night and still bill his three thousand hours. He had always prided himself on being in complete control of his world, but he had soon realized it was only an illusion enabled by Annie. Without her, he was lost and helpless.

The neighbors had tried to help; they brought dinner over several times a week, picked up the kids when he couldn't, and recommended a full-time nanny. But he didn't want his children raised by neighbors or nannies. He was determined to raise them himself because that's what Annie would have wanted. So he arrived late for morning conferences and court hearings, and he left afternoon conferences and hearings early. Over seventeen years of practicing law, Beck Hardin had accumulated a certain amount of goodwill among his partners and the judges, so they tried to be understanding. But there was a limit to understanding, and he was soon pushing the outer limits.

He found himself in a no-man's land: neither father nor lawyer.

Nor. mother. Home life had gotten even worse. Meggie took to carrying a black-haired doll with her everywhere and conversing with it as if it were her mother; but at least she was happy in her denial. When she started wetting the bed, he took her to a therapist; when the therapist told him to take the doll away, he found another therapist.

But the therapists couldn't help Meggie, and they couldn't help Luke. He was neither happy nor in denial. He understood his mother was never coming back, and it made him sad and then it made him mad. And it changed him. The happy-go-lucky kid who loved school and sports was replaced by a stranger given to dark moods. His teacher said he'd just sit and stare and sometimes he would cry. And sometimes he would hit things

19

and other kids. He got into fights, and his grades plummeted. He withdrew deeper and deeper into himself; he quit sports, refused to play with friends, and retreated to his room. Each night Beck would stand outside Luke's door and hear him crying. Beck saw his life replaying itself through Luke; he couldn't let that happen to his son. Beck knew he had to do something soon or he would lose his children, too. But what? He prayed for Annie to show him the way.

He woke one morning with the answer clear in his mind: Texas.

Beck Hardin would go home and take his children with him. As soon as school let out, he quit the firm, sold the house and his Lexus and most of their possessions, packed the Navigator, and headed south to a place he hadn't seen in twenty-four years. He had left at eighteen, a football scholarship in hand and a chip on his shoulder, vowing never to return to Texas, a vow he had faithfully kept. Until now.

To save his children, he would go home.

"Are we there yet?"

He glanced back at Meggie, propped up high in her booster seat like a queen on her throne.

"Soon, baby."

She put the doll to her ear, nodded, and said, "Mommy says we've been in Texas a long time."

"Tell her . . . It's a big state, honey."

They had crossed into Texas early that morning driving south on Interstate 35, which extends from the Red River to the Rio Grande. Twenty-four years before, Beck had been angry and wanted out of Texas; when he had crossed that state line heading in the opposite direction, he had felt like a lifer getting out of prison. Now, his life had brought him full circle.

Beck Hardin was back in Texas.

So he sped up. The posted speed limit in Texas was seventy, but Texans had always regarded the posted limit as the minimum

20

speed. That hadn't changed. They had just been passed by a young woman driving eighty miles an hour and steering with her knees while filing her nails and talking on a cell phone tucked under her ear. So he had had the cruise control set on seventy-five for five hours now—not counting two potty stops— and they had just entered the city limits of Austin, the state capital in the geographic center of Texas.

It's a very big state.

"We've got just over an hour to go. You guys want to eat lunch here or wait until we get there?"

Meggie looked to Luke for a decision, as she often did, but Luke did not look up from the Gameboy. So Meggie whispered something to the doll, nodded, and said, "Mommy says wait."

Beck stayed on the interstate that bisected Austin, barely recognizable after twenty-four years, like a high school buddy who had packed on the weight: the sleepy college town had become a bloated city. When he had last driven through Austin, the pink granite dome of the capitol had loomed large over the skyline; now he only caught quick glimpses of it between towering skyscrapers. Back then, environmentalists had waged war with developers for the soul and skyline of Austin; now, seeing the granite-and-glass skyscrapers, it was obvious who had won.

But a few familiar landmarks had survived. The three-hundred-foot-tall white sandstone clock tower on the University of Texas campus still stood watch over the city; no doubt the tower lights still shone burnt orange on game nights when the Longhorns won. And no doubt the observation deck still remained closed, as it had since 1966 when an ex-Marine with a brain tumor and a marksman's skill stood up there with a high-powered rifle and killed sixteen people on the campus and streets below.

The UT football stadium still stood adjacent to the interstate but had been enlarged to accommodate corporate skyboxes; the stadium had been renamed after Darrell Royal, the legendary Longhorn coach, and the playing field after Joe Jamail, the billionaire plaintiffs' lawyer from Houston, surely the quid pro quo for a sizable donation to the football program.

Football had been Beck's ticket out of Texas, and he had punched it. But he couldn't drive past the UT stadium without a twinge of regret: he had been destined from birth to play in that stadium. His last visit to Austin had been a recruiting trip to UT as the top high school quarterback in the state, a country boy courted by rich and powerful businessmen and politicians who had come to him like the wise men to Baby Jesus; but Beck Hardin had held more than the mere promise of eternal salvation. He held the promise of another national championship for their alma mater. But he had chosen Notre Dame instead, no lesser a betrayal than if Davy Crockett had fought for the Mexicans at the Alamo.

Beck Hardin had never figured on coming back to Texas.

He crossed over the Colorado River and exited the interstate at Highway 290 in south Austin and turned right. Home lay seventy miles due west, in the Texas Hill Country.

Chapter 2

The movie *Giant* gave the world the image of Texas that persists to this day: flat, dusty, and desolate, a land best left to longhorns, rattlesnakes, and armadillos, a place where oil rigs and barbed wire were distinct improvements on Mother Nature. And that would be true for much of Texas.

But not the Hill Country.

Mother Nature had gotten it right here, in the land west of Austin, a landscape formed by a great tectonic event twenty million years ago. It happened after the last dinosaurs had died off and the great sea that once covered most of Texas had receded and the North and South American continents had split apart. The earth's crust fractured along a fault zone extending three hundred fifty miles in a sweeping arc from Del Rio on the Mexican border east to San Antonio and then northeast to Austin and beyond, bisecting the state. The land mass to the south and east of the fracture dropped—the geologists call it a "downwarping"—and the land to the north and west rose—an "uplift"—creating a three-hundred-foot-tall escarpment, a white limestone wall rising from the plains in terraces that appeared to the first Spanish explorers as balconies. They named the escarpment *Los Balcones*.

The Balcones Escarpment divides Texas to this day.

East of the escarpment lies the Blackland Prairies where rain running off the escarpment made the land fertile and cotton king. West of the escarpment lies the parched High Plains of West Texas, the cattle baron land of *Giant*. But between the two lies the Balcones Canyonlands, the rugged terrain above the escarpment that long served as the narrow DMZ of the great Texas range wars: sodbusters to the east, open-range cowboys to the west.

That land is known today as the Texas Hill Country.

As Texas goes, it's a small area, only about ten thousand square miles, bigger than New Jersey and Delaware combined, but not *big* in a state of 268,000 square miles. But it's the best land in Texas. The Hill Country has artesian springs where crystal-clear waters escape from underground aquifers, rivers called the Blanco and Pedernales and Guadalupe, and lakes called Travis and Buchanan and, of course, LBJ. It has hills and ravines and valleys with bald cypress trees shading lazy creeks. It has thick forests of oak and pecan and hackberry trees in the lowlands and stands of dark green cedar on the canyon slopes that give off a deep purplish tint in the sunlight. And it has wildflowers. In the spring the fields become carpets of bluebonnets so unbelievably blue you'd think the sky has settled down on the land.

Mother Nature got it right here.

And Texans hadn't messed it up, not much anyway, probably because neither oil nor gas had ever been discovered in the Hill Country; so industry, interstates, and people had never been lured to this land. Now, as Beck drove west on Highway 290 and the last outlying subdivisions of Austin receded in the rearview and the Navigator carried the Hardin family up and over the Balcones Escarpment, his thoughts were of this land, the land of his youth.

Beck Hardin was home.

This land had always maintained a strange hold over him, like a first love a man never completely gets over; sitting in his

Chicago office and staring out at the adjacent skyscrapers, his thoughts had often returned to this land even though he never had. Now, for the first time in twenty-four years, his eyes beheld the Texas Hill Country. It took his breath away, like the first time he had laid eyes on Annie, and brought a sense of regret to his thoughts: she had asked to see the land he had once called home. It was the only time he had ever said no to Annie Parker.

He had tried to run from this land and the life he had lived here, but he might as well have tried to run from his own shadow.

An hour later Beck said, "That's the LBJ Ranch."

They had driven fifty-five miles due west of Austin and were now driving past the vast ranch in Stonewall that had been the Texas White House when Lyndon Baines Johnson had been president. It was now a state park. He glanced back in the rearview: Luke's eyes remained fixed on the Gameboy and Meggie's on the doll; she was brushing its hair and talking softly to it.

"A president lived there."

That got Meggie's attention. She looked out the window.

"George W. Bush lives there?"

She had learned about the president in her pre-K class. At the last open house, her teacher had questioned the kids in front of their proud parents: "Does anyone know the president's name?"

"George W. Bush," the children had recited in unison.

"And what's his wife's name?"

That had stumped them. The kids had glanced around at each other with confused expressions until Meggie had finally said, "Mrs. Bush." Which had seemed like a perfectly reasonable answer to Beck, the only father at her open house.

"No, honey," he said, "another president from Texas. Lyndon Johnson. He was born and raised right there."

"Are all the presidents from Texas?"

"No, thank God."

Beck chuckled at his own words, downright treasonous in Texas. He had been away a very long time.

"Was he a good president?"

"Well, some people would say yes, some would say no."

"What do you say?"

Beck had been born in 1965, so what he knew about LBJ he had learned in history classes and from the old-timers in town. His father had talked of seeing LBJ—after his presidency had ended and he was back living at the ranch—driving around town in his convertible Cadillac with his long white hair and much younger girlfriend. And Beck the boy had asked, "I thought Lady Bird was his wife?"

"She was," his father had said.

"Did he bring her along?"

"Nope, he left her back at the ranch."

Beck had studied on that for a while, then had asked, "How does that work, a man having a wife *and* a girlfriend?"

His father had chuckled. "Well, for most men it wouldn't work so good. It'd damn sure complicate things. But if you're an ex-president who happens to be one mean son of a bitch, I guess it works okay, particularly if you happen to be married to a saint."

"Was he?"

"Yep, LBJ was about the meanest SOB to come down the pike."

"No. Married to a saint?"

"Oh. Yeah, matter of fact, he was." His father had paused, Beck recalled, and then had said, "Never realized I had something in common with LBJ."

As had Beck.

"No, baby, I don't think he was a good president."

They drove on westward. The sleek foreign cars of Austin with bumper stickers that read WHO WOULD JESUS BOMB and IMPEACHBUSH.ORG had been replaced by bulky diesel pickups with grill guards to protect against unexpected encounters with deer, and bumper stickers that read LUV YA DUBYA and SUPPORT OUR TROOPS; and the dense subdivisions had given way to open pastures where horses, cows, sheep, and goats grazed peacefully under the July sun as if they were the happiest creatures on earth even though the Navigator's outside temperature gauge registered 98 degrees. Weathered homesteads with windmills sat back off the highway, and a series of cell towers ran parallel to the highway. A sign affixed to a fencepost offered "Hay-4-Sale."

"What are those big round things?" Meggie asked.

Beck glanced out her side at a field of hay being cut by a farmer driving a tractor and holding a cell phone to his ear.

"Hay bales."

A mile later, she said, "Mommy says those are big moo-cows."

She was holding the doll up so it could see out the left side of the car. Beck glanced that way.

"Tell her . . . No, honey, those are buffalo."

"Are *those* cows?"

She was now looking out the right side.

"No, those are horses. Says 'Eureka Thoroughbred Farm'." Beck pointed out the other side. "Now those are cows."

A small herd was grazing in a field. It wasn't a real cattle ranch; those were out west. This little ranchette was just a tax deduction for a Houston lawyer or a Dallas doctor.

"And what's that?"

Back to the right side. "Well, that's a one-hump camel. I'm not sure what it's doing here."

Meggie asked and Beck answered as they drove past two ostriches, three wineries, and four turkey farms; the Hummingbird Farm, the Lavender Farm, and the Wildseed Farm; Engel's Peaches, Turner's Tractors, and Vogel's Peaches & Tractors; the steel-blue Lutheran Church with its tall white steeple; and longhorn cattle. They passed bare peach orchards and shuttered peach stands, vacant deer blinds waiting for hunting season, and the same abandoned houses and roadside stores that Beck had seen when he had last driven this highway twenty-four years before. They drove past Upper Albert Road and Lower Albert Road, Gellermann and Goehmann Lanes, Old San Antonio Road and the road to Luckenbach. They crossed over Flat Creek, Tow Head Creek, Rocky Creek, Three Mile Creek, South Grape Creek, Baron's Creek where it turned south, and the Pedernales River where it turned north; all had run dry. And then Beck said, "Plus three."

Meggie said, "Plus three what?"

Beck pointed at the city limits sign: FREDERICKSBURG, TEXAS, POP. 8,911. "Plus three. Us."

"Why's that white cross stuck in the ground?"

Under the sign was a short cross with a vase of flowers.

"Someone must've . . . there must have been a car accident right here."

"Did someone die?"

"Maybe."

"They'll be back. Like Mommy."

Beck sighed. How do you explain death to a five-year-old?

They drove past a new Wal-Mart on the left, Fort Martin Scott with a teepee on the right, and horses grazing around a new sewage treatment plant. Highway 290 became Main Street, and Beck slowed as they entered town; he stopped at a red light fronting the old Nimitz Hotel, now the National Museum of the Pacific War, but once a hotel, brewery, and frontier landmark with its upper stories shaped like the bow of a Mississippi steamboat complete with a hurricane deck, pilot house, and a crow's nest. The original German owner had been a sailor, as had his grandson, Admiral Chester Nimitz, the commander of the Pacific Fleet during World War Two. Back in the late 1800s, the ten-room hotel had been a traveler's last chance for a cold beer, a hot bath, and a clean bed until El Paso five hundred miles farther west. The Nimitz marked the eastern boundary of downtown Fredericksburg.

Main Street was blocked off west of the Nimitz. American,

28

Texas, and German flags flew from standards on every building on both sides of the street. Stretched over the street was a banner that read FREDERICKSBURG SALUTES OUR ARMED FORCES AND THEIR FAMILIES. And Beck remembered what day it was.

"Hey, guys, it's the Fourth of July. I think we're in time for the parade."

Beck pulled around the corner and parked a block north of Main Street. Meggie jumped out, but Luke had to be coaxed.

"Come on, son, this'll be fun."

Luke sighed and climbed out. They walked back to Main Street and crossed over to the south side—the shady side in the summer. Spectators crowded the sidewalks and stood on the second-story balconies that overlooked Main Street and sat on the tailgates of pickup trucks and SUVs that lined the street. Some wore flags—hats, caps, shirts, and shorts; others waved flags. The sun was blazing hot, the sky was clear blue, and the flags were flying: it was the Fourth of July in Fredericksburg, Texas.

They settled into a shady spot out front of what had been the Fredericksburg Auto Parts; it was now a brew pub and restaurant called the Fredericksburg Brewing Company. They stood among white-haired folks sitting in folding chairs, wholesome looking country kids hunkered down on the curb holding red, white, and blue balloons, and their sturdy parents standing behind them holding video cameras and dogs on leashes. Customers carried beer out of the brewery and took up viewing positions; drinking on the sidewalks had been legal in Fredericksburg since the days when thirteen saloons lined Main Street, and apparently it still was. Beck had given up alcohol when he had left this town, so he bought three bottles of cold water from two girls about Luke's age who were selling it out of a red wagon and passing out little flags; Beck handed a bottle and a flag to each of his children, then pointed down at an iron ring embedded in the concrete sidewalk. "Luke, cowboys used to tie their horses to these rings." Luke looked, but only grunted in response.

The four asphalt lanes of Main Street were unoccupied except for two cops on bikes and a long-legged blonde girl wearing cowboy boots and stars-and-stripes short-shorts and making a show of sashaying back and forth across the empty street. Texas girls liked attention; pretty Texas girls demanded it.

Cowboys hats, gimme caps, and umbrellas served as sunblocks for the spectators, all of whom, young and old, now abruptly stood and placed their right hands and hats over their hearts. The parade was upon them, led by a lone bagpiper wearing a kilt and followed by a military color guard, five uniformed soldiers and sailors carrying the U.S. flag and the Army, Navy, Marine, and Air Force colors flanked by Army and Marine riflemen. The high school ROTC marched behind the color guard and were followed by World War Two veterans manning a .60-caliber machine gun mounted on a half-track pulling a flat-bed trailer with national guard soldiers just back from Iraq. The crowd applauded and cheered like they were the Chicago Bears just back from the Super Bowl. A sign listed the names of soldiers in their company killed in action. There were a lot of names. Another sign read FREEDOM IS NOT FREE.

The high school band marched past playing the "Star-Spangled Banner" followed by vintage fire trucks, antique cars, and pickup trucks with pretty girls in blonde braids tossing red, white, and blue bead necklaces into the crowd and up to the people on the balconies. Beck caught a red one and put it around Meggie's neck. She showed it to the doll.

More military vehicles and farm equipment rolled past followed by floats for a ministry with a sign that read KEEP CHRIST IN CHRISTMAS and the Knights of Columbus with a sign that read ONE NATION UNDER GOD. Separation of church and state had never been a major topic of debate in Fredericksburg, Texas. A long RV decked out in red, white, and blue drove by with loudspeakers blaring the Lee Greenwood song "God Bless the USA"; it was trailed by a 1921 Stanley Steamer, an old Cadillac convertible with longhorns on the hood, and a Boys and Girls Club float playing "Yankee Doodle Dandy." The Gillespie County Farm Bureau Queen and her court wore prom dresses and waved as their float passed by. Meggie asked, "Are they supermodels?"

Beck said, "No, honey, they're just high school girls."

Next up were clowns, kids on bikes, cowgirls on horseback, and a University of Texas cheerleader prancing like a show horse alongside a tall burnt-orange replica of the UT clock tower with NATIONAL CHAMPIONS 2005 on the side. The University of Texas had won its national championship without Beck Hardin.

A float for the Gillespie County Democratic Party was manned by five brave souls followed by a standing-room-only float for the county's Republican Party. Gillespie County had always been as red as Austin was blue; LBJ had been the only Democrat to carry the county in the last seventy-five years. The American Legion float played the Marine service hymn, and the last float had men dressed as Revolutionary soldiers. The parade ended with a truck toting a big sign that read DAS IST ALLES, Y'ALL.

God, country, and German beer: the Fourth of July parade in Fredericksburg, Texas, had been exactly as Beck had remembered. And he thought how much Annie would have loved it. She had never lived in a small town but had always thought it would be perfect. He had always told her it wasn't. But standing here now in this Norman Rockwell painting, maybe it was.

As soon as the parade had rolled out of sight, Main Street reopened for business and traffic; it quickly became crowded with cars, pickups, and eighteen-wheel rigs heading out to or in from West Texas. A semi pulling a cattle trailer braked to a stop at the Lincoln Street light. The cows were mooing woefully, as if begging for mercy.

"Daddy, look!" Meggie cried. "Moo-cows! That nice man is taking them for a ride."

"He sure is."

"Where are they going?"

Beck figured a five-year-old didn't need to know about slaughterhouses, so he said, "Well, they're—"

"Hamburgers, little lady. You can eat 'em at McDonald's next week."

Beck turned. An old coot in a cowboy hat was standing there with his thumbs in his pockets and a grin on his face.

"*HAMBURGERS?*" Meggie's face was stricken. "The moo-cows?"

The old coot realized his error. "Uh, sorry about that."

Beck pulled Meggie away from the cows and walked the children west down Main Street. They passed sun-hardened locals wearing Wrangler jeans, cowboy boots, plaid shirts, and caps with *John Deere* and *Caterpillar* on the front. Twenty-four years later, Beck could still recognize the goat ranchers, turkey farmers, and peach growers; they carried the smell of their trades with them.

But he didn't recognize the other people walking down Main Street, sleek women sporting tattoos, designer jeans, and high heels, holding leashes connected to puffy French poodles and hairless Chihuahuas, and carrying stuffed shopping bags . . . teenage girls wearing short-shorts with their lace thongs showing in the back and tank tops stretched across their precocious chests up front with cell phones stuck to their ears . . . long-haired boys wearing baggy shorts, tee shirts, and headphones wrapped around their skulls . . . and pale-skinned, soft-bellied men looking as if they longed for the office.

Who are these people?

They walked on and something began bothering Beck in the back of his brain. Something wasn't right. Something was missing. And then he realized: the people were missing. The *other* people. He had become so accustomed to the diversity of downtown Chicago—Latinos, African-Americans, Asians, Arabs in burkas, Indians in turbans, Orthodox Jews, homeless people pushing

32

grocery carts, and cops, trash, and graffiti—and to hearing loud *Tejano* and rap music pounding out from boom boxes carried by kids who dressed like gangsters and spouted profanity like rappers, that it had all just become part of the landscape that he no longer noticed, like elevator music.

But when all of that is suddenly not there, you notice.

He noticed. None of that was here in Fredericksburg, Texas. The people were white, the streets and sidewalks were clean and quiet, and the cops were two guys in shorts riding bikes. This was not downtown Chicago. But it wasn't his old hometown either.

Fredericksburg had changed.

The same historic buildings still lined Main Street—*Hauptstrasse* to the locals—but all the vacant, dilapidated buildings had been restored and were now occupied, and the names on the buildings were all different. Gone were the old German businesses like the Weidenfeller Gas Station, Otto Kolmeier Hardware, Dorer Jewelers, Haas Custom Handweaving, Langerhans Mower & Saw, Engel's Deli, Freda's Gifts, and Opa's Haus. In their places were fancy boutiques called Haberdashery, Lauren Bade, Root, In-Step, and Slick Rock and shops called Cowboy Eclectic, Divinely Designed, Bath Junkie, Rather Sweet, and Phil Jackson's Amazing World of Things.

Doc Keidel's two-story limestone home still stood on Main Street, but Keidel's Drug Store was now a "vintage western boutique" called Rawhide and the Keidel Memorial Hospital was a kitchen emporium called Der Küchen Laden. In the basement was a restaurant called Rathskeller. The White Elephant Saloon was now the Lucky Star Boutique, and the Domino Parlor where the old-timers had gathered to play dominoes and drink beer all day was now a store called Grandma Daisy's. Lee-Ed's FolkArt & Decoys was a wine cellar. And the Western Auto was a store just for dogs called Dogologie.

The Stout Shop still served the sturdier women of Gillespie County, but the newspaper had been replaced by Spunky

Monkey Toys and a store called Zertz that sold $250 hand-painted jeans for girls. Hill Country Outfitters sold kayaks. And the Pioneer National Bank had been replaced by a Chase branch.

Ausländer Biergarten, the old Herbert Schmidt Electric shop, Dooley's 5-10-25¢ store, and Dietz Bakery still occupied their same spots on Main Street, but the Jenschke Furniture Store was now a live music theater called the Rockbox, and the Nut Haus and the Wilke Barbershop where Beck had gotten his hair cut had been combined for a store called Grasshopper & Wild Honey. And the old Palace Theater where Beck had watched John Wayne in *Rooster Cogburn* was now a store called Parts Unknown, A Fashion Adventure. They sold expensive English loafers and loud Hawaiian print shirts.

Beck shook his head. *Who would have the balls to wear a Hawaiian print shirt in Fredericksburg, Texas?*

Beck turned and came face to face with a white-haired man wearing a bright maroon shirt printed with multicolored parrots perched on floral patterns of yellow and white flowers sprouting amid long green leaves.

Beck said, "You look like the bird exhibit at the zoo."

"I was in a rut."

"Well, you're out of it now."

The two men sized each other up like gunfighters looking to draw. The old man's hair was cut short and the white contrasted sharply against his weathered face. He was wearing the parrot shirt over Wrangler jeans and brown work boots. His bare arms were tanned and sinewy, and his hands were gnarly. His blue eyes were as clear as the sky and were looking Beck over, from his Nike sneakers to his shorts and knit golf shirt to the gray streaks in his hair. The old man finally nodded as if in approval.

"Beck."

"J.B."

"Just get in?"

Beck nodded. "Saw the peach stands out 290 are closed."

34

"Nothing to sell. We're in drought, going on seven years."

"It is hot."

"It's Texas."

"Who are all these people?"

"Tourists. They say we're the next Santa Fe."

"Shopping on the Fourth of July?"

"Every day but Christmas."

The two men fell silent on Main Street. After a long moment, Beck said, "You get married again?"

The old man snorted. "That'll be the day."

After another moment of silence, Meggie's voice rose from below: "Who are you, mister?"

The old man looked down at her, then back up at Beck as if waiting for him to respond. Finally, the old man patted her head and said, "Why, little gal, I'm your grandpa."

John Beck Hardin, Sr., known to all, even his son, as J.B., was sixty-six years old. He stood six feet tall, he weighed one hundred ninety pounds, and he had a handshake that could still bring tears to a grown man's eyes. He was born here and he would die here, as his parents and wife had. He had married Peggy Dechert when he was twenty-four and buried her when he was thirty-seven, left to raise a thirteen-year-old boy alone.

When Beck's mother died, the world had lost all color. Life became black-and-white, J.B. became hard, and Beck became angry—at God, at the world, at his father. By his senior year, the anger was as much a part of Beck Hardin as the color of his eyes or the speed of his legs. He took the anger with him onto the football field; he played with a fury that even he did not understand, a fury that often frightened him. He knew the anger would eventually kill him or he would kill someone— and he almost had; so he left this land and these people and his father. He ran away, as far as his athletic ability would take him. Notre Dame, Indiana, was thirteen hundred miles from Fredericksburg, Texas.

Beck had not spoken to his father in twenty-four years.

"Why didn't you call ahead?" J.B. said.

"Wasn't sure I wouldn't turn around."

Across Main Street from the courthouse was a park where Beck had often played baseball; they were now sitting at a picnic table where second base had been. The baseball diamond was gone, replaced by a covered open-air arena called Adelsverein Halle. Meggie was eating a corn dog, Luke a sausage-on-a-stick, and Beck barbecue. J.B. was sipping a soda.

Playing where home plate had been was the "Sentimental Journey Orchestra," a big band made up of old guys wearing World War Two khaki uniforms. A trio of middle-aged women called the "Memphis Belles" was singing "Boogie-Woogie Bugle Boy from Company B." They were good. Old white-haired folks were dancing, young blond kids wearing bead necklaces and red, white, and blue tiaras were bopping around as if dancing, and their sunburned parents were drinking Weissbier and Bitburger. Germans here were raised on beer and bratwurst, like the French were on wine and cheese. The soldiers from the parade mingled with the locals and were greeted like celebrities; no soldier had ever been spit on in Fredericksburg, Texas. An old-timer in a plaid shirt walked by, slapped J.B. on the shoulder, and said, "Hell of a shirt, J.B."

After the man had walked out of earshot, J.B. said, "Ned don't got the sense of adventure God gave a turtle."

Beck stood and stretched and smelled beef being barbecued and cotton candy being spun. The rural park with a baseball field had been transformed into a manicured Marktplatz, a European-style town square. The white octagonal Vereins Kirche museum stood in the center of the square. Behind it was the Pioneer Memorial Garden with bronze statues of Baron von Meusebach, the town founder, and a Comanche war chief smoking a peace pipe. A Maibaum depicting the town's history stood tall over the square. World War Two-era music, ranchers, farmers, and soldiers in uniform, old folks and young kids, everyone happy and alive on the Fourth of July in small-town America. It all seemed so perfect.

"She was a special woman," J.B. said. "Annie."

Except that. Beck looked down at his father.

"How would you know?"

His words had come out harsh, and Beck saw the hurt on his father's face. J.B. gathered himself.

"Annie and me, we've been emailing for the better part of two years. About every day her last six months."

"*Annie emailed you?*"

J.B. nodded and Beck sat back down. Another secret.

Beck said, "You've got a computer?"

J.B. nodded again. "Down at the winery."

"You've got a winery?"

"That's how Annie found me, buying wine on the website."

"You've got a website?"

"Yep."

"Why?"

"For online sales. We ship wine all across the country—"

"No. Why did Annie email you?"

"Oh. To get me ready."

"For what?"

"For when you and the kids came home."

Chapter 3

Home was eight hundred acres of land on the Pedernales River three miles south of town.

Beck drove through a black iron gate with a hand-painted sign that read: I SIC THE PIT BULLS ON ALL REAL ESTATE BROKERS DAMN FOOL ENOUGH TO TRESPASS ON THIS LAND. He accelerated up the white caliche road that meandered through oak trees fifty feet tall and two hundred years old, leaving a cloud of white dust in his wake. He steered hard right then left then right. When his father had built this road, he had not removed a single oak tree; so the road zigzagged like a snake crawling across hot ground.

The house sat on the highest point of the land; you could see the sun rise over the distant hills to the east and set beyond the distant hills to the west. And every day the sun had fed this land that had fed the goats that had fed the Hardins for more than a hundred years. The Hardins were goat ranchers.

But where were the goats?

The herd had numbered five thousand head. A sea of woolly Angora goats should be grazing in the fields that sloped gently down to the river. But the fields were empty and the goats were gone. The barn, pens, and shearing shed, the pine wood weathered to a steel gray, sat vacant. Beck felt as if he had come home for Christmas only to find that everyone had moved away.

He glanced out both sides of the car, being careful not to drive into an oak tree. He didn't see goats, but he saw horses, a few cows (J.B. Hardin had always raised his own beef), Axis deer, antelope, a peacock, two wild turkeys flapping their wings at a pot-bellied pig lying in the shade of a tree, and standing along the fence line as if planning an escape a . . . *llama?*

Before Beck Hardin had jumped the fence and fled this land, he had lived his life by the seasons—sports and nature's. Summers meant swimming in the river and shearing goats with J.B. in the shed. Falls were filled with football and deer hunting. Winters were basketball and another round of goat shearing. And each spring—his mother's favorite time of the year when the color returned to the land—he had run track, played baseball, and walked with Peggy Hardin through knee-high wildflowers—bluebonnets, Indian paintbrush, and Mexican hat—wildflowers that turned the land into a canvas of blue, red, orange, and yellow. His mother had picked roses but never wildflowers.

Beck braked at a fork in the road. The south fork continued up to the house; a new west fork led over to a two-story structure that hadn't been there when Beck had left home. He trailed his father's black Ford pickup to the house. J.B. got out, followed by a white lab named Butch. Beck parked in the shade of an oak tree and opened the back door for the kids. Luke didn't budge, but Meggie jumped out and held the doll up as if to see.

"Look, Mommy. This is where Daddy grew up."

The home was a one-story structure, simple and sturdy. The main house was constructed of white limestone two feet thick; it faced east. On the north and south sides were rock-and-cedar additions; the one on the north side was new. The house had a porch across the front, a metal standing-seam roof and a massive river-rock fireplace. A windmill stood twenty yards away.

39

J.B.'s great-grandfather had moved to Fredericksburg after the Civil War; he hadn't been German but he had married a German girl—as had every Hardin male until Beck had married a Chicago girl—and had learned from her father everything there was to know about homebuilding and goat ranching. The Hardin males had handed down what they knew, father to son, until J.B.'s son had gone to Notre Dame to play football. The Hardins were goat ranchers by trade, but they could plumb, wire, roof, and build with the best of men. J.B. was no exception.

"Added on again," Beck said to his father.

J.B. regarded the addition on the north side of the house as if he'd just now noticed it there.

"Bedrooms, for you and the kids."

"J.B., we'll find a place in town."

His father gazed off into the distance. "Eagle's been making a nest, down by the river." Then, without looking at Beck, he said, "You didn't come home to live in town."

Beck sighed. J.B. was right.

"Beck, my father told me this land was mine from the day I was born. I reckon it's been yours since the day you were born. It's just been waiting for you to come home. Land's patient."

J.B. Hardin had always believed that a house was a place to sleep, but land was a place to live.

Beck said, "You really got pit bulls?"

"Nah. But those real-estate brokers don't know it."

"They bothering you?"

"Before I put that sign up, three, four of 'em would come knocking on the door every day, wanting to sell this land. Big real-estate play out here these days, Beck, everyone hoping to get rich selling their land to city folk."

"Who's buying?"

"Californians. They come here for a weekend and think twenty thousand an acre is cheap so they buy a hundred acres like they're buying lunch."

40

"*Twenty thousand an acre?* That's the going price? It was under a thousand when I left."

"Yep. Land-poor locals barely making ends meet, all of a sudden they're rich. I was watching TV the other night—"

"You've got a TV?"

"Yep. Anyway, I was watching *The Beverly Hillbillies*. This ol' boy name of Jed Clampett, he goes out hunting one day, shoots at a critter but strikes oil. Well, Jed gets rich and moves the family to California. Struck me, what's going on here is *The Beverly Hillbillies* in reverse: folks are hoping a Californian moves here and makes them rich."

J.B. started walking toward the house.

"That's what I figure, anyway."

Beck said, "Where are the goats?"

"Gone. Sold the herd off ten years back. Kept a few to eat the cedar shoots. Industry tanked when they killed the mohair incentive—not that I ever took a dime from those bastards."

Mean philandering SOB that he was, LBJ had long been beloved in these parts because he had given the goat ranchers of Gillespie County something more valued than good character; he had given them the "mohair incentive." Government money. Every year for forty years, the U.S. Department of Agriculture had mailed checks to Gillespie County goat ranchers totaling tens of millions of dollars. And unlike other farm subsidies, the mohair incentive didn't phase out at a ceiling price; it kept going up. The more mohair a rancher produced and the higher the market price, the bigger his incentive check; at the program's peak, the government paid four dollars for every dollar a rancher earned. The big goat ranchers got annual checks for a million dollars. But Bill Clinton killed the mohair incentive in 1996. He was not beloved in these parts.

"I knew it wouldn't hurt you."

"Ain't but maybe a hundred thousand goats left in the Hill Country," J.B. said.

The mohair incentive had encouraged ranchers to build goat

41

empires; at the peak, over five million Angora goats had grazed on Hill Country land and accounted for fifty percent of the world's mohair production. One legendary goat rancher had even dubbed himself the "Goat King of the World." J.B. Hardin was one of the few goat ranchers in the county who didn't take the money.

His father said, "Hell, I was ready to try something different. Something that don't stink."

"Well, the wine business would qualify on both counts."

"Reckon it does."

"And you can wear that shirt without risking a stampede."

"That's a fact." J.B. nodded toward the building down the west fork. "That's my winery, Beck. Vineyards are on the back side."

"Grapes do okay in a drought?"

"This rocky land and thin soil ain't worth a damn for cattle or cotton, but it's just about perfect for goats, peaches, turkeys, and grapevines. Government and drought killed off goat ranching and peaches."

"That leaves turkeys and grapevines."

"Just so happens I've got fifty acres of the prettiest vines you'll ever see. And they don't need much water—grapes like it hot and dry in the summer."

"So what, you're a wine expert now?"

"Nope. But Hector is. Me and him, we partnered up. He makes the wine, I do everything else."

J.B. sniffed the air. The faint scent of smoke rode the westerly breeze. "Brush fire out west."

Beck nodded toward the fence line. "Is that a llama?"

J.B. nodded. "Named Sue. Got eyes like a woman. Not that we're having any kind of a relationship."

"Llama, peacocks, turkeys, antelope—place looks like Noah getting ready for the flood."

"Flood would be a nice change of pace after seven years of drought."

★   ★   ★

42

The main room of the house had a high cedar-beamed ceiling and a longleaf pine floor. At one end was the kitchen; at the other end a leather recliner and couch fronted a big screen flat-panel TV. "Had a sale over at the Wal-Mart," J.B. said. "Figured the kids might enjoy that."

Beck had grown up without a television; his father hadn't believed in wasting time watching TV when there was work to be done—and there had always been work to be done. Luke plopped down on the couch and pointed the remote at the TV. The screen flashed on and Meggie said, "Can we watch Sponge-Bob?"

J.B. said, "The hell's a SpongeBob?"

Beck said, "You've got cable?"

"Yep."

"For *The Beverly Hillbillies*?"

"And the cooking shows. Hell of an invention, the crock pot."

"You've got a crock pot?"

"Yep."

"J.B., you never cooked an egg in your life. After Mom died, I did all the cooking."

"You left."

Luke found a baseball game, and Meggie started a tour of the house with the doll. Beck went to the kitchen and opened the refrigerator; everything inside was organic, just like their refrigerator back in Chicago.

"Annie?"

J.B. nodded. "Made a run into Austin day before yesterday. Whole Foods. Never seen so many women with tattoos that don't shave their legs."

"How'd you know we'd come?"

"Annie said you would."

"How'd you know when?"

"Annie said this summer, after school let out and you . . ."

"Failed at raising the kids alone?"

"Figured out you needed help. Which ain't a sign of weakness, Beck. Anyway, I knew you'd have to sell the house, so I checked the listing online. When it said the sale had closed, I figured a few days to get packed, few more to get here."

"You always were a figuring man."

Beck walked out of the kitchen and through the doorway leading to the screened-in back porch that allowed the breeze in but kept the mosquitoes out. The same wood rockers still sat there, where J.B. and Peggy Hardin had ended every day of their lives, watching the sun set over the hills and planning their next day of hard work. After she died, J.B. had sat alone out here and his son had sat alone down by the river or in his room.

Where Beck now stood.

His trophies still sat on the shelf, free of dust, and his clothes still hung in the closet, as if he had only left for an out-of-town game. Beck put on his black Gallopin' Goats letter jacket; it still fit. He replaced the jacket and picked up his old black cowboy boots. He had left them when he had left home—he didn't figure on wearing cowboy boots at Notre Dame and he wasn't coming back. The boots had recently been polished. They still fit, too. He pulled the boots off and went over to the window he had climbed through so many nights to go skinny-dipping in the river by moonlight with Mary Jo Meier. She had been his high school sweetheart, blonde and blue-eyed, slim and strong, a goat rancher's daughter. He had asked her to go with him to Notre Dame, but she said she would never leave home. He told her he wasn't coming back, but she had said, "You'll be back. You might leave me, Beck Hardin, but you'll never leave this land."

He wondered if Mary Jo Meier had ever left home.

Beck walked out of his past and into the new addition. One bedroom had an attached bathroom, a king-sized bed, and a nightstand with a framed photo of Annie. It was his favorite one of her, taken on a Hawaiian beach before they had the kids; the setting sun caught her sun-reddened face and made her glow. She was young, she was beautiful, and she was alive. She had written across the bottom: *I'll love you forever from the hereafter.*

Beck stared at the image of his dead wife.

Two other bedrooms were joined by a bathroom. Luke's bedroom had wood floors and a bed with a Chicago Cubs bedspread. Meggie's had thick carpet and walls painted a sky blue. J.B. had recreated home for the children.

"I still do good work."

J.B. was standing next to him.

"You still walk like an Indian."

J.B.'s boots were off and the legs of his jeans rolled up a turn, revealing white socks. Peggy Hardin's rules were few but absolute: don't pick wildflowers and don't wear dirty boots inside her clean house, and it had always been clean.

"Figured you'd want to be near the kids."

"You built all this just because Annie said we'd come home?"

J.B. nodded. "Said she had seen the future. Said she was gone and y'all were here."

"And that was good enough for you?"

"It was."

Beck glanced at his father and saw that his jaws were clamped tight. He turned away. After a moment, his father spoke softly.

"I never met her face to face, Beck, but I loved her like my own daughter."

"Is this our room?"

Meggie was now standing between them with the doll.

"Yes, darlin'," J.B. said. "It is."

Meggie held the doll up and said, "Look, Mommy, it's just like home."

"I'm back, Mama."

The sun was setting and Beck was sitting on the bench inside the white picket fence under the big oak tree in a little clearing overlooking the river. The three white gravestones gave off an

45

orange tint as they caught the last rays of the sun: Henry Hardin . . . Louise Hardin . . . Peggy Hardin. Fresh flowers sat at the base of each stone.

He stared at his mother's marker, and he thought of looking up from the junior high school football field and seeing her in the stands with her hands folded and pressed against her face as if she were praying—and she had been: while everyone else had been cheering her son on to victory, she had been praying that her son not get hurt. A mother's prayer.

He thought how much he had missed her and still did. And how much he needed her now. He wasn't man enough or father enough or mother enough to raise his children alone. He had been a full-time lawyer and a part-time father. A weekend dad. He had two great kids because they had had a great mother.

He felt a presence and knew it was J.B. His father stepped past him, bent over, and brushed invisible dust from his mother's gravestone. Satisfied, he sat beside Beck.

"Luke doesn't say much, does he?"

"Not since Annie. Where are the roses?"

J.B. had planted rosebushes inside the picket fence after they had buried Beck's mother here, but the roses were gone.

"Roses are like pretty girls," J.B. said. "They need constant attention. Yanked 'em up, seeded this whole clearing with blue-bonnets. Figured your mom would like those more."

"How'd you live without her, J.B.?"

"Not so good. I needed her and you needed me. But damned if I knew how to help you, son. Hell, I couldn't help myself."

"I hated you."

"I know."

"Why'd you get so hard, J.B.?"

"I didn't get hard. I got scared."

"Of what?"

"Of not knowing how to raise you alone."

Beck stared at his mother's marker and thought of his wife. The women in his life always died.

46

"I'm afraid, too, J.B. I can't do this alone."

"You don't have to, Beck. I'm gonna help you."

They were almost to the house when J.B said, "Come down to the winery tomorrow. I'll introduce you to Hector. We could use another hand."

"*Me?* No, J.B., I'm a lawyer. That's all I know."

"I was a goat rancher, now I'm a winemaker. Man's never too old to learn something new."

Beck had not thought out his career plan when he had decided to leave Chicago; his only thoughts were of the children. The law had been his life for the last twenty years; now his two children were his life. He had figured on leaving the law behind him, but he had to make a living.

He had almost $1 million in his retirement account, all in stock. The sale of the house had netted $100,000 and his equity in the firm $200,000, which would be paid out over ten years. He had a $1 million life insurance policy on himself, but he had had no insurance on Annie's life. He never thought she'd die first.

Country life would be less expensive than their life in Chicago, but even so, his cash wouldn't last long. So he needed to work. Maybe he could open a small law office in town.

"Hell, Beck, the ten lawyers in town trip over each other every time an ambulance runs down Main Street. Ain't no work for a big-city trial lawyer here. Small town, you sue someone, no one'll ever do business with you again."

"Well, I could've gone back to goat ranching if you hadn't sold off the goats."

"Hell, less money in goats here than in the law."

They walked on in silence, the evening breeze off the river already cooling down the night air.

"You know," J.B. said, "Bruno Stutz up and retired last month, a year left on his term. Heart condition. Which came as a pretty big surprise to most people around here 'cause no one ever figured the son of a bitch had a heart."

47

"Stutz was still on the bench? He was the judge when I was here."

"You know, Beck, you could win."

"Win what?"

"The election."

"What election?"

"To be the new judge. Special election, September fifteenth, to serve out Stutz's term."

"J.B., I've been gone twenty-four years. No one here is going to vote for me."

"Might be surprised. Folks around here, they haven't forgotten Beck Hardin."

They found the children in front of the TV.

"You kids ready?" J.B. asked.

"For what?" Meggie said.

"Fireworks."

J.B. opened the refrigerator and held out a beer to Beck. He shook his father off. J.B. said, "Sorry," then grabbed two root beers instead. He handed them to Beck and grabbed two more. They all went outside and climbed into J.B.'s pickup. It was a Ford F-350 King Ranch Edition with a diesel engine and a double cab with a bench seat in the back; there was a booster for Meggie just like the one in the Navigator.

Annie.

J.B. drove out onto Ranch Road 16 and headed north; he turned into the Lady Bird Johnson Municipal Park. They weren't alone. Hundreds of other cars had already staked out their positions. But J.B. drove deep into the park and then across the creek that cut through the muny golf course like he had done it before.

"Are we by the driving range?" Beck asked.

"Yep. My regular spot."

"You still come out for the fireworks?"

"I like fireworks. Your mother did, too."

J.B. backed in and cut the engine. Everyone bailed out. J.B.

lowered the tailgate and spread old blankets on the grass. Luke and Meggie and the doll sat on the blankets; J.B. handed the root beers down to them. Beck and his father sat on the tailgate and drank theirs.

Nearby, parents were barbecuing in the last light of the day. Kids were eating ice cream. Boys were throwing footballs and Frisbees and flirting with giggling girls. Music was drifting over from the Pioneer Pavilion. The heat had broken, and the evening air was almost cool. There was a soft breeze. This too was just as Beck had remembered. But all the good memories of this place had been blurred by his mother's death.

The sun soon set, and the clear blue sky turned black. Meggie pointed up and said, "Are those the fireworks? All those sparkly things?"

J.B. laughed. "Why, petunia, those are stars."

"We've never seen so many stars before."

"They're up there all right, you just can't see them in the city 'cause of the ground light."

Meggie said, "Can we stay for all the fireworks this time?"

"You bet you can," J.B. said. "I always stay till the end."

"We couldn't last year. Mommy wanted to, but Daddy said—"

Beck interrupted his daughter. "I had a trial. I didn't know it would be her last . . . She loved fireworks, too."

Just then, explosions went off and the sky overhead turned bright with red, white, and blue fireworks. The light faded, and the sparkles drifted downward, as if they would fall down on top of them. Meggie held the doll up.

"Look, Mommy, we're right under the fireworks!"

J.B. said, "You got the catbird seat, little gal."

More explosions followed, one after another. About halfway through the fireworks show, Beck thought he saw Luke smiling.

"We liked the fireworks."

Beck was tucking Meggie and the doll into bed.

"I'm glad, honey."

49

"We like grandpa, too."

"Good."

"We never knew we had a grandpa."

"Well, you do."

"He calls us 'gal' and 'darlin'' and 'petunia.' We like that. And we like our new home."

Beck leaned over and kissed Meggie on her forehead. She smelled like strawberry shampoo.

"Kiss Mommy, too."

She held the doll up, and he kissed it. She then snuggled it close.

"Let's say our prayers, sweetie."

She folded her hands and together they recited: "Dear God in heaven, we bow our heads, here beside our little bed. In your loving care we're blessed, while we sleep safe at rest."

"Sleep tight, baby."

"What if we have an accident?"

Beck had forgotten the plastic sheet. He had kept one on Meggie's bed at home, for her nightly accidents.

"I'll go find the plastic sheet."

"It's already on."

Beck reached down; she was right. A plastic sheet covered the mattress. "If you have an accident, come to me like at home."

"Okay, we will."

She closed her eyes. Beck stood and turned off the overhead light; the room was still dimly lit by a night light. He walked down to Luke's room. His son was lying in bed, staring blankly at the ceiling. Beck went over and sat on the edge of the bed. The boy had been crying again. He brushed Luke's hair from his face.

"We'll make a new life here, son. It'll be a good life."

"If it's so good here, why'd you leave and never come back?"

"Because when my mother died, Luke, I got mad, and I held onto it. I didn't let it go."

50

Tears came into Luke's eyes.

"Did you say your prayers?"

Luke turned his face to the wall and said, "I don't say prayers anymore."

Beck sighed and patted his son's shoulder. He loved this boy, but he didn't know how to help him. Just as J.B. Hardin didn't know how to help his son twenty-nine years before.

Beck found J.B. on the back porch in his rocking chair reading the local newspaper in the light of a gooseneck lamp. The white lab named Butch lay on the floor. Beck sat in Peggy's rocker that still sat next to J.B.'s. His father said, "Got a seventeen-foot Bass Tracker boat for sale in here with a forty-horsepower Mercury oil-injected motor and a fish finder."

"J.B., that's a lake boat. The river's not deep enough to float a lake boat."

"Well, now, that is a drawback."

"You still religious about reading the classifieds?"

"Never know when you might find something you don't need."

"Like a lake boat when you live on a river?"

"Exactly."

The night was quiet, and the breeze through the screen brought the scent of the river up to the house.

"You do much hunting these days?"

J.B. shook his head. "Not since . . ."

"I left?"

"It never was about the hunting."

No, it never was.

"I tell you," J.B. said, "crime around here's getting out of hand. Says right here, six Porta-Potties were knocked over last week, four the week before. That's a damn mess, too. Hope no one was in 'em at the time."

"A Porta-Potty crime spree?"

"Says here Crime Stoppers will pay $1,000 cash for information leading to the arrest of the perpetrators."

51

"A Crime Stoppers reward for a Porta-Potty drive-by? In Chicago, unless there was blood, it wasn't even considered a crime."

J.B. tapped the newspaper with his finger. "Nine divorces last week. That's what happens when people get cable."

"You've got cable."

"But I don't got a wife." J.B. looked up from the paper. "Beck, I'm gonna put Luke to work in the winery, if that's okay."

"That's a good idea. How'd you know about the plastic sheets on Meggie's bed?"

"Annie."

"She didn't start wetting the bed until after Annie died."

"She figured it might happen. Smart woman."

"Yeah. I've got to get smarter at this, J.B., soon. This town got a bookstore yet?"

"Yep. Couple of gals run it, that and the art gallery upstairs. South side of Main Street, just past the brewery."

"I saw that, a microbrewery. The town has really changed."

J.B. smiled and Beck thought it was a good smile. He couldn't remember his father ever smiling after his mother died.

"You ain't seen nothin' yet," J.B. said. "Wait'll you meet those two gals. They're new in town, only been here ten years."

"Lot of new people in town."

"Yep. When Clinton killed the mohair program, he killed all the businesses on Main catering to goat ranchers. So newcomers started all those businesses catering to tourists. Town went from living off Uncle Sam to living off tourists."

"I'm gone twenty-four years and the place turns into Disneyland."

"Santa Fe."

They drifted off into silence. Twenty-four years since Beck had sat on this porch, but it felt like yesterday. Home it had been and home it was again. But his mother was gone and his father was different.

"You've changed, too, J.B."

"Man spends enough time alone, he'll change."

"Being alone does it?"

"Being alone gives a man time to work through every mistake he's ever made in his life. I've sat right here and done exactly that the last twenty-four years. I don't aim to make the same mistakes again . . . if you'll forgive me for back then."

Beck thought about his father's words for a time. Then he said, "J.B., would you mind watching Meggie in the morning? I'd like to take Luke out to the Rock."

"Sure, I'll keep an eye on the little gal."

J.B. went back to the newspaper, and Beck's thoughts went back to his life here. He wondered what his children's lives would be like here; he hoped he had made the right decision.

He said, "Any jobs in that paper?"

"Diesel mechanic out at the granite quarry."

"I can't change the oil in the Navigator."

"You could work at the turkey plant."

"I don't speak Spanish."

"Nursing home needs help."

"I figure watching after one old fart will be enough."

"That'll be the day. Says here they have chair dancing every Monday night. Believe I'd rather not dance than dance with a chair."

His father started chuckling.

"Chair dancing's not that funny, J.B."

"Pretty damn funny, but I'm not laughing about that. I'm thinking about that election, for judge. You could win, Beck."

J.B. returned to his paper, and they sat quietly for a time until Beck said, "J.B., just so you know . . . I forgave you a long time ago. I just wasn't man enough to tell you."

J.B.'s jaws clenched. "Appreciate you telling me now."

"Can you forgive me?"

"A man never has to forgive his son."

"Maybe not, but I'm still sorry. I'm sorry I left here hating you and I'm sorry I didn't bring Annie here, so she could've known you and you could've known her. She was a woman worth knowing."

J.B. sighed. "I knew her."

Chapter 4

*Oh, Beck, I love you . . . I love what you do to me . . . God, I'm
so wet . . . We're so wet . . .*

"We're wet."

Beck woke. And Annie was gone. Again.

"What?"

"We're wet."

Meggie stood beside the bed, holding her doll. She smelled
of fresh urine. She had wet the bed again. He sat up.

"That's okay, baby."

He now kept a damp towel and clean clothes for her next
to the bed. He changed her clothes, and she climbed into bed.

The sunlight through the blinds woke Beck.

He checked his watch: six-thirty. He climbed out of bed,
quietly so as not to wake Meggie, then walked down the hall
and checked on Luke; he was still asleep. Beck took the wet
sheets off Meggie's bed and carried them to the laundry room.
In the kitchen, he found fresh coffee and a note from J.B.: *Gone
to town, then down to the winery. Bring the kids after breakfast. Pancake
batter – blueberry – Annie's recipe – in the fridge.* Utensils and syrup

were on the counter. The sun was just rising, but J.B. Hardin had never wasted a minute of daylight in his life.

Beck poured a cup of coffee and went out onto the back porch. He stepped into a pair of J.B.'s rubber boots and walked outside. He was wearing only pajama shorts, but there wasn't a neighbor within two miles of where he stood. Peggy Dechert had been the girl next door, even though next door had been a mile away. When she and J.B. married, they and their goat ranches had become one.

Beck admired the land. All eight hundred acres had long ago been cleared of brush and Ashe juniper trees, known as cedar to Texans; Beck had cut brush and chopped cedar from sunup to sundown more days than he cared to remember. J.B. Hardin hated cedar like the plague, and in the ground it was just that, with its deep roots sucking the groundwater like a thirsty kid sucking a big soda through a straw. Water had always been more scarce than oil in Texas, and now it was more valuable. Cedar was a water thief.

When goats had free range on this land, they would eat the grass, plants, and brush down to the bare ground and even the shoots six feet up the trunks of the cedar and shin oak trees— the "goat line." But with the goats gone, the native grasses had made a comeback. The land looked good.

There had been a brief rain overnight, not enough to end a drought, just a spit really, but enough to tease the grass into giving off a hint of green hope. The rain droplets on the blades of grass shimmered like diamonds in the first light of the sun over the eastern hills. By mid-morning, the sun would burn off the water and all hope; but now Beck welcomed the sun.

He didn't dream of Annie while he was awake.

He sipped the coffee and inhaled the morning air. The birds were awake and singing, and just past the house fawns were standing on shaky legs and foraging for breakfast. Beck walked down the gently sloping land and across a wood bridge that spanned Snake Creek; it was bone dry. He went down to the

56

river. Cypress trees and willows lined the near riverbank; the far side was a sheer white limestone bluff fifty feet high. Growing up here, this had been his back yard, this land and that river.

The Pedernales River—named "River of Flint" because the Spanish explorers had found flint arrowheads along the riverbank—had its headwaters in springs out one county west and flowed east a hundred miles to Lake Travis. The river was eighty feet wide here but not two feet deep. The clear water coursed gently between large flat rocks that spanned the river and formed a natural bridge; Beck stepped from rock to rock until he was in the middle of the river, where he had often found himself as a boy.

The wind had yet to pick up, so the surface of the water was still as smooth as glass. Beck bent over and grabbed a small flat rock. He hefted it and decided it would do. He gripped the rock between his thumb and index finger like J.B. had taught Beck the boy; he threw the rock sidearm. The rock flew low then skipped across the surface of the water four times before disappearing from sight. Beck watched the ripples spread out until they blended back into the water and the surface became smooth again, as if the rock had never been a part of the river's life.

His life had been perfect here, for a while, and then he had found perfect again in Chicago. Thirteen years here, twelve years there; maybe twenty-five years of perfect out of one lifetime were all a man could rightfully expect. Maybe it was more than a man should expect. And so he felt lonely and afraid but not cheated. It was his children who had been cheated.

"We're hungry."

Meggie was standing on a big rock on the riverbank in her white nightshirt with the doll tucked under her arm.

The Trail's End Winery was exactly what Beck would have expected of his father: built to perfection. The front and back sections of the building were one story, constructed of limestone, and angled up about forty-five degrees to meet a two-story all-cedar center section just below a row of windows that ran the length of the structure under a green standing-seam metal roof.

They found J.B. inside, behind a long wooden bar that looked like it belonged in an old western saloon; a mirror on the back wall stretched the length of the bar. Under the mirror were neat rows of wine glasses; on the bar were a dozen bottles of wine. J.B. said, "You kids like those pancakes?"

"Yes, we did," Meggie said. She was carrying the doll.

The floor was pine and cedar beams spanned the open space. The limestone walls came together in one corner to form a fireplace fronted by a leather sofa and chairs. Stacked on wood shelves were tee shirts, sweatshirts, and caps in all colors with *Trail's End Winery, Fredericksburg, Texas* stenciled across the front.

"I don't remember you ever drinking wine, J.B."

"Never touch the stuff."

"You don't drink wine?"

He shook his head. "Don't like it."

"You own a winery but you don't like wine?"

"I own a winery 'cause I like the wine business. I like the pace of it, the order, the vines in perfect rows in the vineyard. I like planting new growth, tending to it. I like the harvest, crushing and pressing the grapes, fermentation, aging, bottling—it's got a rhythm all its own. I like that. I like people that like wine. I just don't like wine."

"You're a piece of work, J.B."

A door next to the bar opened, and a middle-aged Hispanic man walked through just as J.B. added, "And I like Hector."

The Hispanic man stopped, cocked his head, and smiled. He said, "I like you too, J.B."

"Hector," J.B. said, "meet my son, Beck. The lawyer."

Hector said to Beck, "He says this as if he has another son who is 'the doctor.'" He stuck his hand out to Beck. "I am Hector Aurelio . . . the winemaker."

Hector was a short man with a pleasant face. He wore khaki shorts, huaraches without socks, and a yellow *Trail's End Winery* shirt. He smelled like wine.

"J.B. says you make the wine."

Hector smiled again. "My family first came north from Matamoros to pick the peaches and stayed to pick the grapes. I discovered that I have the taste for wine. So now I make the wine. But I still pick the grapes." He glanced down at Meggie. "And who is this beautiful little *señorita*?"

"My daughter, Meggie."

"Señorita Meggie, perhaps you would like to meet Josefina . . . she is my daughter. She is six."

"Can she play with us?"

"Us?" Hector appeared confused, then he realized. "Ah, the doll. Yes, J.B. said you might need a playmate."

Meggie glanced up at Beck. "It's okay, honey."

Hector turned to Luke. "And you must be Luke. So you would like to learn to make the wine?"

Now Luke glanced up at Beck. "J.B. thought you might like to work down here, Luke, learn a few things."

Luke shrugged his shoulders. Hector looked at Beck and nodded, then he held his hand out to Meggie. "Come, let us find Josefina. She is in the vineyards, with Butch."

Hector, Meggie, and the doll walked off hand in hand in hand.

J.B. came out from behind the bar; he was wearing a gray-blue Hawaiian shirt with a red, yellow, and orange jungle floral print stretching from shirttail to shoulder.

Beck said, "How many of those shirts you got, J.B.?"

"One for every day of the week plus a few spares." J.B. gestured at the room. "This is our tasting room. We got the Harvest Wine Trail end of next month, pretty big deal around here. Tourists drive from winery to winery tasting, like in that movie a few years back. A dozen wineries in the Hill Country now. They say we're the next Napa Valley."

59

"Santa Fe."

"That, too."

J.B. led them into the two-story section of the building. Massive wood trusses and cross beams overhead were supported by floor-to-ceiling rough-hewn logs embedded in the foundation. Sunlight shone through the row of windows on each side of the top wall. Six stainless steel tanks stood in two rows; above the tanks was a catwalk. At one end of the room were barn doors.

"Vat room. Each vat holds fifteen hundred gallons."

"That's a lot of wine."

"Takes a lot of grapes. Right here is where the winemaking happens. Hector'll take you through the whole process, Luke— it's like a science experiment. You like science?"

Luke said nothing, but Beck caught a spark of interest in his eyes; he had made As in science.

"Come on, I'll show you the barrel cellar."

They followed J.B. down a set of stairs into a basement dug out of the limestone bedrock. Hundreds of wood barrels stacked on metal stands filled the cool cavern.

"We keep it at sixty degrees down here," J.B. said. "While the wine ages."

"How do you know when the wine is ready?"

"When Hector says it is. Winemaking's part science, part art. There ain't no gauge or computer program tells you when wine is ready. Takes a vintner with the taste. That's the art of it."

J.B. led them back upstairs into another room with a stainless steel contraption stationed in the middle.

"Bottling room. Each barrel holds fifty-nine gallons. Standard-size wine bottle holds seven hundred fifty milliliters. That comes to twenty-four cases per barrel. Each case is twelve bottles, so that's two hundred eighty-eight bottles of wine per barrel. We'll bottle twenty thousand this year."

"Bottles?"

"Cases."

"*Cases?* That's . . ."

60

"Two hundred forty thousand bottles."

"That's a lot of wine, J.B."

"Nah. Big wineries here, they do twice that. And that's nothing compared to the California outfits."

"J.B., you've got quite an operation here."

"Me and Hector, we've come a long way in ten years."

They followed J.B. up another set of stairs to the second story of the building. Hanging on the walls were antique implements. J.B. stopped and removed a hammer from a hook.

"Bung hammer. Five pound cast-iron head. They used to stuff a leather roll into the end so it wouldn't break the wood bung. We use silicon bungs now."

J.B. replaced the hammer and led them into an office with a wall of windows overlooking the vineyards and the river beyond.

"This is my office."

Beck looked out the windows at the uniform rows of thick green vines. Meggie and Josefina were playing in the shade of the vines. The white lab lay nearby.

J.B. said, "Now Butch's got two little gals to watch over. Makes him feel useful." He gestured at the vineyard. "Fifty acres of vines, ten different varietals . . . types of grapes. We harvest a little later here, so the sugar content of the grapes is higher. Texans like their women and wine sweet. First harvest will be in a few weeks, last harvest first week of September. We throw a big party. Lots of folks come out, we pick till sunset, then we eat Mexican food and Hector plays the guitar and everyone dances. The kids'll have fun."

Southwestern style paintings signed by "Janelle Jones" hung on the walls, a leather couch sat along one wall, and a leather chair was behind a big wood desk. On the desk were a stack of invoices, several unopened bottles of wine, a ledger book, a framed photograph of the Hardin family of Chicago, and a computer. Beck stared at the computer: *Were Annie's emails still on that computer?* Beck looked up and saw J.B. looking at him.

★   ★   ★

Beck turned the Navigator north and drove into town. Luke was sitting in the passenger's seat and staring out the window; he hadn't said a word the entire morning. Beck stopped for a red light at Gallopin' Goat Drive, the intersection fronting the high school. He instinctively glanced over at the adjacent football stadium. It was only the fifth of July, but the team was already practicing for the upcoming season.

"You want to watch the boys practice?"

Beck took Luke's shrug for a yes and pulled into the parking lot of the Gillespie County Consolidated School District stadium. They got out and walked through the main gate and past a sign that read DRUG FREE, GUN FREE, TOBACCO FREE, ALCOHOL FREE SCHOOL ZONE. VIOLATORS WILL FACE SEVERE FEDERAL, STATE, AND LOCAL CRIMINAL PENALTIES. That was different.

They continued on past the concession stand and stepped onto the eight-lane running track that circled the field. Drought had turned the Hill Country brown, but the football field was as green as money and carried the same hopes. Twenty-five summers before, Beck Hardin had practiced, played, and dreamed on that field. It seemed like someone else's life.

Big white boys in black shorts and no shirts were throwing, catching, and kicking footballs; boys were running and balls were flying. The wind was down and the humidity was up; the air in the bowl of the stadium was thick with sweat and testosterone. The boys' voices sounded manly.

Beck spotted the quarterback at the far end of the field. He was a tall kid. He grunted a deep "Hut!" and the center snapped the ball back to him. Five receivers raced down the field toward the south end zone where Beck and Luke were standing. The quarterback waited for a three-count, then his right arm suddenly shot forward and the ball rocketed downfield as if fired from a cannon; it flew in a perfect spiral on a high arc and dropped right into the outstretched hands of a receiver running full speed down the sideline—and he dropped it. A voice bellowed out from above like the voice of God—"Catch the damn ball!"—except God didn't cuss like a football coach. The boys turned in unison and looked up at a solitary figure sitting on the top row of the home bleachers in the shade of the small white press box under a black sign: LAND OF THE GALLOPIN' GOATS. The man seemed familiar.

"Is that . . . ? Come on, Luke."

They walked around the track to the concrete bleachers, then climbed the twelve rows to the top and cut over toward the man. He was wearing black knit shorts, a white knit shirt, and a black cap over short blond hair. He was leaning back against the press box with his legs stretched over the bench in front; his thick arms were folded across his chest, and he was studying his players so intently that he didn't notice he had company until Beck called out to him from twenty seats away.

"Aubrey!"

The man's head swiveled their way; his left cheek bulged like he had a tumor the size of a golf ball. His face remained blank for a beat, then he broke into a big smile. He didn't stand; instead, he spat a brown stream of tobacco juice in the opposite direction, then held a big hand up to Beck. They shook.

"Beck Hardin. Heard you finally come to your senses and got your butt back to the country where you belong."

"Word travels fast."

"Ain't every day a local hero comes home."

Beck Hardin had been the star quarterback and Aubrey Geisel his favorite receiver; they had been the best players and best friends. Their senior year they had won the state championship for the first and only time in the school's history.

"Real sorry to hear about your wife, Beck."

Luke turned and walked back down the bleachers; he stood at the railing and faced the field. Aubrey said, "I say something wrong?"

"Luke's having a tough time. We all are."

Beck sat next to his high school buddy. From twenty-five

63

feet above ground level, they caught a hot breeze and a clear view of the distant hills etched against the blue sky. Beck could see the tall screen of the old Highway 87 Drive-in Theater where he and Mary Jo had made out in his truck.

Aubrey turned away and spat, then drank beer from a can. Four empty cans littered the concrete under him. Beck said, "Sign says this is an alcohol and tobacco free zone."

Aubrey said, "Beer and chewing tobacco ain't free." He smiled. "I'm the coach . . . and I'm not officially here."

"Head coach of the Goats?"

Aubrey nodded. "Ten years now."

"You're starting practice early."

"We can't hold organized practices till August one, but the boys can work out on their own and I can sit up here and cuss at them. Hell, fact is, we never stop practicing. Only two sports seasons in Texas, Beck—football season and football off-season."

"Boys here don't play soccer now?"

Aubrey spat. "Only the Mexicans."

"Luke played up in Chicago, all the boys did. No interest down here?"

"No scholarships down here, except for girls. That Title 9 forced the colleges to equalize scholarships on gender, so they had to cut scholarships for all the boys' sports to keep football and basketball. Black boys from the cities get the basketball scholarships. If you're a white boy and you want a full scholarship in Texas, you don't play soccer. You play football." He gestured at the field. "And every white boy out there wants a scholarship, just like we did. It's their ticket out."

"No black players on the team?"

"No black kids in the school. Hell, even the Katrina kids wouldn't stay, went down to Houston. Sauerkraut and bratwurst, that's a big-time culture shock after crawfish étouffée." Aubrey's attention was drawn to the field; he yelled out, "Catch the damn ball!" He spat. "You staying out at the old place?"

Beck nodded. "J.B.'s putting us up."

"You and him back on the same page?"

"Working at it."

"Wish my dad was still alive so we could work at it. Me and him, we fussed every chance we could. Now I'd give anything just to have a chance to fuss with him again."

"I didn't know he died."

Aubrey nodded. "Thirteen years ago. Now they're both gone, mom and dad." He spat. "Anyway, you went up to Notre Dame, I went over to Southwest Texas, got a degree in education so I could coach. When Otto died—"

"Coach Otto?"

"Yep, heart attack right out there on the field. Boys busted a play, Otto went into one of his cussin' tirades . . . keeled over dead as a doornail. But hell, you can't eat kielbasa and eggs every morning like Otto did and live to be eighty. I was his offensive coordinator, so the school board made me head coach. We're favored to win state this year."

"Your boys are big, Aubrey."

"That's the game now, Beck. Bigger, stronger, faster. Boys start pumping iron when they're ten these days, gotta bulk up to move up. Pro offensive lines, they average three-thirty. Colleges, three hundred. Mine averages two-seventy. And it ain't just linemen. My quarterback is six-five, two-thirty-five."

Beck watched the big kid rifle another pass downfield.

Aubrey said, "Runs a four-five forty in full pads and can throw a football through a brick wall. Number one prospect in the nation. Before he committed to UT, every coach in the country came here to watch him play. He's the real deal. Two years of college, he'll jump to the pros. Name's Slade McQuade."

"*Slade?* What kind of parents name their son Slade?"

"His kind of parents. It's a football name. People name their boys Colt, Chase, Shane, Slade—movie star names that'll sound cool when they're playing on national TV."

"But that's not going to happen for most of these boys."

Aubrey spat. There was a brown puddle on the gray concrete on his far side. "It's gonna happen for every one of these boys, Beck. November nine, we play Kerrville right here, the Nike High School Football Game of the Week. On national TV."

"High school football on national TV?"

"Yep. High school ball is big-time now, Beck. Schools spend whatever it takes to win. And colleges only recruit the best players, so the dads spend whatever it takes to make their boys the best. Slade's dad—name's Quentin McQuade—says he's spent a half-million bucks on private trainers and coaches."

"That's a lot of money."

"He's got a lot. Real-estate developer. Come rolling in here five years ago from Austin, bought the old Hoermann place."

"That was a big spread."

"Almost three thousand acres. Heard he paid twenty million, cash. Built himself a mansion, now he's developing the ranch, a high-falutin' gated golf community."

"*Gated?* Who's he trying to keep out?"

Aubrey spat. "Goats, I guess. They say he spent ten million on the golf course, figures on selling two hundred homes out there, one million and up. We're in a goddamn drought, ain't enough water for the people and livestock as it is, much less to feed a fancy golf course"—he spat—"but Quentin's money cut a wide swath through city hall so he gets what he wants. He ain't someone you cross."

"What brought him out here?"

"He wanted a pro offense for Slade. Shopped high schools around the state, picked us."

"He moved here for your offense?"

"Yep. We spread five out, shotgun, no huddle, throw fifty times a game. Call it the NASCAR offense 'cause we never slow down. Averaged four hundred yards passing per game last year. Figuring on five hundred this year with Slade pulling the trigger." Aubrey abruptly yelled out to the field: "Catch the damn ball!" Back to Beck: "If they'll catch the damn ball."

Beck watched Slade throw a few more passes and said, "He's got an arm."

"He's got a publicist."

"What?"

"Quentin hired the boy a publicist. When he announced he was gonna play college ball at UT, he held a press conference over in Austin. A hundred media people showed up, a thousand students, cheerleaders, coaches . . . all the cable sports channels ran it live. You'd think he found the cure for cancer."

Aubrey grimaced and glanced at Beck.

"Sorry." He spat. "Anyways, I got sports writers come here from all over the country. My secretary, that's all she does now, schedule Slade's interviews. He's gonna be on the cover of *Sports Illustrated*. Other kids, they ask him for autographs, want photos with him, like he's Tom Cruise or something. It's crazy."

Aubrey spat then cupped his mouth and yelled out toward the field: "Slade!" He got the boy's attention, waved him over, and said, "They've already got him in a Gatorade commercial."

The boy jogged across the field and the running track and in one movement grabbed the bleacher railing and vaulted himself up and over. He ran up the stands two rows at a stride.

Beck stood to meet Slade McQuade.

Beck was six-two, but the boy towered over him. Slade outweighed him by fifty pounds, but his body mass seemed twice Beck's. His shoulders were wide and his arms thick with knotty muscles; his veins stood out like blue ropes running down his arms. His chest was broad and looked like a rock sculpture, and his torso angled sharply down to a narrow waist. Slade didn't have a six-pack; he had a twelve-pack. His skin was tanned and shimmering in oily sweat and seemed to be stretched to the breaking point by the muscles underneath. His shorts strained against muscular thighs.

Beck felt small.

Slade's entire body appeared to be chiseled from stone, including his angular face. Acne was his only flaw. Looking at Slade

McQuade was like looking at a statue of a Greek god—except a Greek god didn't wear mirrored sports sunglasses and a black doo-rag or have long black hair hanging to his shoulders or diamond stud earrings stuck in each ear lobe or barbed-wire tattoos wrapped around each bulging bicep.

Beck realized he was staring.

Aubrey spat and said, "Slade, meet Beck Hardin." Aubrey pointed to the face of the press box above them where Beck's number 8 jersey hung encased in plexiglass; the school had retired his jersey after his senior season. "That's his jersey."

Slade said, "They'll have to move it over for mine in a few months." He stuck a hand out. "Beck."

Not "Mr. Hardin."

"I'm looking forward to seeing you play, Slade."

"You and the whole State of Texas—for the Longhorns next year."

Aubrey said, "Let's win state this year first, Slade."

"That's a done deal, Coach."

"Still gotta play the games."

Beck said, "Well, good luck this season."

Slade smiled. "Beck, I'd rather be big, strong, and fast than lucky."

Aubrey spat and said, "Get 'em running sprints, Slade."

Slade jogged down the bleachers, vaulted the railing again, and ran out to the field. Beck sat down and leaned back; he and Aubrey crossed their arms like two old men; they stared at the field. Beck finally said, "Nice kid."

Aubrey chuckled. "Yep, he's a real peach. That's what you gotta put up with these days, Beck, buncha prima-goddamn-donna boys." He spat. "Slade's already got a slogan."

"A slogan?"

Aubrey nodded. "You know, like Nike's 'Just Do It'? His is, 'Number Twelve on the Field and Number One in Your Heart.' Quentin copyrighted it or registered it or whatever you do with a slogan so no one can steal it."

68

"Trademarked."

Aubrey spat. "That's an idea, Beck. Maybe Quentin could use a big-time Chicago lawyer like yourself to further Slade's career."

"I'd rather pick grapes at J.B.'s winery."

"See, that's the thing, Beck, you always had options. Me, I only know coaching, so I gotta put up with Slade."

Beck said, "Bench him."

Aubrey laughed. "You mean quit coaching? 'Cause if I benched Slade, that's what I'd be doing. Been twenty-five years since this town had a state championship, Beck, and people here, they want it bad. And Slade's the ticket." He spat. "Easier to find another head coach than another quarterback like him."

"Maybe he'll flunk out."

"Of what? PE? He's a fifth-year senior. Turns nineteen September three, so he's still eligible and he's taking one PE class to stay eligible."

"He's two months from nineteen?"

"Yep. Quentin held him back in kindergarten and again in seventh grade so he'd have two extra years to get bigger. He did. Lots of dads do that now. Soon as the season's over, he's enrolling at UT."

"In the middle of his senior year?"

He spat. "All the big football factories get their quarterback recruits enrolled for the spring semester, so they'll be there for spring training. Get a jump on next season."

"What about being a kid—senior class trip, prom?"

"Don't mean squat when you're on the fast track to the NFL."

"Doesn't sound like much fun."

"It ain't supposed to be. Slade goes first in the draft, he'll get sixty million with a ten-million signing bonus. How'd you like to be twenty-one with ten million bucks in your pocket? Football ain't about having fun. It's about making money."

Beck shook his head. "High school football is more complicated these days."

69

"You don't know the half of it." Aubrey stared out at the field where the boys were now running sprints the length of the field; Slade was out in front by twenty yards. Aubrey spat. "But if we do win state, I might quit anyway. Figure I could trade up for a college job, maybe ride Slade to an assistant spot with UT. Better pay, might be able to get Randi back."

"Randi Barnes?"

Beck and Mary Jo and Aubrey and Randi had double-dated all through high school. Randi was two years younger.

Aubrey nodded. "We dated till she graduated, got married that summer. But you know Randi, she always wanted more. Left me a few years back, moved to Austin. Ain't seen her since."

"Do y'all have kids?"

Aubrey recoiled almost as if Beck had hit him.

"J.B. didn't tell you?"

"Tell me what?"

Aubrey's eyes dropped and he stared down, as if searching for an answer in the brown puddle of tobacco juice. He spat.

"We had a girl. She died . . . four years, six months, five days ago today. On New Year's Eve. She was only sixteen."

"Jesus, Aubrey, I'm sorry."

Aubrey's jaw muscles flexed like he was chewing on the past. He spat. "She was murdered, Beck."

"*Murdered?* By whom?"

"Don't know. He gave her cocaine, she OD'd."

"How do you know he gave it to her?"

"She didn't do drugs, Beck. She was a good girl."

"No, I mean, how do you know she was with a guy?"

"They got his DNA."

"From what?"

Aubrey looked like he might cry. "Semen."

"Was she raped?"

"Same difference, drugging her like that. She couldn't have known what she was doing or she wouldn't have done it. But it don't matter—she was sixteen and that ain't legal." Aubrey stiffened up. "We got his DNA, Beck, we just don't got him. And we've only got five months and twenty-six days to get him. I keep a calendar."

"What do you mean?"

"I mark off each day since she died—"

"No. The 'five months and twenty-six days'?"

"Oh. Five-year statute of limitations on statutory rape. Runs out midnight New Year's Eve."

"Aubrey, I'm not a criminal lawyer, but if he gave cocaine to a minor and she died, that's got to be murder, or at least manslaughter. And there's no statute of limitations on murder or manslaughter."

Aubrey was shaking his head. "That's the problem—gotta prove he gave it to her. He'll just deny it and who's to say otherwise? D.A. says no way he could get a conviction on murder or manslaughter."

He spat.

"But he can't deny the DNA. If he was three years older than her, ain't no defense to stat rape, even if she let him. He's going to prison—if we find him in time. D.A. says if he's not indicted by midnight on New Year's Eve, he's a free man forever." Aubrey stared out at the field, then said in a quiet voice, "He dumped her in a ditch, Beck. Out 290 East by the city limits sign."

"The white cross."

Aubrey nodded.

"So what's happening with the case? Are the police still looking for this guy?"

Aubrey shook his head. "Sheriff—she was on the county side of the line—he says there's nothing left to do. They got DNA from every male in the county fifteen and over. No matches."

"Stutz ordered that?"

"Nope. Sheriff asked. Everyone came forward on their own, even the Mexicans, at least the legals. Dads brought their boys in. No one wanted to be a suspect."

71

"That wouldn't have happened in Chicago."

"Small town, Beck. Everyone would know who refused."

"So this guy was an outsider? Or an illegal?"

"Mexicans know better than to come around German girls. He was an outsider, I'm sure of it."

Aubrey stared at his players for a time. Then he spat and turned to Beck. "You do me a favor, Beck, for old times?"

"What kind of favor?"

"Look into her case. Smart lawyer like yourself, you might see something the sheriff didn't."

"Aubrey, I'm a civil trial lawyer. I'm not even that right now. I don't know what I could do."

"You can do anything you want to do when you're the judge. Word around town is, you're gonna run."

"Word around town?" Then Beck remembered. "J.B. was in town this morning."

"I heard about it over at the Java Ranch. Coffee shop on Main. Got the whole town talking."

"I haven't decided yet."

"Well, now, that creates a bit of a problem."

"Why's that?"

"'Cause I told everyone I'm backing you."

"Aubrey, every lawyer in town is going to file."

"Every lawyer in town didn't win the state championship."

Aubrey gazed into the sky. Beck looked up: a red-tailed hawk was circling in the distance like a kite on a string.

"You're her only hope, Beck."

"Her hope for what?"

"Justice."

There was that word. Beck Hardin knew all about justice. At Notre Dame, Beck the law student had asked about justice; an old professor had said, "Justice? Mr. Hardin, justice is God's domain. Our domain is the law. A good lawyer never confuses the two." So Beck the lawyer had not expected justice. But Beck the man had, only to learn that there was no justice in

72

this life, not for his wife or his mother . . . or for Aubrey's daughter. But he saw the same hope in Aubrey's eyes that he had seen in Annie's eyes and in the eyes of the other patients in the chemo room when he had taken her in for treatments, the desperate hope that there was still justice to be had in life. The same desperate hope he now saw in his own eyes each morning when he shaved.

"Aubrey, even if I won, by the time I took office, there'd only be three months left before the statute runs."

"How much do you charge, as a lawyer?"

"Eight hundred an hour."

He spat. "I can hire you for six hours."

"Aubrey, you're not paying me."

"The sheriff's holding back on me, Beck, not telling me everything he knows. He might talk to you."

"Why would he withhold information?"

"I don't know. You're my lawyer—ask him."

Aubrey reached to his other side and grabbed a cane. He struggled to his feet. Surgical scars ran down both sides of his right leg, which was noticeably thinner than his left leg.

"You are my lawyer, aren't you, Beck?"

Beck exhaled and pulled his eyes off the scars. He looked up at his old friend and nodded. "Yeah, Aubrey, I'm your lawyer."

"Thanks, Beck. I'll pay you, least until you're the judge."

"I don't want your money, Aubrey."

Beck stood, and they shook hands again. Aubrey nodded down at Luke. "He your only kid?"

"I've got a girl, Meggie. She's five."

"And you don't have a clue about raising girls?"

"No."

"I didn't either. Mine died in a ditch—and I don't know why." Aubrey wiped his eyes. "Find out what happened to my girl, Beck, so yours don't end up in a ditch, too."

Beck stepped down the bleachers. He and Luke turned to

walk away, but Beck stopped and turned back. He called up to Aubrey.

"What was her name, your daughter?"

Aubrey spat then called down to him.

"Heidi."

Chapter 5

Drive north out of town on Ranch Road 965 and the landscape turns from white to pink—from limestone to granite—as you climb onto the Llano Uplift, an underground granite mass seventy miles wide. Granite outcroppings dot the rugged terrain, granite bluffs rise from low creeks, and granite boulders lie scattered across the land like God had smote his kitchen countertop into a million little pieces. And the biggest piece of granite in these parts is the Rock.

"We're gonna climb that?"

Directly in front of them stood a four-hundred-twenty-five-foot-tall pink granite dome jutting out of the earth like the round tip of a granite iceberg. The above-ground portion comprised one square mile, the underground portion one hundred square miles. It'd been there a billion years.

Eleven thousand years ago, the first human climbed the Rock. More followed: the Spanish explorer Cabeza de Vaca; the Indians, first the Tonkawa, then the Apache, and finally the Comanche; and then the Texans. Officially known as "Enchanted Rock" because the Indians believed magical spirits inhabited the caves in the granite, it's now a state park.

Beck's mother had first taken him up when he was five. The Rock was her special place; her body was buried on the homestead, but her spirit lived on here. They had climbed to the summit many times and had sat and talked, mother and son. She had spoken of life and love and the land. Beck had often looked at her and thought how beautiful she was; he knew now that she had been only in her late twenties. Her skin was red from the sun, her hair blonde from her German heritage, and her hands rough from working goats all her life. But her heart was as soft and gentle as the warm summer breeze.

After she died, Beck had hitched rides out. When he turned fourteen and started driving off the homestead, he came out once a week, sometimes twice. He had climbed the Rock over two hundred times; the last time was the day before he had left for Notre Dame. But by then, his heart had become as hard as the granite. Now his son's heart had been hardened by life.

"That's a big rock," Luke said.

But Beck saw the sense of challenge in his son's eyes. So he said, "Let's do it."

They were wearing sneakers, shorts, tee shirts, and Chicago Cubs caps. They each packed a bottle of water. It was a hundred degrees, but a fresh breeze always blew out here, and there were at least fifty acres of open land and a thousand trees for every human being in the Hill Country. There was no smog, no concrete reflecting the heat, no brown haze hanging over the farm-to-market roads, and no heavy industry dumping pollutants into the air that trapped the heat like a blanket.

There was only the land.

They walked through a gazebo that had been added since Beck's last visit and onto a crushed granite trail. Small granite blocks served as steps up a path wandering through the native grasses, cacti, mesquite, and oak trees, and massive blocks bordered both sides like a granite gauntlet. Beck pointed to the yellow blossoms of the cacti.

"Prickly pear."

Beck's mother had educated him about the Rock's ecosystem. He could distinguish a live oak from a post oak from a blackjack oak; a Texas persimmon from an agarita shrub; bluestem grass from grama grass; rock squirrels from fox squirrels. Farther up the trail, Beck spotted a gray creature darting into the underbrush.

"Look, Luke, an armadillo."

They soon arrived at the mushroom rock, a granite boulder shaped by weathering into the form of a giant mushroom. It marked the base of the Rock, where the tree line ended and the dome turned barren like the hairline on an old man's bald head. They stepped around the mushroom rock and began the ascent. The grade steepened so they leaned forward for leverage; the wind quickened. Beck turned his cap backward so the current didn't sweep it up into the blue sky where two black turkey vultures circled overhead in hopes of a fat rodent or a fallen climber.

They climbed around sheets of granite three feet thick and fifty feet long that had sheared off and slid down the dome like sheets of ice down a glacier until friction had finally halted their descent. They stepped over small patches of cacti and fairy sword ferns sprouting from fractures in the granite face and granite blocks on which lichens had taken root and spread out like a nasty orange-and-yellow rash. Luke's young legs were taking the climb with ease; Beck's surgically repaired knees throbbed with each step. When he was eighteen, he had run the Rock.

By the time they made the summit, they had sweated through their shirts. But the wind at 1,825 feet above sea level soon dried them. They drank the water and took in the view. Luke's head turned in every direction and his eyes were alive; for a brief moment, he was that adventure-loving boy again. He pointed northeast. Over on Turkey Peak two climbers were standing on the summit with their arms spread like Rocky Balboa.

Beck turned in a circle, a 360-degree view of the Hill Country. Smaller granite hills—Little Rock, Freshman Mountain, Buzzard's Roost, Flag Pole—looked like Rock wannabes; across

Echo Canyon over on Little Rock huge granite chunks hung on the side of the rock as if daring gravity to pull them down. The distant ridgeline stood in sharp relief against the blue sky. The water of Moss Lake glistened in the sunlight.

Beck's office in Chicago had been on the forty-second floor, four hundred twenty feet above street level. He could stand at the floor-to-ceiling window and see nothing but man—his buildings, cars, and pollution. Now he looked out and saw the land before man. Only the narrow ribbon of black asphalt that was Ranch Road 965 snaking through the terrain evidenced man's presence. The land was as it had been.

He saw what the Comanche had seen; he inhaled the same untainted air, and he felt the same sun on his face and the same hot wind against his body. And he felt the same about the Rock: it was a sacred place. He felt his mother's spirit, and he thought of his wife: Annie would have loved this place.

Vernal pools, small pits in the granite where rainwater collected and a few hardy plants like cacti and yucca survived, dotted the summit; the pits were bone dry and the patches of plants smoldered. A lone dead oak tree that had grown in one vernal pool stood guard over the summit. The wind had sanded its bark smooth, and the weather had given it a silver sheen. Shallow furrows wound their way down the dome, cut into the granite by rainwater running off the Rock over millions of years. They sat down, and Beck saw the life fade from Luke's eyes; and he knew his son's thoughts had also returned to Annie.

"It sucks," Luke said.

Beck reached over and put his arm around his son, a man in a boy's body. A mother's death will age a boy.

"Luke, after my mother died, I came out here and ran the Rock to burn up the anger inside me. I'd run all the way up here and I'd stand all alone and I'd scream and cuss—"

Beck stood.

"Stand up, Luke."

Luke stood.

"Now scream."

Luke shook his head.

"Go ahead, son, scream. We're the only people here."

Luke shook his head again, so Beck spread his arms and screamed: "AHHHHHHH!"

Luke was looking at Beck like he'd lost his mind. Maybe he had. He screamed again. It felt good, just as good as it had felt back then.

"Scream, son. Get it out."

But Luke refused, so they sat again. Beck said, "I'd sit right here for hours . . . trying to figure things out. To understand why life isn't fair. But I know now there's no figuring it out. All you can hope is that your mother's life had meaning to your life, otherwise her life was wasted. I look at you and Meggie, and I see her. Up here, I feel my mother's spirit. She lives on in me. Luke, your mother's spirit lives on in you. You just have to let yourself feel it.

"But if you keep up like this, you'll drive her spirit out of you. Don't do that, son. Keep her inside you. Remember her in the good days, before she was sick, at your games cheering like a crazy woman when you got a hit or scored a goal or nailed a jump shot. She loved to watch you play. Because that's who you are, Luke. You're an athlete. And she's still watching you. Make her cheer for you again, son."

Luke leaned his head into Beck's chest and cried; his son's tears wet his shirt. Beck had tried and failed to find his peace on this Rock; he hoped his son could find his here. When they stood to head down, Luke surprised Beck. He screamed.

"I hate you, God!"

"Luke, hating God won't make it any better. I know that for a fact."

In April of 1842, the great Comanche war chief Buffalo Hump stood atop the Holy Rock on a fine spring day and surveyed the glorious land laid out before him. Buffalo Hump and his

79

brave warriors had first killed the Lipan Apaches, and then the men, women, and children at the *Misión Santa Cruz de San Saba*, and finally those Spanish morons who had wandered about the land searching for the legendary lost silver mines of *Cerro del Almagre* that had so captured the white man's greedy imagination.

Then the Texans had come also with dreams of silver, and he had killed them. Even Jim Bowie of the long knife had come to search for the silver; Buffalo Hump had admired Bowie and so did not kill him. But the Mexicans did, at the Alamo.

Buffalo Hump's bravery had earned him the right to stand atop the Holy Rock nearer his father, the sun, and to bask in his father's glow. Buffalo Hump felt proud, for this had been his vision and it had come true: all that his eyes could behold now belonged to the Comanche. He knew it would always be so.

But he couldn't know that an ocean away, Prince Frederick of Prussia and twenty other German noblemen meeting in a castle at Biebrich on the Rhine were at that moment organizing the "Society," officially known as the "German Emigration Company," with the intent of establishing a new German state in the Republic of Texas through mass emigration. It would be called "Germania."

The Prince had read about Texas—the vast unsettled land, the natural resources, the Enchanted Rock, and, of course, the lost silver mines—and, like so many men before and after him, Texas had captured his imagination. The Prince and his noblemen soon became the first out-of-towners to be duped by a Texas real-estate speculator. The Germans paid $9,000 to Henry Francis Fisher for a half-interest in the 3.4 million-acre Fisher–Miller Land Grant located north of the Rock between the Llano and Colorado Rivers—sight unseen. They relied solely on Fisher's word. Which was a mistake. Fisher had promoted the land as paradise on earth—water, timber, wildlife, fertile soil, silver mines—but failed to mention one minor drawback: the land was right in the middle of Comanche territory. And, truth be known, Fisher didn't even own the land; the Republic of Texas was giving it away for free to anyone with the guts and guns to settle the hostile land.

But the Germans paid their money and came to Texas. They established settlements at New Berlin, Solms, Nockenut, and New Braunfels on the Comal River east of San Antonio. But they never got all the way to the Fisher–Miller grant. So in 1846, the prince sent Baron Ottfried Hans Freiherr von Meuse-bach to Texas with strict orders to settle the land he had bought. The Baron arrived in Galveston and traveled to New Braunfels; from there he departed with one hundred twenty German settlers for the Fisher–Miller grant. Sixteen days and sixty miles later, they arrived in the Pedernales River Valley, halfway to their destination. His people were sick with cholera, so the Baron decided to settle there on ten thousand acres where two creeks joined the Pedernales. He named his new town Fredericksburg.

Buffalo Hump became angry at the sight of white men on Comanche land; so, in accordance with his strict anti-immigration policy, he promptly raided and killed many of the settlers (cholera and Comanche were known as the two most common causes of death among the Germans.) After enduring a year of Comanche raids, the Baron led an expedition to meet with Buffalo Hump and the other Comanche chiefs; normally, the Comanche would have killed and scalped the Baron, but his red hair and beard captivated them. They called him *El Sol Colorado*—the Red Sun. The Baron proposed a peace treaty: in return for an immediate cessation of war parties, the Germans would give the Comanche $3,000 worth of presents in Fredericksburg. Buffalo Hump might have been a savage but he wasn't stupid; he signed the treaty and took the gifts. The Comanche became Fredericksburg's first tourists.

Seven thousand Germans emigrated to the Hill Country of Texas; over half died in the first year. They never settled the Fisher–Miller Grant land. The Society went bankrupt. Prince Frederick's dream of a German state in Texas was never realized.

And to add insult to injury, the Texas legislature refused the Germans' request to name their new county Germania; instead, it was named Gillespie, after a soldier who had died in the Mexican–American War. But through it all, the town of Fredericksburg survived as a close-knit community of Germans isolated in the middle of Texas.

It wasn't the same town today.

Twenty-four years before, Beck had left a rural Main Street lined with pickup trucks and German businesses. Today, Main Street was about as rural and German as the Lexuses lining the curbs and the city slickers strolling the sidewalks. If Austin was the high school buddy who had packed on the weight, Fredericksburg was the ugly duckling who had undergone an extreme makeover—from a down-home ranching town to a high-falutin' tourist trap.

They had stopped in town on their way back from the Rock for lunch and were now caught in buckle-to-butt sidewalk traffic. The tourists had apparently come for the parade and stayed for a long weekend. Now, walking again among the tattoos and thongs on Main Street, Beck's greatest fear as a single father rose in his thoughts like a recurring nightmare: was he mother enough to raise Meggie alone? He didn't fear raising a son alone: Luke was a male; he was a male; ergo, he could raise Luke. (Or so he hoped.) But Aubrey was right: he didn't have a clue about girls.

Before Annie had gotten sick, they had gone to several football games at the high school in Winnetka. He had been shocked to see affluent teenage girls dressed like high-class call girls—breasts and butts, thighs, torsos, and thongs, all bared to the world; but he had been completely unconcerned about Meggie dressing like that when she was a teenager—because it wasn't his problem. It was Annie's problem. Raising a girl was a mother's job.

But now Annie was gone, and it was his job. Now it was his problem. So Beck Hardin would do what he had done for the last twenty-four years whenever he needed an answer:

he would hit the books. He would read about raising children. He would learn about girls.

Just past the brewery, they turned down a narrow stone path between two buildings. Twenty paces in, the path opened onto a grassy courtyard with a fountain and chairs and a two-person metal bench under shady trees where several people sat reading beside an old rock water well that was now a wishing well. The noise of Main Street seemed distant.

The Cowboy Eclectic shop formed the east wall of the courtyard and the brewery the west wall. At the south end stood a restored two-story limestone house with beveled-glass doors and a sign that read: BOOKED-UP & ARTFUL, COFFEE BAR. Tables and chairs sat on porches up and down; an outside staircase led to the second-story porch. Books were visible through the first-floor windows. They went inside. Luke walked over to the sports section of the magazine rack, and Beck to the checkout counter/coffee bar. On the counter were three "Death Notices," single-page obituaries of locals who had died the preceding week. Death Notices had been hand-delivered to Main Street businesses back when Beck was a boy.

Behind the counter stood an attractive woman wearing narrow black-framed glasses, a black tee shirt, snug Lee Rider jeans, and red cowboy boots with black toecaps; she had long legs, lots of red hair, and silver-and-turquoise jewelry. She was sticking price tags on a stack of books. Beck said, "I need help, please."

Without looking up the woman said, "Spiritual, mental, or physical?"

"Parental."

She now turned to Beck and gave him a quick once-over. He nodded at the espresso machine and said, "And I need caffeine."

She stuck her hand out and said, "Judge Hardin, I presume."

"You know J.B.?"

"Everyone knows J.B."

"Well, I'm just Beck."

"Jodie Lee." She had a strong grip. "What's your pleasure?" She quickly added, "In regards to caffeine."

"Small nonfat latte."

She turned to the espresso machine, but said, "So you're the prodigal son." She grimaced and glanced at him. "Sorry. J.B. and I, we've talked a bit, probably too much. He started the winery right after we opened, came in and bought every book I had or could order about winemaking and growing grapes."

"And he doesn't even like wine."

"Hector does." Beck tried not to stare when she bent over to get milk out of a small refrigerator. When she came back up, she answered his unasked question. "We go out every year for J.B.'s last harvest party."

"You and your family?"

She pointed at the ceiling. "Janelle Jones. My partner, the artist upstairs. And our kids."

"When I was here, there wasn't a bookstore or an art gallery in town."

"One bookstore, six galleries now. Western, European, American, contemporary, Southwestern . . . we had an African art gallery for a while, but that was pushing the envelope."

"Maybe just a little."

"But we've got writers, artists, movie stars living here now . . . Tommy Lee Jones lives out north. Madeleine Stowe, she was in *Last of the Mohicans*—she lives on a big ranch south of town. Linda Obst, the movie producer—she did *Sleepless in Seattle*—she lives out west. G. Harvey, the western artist, he lives in town. Robert James Waller, he wrote *The Bridges of Madison County*—"

"I saw the movie, with Clint Eastwood."

"He lives here."

"Eastwood?"

"Waller. He comes in and signs his books."

Beck said, "Dale Evans was born south of here."

"Who's Dale Evans?"

"Roy Rogers' wife."

"Who's Roy Rogers?"

"How old are you?"

"Sorry, we don't know each other well enough." She handed the coffee to him across the counter. "First one's on the house."

"Thanks. Twenty-four years, the town has changed."

"Ten years and it's changed. When we first got here, only food was Dairy Queen or Wiener schnitzel. Now we've got cuisine—Navajo Grill, Herb Farm, Lester's on Llano, three or four other high-dollar places. And you can get aromatherapy, lypossage, salt rubs, Aqua-Chi ionic foot baths, Reiki, Chakra balancing . . ."

"In Fredericksburg, Texas?"

"He is so hot."

Beck turned to the young voice behind him. A pretty teenage girl with red hair had walked up; she was reading a magazine. Jodie said, "He's going to be the next judge."

The girl looked at Jodie then at Beck; she held up the magazine. "I meant Teddy Bodeman. He's the sexiest man alive."

"Well," Jodie said with a slight smile, "Judge Hardin's kind of sexy, too, don't you think?"

Beck wasn't sure if Jodie was flirting with him or being funny. The girl turned to Beck and looked him up and down. She shrugged. "For an old guy." Then to Beck: "I didn't do it."

"You didn't do what?"

"Whatever you're talking to my mom about."

"Bed-wetting."

The girl blinked hard. "Oh. Then I really didn't do it."

Jodie said, "This is Libby, my daughter." To Libby: "Did you shelve all the books, honey?"

"Yes, Mother."

Libby walked away and Jodie said, "She's thirteen."

"I've got a daughter, too. And Luke over there." He nodded at the magazine rack. "So, are y'all from here?"

85

Jodie shook her head. "Austin. Janelle and I, we were both married to lawyers in the same firm. They spent their billable hours together, we spent our days together. Turns out they were both screwing the same secretary." She shrugged. "But we liked being with each other more than with our husbands anyway. So we divorced them, took our community property and moved out here, opened this place. Books, art, and coffee. We make money on the coffee."

Beck held up the latte. "I cut into your profits. Why'd you pick Fredericksburg?"

"We decided it was time to leave Austin when the middle school girls formed a Rainbow Club. Figured a small town might be a better place to raise our kids."

"What's a Rainbow Club?"

"How old is your girl?"

"Five."

"You don't want to know." She stuck her hands in her jean pockets and said, "So, Judge Hardin, how long have you been wetting the bed?"

"My daughter, Meggie. Since my wife died."

"Sorry. J.B. mentioned about your wife, how she emailed him, to get him ready for you and the kids. That's amazing."

"He told you?"

"Was it a secret?"

"Apparently just to me."

"Oh."

"Meggie's wetting the bed, and Luke won't talk. You got a book that'll tell me how to raise two kids alone?"

"Maybe."

Jodie tapped on her computer, then led Beck to the other side of the store. Fifteen minutes later, he left with a bag of books with more on order.

Beck said, "I'll see you at last harvest."

She waved and said, "Oh, you'll see me before then."

★   ★   ★

J.B. said, "Little gal, she needs a pet."

Meggie and Luke were in bed; Beck and J.B. were sitting on the back porch. J.B. was reading the same newspaper as the night before; Beck was reading a book about parenting.

"A pet?"

"You know, a little animal to care for."

"I know what a pet is, J.B. What are you thinking, a cat?"

"A goat."

"A *goat?*"

"Thought maybe I'd take the little gal over to the auction house, let her pick one out."

"You thinking if she had a pet to care for she might let go of the doll?"

"I'm thinking. How'd it go with Luke?"

"Says he hates God."

"Been there."

Beck said, "I bought some books down at the bookstore, about raising kids."

"You meet Jodie?"

"Yeah."

"Good-looking gal, ain't she?"

"Yeah."

"She's a lesbian."

"You're kidding?"

"Nope. Her and the artist upstairs, they're the town lesbians."

"Jodie said they were partners. I thought she meant business partners. She doesn't look like a lesbian."

"What do they look like?"

"Not like her."

"She's got a mane of red hair, don't she? And believe me, she don't have it for nothing—she's a pistol, always down at city hall raising hell with the Germans about something."

"A lesbian . . . J.B., you sure about that?"

"Well, I never asked her straight out, but that's what everyone says. They live in the house back of their store."

"I thought she was flirting with me."

J.B. chuckled. "You ain't her type."

"They must've created quite a stir when they showed up."

"That's a fact. Every goat rancher in the county without a wife all of a sudden got real interested in reading. Jodie had to beat 'em off with a stick, even Janelle got suitors. 'Course, goat ranchers mostly want a cook, so Jodie being good-looking was considered a bonus, like a two-fer sale. Once word got around they were lesbians, goat ranchers gave up reading just as fast."

"Why'd you tell her about Annie?"

"'Cause Jodie's the only person I had to talk to about anything."

"The prodigal son?"

J.B. looked up from the newspaper. "She said that?"

"Yeah, she did."

J.B. shook his head. "You'd think a lesbian could keep a secret."

"J.B., why would a lesbian be better at keeping . . . never mind. Was there really an African art gallery here?"

"Yep. When I heard about it, I drove downtown just to shake the man's hand. Figured anyone with a good enough sense of humor to open an African art gallery in the middle of Texas had to be a man worth knowing. He was."

J.B.'s eyes dropped to the paper, but he said, "'Course, he didn't have a lick of business sense—who the hell was gonna buy that stuff here?" He was shaking his head until he whistled. "For sale: John Deere bulldozer, six-way hydraulic blade, rear ripper, limb risers, side brush guards . . ."

"All he needed to do was put an ad in the paper and you would've bought his stuff."

"Whose stuff?"

"The African art."

"What would I do with African art?"

"What are you gonna do with a bulldozer?"

"That's the thing, Beck, you don't know until you got one."

88

"J.B., why does it take you a whole week to read one news-paper?"

"'Cause it only comes out once a week. That's why they call it a 'weekly,' Beck. If it was a daily, I'd read it in one day."

"J.B., that doesn't make a damn bit of sense."

But his father had already moved on to the next ad.

"The hell's a 'personal climber'? Someone climbs up and gets stuff down for you?"

"Exercise equipment. Like a StairMaster."

"The hell's a StairMaster?"

"It's a stair-climbing machine. Like I used to run the stands at the stadium."

"You climb stairs but don't go anywhere?"

"Like a stationary bike."

"You ride a bike and don't go anywhere?"

"You get in shape."

"In case you need to climb real stairs or ride a real bike?"

Beck knew this conversation was going the same place some-one went on a StairMaster or stationary bike: absolutely nowhere. So he changed the subject.

"Ran into Aubrey today, over at the stadium. Said his daughter was murdered."

"Aw, hell." J.B. sighed. "Didn't want to hit you with that your first day back. Figured on telling you before you saw him. Didn't figure on you seeing him today."

"To lose your daughter like that . . . might drive a man to drinking. He was hitting it pretty hard at the stadium."

"That's the word."

"What do you know about her?"

"His daughter? Just what I read in the paper. Pretty girl, got in trouble with drugs, ended up in that ditch. Then that no-count wife of his divorced him."

"He said she lives in Austin."

"Figures."

"Why?"

"There's money in Austin."

"And?"

"I always figured her for money. That she'd find some one day."

"He hired me as his lawyer, to look into her case."

"That a paying job?"

"He offered. I refused."

"You do a lot of free work in Chicago?"

Beck chuckled. "Free isn't part of the rate structure at a corporate law firm."

"Figure you owe him?"

"Maybe."

J.B. grunted.

Beck said, "And he said something that made me think."

"What's that?"

"Said he didn't know why his daughter ended up in a ditch. Said to find out what happened to his girl so mine wouldn't. Made me think maybe the answers I'm looking for aren't in these parenting books. Maybe they're in that ditch."

"May be. So what are you gonna do?"

Beck shrugged. "All I can do is ask around."

"When you're the judge, you can do more than ask."

"Which reminds me, J.B., Aubrey said word's all over town that I'm running. So exactly how many people did you tell?"

J.B. scratched his chin. "Well, I might've mentioned something about that over at the post office."

"That the only place?"

"Might've said something at the barber shop."

"Unh-huh. And you didn't stop over at Rode's and mention it to all the regulars there, did you?"

Rode's was a welding shop south of Main where old-timers gathered each morning to drink coffee and gossip. With only a weekly newspaper in town, Rode's was where you got the daily news.

"Well, now that you mention it . . ."

"J.B., now everyone in town is talking about me running."

J.B. furrowed his brow and turned to his son.

"And that's a problem because . . . ?"

Beck didn't answer, so J.B. went back to the classifieds. Beck was trying to think why that was a problem, when J.B. said, "The hell's a 'futon'?"

Beck turned off the late news. He walked to the kids' bedrooms and checked on them; both were sound asleep. He knew J.B. would be asleep; he had always hit the sack at ten sharp. Beck went outside and walked down the caliche road; the light from the full moon reflecting off the crushed white rock provided ample light. He felt like he had all those times when he had snuck out to meet Mary Jo, except hormones weren't driving him out tonight.

He had to know what Annie had told his father.

He entered the back door of the winery—there was no need to lock doors in the country—and found the light switch. He climbed the stairs and entered J.B.'s office. He turned the light on and sat in J.B.'s chair.

He stared at the computer.

After a long moment, he reached over and turned it on. When it had loaded and the homepage had come up, he clicked on the email icon. No need for door locks or passwords in the country.

He clicked on Inbox. A string of emails filled the screen. Annie had died on January 17. Beck scrolled down the list until he came to emails dated back in January. He slowly clicked down until he saw it: *Annie Hardin*. He slid the cursor over that entry. He clicked. An email came up on the screen.

My dearest J.B.,

I'm lying in bed. It's late and Beck's asleep in the chair next to me, holding my hand, his head on the bed. I always told him I would love him until the day I died. I did.

Julie is typing this for me on the laptop. J.B., this will be my last email. When I close my eyes, I won't open them again. I'm trying not to close them, but I'm so tired. I feel life leaving me. It's my birthday. I'm 37.

When I practiced law, I wrote wills. My clients worried so much about giving away their possessions. Meggie and Luke, they were my only possessions in life. They prove I was here. Tell them I love them.

They will come to you this summer. Beck will try to do everything himself that long, then he'll accept the fact that he needs help. He'll take the children and go home to Texas. That's where he belongs.

When the time is right, tell Beck I want to be there with them. I want to be buried on the land he loves. I want those bluebonnets on my grave.

Closing my eyes now. I always wondered if there really is a God. Now I'm going to find out. I'll let you know. I love you, J.B. Hardin.

(Mr. Hardin: I'm Julie, the hospice nurse. Annie passed at 3:12 A.M. She was a very brave woman. She was also right about Beck. He will need help. He's never accepted that she would actually die. Now I've got to wake him and tell him.)

When the nurse had woken Beck that day, he was still holding Annie's hand or she was still holding his; but she was gone.

Beck now exited the email program, turned off the computer and the lights, and walked outside and down to the river. He sat on the same flat rock he had sat on so many nights after his mother had died and just as he had cried then he cried now— for his dead wife, for his children, and for himself.

Chapter 6

Beck Hardin was on his knees in the girls' department at the
Wal-Mart. It was three weeks later, and he was shopping for
school clothes for Luke and Meggie. It was also his first time
inside a Wal-Mart. There hadn't been one in Fredericksburg
when he had lived here, and Annie had always done all the
shopping for the kids. But since his only client was a nonpaying
one, he had decided against paying tourist prices on Main Street;
instead, he had brought the kids to the Wal-Mart, where the
locals shopped.

"We like this," Meggie said.

She was holding the doll in one hand and a pair of overall
shorts in the other. First day of school was only a few weeks
off, and Beck didn't have a clue how to buy clothes for kids.

"That looks too big."

"What size do we wear?"

"I don't know. Just try some stuff on and we'll find out."

"Call J.B. He'll know."

Even the kids had taken to calling their grandfather J.B.

To his daughter, he said, "We don't need to call J.B. We
can figure this out on our own." To himself, he said, "I hope."

Meggie said again, "Better call J.B."

"Need some help, Beck?"

Beck looked up to a middle-aged woman standing over him; she seemed vaguely familiar. She had blonde hair and blue eyes, a stocky build, and a full round face; she was wearing a summer dress and sandals. Four young blonde children surrounded her like kids around their nanny goat. Beck stood.

The woman said, "I recognize those boots."

Beck had worn jeans and his old cowboy boots. They were going to meet J.B. at the goat auction after shopping, and you don't wear Nike sneakers to the goat auction. It was easier to scrape goat shit off leather boot soles than rubber sneaker soles.

"But you don't recognize me," she said. "I know, I'm fat now. Four kids'll do that."

A little girl about Meggie's age licking on a sucker said, "You're not fat, Mommy."

"Yes, I am, honey." She then leaned close to Beck and whispered, "All those nights in the river?"

"*Mary Jo?*" Mary Jo Meier. "Wow. And these are your kids?"

"Yep." She pointed them out: "Bobby, Sally, Arlene, and Stanley Junior. Ten, eight, six, and four. Stanley wanted them exactly two years apart. I told him it's not like buying goats at the auction, but Stanley, he's kind of anal. You remember Stanley Jobst, he was a year older than us?"

"His folks owned the spread next to your place?"

"We own both places now."

"Stanley Jobst. Wasn't he your . . .?"

She nodded. "Cousin. Second cousin." She shrugged. "We kept the land in the family. So I hear you're running for judge."

"I've heard that, too."

"Saw the article in the paper."

"What article?"

"About you. Big deal in today's paper, how you're back and want to be judge. You haven't seen it?"

94

"No. I guess J.B.'s been out campaigning again." Beck stared at his old girlfriend and said, "So how are you, Mary Jo?"

"I'm good." The kids had engaged each other, so Mary Jo stepped closer and spoke softly. "I waited for you, Beck. When I read you stayed on at Notre Dame for law school, I stopped waiting. That's when I knew you weren't coming back."

"I'm sorry, Mary Jo."

She shook her head. "You didn't lie to me. You told me you weren't coming back. I just didn't believe you. Beck, I'm real sorry about your wife. Did you hear about Aubrey's daughter?"

Beck nodded. "Saw him at practice."

"She was a beautiful girl . . . drugs."

"What do you know about her?"

"Heidi?" She shrugged. "She was special . . . like you." Mary Jo hesitated, as if she wanted to say more but thought better of it. She backed up a step and her face brightened. "So, first time buying school clothes?"

"Does it show?"

"Like a tourist on Main Street. All right, let's figure this deal out." She turned to Luke. "You must be Luke. You need jeans. Wranglers or Levis?"

Luke shrugged.

"Wranglers," Mary Jo said. Then to the older boy: "Bobby, you take Luke over to the boys' department, show him the Wranglers. He looks about your size. Slim cut."

Luke followed Bobby down the aisle. Mary Jo now faced Meggie and leaned over and put her hands on her knees.

"And this is Meggie."

Meggie nodded and held up the doll. "And this is Mommy."

Mary Jo's head swiveled and her eyes turned up to Beck. "She, uh . . ."

Mary Jo waved him off. Back to Meggie: "Okay, Meggie, let's find you some pretty things to wear to school. Come on, kids."

She took Meggie's hand and led her to a rack of girls' clothes. Beck and her children followed.

"We'll start with the sale rack first. Your daddy, he's not a rich Chicago lawyer anymore. He's gonna be a poor small-town judge, so we gotta save him some money."

Meggie smiled. "Mommy likes sales, too."

An hour later, Mary Jo had outfitted the children up with clothes, backpacks, lunchboxes, and supplies. Before they parted, she said, "I'm happy, Beck. I'm happy how my life turned out, and I'm happy you're back. This is where you belong."

Mary Jo checked out first. Just as Beck and the kids walked out of the Wal-Mart and into the blazing sunlight of a hot July day, Mary Jo drove by in a red Suburban. She waved and her kids waved, and Beck and his kids waved back. On the back bumper were JESUS LOVES YOU and BECK HARDIN FOR JUDGE stickers.

They met J.B. out front of the auction house on Longhorn Street a few blocks south of Main Street, down from the Lochte Feed Store. The Gillespie Livestock Co. auction house was an old metal building with a split-rail fence out front, livestock pens out back, and a satellite dish on the roof. The place looked like a pickup convention; trucks and goat trailers packed the dirt parking lot and surrounded the building.

Goats were auctioned off every Tuesday in Gillespie County.

J.B. was talking to two old-timers wearing plaid shirts. Just as all the old Volkswagen Beetles in the world had found their way to Mexico, all the plaid shirts had found their way to Fredericksburg. J.B. was wearing another Hawaiian shirt; this one had a bright floral print of gold, yellow, red, and green. As they walked up, Beck heard one old-timer say, "J.B., looks like someone throwed up on that shirt."

The old-timers laughed; J.B. shook his head. "You old Germans ought to get out more."

"You're one to talk, J.B.," the other one said. "We ain't seen you in so long, we figured you died."

"That'll be the day."

It was all smiles and good times until one old-timer said, "Still can't believe you gave up the goats to make wine, J.B. . . . and with a Mexican."

The man's last words had the same effect on J.B. Hardin as a punch in the nose. The smile dropped off his face, and the old fire came into his eyes.

"His name's Hector Aurelio and he's a damn fine man. And he ain't never taken no government money, welfare or mohair."

The old-timer said, "Now, J.B., don't get all righteous on us."

"You boys been bitching about Mexicans long as I can remember. Wish to hell you'd come up with something new to bitch about, just for a change of pace."

J.B.'s face was redder than normal, and when he pointed a big finger at the old-timers, Beck knew he was about to tell them what he really thought; but he noticed Meggie standing there with the doll and his face softened. He turned away from the old-timers without another word.

"Why, here's my little *schatzy.*" His little sweetheart. "Now, honey, I want you to pretend you didn't hear your J.B. say those bad words, okay?"

"Okay, J.B., we'll pretend."

"That's a good little gal."

They walked over to the metal stairway leading up to the catwalk above the open pens, and J.B. said to Beck, "Used their mohair money to buy more land, now they're selling to Californians, making millions. Had their hands out to the government for forty years, but they bitch about welfare for Mexicans."

Meggie was walking between them. She said, "J.B., what's a Mexican?"

"A human being, honey, just like you and me. Some folks around here just ain't figured that out yet." J.B. took her hand and said, "All righty, little darlin', let's find you a goat."

And Beck thought, they say a man never really respects his father until he's a father himself. They're right.

Meggie and the doll went up the stairs to the catwalk with J.B. Beck followed with Luke. Beck had climbed these same stairs every Tuesday of every summer from the day he could walk until the day he had left for Notre Dame. Below them, thousands of bleating goats—Angora and Boer; kids, nannies, and billies; brown, black, white, tan with black highlights, black with tan highlights—huddled in pens tended by old men in cowboy hats. It looked like a scene from a John Wayne movie— *Red River*, but with goats instead of cattle. The smell was no better. The goat stink was strong enough to taste. Meggie was pinching her nose.

"J.B., it stinks!"

J.B. laughed. "It does at that, honey."

A squat three-legged brown mutt waddled over to Luke and started licking his legs. Luke backed off.

"That's Killer," J.B. said. "He's harmless . . . 'cept he'll lick the hair right off your legs." To Meggie: "Look around, doll, pick one out. A little one."

"We can have a baby goat? For our very own?"

"Yep, for your very own."

"What are we going to do with a goat?"

"It's gonna be your pet."

"We had a goldfish for a pet in Chicago."

"Well, petunia, in the country we have fish for dinner, not for pets. We have animal pets."

"It died."

"The goldfish?"

"Unh-huh. Will our goat die?"

"Nope. Goats are tougher than bark on a shin oak."

"They don't get cancer, do they?"

"No, honey, they don't."

"That's good."

Meggie walked along the catwalk, peering down into the pens and carrying on a conversation with the doll. She waved at a girl about Luke's age who was tending goats.

"Is she a goat girl?"

J.B. said, "I reckon she is."

"Can I be a goat girl one day?"

"I reckon not. We're in the wine business now, honey."

Beck followed J.B. and Meggie around the catwalk. It was like going back in time, except that twenty-four years before the hundreds of pens had been full; today, many were empty. Meggie moved on around the catwalk until she suddenly cried out, "J.B., that's the one we want!"

She was pointing down at a black kid with a tan face.

"Then that's the one it'll be, sweet pea," J.B. said.

He wrote the pen number on his palm and pointed the goat out to the man tending that pen. They followed the catwalk around to the door leading into the auction arena. Inside, a dozen spectators sat in plastic seats bolted to a wood platform that stepped down to fashion theater seating; the auction pen was down front. Goats were being herded into the pen through a sliding door to the right and out through a sliding door to the left.

The auctioneer sat above the pen; the bidders, old men wearing straw cowboy hats and boots with goat shit stuck to the soles—a buyer's degree of savvy could be determined by the amount of goat shit on his soles; savvy buyers examined the goats in the pens outside before bidding inside—sat directly in front of the pen. Their plaid shirts glowed under the exposed fluorescent lights fixed in the yellowed acoustical ceiling tile. An air conditioner and two ceiling fans were blowing but couldn't blow out the goat stink. The auctioneer was calling into a microphone: "Ninety-five, ninety-five . . ."

One old-timer gave a little wave.

"Ninety-six, ninety-six . . ."

Another nodded.

"Ninety-seven, ninety-seven . . ."

No heated bidding contest broke out among the old-timers. They just nodded or raised a finger or touched the brim of their hats to up the bid while a young girl in short-shorts took the bidders' lunch orders; a small grease board on the wall noted that day's lunch special: King Ranch casserole and pinto beans. Beck picked up a few German words spoken by the same men he had last seen here; they were just twenty-four years older. It was as if these old goat ranchers were just going through the motions, buying and selling goats just for the sake of buying and selling, trying desperately to prolong a way of life, like a dying patient on life support.

After a few more rounds, the auctioneer announced, "Sold to John Ed for ninety-eight."

That lot of goats was prodded out. The door to the outside pens was slid open and a fresh blast of goat stink blew in like a norther. Beck wondered how he had ever gotten used to the stink.

A few sales later, a dozen kids were led into the auction pen by the nanny goat. J.B. said, "That's us, honey."

J.B. walked down the steps hand in hand with Meggie. When they arrived, he waved at the bidders, then said something to the auctioneer. He pointed at the kid that Meggie had picked out and shook hands with the man tending the auction pen.

"Boys, we got us a special guest today," the auctioneer said. "J.B. Hardin. Yep, that's him looking like a tourist on Main Street. J.B., you ain't gone Democrat on us, have you?"

J.B. said, "I hate to break it to you boys, but I've always been a Democrat."

That brought a big round of laughter. The auctioneer said, "J.B., you always been a kiddin' son of a gun. Say, is that your boy Beck back there?"

The bidders turned in their chairs and waved at Beck. He waved back. The auctioneer said, "We're gonna win state again this year, Beck. We got Slade."

J.B. said, "Beck's running for judge."

The bidders chuckled as if sharing a private joke, and the auctioneer said with a smile, "Well, J.B., we can help you with the goat, but ain't much we can do about that election." To the bidders, he said, "J.B.'s little granddaughter come to buy herself a goat. She fancies this pretty little kid here. We'll start the bidding at ninety-five."

J.B. leaned down to Meggie. She held her hand up.

The auctioneer called out: "Ninety-five to Miss Meggie. Ninety-five, ninety-five . . ."

One old bidder held a finger up and everyone froze. J.B., the auctioneer, and every other bidder turned and stared at him as if he were Bill Clinton just walked in. He glanced around, then lamely withdrew his finger. The auctioneer banged his gavel. "Sold, to Miss Meggie Hardin for ninety-five. And good to see you, J.B., if not that shirt."

J.B. waved at him, then he and Meggie walked back up.

Meggie said to the doll, "Mommy, we own a goat!"

J.B. said to Beck in a low voice, "I wasn't kidding. I've always voted Democrat."

J.B. took Luke, Meggie, and the goat back home for lunch. Beck drove to the bookstore to get a coffee and collect the books he had ordered. Taped to the front door was a hand-painted campaign sign: BECK HARDIN FOR JUDGE.

He opened the door and stepped inside. He hadn't been back since he had learned about Jodie and Janelle, so he tried not to act differently. He walked up to the counter/coffee bar where Jodie was working and said, "Small nonfat latte, please."

She looked up and stared at him. "You heard?"

"Heard what?"

"About the town lesbians."

"Does it show?"

She nodded. "You okay with that?"

Beck shrugged. "Sure. Now I don't have to worry about you hustling me."

She smiled. "What does J.B. say? 'That'll be the day'? So, have you decided yet?"

"Decided what?"

"Whether you're running for judge?"

"No."

She walked around the counter. "Come with me."

"Can I have that coffee first?"

"There's not time." She called to an older woman in the stacks. "Ella, watch the store!"

She grabbed his hand and yanked him back outside. She didn't let go until they hit the Main Street sidewalk; he hadn't held a woman's hand since Annie's last night. Jodie turned east and walked fast; Beck followed her red hair and boots across Lincoln Street and down to the Ausländer Biergarten where back in high school Beck had often listened to live country-western music. She stopped so he stopped. She pointed inside.

The biergarten was open to the street and the smell of sausage and sauerkraut wafted out. Just inside customers sat at small wood tables on a gravel floor and ate German food and drank German beer below a mural of the blonde St. Pauli girl holding six mugs of beer. A long wooden bar stretched down one side of the room. On the back wall hung a big sign that read WARSTEINER. Below the beer sign stood a young man. He had blond hair and wore a suit. He was addressing the crowd of locals in for lunch.

"If you commit the crime, you will do the time. Criminals belong in state prison in Huntsville, not on our streets in Fredericksburg. Our streets are for tourists, not criminals!"

The crowd applauded and whistled.

"Who's that?"

"Niels Eichman, the D.A."

"Junior?"

"Yep."

Niels Eichman, Sr., had been the Gillespie County District Attorney back when Beck had lived here. In keeping with the long-standing local tradition, he had apparently handed down his public office father to son, German to German.

102

"He's running for judge," she said. "Unopposed . . . unless you run."

"The old Germans backing him?"

"Of course."

"He'll be tough to beat then."

Inside, the D.A. was saying, "I'm not going to stand by while the criminal element destroys this town!"

Beck turned to Jodie: "What criminal element? Crime of the week was a Porta-Potty drive-by."

Inside, the D.A.: "Our town is being inundated by illegal Mexicans and their illegal drugs . . ."

Beck, to Jodie: "Is there a drug problem here?"

She shrugged. "Not much, but more than there used to be."

Back inside, the D.A.: "And we all know who killed the coach's daughter with drugs—an illegal Mexican! And he's still walking our streets!"

"Is he talking about Heidi?"

"How'd you know about her?"

"Her dad, we were buddies back in high school."

She nodded inside. "That's why people like him, promising to keep drugs out of our town. Like their kids aren't using."

"What do you know about her?"

"Heidi? Just what I read in the paper."

"Can I get the papers from back then at the library?"

"You can get them from me."

"You keep old newspapers?"

"One a week, fifty-two a year. One box for each year."

Back inside, the D.A. was saying, "We are a God-fearing, law-abiding people, but illegal Mexicans are criminals. They commit a crime when they step across that border and they commit a crime when they smuggle drugs into our town . . ."

Jodie said, "Praise the Lord and blame the Mexicans."

"It's worked for Texas politicians since the Alamo."

Jodie shook her head and sighed. "You know, I like living in a small town, being able to walk down Main Street after dark

103

and not having to look over my shoulder, not having gangs and drive-by shootings and murders every day and police cars running up and down the streets at all hours—"

A shrill siren went off down the street.

Jodie said, "Grass fire, calling in the volunteers. I like all that, but I still believe in civil rights. See, the Main Street business owners, we fled the big city . . . the crime, the lousy schools, Rainbow Clubs . . . we moved out here to the country but we didn't move to *another* country."

"Locals lived here all their lives, they don't appreciate diversity."

"Diversity to an old German is eating Mexican food at Mamacita's on Saturday night." Beck laughed. "But it's not just them, Beck. We have friends—white friends—from the city, they come out here for the first time and walk Main Street and they start to realize something's different, but they can't put their finger on it. But you can see it on their faces when it hits them: there aren't any black or brown people here. And this funny little smile comes over their faces, right before they say, 'We want to move here.' They want to live here because everyone's white."

"Like joining a private country club."

"Without the dues."

"But there were Latinos here when I was growing up. Did they all move away?"

"No, but they stay off Main Street because they don't want any trouble. They got in trouble, Stutz threw them in prison. Now he's finally gone after forty years, but his clone wants his job."

Back inside, the D.A. shouted, "Elect me your judge and I'll guarantee you that illegal Mexicans who come to our town won't be in our town for long!"

Jodie now leaned in close and grabbed Beck's arm tightly. Her eyes were green and her face was now as red as her hair. She pointed a long finger inside.

"And Beck, if you don't run, that little prick's gonna be our judge for the next forty years!"

BECK S BACK AND HE WANTS TO BE JUDGE the headline of that week's newspaper read. The article detailed his life from quarterback of the Gillespie County Gallopin' Goats to quarterback of the Notre Dame Fighting Irish to top law student to partner at a big Chicago law firm. Honors, awards, important cases, his Supreme Court appearances, his children. Annie's death. His return home. Beck turned to his father. They were in the rockers on the back porch.

"J.B., how'd you know all this?"

"I kept up."

"Annie?"

"She filled in the blanks."

"So you took it on yourself to go to the paper?"

"Someone in the family's got to do the campaigning."

"What campaigning?"

J.B. nodded at the paper. "That . . . and the bumper stickers. Janelle designed them, got 'em printed up."

"You been putting that bumper sticker on cars?"

"A few."

"Did you ask the owners if it was okay first?"

"A few."

"J.B. . . ."

"Jodie put up a big campaign sign on her door. Janelle hand-painted it."

"I saw it. Stopped in to get the books I'd ordered. Jodie dragged me down to Ausländer to hear the D.A.'s stump speech. The crowd liked him."

"Too much like his daddy."

"He'll be hard to beat."

"You could beat him."

"Maybe."

"You want Meggie and Luke to grow up in a town with

105

Niels Eichman as their judge?"

"No."

"Then do something about it." J.B. flipped through the paper and said, "Meggie says you bought 'em school clothes today."

"Over at the Wal-Mart."

"Why didn't you say something? I would've gone with you."

"J.B., I can do a few things on my own."

"You know their sizes?"

"No, but we figured it out."

"Mary Jo figured it out, way I heard it."

"Meggie can't keep a secret."

"Neither can lesbians. So how'd it go with Mary Jo?"

"Good. She's happy. Got four kids."

J.B. grunted and returned to the classifieds. Beck went back to the newspapers Jodie had given him. He started with the paper dated January 8, 2003, one week after Heidi's death; color images of her covered a big portion of the front page, one of her in a cheerleader uniform and another of her lying in the ditch with a white sheet over her body; the sheet did not cover her bare feet. She had been spotted by a trucker heading east out of town early on New Year's Day. He called 911. The sheriff came, the Texas Department of Public Safety mobile crime scene van came, and the justice of the peace came and pronounced her dead.

The lack of murders in Gillespie County made a medical examiner an unnecessary county expense. So the county hired out autopsies to the Travis County Medical Examiner in Austin. The ME ruled that the cause of Heidi's death was cardiovascular failure due to acute cocaine intoxication. No mention was made of the semen sample obtained from her body.

The sheriff requested that all males age fifteen to sixty-five provide a confidential DNA sample. All cleared samples would be destroyed; results would not be submitted to the FBI DNA database. He assured Mexican nationals that he would not check their immigration status. He confirmed that a DNA sample had been recovered from Heidi's body, but he refused to elaborate.

Beck found the next week's paper, dated January 15, 2003. It was still all about Heidi. Over five hundred males had given DNA samples in the preceding week. The samples had been sent to the DPS crime lab in Austin. Test results were expected back in eight weeks.

By the third week, over one thousand males had given samples. The sheriff acknowledged that few Mexicans had come forward to provide DNA samples and that given the number of illegals in town, the perpetrator might be a Mexican—who might have returned to Mexico.

With each passing week, there were fewer mentions of Heidi in the papers. By the tenth week, all samples had been tested; there was no match. The sheriff concluded that an outsider had dumped Heidi in that ditch and left town. He vowed to continue his investigation as long as there was any hope of finding the perpetrator. That was four and a half years ago.

Beck stared again at the image of Heidi Geisel, all-American cheerleader. How did that beautiful girl end up in a ditch?

Chapter 7

Beck threw up in the gutter.

It was the tenth day of August, and the dog days of summer had descended on the Hill Country. The temperature sign on the bank building read 97 degrees—at eight in the morning. His feet hurt, his knees ached, and his body was drenched in sweat. He had picked that day to start running again.

He had fixed breakfast for the kids and walked them down to the winery. Then he had run the three miles into town. When he hit Main Street, he had crossed over to the north side and ran east on the sidewalk. The shops didn't open until ten so the sidewalks had been empty except for the customers lined up out the door at Dietz Bakery, waiting for fresh sausage rolls. He ran around them and crossed over to the south side of Main at the light fronting the Nimitz.

He ran west past a shop called the Garden of Beaden and the vacant Crenwelge Buick & Olds building. It was Friday, but the weekend tourists didn't start arriving until noon; so pickup trucks instead of Lexuses were parked at the curb and tractors, farm equipment, and eighteen-wheelers rolled down Main Street past the expensive restaurants and fancy boutiques. When Beck hit the Llano Street intersection, he had to stop for a rig pulling a cattle trailer. The breeze brought the smell straight to Beck— and he threw up.

"I think that's illegal. Littering on Main Street."

Beck's hands were on his knees. He looked up to a red Jeep Wrangler 4x4 pulled alongside the curb; it had no doors and a roll bar instead of a top. Jodie Lee was sitting behind the wheel wearing sunglasses and a smile. Her red hair blew in the breeze.

"Careful you don't get run over by a local. They don't brake for joggers."

"Why?"

"They figure only liberals jog. And they figure if God wanted us to run everywhere He wouldn't have invented the pickup truck. You run up here from the ranch?"

He nodded.

"You won't make it back. Climb in."

She was right. He climbed in. Jodie reached back to a cooler behind them and handed a cold bottled water to Beck.

"This hot, you've got to hydrate."

Jodie shifted the Jeep into gear and turned west on Main. Beck drank half the bottle and said, "Thanks."

The wind was the only air-conditioning the Jeep offered, but Beck's body soon cooled down.

"I haven't run since Annie . . . I've got to get back in shape."

"Tough in this heat. Try the Athletic Club, out 290 East across from the Wal-Mart."

Jodie worked the stick shift again, and Beck drank more water. She said, "Have you decided?"

"On the gym?"

"On running for judge."

"No."

"People here are afraid."

"Of what? This is Disneyland."

She gestured at the Main Street shops. "This is a façade town, Beck. It's all fake, like a movie set . . . like Disneyland. That's all show for the tourists. But the people who live here, they're afraid."

"Afraid of what?"

"City hall, the cops, the judge. This town is ruled with an iron fist, Beck. The old Germans, they're big on law and order— more order than law. You get on their wrong side, you either leave town or they'll run you out."

"You mean the Latinos?"

"This is Texas, so they take the brunt of it. But it's also Fredericksburg, so anyone who isn't from an old-line German family with money gets run over if they get in the way. I know Main Street business owners who wouldn't call a cop to save their lives. Literally."

"If the cops are harassing people, why don't they file civil rights suits?"

"And seek justice from Stutz?"

That word again.

They turned south off Main and onto Adams Street. They drove past the courthouse. Beck looked up to the second floor, where the courtroom was located. And he remembered that day twenty-five years before when he had witnessed justice dispensed by Judge Bruno Stutz.

Jodie said, "You could change that, Beck. A good judge could make the people feel safe."

"Safe from what?"

"The law."

When Adams became Ranch Road 16, Jodie accelerated. The wind noise was too loud to talk, so Beck leaned back and thought. He thought about the law and he thought about justice.

And he thought about Miguel Cervantes.

Chapter 8

The spoils of Texas politics have long been divided equally between Republicans and Democrats. The two-party system makes life so much simpler for lobbyists; at all times political they know exactly whom to bribe with campaign contributions, parties, trips, dinners, golf, and girls.

Independent candidates confuse lobbyists—something to be avoided at all costs—so Republicans and Democrats, in a rare showing of bipartisanship, passed election laws making it difficult (if not downright impossible) for an independent candidate to get his or her name on the ballot in Texas. The major obstacle is the petition requirement.

To get his name on the 2006 ballot for governor of Texas, Kinky Friedman had to get signatures of registered voters equal to one percent of the total votes cast in the prior gubernatorial election; in his case, 45,540 signatures. Those voters could not have voted in either the Republican or the Democratic primary that year; and all 45,540 signatures had to be collected in the sixty days following the primary election. He did it.

Of course, Kinky lost.

Under the election code, Beck had needed the "lesser of five hundred or five percent of the total vote received in the district, county, or precinct, as applicable, by all candidates for governor in the most recent gubernatorial election." The votes cast for governor in Gillespie County in the prior election totaled 8,403, so 420 registered voters in the county had to sign his petition.

He hadn't liked his odds.

But if a Jewish country-western singer whose biggest hit was "They Ain't Makin' Jews Like Jesus Anymore" could convince 45,540 Texans to sign his petition, surely a local football legend and honors graduate of Notre Dame Law School could convince 420 voters in Gillespie County to sign his petition. He did it. Or, actually, Jodie and Janelle did it.

Beck Hardin had decided to run for judge.

He had specialized in complex civil litigation at a seven-hundred-lawyer corporate law firm in Cook County, Illinois. But the most complex civil cases in Gillespie County, Texas, were divorces contesting whether husband or wife would get the hunting lease. Which rendered an $800-an-hour trial lawyer about as useful in Fredericksburg as a goat rancher in Chicago. He needed a job, but he wasn't running for a job. He was running because he didn't want his children to be afraid of the law. He was running because no one should be afraid of the law. He was running because Miguel Cervantes had been afraid of the law.

So at 4:45 P.M. on August 15, Beck was standing at the counter in the district clerk's office in the Gillespie County Courthouse on Main Street and completing the filing form for an independent candidate. The filing deadline was five P.M.

Beck handed the filing form to the district clerk. Mavis Mooney was pleasant and plump with a beehive hairdo. She reached to her hair and pulled out a pen like a magician pulling a rabbit out of her hat. She glanced around then whispered, "Jodie asked me to sign your petition. I would've, but I'm elected, too." She looked over the form then said, "Please take the oath."

112

Beck recited from the form: "I, John Beck Hardin, Jr., of Gillespie County, Texas, being a candidate for the office of the 216th District Judge, swear that I will support and defend the Constitution and laws of the United States and of the State of Texas. I am a citizen of the United States eligible to hold such office under the Constitution and laws of this state. I have not been finally convicted of a felony for which I have not been pardoned or had my full rights of citizenship restored by other official action, nor have I been declared mentally incompetent as determined by final judgment of a court."

"If you think you can win, you're damn sure mentally incompetent."

Beck turned to the voice behind him. The Gillespie County District Attorney was standing there wearing a stylish suit. He was younger and shorter than Beck; he looked like a fraternity boy dressed up for a night at the country club.

"It's just the two of us then," the D.A. said.

Beck extended his hand and they shook. "Beck Hardin."

"Niels Eichman . . . Junior. So the football legend wants to be the judge?"

"Is that a problem?"

"It'll be a problem for you to get elected." He smiled. "You've been gone twenty-four years, Beck, and this town's changed— but not that much. The names on Main Street might not be German, but the name of every elected official in this county damn sure is, from the mayor to the dogcatcher. Full-blooded Germans, every one of them. And you're not."

"My mother was."

"Your daddy isn't. And public offices here are handed down father to son, not mother to daughter. We don't elect non-Germans and we don't elect women."

"Except Mavis."

"That judgeship was mine from the day I was born."

"Your father was the D.A., not the judge."

"Stutz doesn't have a son."

113

"So what, he adopted you?"

"You could say that. He's backing me. All the Germans are."

"Yeah, well, the football coach is backing me."

"Him and the town lesbians, now that's a winning team."

"Four hundred twenty-two voters signed my petition."

The D.A. snorted. "The Main Street crowd. Democrats spitting in the wind. They never win."

He shook his head.

"Beck, come on, you grew up here, you know how it is. Germans have controlled this town and everything in it for a hundred sixty years, since the Baron settled this place. Still do. We still say what will be or won't be in this town and out in the county and over at the schools. Sure, you'll get the newcomers' votes, but the Germans will mobilize to defeat you just like they've defeated every other non-German stupid enough to waste good money running for public office here. You may be a legend, Beck, but you'll never be the judge." He chuckled. "But don't feel bad, Jesus Christ Himself couldn't get elected here . . . well, especially not Him, He was Jewish."

Beck turned back to the district clerk. "We good, Mavis?"

"Yep. Say hi to J.B."

Beck started to walk out, but turned back to the D.A.

"What do you know about Heidi Geisel?"

"Why do you ask?"

"Aubrey and I, we go back to high school."

"And he wants you to find the guy?"

"Something like that."

"Knowing Aubrey, exactly like that. Well, you've got until New Year's Eve to find him and indict him, because when the clock strikes midnight, that guy won't ever turn into an inmate."

"You really think an illegal Mexican killed her?"

The D.A. shrugged. "Who knows? But it makes for a good stump speech. A scared voter votes."

"Playing the race card?"

114

"It's a winning hand here. Illegal Mexicans, they're a hot-button issue, so I'm pushing that button hard."

"Watch out you don't push it too hard."

"Beck Hardin!"

Beck had just walked out the rear exit of the courthouse when a thick man wearing jeans and a plaid shirt and leaning against a pickup truck called out to him. The man stepped over and stuck a meaty hand out to Beck; they shook. His arm didn't taper down to the wrist; from shoulder to hand, it was one size, like a log. He smelled of goats.

"Stanley Jobst."

"Stanley . . ."

"Jobst. I married Mary Jo."

"Oh, yeah, Stanley. Good to see you again."

"Saw you going into the courthouse, figured I'd wait for you. Mary Jo said you were back in town."

Beck smiled. "Yeah, I saw her over at the Wal-Mart. I was trying to buy clothes for my kids and—"

Stanley wasn't smiling. "Look, Beck, here's the deal. I know you and Mary Jo had a thing going back in high school. But I love her and she's happy now and I—"

Beck gave him a timeout signal. "Whoa, Stanley, hold on. It's not like that anymore."

"It's not?"

"No. I love my wife."

"Thought she died."

"She did."

"Oh. Well, so I got nothing to worry about?"

"Just getting arrested for wearing that shirt in public."

Beck smiled; Stanley didn't.

"No, Stanley, you've got nothing to worry about from me."

Stanley seemed relieved. "Well, that's good to hear, Beck, 'cause if I ever found out you were screwing Mary Jo again,

115

judge or no judge, I'd kill you and bury you where the best tracking dog in the county couldn't find you."

Beck maintained eye contact with Stanley for a long moment, hoping he'd break into a smile. He finally did, then slapped Beck on the arm so hard that Beck had to regain his footing.

"Hell, Beck, I'm just joshing you. About the killing part, not the screwing part."

"Won't happen, Stanley."

"Well, fine then. That's just fine and dandy. Wanted to clear the air, that's all."

"Consider it cleared."

"All righty then, you have a good day." Stanley Jobst walked back to his truck and said over his shoulder, "Say hidi to J.B."

Beck shook that off and continued across the asphalt parking lot and went inside the Gillespie County Law Enforcement Center, a squat one-story building with a brick façade the color of goat crap. It housed the county jail and the sheriff's office. A young woman sat behind the counter. Her head was down, and she was writing.

"Be with you in a minute," she said with the enthusiasm law enforcement personnel saved for defense lawyers. After a very long minute, she finally looked up.

"I'm Beck Hardin. Is the sheriff available?"

She glanced at the clock on the wall. "It's after five."

"Is that a yes or a no?"

"That's Doreen's way of saying 'come back tomorrow.' But she don't know she might be talking to our next judge."

Standing there was the Gillespie County Sheriff. Grady Guenther had been a deputy sheriff back when Beck was in high school; he would be in his early fifties now. He sported a bratwurst-and-beer physique, and he was chewing on a toothpick and fiddling with a little pocketknife; the legs of his trousers were partially tucked into his tan cowboy boots. In his green-and-tan uniform, he looked every bit like Rod Steiger from *In the Heat of the Night*. A small-town Texas sheriff, just like his

116

daddy before him; the old man had inspired fear in the kids back when Beck was in high school. Apparently, the sheriff had inherited the job from his father, same as the D.A. They shook hands.

"Grady Guenther."

"Sheriff . . . Beck Hardin."

"Just Grady. So, you running?"

"Just filed my papers."

"Well, you don't have a snowball's chance in hell of winning, but I'll vote for you anyway."

"Why would you vote for me?"

"Have you met the D.A.?"

"Just now, in the courthouse."

"And?"

"Some ageing will do him good."

"Getting his ass kicked would do him more good." Grady smiled at that. "Junior took over from his daddy. Real ambitious boy, figures on being governor one day. 'Course, ambition ain't generally a good thing in a D.A. So, what can I do you for?"

"Heidi Geisel."

Grady nodded like he had expected that answer. "Aubrey want you to solve her case?"

"Something like that."

"Few years back, he tried to get that *America's Most Wanted* to do a show on her. When I read you were back in town, knew it wouldn't be long before he got you involved. Old debts never go away, do they?" To Doreen, Grady said, "Bring me Heidi's file."

He motioned with the pocketknife for Beck to follow. They walked down a hallway and into the sheriff's office.

"Take a load off."

Beck sat in a visitor's chair. Grady remained standing until Doreen arrived with a thick file. He took the file from her and dropped it with a loud thud on the desk in front of Beck. Then he sat behind his desk.

117

"Did everything we could," Grady said. "Called in DPS to work up the crime scene, handle all forensics—we ain't had but one murder in Gillespie County the last thirty years and that was a mental case, so we use criminologists from Department of Public Safety. They came up empty. Travis County ME did the autopsy, got the DNA, but we got no matches from the FBI database or our local samples."

"Aubrey thinks you're holding back on him, not telling him everything you know."

"He's right."

"*Why?*"

"'Cause he don't want to know what I know."

"And what do you know?"

"I know Aubrey."

"Grady, I'm his lawyer."

Grady glanced around at the objects in his office—two stuffed deer heads on the wall, framed hunting photos, and a glass-fronted case holding hunting rifles. He exhaled and looked back at Beck.

"They found two DNA samples on her."

"You mean semen?"

Grady nodded. "From two different men."

"On the same night?"

Another nod. "One sample was from her vaginal cavity, I figure that's our man. The other was from her shirt. Way I figure, she gave oral to the first guy, then the guy that killed her came second . . . so to speak. She had intercourse with him."

"Why not the other way around?"

"Well, according to the autopsy, she died within fifteen, twenty minutes of inhaling the cocaine. Massive heart failure. Apparently she was taking diet pills, which are stimulants, so the effect of the cocaine was multiplied. Soon as she snorted the stuff, it was like she had slit her wrists and was just waiting to bleed out. Anyway, unless the guy likes to screw dead girls, I figure she

118

was alive when they had intercourse. And the autopsy report said the amount of semen still in her vaginal cavity meant she wasn't upright for any extended period of time following intercourse. Gravity. So I figure the second guy gave her the alcohol and cocaine, they had sex, and then she died. Probably her first time. The coke, not the sex."

"Why do you say that?"

"How many virgins would start with two men?"

"No, the cocaine."

"Oh. My older boy, he was in school with Heidi. If she was a cokehead, everyone would've known it. Small town. My boy said she was obsessed with staying gorgeous, wouldn't even drink beer 'cause it might hurt her looks."

"Was she? Gorgeous?"

"Drop-dead. She was our beauty queen." Grady shook his head. "I kid you not, Beck, every time she walked down Main Street, we had three traffic accidents. No one had ever seen anything like her around here before . . . or since. We all figured she'd be Miss America one day."

"Then how'd she end up in that ditch?"

Grady shrugged and turned his palms up. "Wish I knew."

"Did she have a boyfriend?"

"Nope. She wouldn't have nothing to do with the local boys. Rumor had it she liked girls, like our lesbians over at the bookstore. She hung out there some. But her best friend says she wasn't like that, said she was just too mature for high school boys."

"So this guy could've been a college boy?"

"Could've been."

"Two guys at the same time?"

"Forensics said the semen on her shirt had caked before the rain hit it. So some time elapsed between the two encounters."

"And she was only sixteen?"

Grady nodded. "Sad, ain't it? And playing Russian roulette, sex without a condom. Kids think they're bullet-proof."

119

"So she either knew this guy well enough not to be worried about contracting a disease or—"

"She was too drunk and stoned to care. But we got his DNA. We just don't got him."

"The paper said you got samples from every male in town."

"Yep. We even accounted for every college boy home for the holidays."

"They all came in voluntarily?"

"It was like a blood drive, everyone asking each other if they gave yet. She was the coach's daughter, whole town wanted the guy found. We had to use our emergency fund to pay for the tests, over a thousand."

"That's all?"

"Males fifteen to sixty-five. Hell, half the population is over sixty-five, Beck. This is a retirement place now, like Florida without the hurricanes."

"Or the ocean."

"That, too. Results started coming in a couple months later. Aubrey would be here waiting for the FedEx truck like an old-timer waiting for the mailman to bring his social security check. But no matches, so he ain't a local. Which is about the only good thing in this damn case, at least one of our boys didn't do it."

"Aubrey said illegal Mexicans didn't give samples."

"Nope. Scared they might get deported. I told them I wouldn't give their names to the Feds, but they didn't go for it."

"D.A. seems to think an illegal did it."

"He's just politicking. Mexican boys are too scared to even look at a German girl. And if Heidi was hanging with a Mexican, whole town would've known."

"Is the autopsy report in the file?"

"Yep. Cause of death was acute cocaine intoxication."

Grady was now cleaning his fingernails with the pocketknife.

"Did they check under her nails?"

Grady stared at his handiwork a moment, then looked up at

Beck. "No tissue under her fingernails, no bruising around her genitals, no scratches, no fight marks—ME says sex was consensual. He found a few fibers, probably from a towel, inside her underwear. Figures the guy wiped her."

"Why?"

"Must've figured it all come out and he could wipe his DNA off her." He shrugged. "That's why they call it dope. That's also what tells me he wasn't a Mexican."

"Because he wiped her?"

"Because he thought about it. Means he watched those *CSI* shows."

"And?"

"And most Mexicans here can't speak English. They watch the Spanish channels and Mexican soccer on satellite. They don't watch *CSI*."

Beck nodded. "No other evidence?"

"Nope. No fingerprints, no other trace evidence of any kind. It was raining that night, so any trace evidence would've washed away."

"So what's your theory?"

"Not sure it qualifies as a theory, but way I figure, she was at a party, snorted coke, had sex with a couple college boys from UT. Gets in a car with the second boy, then she ODs. He panics, dumps her, hightails it back to Austin."

"She was only sixteen, Grady. That's statutory rape."

"Only if the boy was more than three years older than her. College boy, might not be."

Grady inhaled and blew out a breath.

"Look, I know Aubrey wants this guy caught and put in prison, but Heidi looked twenty-five and snorted coke like she was twenty-five and screwed like she was twenty-five. Now we're gonna make out like she was the Virgin Mary and put some kid in prison for twenty years for thinking he was screwing a twenty-five-year-old girl? Is that justice? When the stat rape age was put on the books, sixteen-year-old girls were virgins.

Today, you got a better chance of winning the lotto than finding a sixteen-year-old virgin." Grady pointed the pocketknife at the window. "You walk down Main Street when the tourists are in town? Looks like a goddamn hooker convention."

"I saw that."

"We ain't isolated anymore, Beck. We got cable, we got the Internet, we got kids on MySpace, we got 'em freak dancing —"

"Freak dancing? What's that?"

"How old are your kids?"

"Ten and five."

"You don't want to know."

"Grady, how do you raise your kids with all that around them?"

"It ain't easy. Not like when we were growing up here— worst trouble we could get into was drinking beer and skinny-dipping in the river. Coke was something you drank from a bottle and you couldn't die from getting laid." He exhaled. "It's a different world now."

"I've got a girl."

"Raising girls is double-tough. They're a different breed, Beck. I can't figure mine out. Hell, if not for the wife—" Grady grimaced. "Sorry."

Beck said, "How'd you learn so much about kids?"

"Hand-to-hand combat." A little smile. "I got four of 'em, two teenagers. And I'm the sheriff. You're gonna find out, Beck, if you're the judge, you learn a lot more about people in town than you want to know."

Beck picked up Heidi's file. "Mind if I borrow this?"

Grady waved the pocketknife at Heidi's file. "Knock yourself out." He then closed the pocketknife and stuffed it into his pants pocket. "Beck, I never had the heart to tell Aubrey, about the two DNA samples. He was real proud of her. Figured I'd let him keep on being proud. Every morning driving in, I see him stopped by the city limits sign out on 290, putting fresh flowers by that white cross. Every day going on five years now."

"Four years, seven months, and fifteen days. He keeps a calendar. Called me this morning, to see if I had talked to you yet."

Grady shook his head. "All he's got left is football and dreaming of finding that guy . . . and drinking."

"I've noticed."

"If I arrest him for DUI, Beck, he'll lose his coaching job."

"Maybe if he knew what happened to Heidi, he wouldn't need to drink."

"Maybe."

Beck pushed himself out of the chair and turned to the door. Grady said, "Guess you can decide now."

Beck turned back. "Decide what?"

"Whether Aubrey wants to know what's in that file."

"Thanks."

"You asked."

"Yeah, I asked."

"Good luck with the election. Say hi to J.B. for me."

J.B. Hardin was standing at the open barn doors at the rear of the winery and gazing out at the vineyards. He and Luke had spent the day picking ripe grapes and dumping them into the destemmer for Hector. He now called over to his grandson.

"Luke, let's take a last run through the vineyards."

The boy met J.B. at the two-seater Gator. J.B. got in behind the wheel; Luke jumped into the passenger seat.

"Buckle up."

J.B. shifted the John Deere utility vehicle into gear and drove into the vineyards.

"You put in a man's day of work, Luke."

The boy didn't say much; he was a lot like J.B. He didn't talk just to hear his own voice.

"You gonna play baseball this year?"

"No."

"You're not gonna play your favorite sport?"

"I quit."

"Oh, can't hit?"

"I can still hit."

"Can't catch?"

"I can catch."

"Throw?"

"I had the strongest arm on the team last year."

"So why'd you quit?"

"Mom."

"She wanted you to quit?"

"She died."

"You quitting baseball 'cause your mama died?"

"It's not right for me to play when she's dead."

"Oh, I see. You're punishing yourself."

"God."

"You're punishing God?"

"Because He took her."

J.B. stopped the Gator. "Yep, He sure did, Luke, and I don't have a clue why. But that's the way it is, and there ain't nothing we can do about it. I'd trade places with your mother if I could—I guess maybe I have. But life is for the living, Luke. Your mama emailed me many times before she died, and she told me to tell you she's cheering for you from heaven."

Tears came now, so he reached over and pulled the boy in next to him the way he should have pulled his own son next to him twenty-nine years before, but didn't. J.B. let the boy cry; sometimes a good cry is the best thing for the human soul. Many were the times J.B. Hardin had stood on this land and cried after his wife had died, and then again when his only son had left here hating him. He didn't want this boy to hate his daddy; and he didn't want the boy's daddy to feel the hurt of a son's hate. After the boy's tears had run out, J.B. got out and walked around to the passenger side and said to his grandson,

124

"Scoot over. You're living in the country now, time you learned to drive."

The boy took the wheel but said, "I miss her."

J.B. sighed and said, "I know you do."

Heidi Geisel might have been a beauty queen in life, but she wasn't in death. Beck had never before looked at crime scene photographs. It wasn't a pleasant experience. The DPS crime lab technicians had taken color photos of Heidi's body lying in the ditch: location shots, full-length shots, and close-up shots of her face and arms and legs and torso and hips from every conceivable angle; and the file included a DVD in a plastic pouch containing even more photos.

She had been found lying face-down on the county side of the city limits sign. Her blonde hair was dirty and wet from the previous night's rain. Her clothes were soaked and stuck to her body and did not completely cover her pale flesh; her wet mascara had made black lines across her face. Her eyes were closed, as if she were sleeping peacefully.

Beck knew how it felt to lose a wife to death; how would it feel to lose a child? To be awakened early one morning with a call and learn that your child was dead—that you would never see or touch or hold or speak to your child again? How had Aubrey and Randi survived that call? Or had they?

And how had Heidi ended up in that ditch?

The six-inch-thick file contained the photos, the Offense Report, the DNA Report, the Autopsy Report, the Evidence Report, and sworn statements from family and friends. The Offense Report detailed the facts surrounding the discovery of her body: the trucker's 911 call; the units dispatched to the scene; the crime scene diagram; statements of officers. But there was no more information than had been in the newspapers.

The DNA Report stated that none of the 1,017 samples obtained from local males matched the DNA samples obtained from Heidi's clothes and body.

125

The Evidence Report listed the personal effects recovered from Heidi's body and at the crime scene: white shirt, black skirt, black undergarment, three silver loop earrings, silver ankle bracelet. That's all? Beck flipped through the pages and thought of Annie: what had she worn when they had gone out? Glasses, earrings, necklace, bracelet, wedding and engagement rings, watch; bra and panties and sometimes pantyhose, dress or blouse and slacks, shoes; purse, keys, and cell phone.

Heidi was sixteen, so she might not have needed glasses, she wouldn't have had a wedding or engagement ring, and she might not have worn a bra or pantyhose. But wouldn't she have worn shoes and carried a purse? And every teenage girl Beck had seen in Chicago had had a cell phone stuck to her ear. Wouldn't Heidi have had one? Beck shut the file.

Where were Heidi's cell phone, purse, and shoes?

Chapter 9

Beck was double-knotting the laces of Meggie's shoes.

"Now, don't be nervous, honey."

"We're not nervous. Mommy says school is fun."

The doll was in her backpack.

Beck stood. Meggie's kindergarten teacher was looking at him with a sympathetic expression that said, *Father's first day of school.* Beck Hardin had never before taken his children to their first day of school. But he had taken them to their last.

The Gillespie County Consolidated School District covered the 1,061 square miles in the county and educated four thousand students at four campuses: primary, elementary, middle, and high. Beck and J.B. had already dropped Luke off at the elementary school. They were now delivering Meggie to the primary school. She said to the teacher, "My mommy's visiting Jesus. She'll be back soon, probably by Christmas."

"Welcome to kindergarten, Meggie," the teacher said. To Beck: "Hi, I'm Gretchen Young."

She was young, a slim blonde woman wearing a denim skirt and a colorful shirt; she looked like Mary Jo Meier in high school.

"I'm Beck Hardin. This is my father—"

"Oh, I know J.B." To his father, she said, "The merlot was wonderful."

J.B. said, "Guess I know what to get the teacher for Christmas."

Ms Young smiled, then consulted her clipboard; her smile turned into a frown. "There must've been a mix-up. I'll get Meggie moved to another class today."

"Why?"

"Didn't you request an Anglo class?"

"You can do that?"

"You can here. All the rich German parents request the same teachers so their kids' classes will be all-Anglo. Mine's a Latino class. Well, officially, it's a bilingual class, but that's how they separate the kids."

Beck looked into the classroom. It was bright and colorful, with posters and artwork on the walls and mobiles hanging from the ceiling. The children were chattering in Spanish; all of their faces were brown. He turned back to the teacher.

"This is a public school, isn't it?"

"Don't tell the Germans that." She glanced around and lowered her voice. "Our principal, Ms. Rodriguez, she came here from San Antonio. When she hired on last year, she told admin it was illegal to segregate the kids, so she stopped all requests and mixed the classes. The German parents went ballistic, complained to the school board. So admin took over our class assignments—and they let the Germans pick their teachers."

"But if that's illegal segregation, how can they get away with it?"

"Because no one complains."

"What about the Latino parents?"

"Especially not them. Most of our Latino parents are illegal— and who would they complain to here anyway? And if they filed a complaint with the state, word would get around and the German employers would blacklist them—they'd never get work here again. Small town. They need to work, so they don't complain."

"So their kids get dumped into all-Latino classes?"

"Over at the elementary school they get dumped into Special Ed classes."

"Because they're Latino?"

"Because they can't speak English. That way they don't have to take the state achievement tests. The Latinos don't score as well, so admin games the system, dumps them into Special Ed. If they can keep the Latinos from being tested, the district will rank higher. I overheard an administrator saying he was glad the city finally took down that big 'welcome-willkommen-bienvenidos' banner over Main Street. Said he wants them to put up another one saying 'No More Mexicans.' Said the Mexicans are ruining our scores. Public school today, Beck, it's all about test scores."

"What about that 'No Child Left Behind' law?"

Ms. Young pointed at the brown faces in her classroom.

"That's what the law looks like in a school."

"The law of unintended consequences."

"The law doesn't mean anything to those kids, Beck. They just want to learn. You should see their faces when they learn to read English. When it clicks in their mind, all the words in the books come alive for them. They're so happy. That's why I teach."

Beck thought she might cry.

"People can argue all they want about illegal Mexicans, but those kids"—she pointed at her classroom—"they were born here. They're American citizens and they're entitled to an education same as the German kids." She calmed and sighed. "I have to fight for these kids every day, to give them a chance."

She turned when a little Hispanic girl walked up with a young Hispanic woman. "*¡Hola*, Graciela*! ¡Buenas días!*" She said to the woman, "*Señora* Gomez. *¿Le gusto el verano?*"

The mother: "*Sí.*"

"*Este año será maravilloso.*"

The mother bent over and kissed the girl then walked away. Ms. Young said, "Meggie, Graciela, why don't y'all find your desks? You're next to each other."

The children went into the classroom, each with a backpack over her shoulder and a big smile on her face. Ms. Young nodded toward Señora Gomez walking away and said, "She's illegal, but Graciela's a citizen."

J.B. said, "Your Spanish is pretty good."

"I'm working at it. We don't have any Latino teachers, so someone's got to speak the language. Ms. Rodriguez has the kids saying the Pledge of Allegiance in English and Spanish each morning. Anglos learn Spanish, Latinos learn English. They pick it up pretty fast at this age."

J.B. said, "Smart move."

"Smart principal." Ms. Young again glanced around and dropped her voice to a whisper. "But the Germans went Gestapo. The school board said they wanted the schools to promote the German heritage, not the Mexican heritage. If they'd said that in Austin, they'd have to resign. Not here. They told Ms. Rodriguez 'no more Spanish Pledge and no more Spanish in the schools'—forty percent of our students are Latinos, but the board wants her to stop all Spanish in the school. How stupid is that?"

"So she stopped the Spanish Pledge?"

"Nope. Ms. Rodriguez, she won't back down."

"How'd she ever get hired here?"

"She was just for show. The state was all over admin to do something to help the Latino students, so they figured if they hired a Latino principal, the state would back off. The state did, but Ms. Rodriguez won't. It's a war zone here, between her and the Germans. She'll be at the front door greeting the kids and the German parents won't even acknowledge her. They're trying to get her fired." Ms. Young exhaled and shook her head. "So, you want me to move Meggie?"

"No. I want you to be her teacher. But can I ask you something?"

"Sure."

"Why did you tell me all this? How do you know I'm not like those German parents—you don't even know me."

She smiled. "I know J.B." She consulted her clipboard. "I still need Meggie's immunization records."

"Immunization records? Oh, well, I'll have to get . . ."

J.B. held out a document. "She's had all her shots."

Ms. Young laughed. "She's not a goat, J.B."

J.B. said, "I packed her lunch and snack. No sodas, no sugar. Got a spare set of clothes in a ziplock bag with her name on it in the backpack and a pillow and her blankie for rest time."

Beck looked at his father. "Her *blankie*?"

His father looked back. "You got a problem with that?"

"Why spare clothes?"

Ms. Young said, "In case she has an accident."

"That only happens at night."

"Kids her age, sometimes they have accidents during rest time. We like to be prepared."

The intercom crackled on. Ms. Young said, "I hope you win, Beck. You won't, but I'll vote for you anyway." She stepped inside the classroom and instructed the students to stand and place their hands over their hearts. Meggie waved at Beck and J.B. They waved back and walked down the hallway. A child's voice came over the intercom and recited the Pledge in English; then another child's voice came over and recited the Pledge in Spanish: "*Yo prometo lealtad a la bandera de los Estados Unidos de América . . .*"

J.B. said, "Your grandfather—on your mother's side—he told me when his people first got here, they spoke only German, refused to even learn English. They wanted to live out here on the frontier, isolated, didn't want any part of being American."

"Then why'd they come here?"

"'Cause they couldn't own land back in Germany. Here they

131

could. They came here 'cause they could work hard and make a better life for themselves. Now their heirs begrudge the Mexicans doing the same thing."

"They're not so different, Germans and Mexicans."

"Difference is, Germans will eat Mexican food."

Hundreds of bikers had invaded Fredericksburg, Texas. Not a gang of Bandidos looking for trouble, but middle-class, middle-aged mom-and-pop bikers wearing black leather vests, pants, and chaps, riding designer Harleys, and looking for a good place to eat.

Jodie said, "You'd think leather in August would be hot."

Beck said, "Women in chaps—why's that so interesting?"

She gave him a look. "Because you're a male of the species."

Janelle said, "Jodie, you really think our campaigning for Beck is helping him?"

Janelle Jones was a frumpy woman; her hair was frizzy and black with gray streaks, and she had apparently sworn off makeup. She wore a blue denim shirt that she had worn when painting and a jean skirt; she had pink Crocs on her feet. Jodie, on the other hand, was slim and wore jeans, the red boots with the black toecaps, and a black tee shirt. Janelle drove a turquoise Thunderbird sportster; Jodie drove the Jeep 4x4. They made for an odd couple.

"Janelle, if we don't campaign for him, who will?" To Beck: "No offense, Beck."

Beck nodded.

Janelle said, "You know what I mean, what everyone thinks about us."

"They think we're a couple of crazy liberals when we raise hell at the council and school board."

"And the old-timers can't abide that."

Jodie said, "Praise the Lord and vote Republican."

"In Austin, we were mainstream. Out here, we're like animals in a zoo, something to point at."

"Janelle, Beck doesn't want close-minded right-wing conservatives to vote for him—do you, Beck?"

"Well . . ."

"Then who's gonna vote for him?" Janelle said. "No offense, Beck."

Beck nodded again.

Jodie said, "Everyone we know is going to vote for him."

"He's gonna get the Main Street votes, Jodie, but he won't get the Germans'."

"So what's he supposed to do, promise to throw all the Mexicans in jail like the D.A.?"

"No. I'm just saying, maybe we're not helping, him associating with us publicly."

Beck said, "I'd rather associate with you two crazy liberal lesbians than with the best people in this town."

They gave him a funny look.

Beck shrugged. "You know what I mean."

Other than the bikers, downtown was quiet and would remain so until noon Friday when a stream of tourists in SUVs and motor homes would begin arriving. Downtown on the weekends belonged to the tourists, so locals came into town during the week. That Monday morning Jodie and Janelle were introducing Beck the candidate to the Main Street business owners, most of whom had moved to town from Austin and voted Democrat and none of whom spoke German.

"Every election, it's the same deal," Janelle said. "Main Street versus the Germans. We always lose. Last county election, nine Germans ran unopposed. We couldn't even get anyone to run against them . . . why bother?"

"We're gonna win this time," Jodie said. "We've got Beck Hardin." To Beck: "Word around town is, you've got the D.A. worried. He's hitting the Germans up for more money." She pointed down Adams Street. "See that shop—Texas Jack's Wild West Outfitter? When Tommy Lee was filming *Lonesome Dove*, he came in and bought all his clothes for Captain Call there. I

133

don't think Larry McMurtry gets the recognition he deserves as a writer, do you?"

"Uh . . . I don't know."

"I mean, he won the Pulitzer for *Lonesome Dove* and an Academy Award for *Brokeback Mountain* and—"

Janelle yanked Jodie to an abrupt halt. Jodie said, "Not today, Janelle." Back to Beck: "But because he's a Texan—"

" '*Not today?*' "

"*Brokeback* . . . that was the gay cowboy movie?"

"You got a problem with that?"

"Hey, I played quarterback. I had my hands on another guy's butt for twelve years."

" '*Not today?*' "

"Not today, Janelle."

Janelle had her hands on her wide hips and an incredulous expression on her face; Jodie's face was firm. The women were locked in some kind of standoff.

Beck said, "What's up, girls?"

"Mexican Espresso Mocha," Janelle said. "Double-shot espresso, Mexican vanilla ice cream, chocolate syrup, cinnamon, and whipped cream. It's to die for. We never walk past Clear River without getting one."

They were standing outside the Clear River Pecan Co., an old-fashioned ice cream parlor with a candy-apple red storefront and an Elvis poster in the window.

"Why don't you make that at your coffee shop?"

Jodie said, "Yeah, that's what I need, ice cream within arm's reach at all times. At least we have to walk here for one."

"Well, don't change your routine on account of me. I'll sit here and wait."

Beck sat down on a red metal bench in the shade of the awning next to a mechanical bucking horse for kids. Jodie sat next to him and said to Janelle, "I'm skipping today."

Janelle frowned and said, "Why?"

"Because it's fattening."

"That didn't stop you the first thousand times. Hell, Jodie, it's not like we're cruising for cowboys."

"You get one, Janelle. I just don't want one today."

"We always share one."

"Tell John to make you a small one. I've got to get in shape for the Santa Run."

Janelle, to Beck: "Main Street owners put on a race every Christmas. You gotta dress up in a full Santa outfit to run. Jodie won a couple times." Back to Jodie: "You're sure?"

Jodie nodded. Janelle went into Clear River just as a big white diesel pickup with a German shepherd in the back pulled into one of the curbside parking spots and an old-timer got out; he went into Clear River without turning the engine off. Jodie said, "Leave your car running in Austin and it'll be gone time you come back out. But people here leave their homes unlocked at night."

A few minutes later, the rancher returned licking a pink ice cream cone with colored sprinkles like the kind Meggie loved. He nodded at them and said, "Hidi, folks." When he drove off in a cloud of black diesel smoke, Jodie said, "Old-timer like him, he sees me on the side of the road with a flat tire, he'll stop and fix it without a thought. But if I'm driving under eighty on the farm-to-markets, he'll run right over me. Texans are the nicest people in the world . . . until they get behind the wheel of a pickup. Problem is, most Texans drive pickups." She turned to Beck and said, "Thanks for running, Beck. Maybe you can change things around here."

"The law can't make everything right."

"But a good judge can try."

"Why don't all the Main Street business owners get together and change things?"

"Because we've got to win an election first. And because any business owner who bucked the Germans would be blackballed. You need to renovate your store, city council will deny your application. Your lease comes up for renewal, the German owner

135

will raise your rent through the roof. That's how things are done in a small town, Beck. So Main Street votes against the Germans in private, but they won't stand up to the Germans in public."

"You and Janelle do."

She smiled. "We're just crazy liberals. And we own our building."

Janelle returned with her Mexican Espresso Mocha, and they continued down the sidewalk. They had met the owners at the Spunky Monkey, Zertz, and the Earthbound Trading Company with a Buddha in the front window. Jodie had said, "Better chance of selling African art in Fredericksburg than Buddhas."

Beck paused outside Parts Unknown in the old Palace Theater. He recalled making out with Mary Jo in the balcony. In the display window were Hawaiian shirts that cost $100.

"J.B. never wore anything but plaid."

"I gave him his first one," Jodie said. "Five years ago, for Christmas. He was in a rut."

"He likes you."

"I like him."

"He'd probably marry you, if you weren't . . . younger. So how old are you?"

She shook her head. "I'm not that easy."

They came to a store called Bath Junkie. Jodie said, "My favorite shop. They make custom bubble bath, any scent and color."

"Custom bubble bath for goat ranchers?"

"For tourists. Main Street isn't for the locals." She gestured up and down the street. "The 'Three Magic Blocks.' Storefronts rent for ten thousand a month, and the stores on these three blocks bring one-point-five million tourists to town every year. That's why the Main Street business owners stick together, so the old Germans down at city hall don't screw it up."

"How?"

"By allowing chain stores on Main. We're trying to get a

136

'No Chains on Main' ordinance passed so we don't end up with a Starbucks on every corner and a Victoria's Secret next to the Nimitz. Tourists come here because our shops are different. If this place starts looking just like Houston and Dallas, why come here?"

"But if the chains come and the tourists leave, this town will go back to the way it was when I was here, vacant buildings up and down Main Street."

"Some of the old Germans, they'd like nothing more than to chase the tourists away. And all us newcomers with them."

"Why?"

"Because they don't like this town anymore. Liberals coming from Austin and Latinos from Mexico, they figure their town's going to hell in a hand basket. For the old Germans, it doesn't get any worse than liberals and Latinos."

They walked past the Jeep Collins jewelry store and arrived at Dogologie—pronounced like psychology—a store just for dogs. In the window was a tee shirt that read *You Had Me at Woof*; inside there were doggie beds, doggie toys, doggie strollers, doggie treats with fancy icing like you'd buy in a bakery, and doggie tutus. The pink tutus were kind of creepy. But Beck stuck his hand out to the woman behind the counter and said, "Hi, I'm Beck Hardin. I'm running for judge."

Hi, I'm Annie Hardin, Beck's wife.

It had been six weeks since Beck had read Annie's last email to J.B. He hadn't been able to go back—until now. The thought of her emails stored on this computer burned in his brain. He had to know. It was past eleven, and J.B. and the kids were asleep. Beck had decided to start back at the beginning, with Annie's first email to J.B. He had just found it, dated two and a half years ago.

Dear Mr. Hardin,

Hi, I'm Annie Hardin, Beck's wife. I can't believe I found you!

I was searching the Net for new wines to try—no, I don't drink a lot, but I like wine and Beck doesn't have time to go wine shopping with me. And he doesn't drink. Anyway, I came across wineries in the Texas Hill Country, and I knew Beck had grown up there. When I clicked on Trail's End Winery and read J.B. Hardin, I knew I had found his father. That's incredible. I love wine and my father-in-law owns a winery. But Beck said he grew up on a goat ranch?

Anyway, a little information. You have two grandchildren, Lucas Beck, 8, and Megan Anne, 3. They're great kids. I've attached our last family photo.

Beck and I married 10 years ago, after I graduated from Notre Dame Law School. I practiced almost two years, then decided to be a full-time mother. Beck is a partner in a big Chicago firm. We live in Winnetka, about 20 miles north of the city. I've begged him to take me to Texas, but he says he'll never go back. I know his mother died when he was young, but what happened between you and Beck?

Please write back. (This will remain confidential between us, okay? Hey, trust me, I'm a lawyer.)

I ordered two bottles of wine.

Annie Hardin

Beck now clicked on Sent and scrolled down the outgoing emails. J.B. had written Annie back that same day.

Dear Annie,

Well now, this was a real nice surprise. Good Lord, those are some good looking kids. And you are beautiful. Beck is a lucky man.

Gave up goat ranching about eight years back, went into the wine business. I was in a rut.

Beck's mother died when he was 13. I didn't handle it so good. Beck was real angry back then, left here hating me. Hard thing for a man to carry.

Never figured Beck for the big city, but I reckon he's happy.

I'll send you the wine you ordered, but the only charge is more photos.

J.B.

Beck found dozens more emails going back and forth over many months. J.B. sent more wine to Annie; she sent more family photos to him. She told him about his son's career, the Hardin family of Chicago, and her parents, who had both died; he told her about Beck's life as a boy and about Peggy, about the Texas Hill Country and those bluebonnets. The tone of their emails gradually became that of close friends.

Dear J.B.:

The chardonnay was wonderful! Give Hector my compliments. I ordered a case this time. Beck has never even noticed the label. Of course, he's never around when I drink.

The kids are at school and Beck's in L.A., another long trial. He's what we call a "high-profile" trial lawyer, with corporate clients all over the country, so he travels a lot. He argued before the Supreme Court once (he won) and he's going back next year. He's very good. You would be proud of him. It's just that he's gone so much, the kids are growing up without him, and I'm raising them alone. That's the world today, I know, and at least they have one full-time parent, but he's missing out on their lives. I know he loves the kids, and me, but I've learned to sleep without him. Of course, a bottle of your wine and I'm out like a baby! (I'm just kidding. Only a glass or two each night. Or three. Four last night. You can't be an alcoholic on wine, can you?)

Okay, that's enough whining for today. Maybe I'll start going to the gym. Time to get rid of that baby fat! (It's only been four years.) Maybe I'll get real skinny (well, not *real*) again and Beck will spend more time at home. First day of school photos are attached.

Love, Annie

PS: J.B., 23 years is long enough. It's time for you and Beck to make up. My children need a grandfather, and I want to hug you. And I want to see your winery and meet Hector. If it's the last thing I do, I'm getting you and Beck back together.

Their great life had not been so great for Annie. But she had kept it a secret from him; instead, she had told his father. He had been so focused on his career that he had failed her as a husband and his children as a father. As if winning another case would have changed his life. He knew now that marriage, children, illness, and death were life-changing events. Everything else was just ripples in the river. And getting J.B. and him back together was the last thing that Annie ever did.

140

Chapter 10

"Beck Hardin hasn't lived here for twenty-four years—he's an *Ausländer* now! He thought he was too good for us, so he moved up north to live with Yankees in *Chicago*."

He said the word as if saying *Shit-cago*.

"I've lived here all my life and I'll always live here, just like you. I'm a full-blooded German, just like you. My daddy was one of you, and I'm one of you. We need a judge who's one of us."

The Gillespie County Fairgrounds were crowded with parents, children, and farm animals. The Hardin family had come for the county fair. It had a carnival, arts and crafts, cooking competitions, and pari-mutuel horse racing. It had live country-western music, a swine futurity, livestock shows, and a beauty queen pageant. It had mutton busting, tractor pulls, agricultural exhibits, and a down-home version of *American Idol*. It had prizes for the Grand Champion Steer, Sire, Doe, Dam, Ewe, Ram, Lamb, Billy, Bull, and Bale of Hay; for the Outstanding Cake and Pie; for the Best of Show Pickles, Pie, Canned Fruit, Crochet, Quilt, Standard Breed Chicken, and Rabbit Buck; and, of course, for the Best of

Show Adult Mohair. It had goats, sheep, cows, chickens, pigs, and politics; the D.A. was campaigning at the county fair.

J.B. gestured at the crowd of men gathered around Niels Eichman and said to Beck, "Those old boys are the richest Germans hereabouts. Goat ranchers, every one of them. They own most of the land in the county . . . and they own all the politicians in the county. Including the judge, until Stutz retired. Now they got to buy a new one."

"They can't buy me."

"But they can buy the D.A."

"You saying I can't win?"

"I'm saying you won't win."

"Why not?"

" 'Cause you're standing here talking to me and he's over there talking to them."

"I didn't get into this to lose, J.B."

"Then go over there and do something about it."

Beck looked down at Meggie holding the doll in one hand and a cotton candy on a stick in the other.

"Honey, you stay close to J.B. Daddy's got to go kick some . . . talk to some folks. Okay?"

"Okay."

J.B. said to Meggie and Luke, "Come on, kids, let's go over to the Show Barn for the swine futurity."

Meggie looked up at her grandfather and said, "J.B., what's a swine?"

"I'm fixin' to show you, darlin'."

They walked off, and Beck strode over to the group of old men—he felt like he had when the Notre Dame coach had him glad-hand rich alumni—and stuck his hand out.

"Hidi, boys—Beck Hardin. Good to see you again. So what's this I hear about winning a state football championship this year?"

They all turned his way and their faces lit up like he was LBJ himself walking in with their mohair checks. Beck glanced over at the D.A. and winked. The D.A.'s face wasn't lit up. His face was red and he was frowning.

Thirty minutes later, J.B. said, "How'd it go?"

"We talked football."

J.B. chuckled. "Well, at least they talked to you."

"Yeah, but I saw it in their eyes, J.B. They're not going to vote for me. They've been living a certain way all their lives. They're not changing now. Doesn't matter if the election is for county judge or county fair queen, result's the same. Always has been, always will be."

The Gillespie County Fair Queen had just been announced to the crowd in the grandstand. Another pretty German girl had won this year. One hundred years the county fair had elected a queen; one hundred years the queen had been German. Always had been, always would be.

J.B. said, "Beck, if you quit—"

"*Quit?* Who said anything about quitting? This game's not over yet, J.B."

Chapter 11

Two weeks later, the game was all but over. The D.A. was leading Beck in early voting by a five-to-one margin. Jodie had coaxed the latest results from Mavis Mooney; she was not happy.

"How many football games did you lose?"

"A few."

"How many trials?"

"None."

"Well, you're going to lose your first election in one week . . . unless . . ."

Beck turned to her. "Unless what?"

"Most people around here are married by eighteen and parents by nineteen—nothing else to do in a small town. The D.A. is thirty-two and single."

"You saying he's gay?"

"No. He's a daddy."

"But he's not married."

"That's not a requirement."

"Explain."

"He's got a child in Austin. Seven years old now. He was in law school at UT, the mother was in college. He sends her money."

"How do you know this?"

"Mavis. Stutz told her one day, she thinks he was drinking. Stutz knows everything about everyone."

Beck shrugged. "Half the movie stars in Hollywood have children out of marriage."

"She's Latina. The mother. That makes him a hypocrite."

"Most of the politicians in Texas are hypocrites."

"Yeah, but the old Germans, they won't elect a judge with a Latino child."

"You want me to use that to win?"

"Yes."

"I never won that way."

"Thought you were a lawyer."

"Oh, I played hardball, but not sleazeball."

"Beck, you haven't lived here the last ten years, seen how it is. I'm tired of living in a town where people are afraid. If you're the judge, you can change that. You can change this town."

Beck shielded his eyes from the low sun. The eighth day of September was still hot, but by five the sun's heat had played out for the day. The heat was bad for humans but good for grapes.

"Jodie, you're expecting a lot from me. You might be disappointed."

She turned and looked up at him. "I don't think you'll disappoint me, Beck Hardin."

They were standing in the vineyard watching Meggie and Josefina carry a basket of grapes between them over to the bins manned by Luke and Danny, Janelle's twelve-year-old son. Luke dumped the grapes into one of the bins sitting on a small trailer. The girls carried the basket back to their picking spot, where Butch was waiting. Meggie's goat followed behind like a duckling following its mother. It was last harvest at the Trail's End Winery.

"They're cute," Jodie said.

"She named the goat Frank."

"Odd name for a goat."

"Especially for a girl goat."

145

"Is Meggie still having accidents?"

"Yeah. I read the books, but nothing's worked."

J.B. drove past on the green Gator. He stopped at Luke's trailer, backed into place, and hitched up.

"You boys hang on."

He gunned the Gator and drove off with the trailer and boys in tow. Hector was in the winery overseeing the grape processing, and his wife was up at the house cooking for the fiesta. The winery hands were helping Hector, and their families were spread out over the vineyard, handpicking the grapes. Aubrey was picking alongside Janelle; the Goats had won their first game the night before, 56–0 in San Antonio. Slade McQuade had thrown for five touchdowns.

Beck and Jodie were picking together. "She didn't think I could raise the kids alone. Said I was a lawyer, not a father."

"Annie?"

Beck nodded. "In her emails to J.B."

"Beck, she—"

"Was right."

By the time they had filled their baskets, J.B. had returned with the trailer and the boys. Beck carried the baskets over to the bin. He heard Danny say, "My dad left us."

"But he's still alive," Luke said.

"Not to me."

When the boys saw him, they went mute like lawyered-up suspects. Luke emptied the baskets into the bin.

"You're doing good, Luke."

He gave Beck the baskets and a half smile.

An hour later the picking was done and all hands had gathered on the patio for the grape stomp. J.B. had dumped grapes into a dozen barrels cut in half; the kids were now giggling and stomping the grapes into mush and getting purple in the process. With the destemmer and press, the stomp was just for fun.

Jodie jumped into the barrel nearest Beck. She was wearing a wreath of purple grapes and green leaves on her head and a

146

traditional grape harvest outfit, a colorful shirt and long skirt, which she now hitched up thigh high. Her legs were muscular and soon purple with grape juice. The setting sun caught her face like it had Annie's on that Hawaiian beach. She was quite beautiful. She bent over, and Beck caught the briefest glimpse of her black panties—and he felt a slight stirring, something he thought had died with Annie. Something he hadn't thought about in a long time. He looked up at her face and saw her looking at him. He felt his face flush. He turned away.

Jesus, you're pathetic. Your wife's been dead eight months and you're looking like that at a lesbian.

"She's a looker, ain't she?" Aubrey had sat down next to Beck with a beer. "How old you figure she is, thirty-five?"

"I don't know."

Aubrey drank from his beer. "Seems a shame, a good-looking woman like her going to waste."

"She's not a dead deer rotting on the side of the road, Aubrey. She and Janelle, they're happy in their own way."

"Aw, I'm just jealous, I guess. They both got something we don't."

"What's that?"

"A woman." Aubrey again drank from his beer, then said, "So what was Grady holding back from me?"

A lawyer has an ethical duty to disclose to his client all the information he learns in the course of his representation of that client. Beck Hardin had never failed that duty. But he had never before learned that a client's daughter had had sex with two men on the same night. So he didn't answer his client.

"Did Heidi have a cell phone?"

Aubrey shook his head. "Wouldn't let her have one. So you ain't learned nothing? Beck, we only got three months and twenty-two days to find this guy."

"Aubrey, the election is a week from today. It's not looking good."

"I never figured you for winning. Hell, those San Antonio boys had a better chance of winning against Slade—he played like a man among boys. He *was* a man among boys." He chuckled. "But you're still my lawyer, Beck. I'll find a way to pay you."

"I don't want your money."

A lanky older black man walked up with a beer in his hand. Beck reached over and shook hands with him.

"Mr. Johnson, how're you doing?"

The man shook hands with Aubrey, then sat. "Beck, I reckon you're old enough to call me Gil now. 'Course, this time next week I'll have to call you 'judge.'"

"Doubtful. Gil, you still build the best rock I've ever seen."

The patio had been laid out like a courtyard. The rear limestone wall of the winery formed one side and a four-foot-high limestone wall the others; the walls joined to form a fireplace constructed of river rock. J.B. had built a roaring fire that didn't seem out of place on a warm September evening. The patio was covered by a pitched cedar roof supported by thick logs fixed in rock beddings. The floor was stained concrete. Every piece of rock had been hand-laid by Gil Johnson.

"Why, thank you, Beck. I'm kind of proud of this patio." Gil Johnson shook his head. "Hell of a thing, ain't it? Saturday night and none of us got a woman. What we should do is, go over to the auction house and buy us one. They got the Fall Female Replacement sale going on. And boys, we need replacements."

Aubrey said, "Shame it ain't as easy as buying a heifer."

"Life is better with a woman," Gil said. Then in a softer voice, he said, "I was married once."

Beck said, "I never knew that."

"Her name was Doris. She died in childbirth. Baby was coming out feet first, midwife couldn't turn it. Lost both of them, her and the child. Boy."

"I'm sorry, Gil."

"I'm sorry about your wife, too, Beck. But they're in a better

148

place now. It's us that are left here to suffer. Don't know why the Good Lord keeps me around." He downed his beer and stood. "Now I'm getting melancholy on a Saturday night. Reckon I'll go help Lillianna with the food."

Hector's wife had pulled up in J.B.'s black pickup truck. Everyone sat at the picnic tables on the patio and ate enchiladas, tacos, guacamole, rice, beans, and handmade flour tortillas until Hector began playing his guitar and singing a Mexican ballad. J.B. grabbed Jodie and pulled her up to dance. Gil and Janelle were next, then Libby dragged a reluctant Luke out. Beck lifted Meggie and danced with her in his arms. Aubrey tapped his cane on the concrete floor. The winery workers and their wives and kids joined in, and they all danced until Hector's hands were too tired to play.

Julio Espinoza was invisible.

He stood right there, yet no one saw him. He was like the movie posters on the wall: an inanimate object. He had often thought of jumping onto the counter and stripping naked, just to get someone to acknowledge that he existed. But he never had, because that would have brought trouble to his family.

His parents were illegals. They had come to Fredericksburg nineteen years before from Piedras Negras to work in the turkey plant. And that was to be his life as well, twelve hours each day killing and gutting turkeys for the Mexican wage. But Julio wanted more, more than the life he had been born into, the life the world told him to accept as his own. Julio was seventeen, he would be the first Espinoza to ever graduate from high school, and he would be the first to go to college.

He wanted to build rockets at NASA.

He was a senior, he made straight As, he had scored 2350 on the SAT, and he had been accepted at the University of Texas at Austin with a full scholarship—but only because he was Latino. Because he served their purpose: "Oh, look, we have found a smart Latino. Let us help him and show the world what good Anglos we are." They wanted to display him like a rare species, as if finding a smart Latino in Texas were some sort of great anthropological discovery—like finding a dinosaur bone!

The school counselor had told him, "Julio, take the free ride. Sure, they're giving you a free college education just because you're Latino, but that's no different than dumb jocks getting free rides just because they can play football." But it felt different to Julio. It felt wrong to get a scholarship just because his skin was brown, just as it felt wrong to walk down Main Street and be viewed as a crime waiting to happen just because his skin was brown.

Julio did not want the Anglos' help. He did not want to go to college on the Anglos' money. He did not want to live his life on the Anglos' terms. He wanted to go to college and live his life on his own terms with his own money.

But he had no money.

So he worked weekend nights here at the theater and weekend days with his father. Rafael Espinoza worked at the turkey plant during the week and built rock for the rich Anglos' new houses on weekends. Julio's hands ached this night from his work that day. His father was from the old school; he spoke only Spanish at home and in his native tongue he had often said, "Julio is not going to build rockets—he is going to build rock!" But his mother, Maria, always replied in her sharp Mexican tongue, "No, Rafael, building rock is not to be his life! Julio must have the education so he will have a better life and so he may help his brothers and sisters to a better life!" Rafael Espinoza was the *hombre* of the house, except when Maria Espinoza was home.

Home was the barrio on South Milam, just five blocks off Main Street but in the part of town the tourists do not see. Tourists drive south on Milam, cross Baron's Creek, and turn right on Whitney Street to dine at the Herb Farm on—and Julio had read this in the newspaper—"Herb & Coffee Bean

Crusted Tenderloin Served with Rosemary & Garlic Potato Mash & Grilled Asparagus with Lemon Herb Hollandaise" and after dinner to purchase aromatherapy bath salts in the gift shop. They do not continue just one block farther south on Milam into the barrio to dine on *cabrito* cooked over an open pit and drink Tecate to the sounds of *Tejano* music and after dinner to purchase marijuana, cocaine, and meth from El Gato, the neighborhood dealer.

Julio lived in the barrio but he hoped one day to taste a Coffee Bean Crusted Tenderloin.

His was a *casa pequeña*: living room, kitchen, bedroom, and bathroom. His father worked the night shift, so his mother slept in the bed with Juan, the baby, and Rosita, the two-year-old. Margarita slept on the couch, and Gilberto and Jorge slept on pads on the floor in the living room. Julio slept in the bathtub. Each night he dried the tub with a towel, then placed a pad and his pillow in the tub. Sometimes he would wake with a crick in his neck. But he had the light so he could shut the door and read after the others were asleep. He had read many books in the bathtub.

But Julio did not complain. Other houses in the barrio were home to three and four families each, often twenty people in four rooms. All Mexicans. All illegal. All invisible. Careful to stay in the shadows so as not to bring trouble to their families. When the girl had been found dead in the ditch, the Anglos blamed the Mexicans; and the Mexicans had been fearful of a raid in retaliation. One phone call could bring ICE into the barrio, immigration agents wearing black jackets and pointing guns and ordering everyone into buses for immediate deportation to Nuevo Laredo. Fear of a raid never left the Latinos; they carried the fear with them always just as the Anglos carried their cell phones.

If trouble came to the barrio, it would come to the Espinoza family. Julio and his siblings had been born in America; they were citizens. But if their parents were deported, they would have to move to Mexico with them. And there were no universities in Nuevo Laredo; there were only the *narco-traficantes*.

So Julio stayed out of trouble.

He did not hang out on the Latino porch during lunch at the high school with the other Latinos, their arms and necks wrapped with white bandages that covered their tatts; gang tattoos violated the school dress code, so tatts had to be covered with long-sleeve shirts or bandages. On hot days when the boys wore short sleeves and bandages, the Latino porch looked like the burn unit at the hospital.

Of course, Julio also did not hang with the sk8rs, the socialites, the jocks, or the rednecks with the LONG LIVE JOHN WAYNE bumper stickers on their new Ford F-150 pickup trucks. He wasn't a skateboarder, he wasn't rich, he wasn't a football player, and he wasn't German.

He was invisible.

Julio was invisible in town, at school, and here at work. He was just the brown boy selling snacks to Anglos, just as invisible as the brown men roofing Anglo homes and the brown women cleaning dishes at the Anglo restaurants. He was as invisible to the Anglos as the hot wind on their faces, and far less important.

Julio did not want to live his life invisible.

His parents had long ago resigned themselves to such a life; it was the trade-off a Mexican must make for a better life in America. An invisible better life. But Julio was an American citizen. He should not have to make that trade-off. He should not have to live his life invisible.

But it would always be so here.

He had often wondered, what is it about a brown face that brought anger to the Anglos? But he had never found an answer, until Juan was born. Julio had walked to the hospital just down the road and gone to the nursery to see Juan lying there in his crib wrapped like a papoose. And Julio then looked at the other new babies; they all had brown faces. His eyes met those of the

152

Anglo nurse; and in her eyes he saw the knowledge that with each brown baby that came into her nursery, her world was changing.

The Anglos' world was changing.

Now when Julio walked downtown and the Anglos looked upon him with disdain, he just smiled, because he now understood: his brown face did not make them angry; it made them afraid. They did not hate him; they feared him. They feared the future. Because his brown face was their future. Because change was upon them.

Change that would threaten their way of life.

But Julio Espinoza did not threaten the Anglos. In fact, he did not threaten anyone: he stood barely five feet eight inches tall and weighed only one hundred thirty pounds soaking wet. He was not a gang member, he did not tag the school campus with gang graffiti, and he did not have gang tattoos all over his back and arms. He did not cause trouble. He was a "good Mexican." So he was tolerated by the Anglos—as long as he stayed in his place. And minded his manners. And did not speak to the pretty Anglo girls. The big German football players always glared at him if they caught him talking to an Anglo girl after an AP class, but he did not glare back and call them *cabrónes* and throw up a gang sign, as did the tough Latinos.

Julio Espinoza knew his place.

His place that Saturday night was behind the snack bar at the Stagecoach Theater just south of town, where he worked weekend nights, serving sodas and buttered popcorn and candy to Anglos before the eight o'clock movie began.

"Thanks, Julio."

He handed the large popcorn to Nikki and tried not to stare. Nikki was a senior like Julio, she was smart like Julio, and she took all the AP courses like Julio. But she was not like Julio; she was blonde and she was beautiful and she was German. She was the head cheerleader and the most popular girl in the school. Julio had loved Nikki Ernst since first grade.

153

"Julio," Nikki said, her white smile blinding him, "after the movie we're all going over to my house to swim. You wanna come? And don't worry, Slade won't be there."

Nikki was also Slade McQuade's girlfriend.

He had often imagined Nikki in a bikini; just seeing her in her cheerleader outfit at school on game days made him feel faint. But Nikki's movie would end at ten; Julio got off work at midnight on Saturdays, after the last movie. Not that he would really be welcome at an Anglo party—he might be a good Mexican, but he was still a Mexican. Julio could only imagine her parents' reaction at the sight of a Latino in their pool: *"More chlorine, Hilda!"* Nikki was nice, but terribly naïve.

"Can't. Working till midnight."

She put the popcorn on the counter, stuck her hand into her purse, and pulled out a five-dollar bill. Julio took the bill, made change, and held a handful of coins out to her. Nikki took his hand, turned it over, and held her purse underneath to catch the change. It was almost as if they were holding hands, something Julio had often dreamed of. Just the touch of her smooth skin on his made Julio's entire body come alive; he inhaled her scent and felt drunk. The last thing he remembered about that incredible moment was how it ended: huge hands grabbing him by the shirt and being lifted off his feet and dragged across the counter by Slade McQuade.

Chapter 12

"*Uno, dos, tres, cuatro, cinco . . .*"

Six days later—the night before the election—Beck was in the kitchen stirring J.B.'s stew, listening to Meggie count to ten in Spanish, and wondering if he should have gone public with the D.A.'s half-Hispanic child. Dirt was part of politics today—but was a child fair dirt? The D.A. had made a youthful mistake when he was young; what if Mary Jo had gotten pregnant when they were in high school? They probably would have married, but he had loved her. The D.A. didn't marry the girl, but he was supporting the child. He was doing the right thing.

But the D.A. campaigned against Mexicans to win the judgeship. Was that the right thing? Illegal immigration was the hottest wedge issue in America today; presidential candidates were wedging for all they were worth. Why shouldn't a local D.A.? Was he to blame or the voters who voted for him?

Beck had faced the same dilemma as a lawyer: Do you work the margins of ethics and the law to win? Most lawyers did because that's where the money is made in the law, at the margins. He never had. But he had still won. And he wanted to win this election—as much as he had ever wanted to win a football game or a trial. He wanted to win for the children, for J.B. and Jodie, and for Miguel Cervantes.

"*Seis, siete, ocho, nueve, diez.*"

"That's very good, honey."

The back door opened, and his father walked in with Luke. J.B. came over and patted Meggie on her head. "Why, you're gonna be the prettiest gal at the game." He then sniffed the stew. "Wasn't sure about the garlic powder, but figured what the heck. I think it's gonna turn out okay." He went to the sink and washed his hands. "Hector says Luke's got the makings of a real winemaker."

Luke almost smiled. "J.B., the Gator's running rough."

"I'll look at it tomorrow."

The phone rang. J.B. dried his hands and picked up the receiver. "Yep?" He held the phone out to Beck. "Jodie."

Beck swapped the spoon for the phone. He put the phone to his ear and said, "Hi, Jodie."

"Beck, Mavis just called me. She said early voting closed out and the D.A. is up by two thousand votes."

He sighed. He had expected that verdict, but it still felt as if he'd been kicked in the gut. He said, "You were right."

"About what?"

"Using the D.A.'s kid."

"No, Beck, you were right. I was mad."

"You worked hard, Jodie. I'm sorry we lost."

"We didn't."

"Didn't what?"

"Lose. You won."

"I won? *How?* You just said he's way ahead, and the election is tomorrow."

"D.A. dropped out of the race."

"*When?*"

"Today."

"*Why?*"

"Mavis didn't know. But you're our new judge. Congratulations. I'll see you at the game."

Beck hung up. J.B. said, "What's this about you winning?"

"The D.A. dropped out of the race."

"I'll be damned." J.B. turned to the children. "Hey, kids, your daddy's the judge."

Beck said, "He's way ahead in early voting but he quits the day before the election? That doesn't make any sense."

"Beck, ain't nothing in a small town makes much sense, especially politics and football."

If you've never played football on a Friday night, you can't begin to imagine what it feels like to be on the field under the bright lights on a warm evening with the fans screaming, the bands playing, cheerleaders cheering, and your body pumping out so much adrenaline that you're actually high on hormones. Every cell in your body—nerve, brain, muscle—is alive. In fact, when you're forty-two and you look back on those nights, you realize that you had never been more alive. And if you've never played high school football in Texas, you haven't lived.

High school football in Texas is more than a game. They say it's a religion. It might be an obsession. But Texans don't win or lose high school football games—they live or die high school football games. Few states spend less on education, but no state spends more on football. High schools across the state boast indoor practice arenas like the pros and stadiums like colleges with artificial turf, air-conditioned press boxes, 20,000 seating capacities, and Jumbotron video screens showing instant replays in living color.

The Gallopin' Goats Stadium did not have a Jumbotron. It had a real grass field, an open-air press box, and a capacity crowd of 2,200 that had come to watch the top-ranked high school football team in the state. The Goats wore Angora-white jerseys and helmets and black pants, socks, and shoes. The players were identified by their last names printed on the backs of their jerseys—except the name on the back of the quarter-back's jersey was SLADE. The sleeves of his jersey were cut short to reveal the barbed-wire tattoos wrapping around each bicep. His long hair was wet and combed straight back. He looked like Samson.

The Goats' opponent for their first home game of the season was the LaGrange Leopards. LaGrange was a small town east of Austin that would forever be famous for having been home to the "Best Little Whorehouse in Texas." Beck, J.B., and the kids were sitting in Aubrey's reserved seats among the coaches' wives and children. Aubrey gave away his tickets each week because he no longer had a wife or child.

The stadium, the team colors, the cheerleaders, the band, the fans dressed in plaid, it was all as Beck had remembered—except J.B. had never worn a Hawaiian print shirt to Beck's football games.

Everyone stood for the opening kickoff. The Goat player returned the kick to the thirty yard line. The Goats offense ran onto the field and lined up without a huddle. The players spread out from sideline to sideline, with three receivers on one side and two on the other. Slade stood five yards behind the center in the shotgun formation; there was no running back. The center snapped the ball back to Slade; the LaGrange defensive line surged forward, but the Goats line held them to a stalemate. Slade stood tall while his five receivers raced down the field. Then Slade's right arm just flicked forward as if he were throwing a dart instead of a regulation-sized football and the ball flew high and far and fell into the Goats receiver's arms at the ten-yard line—*sixty-five yards in the air*—and the receiver ran into the end zone.

One play, one pass, one touchdown.

The players' parents sat as a group and wore Goats jerseys with their sons' names and numbers on the back. Beck spotted a tall man in the group with an unlit cigar clamped between his teeth and a SLADE jersey on his back. The other fathers were high-fiving him like he had sired the second coming of Joe Namath. Maybe he had.

158

LaGrange got the ball but went nowhere against the Goats defense. The Goats were bigger, stronger, and faster. They hit harder and hurt less. They were more aggressive and violent. They knocked the LaGrange running back out cold.

After each big hit, the Goats players slapped and head-butted each other; they were high on adrenaline. The stadium pulsed as the cheerleaders and the crowd chanted "De-fense . . . De-fense . . . De-fense." Beck felt a twinge of sympathy for the smaller LaGrange team, like when Notre Dame had played Navy.

The Goats offense took the field again and put the NASCAR offense into overdrive: they raced to the line of scrimmage, snapped the ball quickly, and ran the play. Slade completed a pass for twenty-two yards. They raced to the line of scrimmage again and ran another play. An eighteen-yard completion. Three more plays and they scored again. Seventy-eight yards, five plays, less than two minutes. It was frantic football, and it was winning football. By the time the bands took the field for the halftime show, Slade had thrown for four touchdowns and the Gillespie County Gallopin' Goats led 42–0.

J.B. said, "Beck, you think the Goats can win state?"

"Only team around here that could beat them plays on Saturdays in the UT stadium."

"Slade's good, ain't he?"

"Yeah, he's good."

"Unreal" was the word that came to mind.

The fans were giving the players a standing ovation as they left the field when Beck heard a woman's voice in his ear: "Do goats really gallop?"

Jodie Lee was standing next to him.

"More like canter."

She wrapped her arms around him and gave him a big hug. "Congratulations, Judge Hardin."

When she pulled back, she had tears in her eyes.

"You okay?"

"I'm happy."

An old man walked by, nodded at Beck, and said, "Judge."

Beck said to Jodie, "Word travels fast."

"Good thing about living in a small town is that everyone knows everything about everyone. Bad thing about living in a small town is that everyone knows everything about everyone." She wiped her eyes and said, "Thank God you won."

"I didn't win. He quit. Why would he do that?"

She shrugged. "Who cares?" She sat and looked away.

He sat and said, "Something tells me I should care. Jodie, you didn't use his kid, did you? To get him to drop out?"

She looked back. "You think I would do that?"

"They say women are the tougher of the breed."

"They're right. But like I said, I was just mad. I didn't use his kid."

Meggie stepped around Beck with the doll and said, "Hi, Miss Jodie."

"Well, hi yourself, girlfriend. What's up?"

"We're sad."

"Why, honey?"

"Josefina asked us to have a sleepover with her."

"Well, that'll be fun."

"We can't go."

"Why not?"

"We might have an accident."

"Oh. Well, you know what you should do?"

"What?"

"Ask Josefina to have a sleepover at your house. Your daddy can put a mattress on the floor for her and you can sleep in your bed. If you have an accident, it won't be a problem."

Meggie's face brightened. "We can do that."

She jumped onto Jodie's lap, and they giggled and chatted about the cheerleaders and the dance team called the Goat Gals, and for a brief moment Beck felt whole again.

★   ★   ★

Beck had read through a year's worth of Annie's emails to J.B. and J.B.'s emails to her. They had become like father and daughter. His wife had told his father more than she had ever told her husband; and his father had told his wife more than he had ever told his son—about his life, his dreams, his love for his wife, and his love for his son. Beck was about to quit when he found an email dated a year before Annie had died. The first part was more family news, but the last part stopped Beck short.

Gotta run. Doctor's appointment. Routine mammogram, first one. Which sounds like a lot of fun, having my breasts squished flat like pancakes. Can't believe I just typed that. Love, Annie

Beck quickly scrolled down for the next email. It was from Annie to J.B. a week later.

They found a lump in my breast. Had an ultrasound. Needle core biopsy tomorrow. That should be fun, getting stabbed in my breast. (Acting brave here.) I haven't told Beck.

His heart rate jumped. He scrolled down fast and found the next one from Annie a few days later.

Pathology came back positive. "Invasive ductal carcinoma." Not good. MRI tomorrow, surgery soon. I'm scared, J.B. I've got to tell Beck. Tonight.

"Perfect" had ended that night for the Hardin family of Chicago.

161

Chapter 13

Alfred Giles died a Texas goat rancher.

But he had been born an Englishman. Alfred wanted to be a minister; he became an architect instead. After studying at King's College in London, he traveled to the United States and settled in San Antonio in 1873. He had suffered rheumatic fever as a boy, and Texas' hot, dry climate suited him.

He arrived just as Texas' two hundred fifty-four counties embarked on a kind of courthouse competition, each trying to one-up the other. They called in great architects to design grand structures: Romanesque, Classic, and Renaissance Revival, Beaux Arts, Second Empire, Art Deco, and even Mediterranean. Now, Texans might not know Romanesque from Beaux Arts, but they know what they like; and they liked their fancy new court-houses.

Gillespie County entered the competition in 1881. But the Germans in Fredericksburg were nothing if not frugal; they simply could not bring themselves to spend good money to hire a great courthouse architect. So they held a contest. Sitting in his office in San Antonio one day, twenty-eight-year-old Alfred Giles opened the newspaper and saw an ad offering a $50 prize for the winning design for a new Gillespie County courthouse. Two architects answered the ad; Alfred was one.

Alfred designed a Renaissance Revival courthouse that would sit on Main Street surrounded by oak trees and one unusual three-trunk deodar cedar tree. His two-story structure had a footprint in the shape of two Ts set end to end. The north and south façades were symmetrical with wide balconies, as were the east and west façades with smaller balconies. The walls would be yellow limestone blocks, the trim white limestone, and the arched windows encased in pine wood and secured in place with square-headed nails. The doors would be pine and the doorknobs copper with a raised hummingbird etching. The building would be topped by a green standing-seam roof above ornamental cornices and a cast-iron cresting. Alfred's design was grand, and it won. The Germans liked the style, the symmetry, and the cost: $23,125.

The Gillespie County Courthouse earned Alfred a reputation as a great courthouse architect. He went on to design ten other courthouses across Texas, including the Presidio County Courthouse in Marfa, generally regarded as the grandest county courthouse in the state. When his mother died in 1885, Alfred sold off her London real estate and bought thirteen thousand acres of land south of Fredericksburg. He named his new ranch Hillingdon, after his birthplace in Middlesex, and stocked the land with Angora goats. He later founded the Texas Sheep and Goat Raisers' Association. Alfred Giles, the Englishman turned Texan, raised goats on his land in the Texas Hill Country until he died in 1920.

Alfred's courthouse still stands on Main Street, shaded by those same oak trees; but that lone three-trunk deodar cedar tree is gone. A year before, James Brazeal, a "chainsaw artist," had carved the dead cedar tree into the image of an eight-foot-tall eagle with its wings spread as if taking flight; smaller eagles sat atop each wing. Locals call it the "Eagle Tree."

Beck walked past the Eagle Tree to the front door and entered the courthouse. The first floor housed the district clerk's office, the district attorney's office, the justice of the peace, and the judge's chambers. Dual staircases led upstairs to the second-floor courtroom where for one hundred twenty-five years justice had been dispensed in Gillespie County.

Beck stood there dressed in a custom suit; the last time he had been in this courtroom he had worn jeans. It was the summer before his senior year. Two boys had been arrested for smoking marijuana—in the same pickup at the same time. One was German; the other was Latino. Both were Beck's friends. The German boy's family hired a good lawyer; the Latino boy had a public defender. Beck had sat in the courtroom on sentencing day and heard old Judge Stutz say "probation" to Merle Fuchs and "one year in the state penitentiary" to Miguel Cervantes, and his face had burned hot. He stormed out of the courtroom and into the fresh air outside. He sat on a bench and watched Merle leave through the front door with his parents and Miguel through the back door with deputies. He had decided then that he would become a lawyer. The matter of Miguel Cervantes haunted Beck to that day.

Justice in Gillespie County would now be dispensed by Judge John Beck Hardin.

He had been in courtrooms hundreds of times. He had tried cases in state and federal courts, and he had argued before appellate courts and twice before the Supreme Court. But he had always been there as a lawyer, and the cases had always been about money. He now wondered if he were up to that task: justice.

But then, he was the judge of a rural Texas county with a population of twenty-three thousand. How hard could it be?

It was eight-thirty and the courtroom was still vacant. He walked up the center aisle past the wooden pews and sat behind the bench beneath an arched wall. The floor was longleaf pine; the walls were limestone and white stucco; the ceiling was sixteen feet high. The courtroom was illuminated by eighteen tall

164

windows with green wood shutters and eight black wrought-iron chandeliers.

To his immediate left was the witness stand; beyond that was the court reporter's desk and the jury box with thirteen chairs bolted to the floor. To his right was the district clerk's desk. Behind him on tall standards hung the American and Texas flags on either side of the limestone arch.

Behind the bench was an alcove with two twelve-foot-tall windows looking out on a balcony. He opened one of the windows and stepped over the low sill and onto the balcony. He had stashed two lawn chairs just inside; this balcony would be his private retreat, a place to be alone and think.

The first day of October had brought a cool front to town. Beck stood at the low wrought-iron railing and faced the Adams and Main Street intersection, the busiest in downtown Fredericksburg. A few pickup trucks were stopped at the light, people were walking to work, and business owners were sweeping the sidewalks out front of their stores. The view to the north across Main Street was of the Marktplatz where preparations for Oktoberfest were underway; to the east across Adams Street it was of the community college building, the Beckendorf Art Gallery, L.M. Easterling boot maker, and Texas Jack's Wild West Outfitter with a wooden cigar store Indian out front of the old stage depot.

He ducked back inside and shut the window. Tucked into the corner of the alcove was a narrow spiral staircase built around a thick pine log. Beck wasn't sure if the architect had intended the stairway as the judge's private escape route should gunfire break out in the courtroom or just as a quicker route to an outhouse since the courthouse had no restrooms at the time it was constructed. It was now his private stairway to and from his chambers on the first floor.

Beck descended the stairs and entered his chambers. The room had limestone walls, a high ceiling, and tall windows that looked out at street level. There were no bars on the windows or other security of any kind. He sat behind his desk. Above the desk was a black wrought-iron chandelier. In front of the desk were visitor chairs. Against each wall were bookshelves with law books; this was also the judge's law library.

"Do I have to call you 'judge' now?"

Aubrey was standing in the doorway, dressed in his coach's uniform and leaning on his cane. The smell of beer drifted over.

"Only in the courtroom."

"Congratulations, Beck. Still can't believe you won."

"I didn't, but thanks anyway. And same to you—four straight wins."

"Slade's unstoppable."

Beck knew that Aubrey hadn't come to talk football.

"I've been in Austin the last two weeks, Aubrey, for judge school. But I'll be able to do more now, about Heidi."

"Four years and nine months ago today, Beck. Ninety-one days left." Aubrey nodded past Beck and said, "You've got company."

Beck turned. Jodie was standing outside, tapping on the window. He opened the window, and she stuck a coffee through.

"Small nonfat latte," she said. "Figured you might need one your first day, Judge."

"Feels like when I was a teenager sneaking out my window to meet Mary Jo."

Her eyes got wide. "*Mary Jo Jobst?*"

"Hey, don't say anything, okay?"

"I can keep a secret."

"J.B. said . . . never mind. Thanks for the coffee."

She walked off, and Beck shut the window. When he turned back, Aubrey was giving him a funny look.

"You're not, you know"—he made a little punching motion with his fist—"with the lesbian?"

"No, I'm not with the lesbian."

The district clerk walked in past Aubrey; he waved and limped out of sight. She said, "He smells like a brewery. You ready, Judge?"

166

"As ready as I'll ever be, Mavis."

Mavis Mooney had served as the District Clerk of Gillespie County for twenty-seven years now; she knew more about being a judge than Beck did. Beck removed his suit coat, donned the black robe, and grabbed the latte. They walked out of his chambers and around the corner to the spiral staircase. Mavis stood aside.

"Go ahead, Mavis."

"You'd better go first, Judge. So you're not tempted to look up my dress."

She said it with a straight face.

"Uh, okay."

They climbed the stairs and entered the courtroom. No burly bailiff bellowed out, "All rise!" when he walked in; Beck just sat down behind the bench like he was chairing a bar luncheon. Mavis sat to his right. The courtroom was no longer vacant.

Six lawyers stood before the bench. Their arms were crossed, and they were eyeing Beck like students taking measure of the new teacher. They were not $800-an-hour lawyers who represented well-dressed white corporate executives in federal court. This was a rural county court, they were country lawyers, and their clients were dressed in black-and-white striped jail uniforms with GILLESPIE COUNTY INMATE stenciled in red across the back. Leaning against the jury box railing like he owned the place was the Gillespie County District Attorney.

Beck didn't figure they would be fishing buddies.

Four female inmates sat in chairs along the wall to Beck's right; they were wearing jail uniforms, white socks, red rubber slippers, and ankle chains. They were young and white, but their faces were old. Their eyes were hollowed out with dark circles, and they wore no makeup. They were chatting casually among themselves like sorority sisters at a chapter meeting. They were meth addicts.

Eight male inmates sat in the jury box to Beck's far left. They were young and brown, tattooed and stone-faced, staring at their

167

cuffed hands as if resigned to their fate. Standing guard next to the jury box was a tall lean deputy sheriff dressed in a tan long-sleeved uniform shirt with epaulettes on the shoulders and a silver badge pinned over his heart, a green tie with a silver hand-cuff tie pin, green cowboy-cut slacks with a crease that looked sharp enough to bring blood if you ran your hand down it, tan cowboy boots, and a tan western-style holster holding a large-caliber sidearm and a cell phone. His hair was cut in a sharp flattop with the sides combed back. He didn't look like an old Rod Steiger. He looked like a young Clint Eastwood ready to draw his big gun on a recalcitrant inmate and snarl through clenched teeth, "Go ahead. Make my day."

The audience consisted of one older Anglo couple and a dozen or more Hispanic females—the male inmates' mothers, Beck figured. They sat as if they had long been accustomed to sitting in courtrooms waiting for their sons' cases to be called.

By statute, state district courts had original jurisdiction over all felony criminal cases, divorces, contested elections, and civil cases exceeding $200 in damages. In the urban counties, those cases were filed in specialized courts: criminal or civil, family or probate. In the rural counties, all cases came to the same court before the same judge. Today, District Judge John Beck Hardin would execute the court's original jurisdiction over felony criminal cases.

It was sentencing day in Gillespie County.

On the desk in front of Beck sat a laptop computer showing that day's docket and thirteen red file folders stacked high. Mavis had color-coded the cases: civil cases were in manila folders, tax in gray, child custody in blue, child support in green, divorce in gold, and criminal in red.

Each red file represented one human being's life history: employment, family, and criminal. Each file represented a life gone awry, usually because of alcohol or drugs, a few because of dark hearts. Beck had read their files and learned their lives;

some seemed destined to end up in court before a judge with the power to send them to prison from the day they had been born poor or illegitimate or to a father who had beaten them or a mother who had abandoned them. Others seemed to have no luck in life except bad. Beck looked at the defendants sitting before him. How had their lives led them to this courtroom?

The D.A. walked up and set a file on the front of the bench. Beck said, "Mr. Eichman."

"Judge."

Niels Eichman, Jr., was dressed as well as any lawyer in Beck's Chicago law firm and he had that same big-firm lawyer look about him. Had he not dropped out of the race, he would be sitting in Beck's chair at that moment. He knew that, and Beck knew that. But when they eyed each other across the bench, and the D.A.'s lips formed a thin smile and then he winked at the new judge, Beck knew that the D.A. knew something that he did not.

Mavis called the first case. "Cause number forty-two thirteen, State of Texas versus Ignacio Perez. Possession of a controlled substance and driving without a licence."

Beck had inherited these cases, defendants who had pleaded guilty or had been convicted at trial before old Judge Stutz but had been awaiting sentencing when Stutz had abruptly retired due to a heart condition. Beck had read the case files, the briefs, and the trial transcripts; he had learned that these defendants were not criminal masterminds, drug lords, murderers, rapists, or even Enron executives. They were just small-time offenders who had turned to drugs because they were down on their luck or to salve life's wounds or just because they were bored. The D.A. wanted the new judge to pick up where the old judge had left off and sentence them to the state penitentiary in Huntsville.

A young Latino in a jail uniform with his hair cut like a Marine stood in the jury box and shuffled over as well as he could with his hands and feet shackled. He stood directly in front of Beck and to the left of the D.A. One of the lawyers stepped forward and stood next to him. Unlike the D.A., this lawyer was not well-dressed; his rumpled suit looked like the cheaper one in a two-fer sale at a second-hand store. He was bald, paunchy, red-faced, and breathing through his mouth like a heavy smoker. Beck inhaled the strong scent of German lager.

"Henry Polk, Your Honor," the lawyer said. "For the defendant."

Henry Polk was a beer-and-bratwurst-for-breakfast man.

"Mr. Polk, what's your client's first name?"

"Who?"

Beck pointed at the defendant. "Your client, Mr. Perez—what's his first name?"

Polk turned and gazed at Perez as if they had never met. Then he looked to Mavis for help.

"Ignacio," Beck said. "His first name is Ignacio."

Polk broke into a big smile. "You knew all along."

"Have you been drinking this morning, Mr. Polk?"

"I'm German, Judge."

"If we can attend to the matters at hand, Judge," the D.A. said. "Mr. Perez pled guilty to possession of a controlled substance and driving without a licence. The state seeks the maximum punishment, two years in the state penitentiary."

Beck opened the red file for Ignacio Perez. He was a Mexican national. He had come here to work in the turkey plant. He was nineteen years old and charged with possession of less than one gram of cocaine. He had no prior criminal record.

"Mr. Eichman, in Chicago this case would never have gone to trial. The defendant would have been fined and released."

The D.A. shrugged. "We don't have a lot of crime here, Judge. We have to make do with what we've got."

The D.A. smiled; Beck didn't. He turned to the defendant.

"Mr. Perez, you've been charged with possession of a controlled substance, a state jail felony, and driving without a license. I want to confirm that you did in fact knowingly and voluntarily plead guilty."

"Yes, Your Honor," Lawyer Polk said, "he pleaded guilty."

"I didn't ask you, Mr. Polk. I asked your client." To the defendant: "Sir, your name is Ignacio Perez, is that correct?"

The defendant stared back at Beck blank-faced. After a brief pause, he abruptly nodded and said, "*Sí*."

"Mr. Perez, did you plead guilty to these charges?"

Beck's question was met with the same blank face.

Then, another nod. "*Sí*."

Beck thought he had seen Lawyer Polk's body twitch.

"And you pled guilty because you did in fact commit this crime and not out of any fear?"

Another little twitch from Polk and another "*Sí*" from the defendant. Beck stared at Ignacio Perez and saw Miguel Cervantes. He pointed to a spot three feet to Lawyer Polk's left—three feet farther away from the defendant.

"Mr. Polk, please stand over there."

"Why's that, Your Honor?"

"Because I don't think your leg is that long."

Lawyer Polk took two steps to his left. The defendant's eyes darted to Polk, then back to Beck.

"Mr. Perez, do you understand English?"

A nervous look from the defendant; he glanced at Polk.

"*¿Sí?*"

"Mr. Perez, do you understand the charges against you?"

"*¿Sí?*"

"Mr. Perez, did you go to Harvard?"

"*¿Sí?*"

Lawyer Polk rolled his eyes. "Your Honor—"

"Your client doesn't understand English?"

Polk shrugged. "He's Mexican."

"Do you speak Spanish, Mr. Polk?"

"Nope."

"Then how did you communicate with your client?"

He shrugged again. "Not so good."

"Your Honor," the D.A. said, "Mr. Perez was caught red-handed. The cocaine was found in his car."

"Pursuant to a consent search?"

"Yes, sir."

"Mr. Eichman, how did Mr. Perez knowingly consent to the search of his vehicle if he can't understand English?"

The D.A. frowned. "Well . . ."

Polk's bloodshot eyes lit up. "Good point, Judge."

"Thank you, Mr. Polk." To the D.A.: "Mr. Eichman?"

"I'm thinking."

"While you're thinking, think about this: the car was registered in the name of a"—Beck flipped through the pages in the file—"Juan Hermoso. Was Mr. Hermoso apprehended?"

"He fled the jurisdiction. He was a Mexican national."

Illegal aliens could not legally hold jobs in the U.S., but they could legally own cars in Texas.

"Perhaps the cocaine belonged to Mr. Hermoso just as Mr. Perez claimed."

"Yeah, and maybe Ignacio here is the son of Santa Anna."

"Careful, Mr. Eichman. And please address the defendant as 'Mr. Perez.' "

The D.A. gritted his teeth and glared at Beck.

Beck said, "Have you thought of anything sustaining Mr. Perez's ability to give an informed consent to search his vehicle?' "

"Maybe the cop spoke Spanish."

Polk: "That's a thought."

Beck flipped through the file to the arrest report. "The arresting officer—a city cop, I see—his name is Gerhard Goetz. Mr. Eichman, you think Officer Goetz is fluent in Spanish?"

"Well . . ."

Polk, with a big grin: "Gerhard, he's still working on English."

"Anything else to add, Mr. Eichman?"

The glare again: "No . . . Your Honor."

Beck said, "The court finds that the search of Mr. Perez's vehicle was illegal due to an invalid consent and thus the cocaine found in the vehicle is inadmissible as evidence."

The D.A.: "But he confessed."

"In Spanish? The court also finds that his confession is inadmissible due to inadequate counsel. His guilty plea is not accepted. The controlled substance charge is dismissed."

Polk: "Thank you, Your Honor."

"You're welcome. Mavis, when is the next available trial setting for the driving without a license charge?"

Mavis turned to her calendar, but stopped short when the D.A. said, "Your Honor, the state drops all charges."

Beck now glared at the D.A. "You wanted me to sentence the defendant to two years in prison, now you're dropping all charges?"

"Not worth the expense to try him on the remaining charge, Your Honor. Besides, he'll be back. They all come back."

Beck shook his head. "Case dismissed. And Mr. Eichman, don't bring me drug cases predicated on searches of vehicles pursuant to consent given by Latinos who can't speak English."

"Why, thanks, Judge, you just cleared my docket. Guess I'll go play golf."

The D.A. shook his head; he and Lawyer Polk went over to the prosecution table. Ignacio stood alone in front of the bench; his face was that of a man about to be led to the firing squad. He recoiled slightly when Deputy Clint came toward him, but smiled broadly when the deputy spoke to him in Spanish and unlocked the shackles. Ignacio Perez was crying when he turned to Beck.

"*Gracias, el jefe. Mucho gracias.*"

"Good luck, Mr. Perez."

The other inmates suddenly perked up, as if they had witnessed a miracle. They exchanged glances and spoke excitedly in Spanish. Beck wondered what had happened to Miguel Cervantes.

Mavis called the next case, but Beck's thoughts remained on

Miguel. When he snapped, he was looking at the D.A., another brown-faced defendant, and the same defense lawyer.

"You again, Mr. Polk?"

Lawyer Polk shrugged. " 'Fraid so, Your Honor."

Beck leaned down to Mavis and whispered, "What's the deal with Polk? Does he represent every Hispanic defendant?"

"Most. 'Cause they're poor and he works cheap. It's him or the public defender. If their folks own land, they can hire a good lawyer, but he'll take their land for his fee. Lawyers here, they've acquired a lot of land that way." She shrugged. "Deed your land over or hire a drunk. That's how things work here, Judge."

Beck turned back to Polk, who said, "But, Jesus"—*Hay-Zeus*—"here, he speaks English real good, Judge."

The D.A. added, "And he signed a written confession."

Jesus Ramirez was a short wiry Mexican national. He was not a county inmate; he was neatly dressed in jeans, boots, and a work shirt. Beck opened the red file. Jesus was charged with assault with a deadly weapon. He had gotten drunk on a Saturday night and battered his wife. The deadly weapon was a burrito.

Beck looked up at the D.A. "A burrito?"

"It was frozen."

Beck turned to the defendant. "You hit your wife with a frozen burrito?"

"Yes, sir." He spoke with a heavy Latino accent.

Beck glanced at Lawyer Polk, who quickly said, "I didn't kick him, Your Honor. I swear."

Back to the defendant: "Why?"

"Oh, Macarena, she has the mouth. Sometime, she drive me *loco*."

"Is she here?"

"Yes, sir." Jesus turned and pointed to a Latino woman sitting in the audience with six young children.

"Are those your children?"

Jesus smiled. "Yes, sir, those are my *niños*." He pointed. "Marita, Manuel, Maribel—"

The D.A. sighed: "Your Honor . . ."

Beck held an open hand up to the district attorney.

"Marco, Miguel, and Marvin."

"*Marvin?*"

"After the landlord."

"And what do you do, Mr. Ramirez?"

"Kill line at the turkey plant. Hang the birds by their feet and cut their scrawny necks, to let them bleed out."

"And you go home and drink?"

"Judge, I see now the dead turkeys in my sleep . . . Monday, Tuesday, Wednesday, Thursday, Friday, and now we work the Saturday because of Thanksgiving coming. Twelve hours each day I kill the turkeys. I must drink to forget the turkeys."

"And you are still employed?"

"Oh, sure."

"Has your wife filed for divorce?"

"*Macarena?* No, she no file for divorce. She love Jesus."

"But you hit her with a frozen burrito."

Jesus turned his palms up. "I was drinking, she was yelling, the *niños*, they were screaming, I was watching the *fútbol* on the satellite, Mexico *y* Brazil . . . I throw the burrito, but I did not mean to hit her. She call the *policía*."

Macarena Ramirez stood in the audience. "Señor Judge, I love Jesus!"

"Mr. Ramirez, do you love Macarena?"

"Oh, yes, *mucho*."

The D.A.: "What is this, a courtroom or Dr. Phil?"

Beck ignored the D.A. "Mr. Ramirez, do you promise the court that you will stop drinking?"

"Oh, yes, sir. No more drinking for Jesus."

"And you will not throw frozen products at your wife again?"

"No, I will not do that no more."

"All right, Mr. Ramirez." Beck turned to Lawyer Polk. "Do you have anything to say on behalf of your client, Mr. Polk?"

Lawyer Polk shrugged. "No, sir."

Beck stared at Lawyer Polk a minute and shook his head. He turned back to the D.A. "Mr. Eichman, the defendant is the sole support for his family. If I put him in jail for six months, he'll lose his job. What will happen to his wife and children?"

"Your Honor, that is not the state's concern."

"Does the state really want to prosecute this case?"

"Not unless you're going to send someone to jail today."

"No one yet, Mr. Eichman. So the state dismisses the charges against Mr. Ramirez?"

The D.A. shrugged. "Why not? He'll smack her around another Saturday night."

Two hours later, Beck had sentenced the Latino defendants and three of the women, all charged with possession of small amounts of marijuana, meth, and cocaine and other minor violations of parole, to fines, probation, and community service. He saw no sense in sending poor people to prison for non-violent crimes. The D.A. saw red.

Beck now had to send someone to prison.

The last defendant of the day was a twenty-year-old woman named Dee Dee Birck. She was the descendant of a wealthy old-line German family. She had been given everything in life, and she had sold everything for drugs. When her family had cut her money off, she had stolen for drug money. This was her sixth trip through the system. On her last trip she had been sentenced to two years, but Stutz had probated her sentence. Dee Dee Birck had then violated probation: she had robbed her mother at gunpoint. She needed money for meth. She would be boarding the bus to Huntsville tomorrow morning.

She was short and skinny; her hair was brown and ratty. Her face had been ravaged by five years of methamphetamine use: she looked twice her age. She stood before Beck, and her lawyer stood beside her. Beck glanced at the older white couple sitting in the front row. The woman was crying. Mavis leaned in and whispered, "Her parents." Dee Dee had put a gun to her mother's head, but her mother cried when she was being sentenced to prison. A mother's love.

Beck said, "Ms. Birck, you are charged with violating your probation, do you understand that?"

"Yeah."

"Do you plead true or false?"

"Yeah."

"Yes, you plead true?"

"Yeah."

"You understand that because you violated your probation, I must now enforce your original sentence?"

"Yeah."

"Which was two years in the state penitentiary?"

"Yeah."

Beck leaned back in his chair and stared at this young woman. She just stood there. She wasn't crying or begging for mercy or showing any emotion at all. She was about to be incarcerated for two years—and she just stood there! What had happened to her?

What if fifteen years from now, that were Meggie standing there? What if Meggie got off track in life because of drugs? It broke Beck's heart to think of that, just as it was breaking his heart to send this young woman to prison. He sighed.

"Ms. Birck, your probation is revoked. You are hereby remanded to the custody of the Texas Department of Corrections for confinement in the state penitentiary for a period of two years pursuant to your original sentence. Good luck to you."

Dee Dee Birck broke into a big grin, turned around, and waved at her parents like they had just dropped her off at summer camp. Deputy Clint escorted her to the door. Beck's eyes followed her all the way out of the courtroom.

She was grinning!

Mavis was crying.

"What's wrong, Mavis?"

"Nothing."

"Why are you crying?"

177

"I always cry at weddings, funerals, and sentencings."

"Okay. Why was Dee Dee Birck grinning?"

Mavis dabbed her eyes. "Because she's been in the system. She knows TDC can't afford to keep her in prison for her full sentence and she knows she gets credit for time served in the county jail. She knows she won't spend more than sixty days in prison." Mavis shrugged. "She did the math."

Chapter 14

Sentencing day was over.

Dee Dee Birck's grin—and the fact that a twenty-year-old girl knew how to do the time-served math—had so disturbed Beck that he had no appetite for lunch. So he walked out the back door of the courthouse and across the rear parking lot and into the Gillespie County Law Enforcement Center; he was carrying the Heidi Geisel file. Doreen jumped up this time.

"Judge Hardin, sir."

"Grady in?"

"Yes, sir. I'll get him for you."

She almost ran to the back offices. When she returned, she was followed closely by Gillespie County Sheriff Grady Guenther with a toothpick in his mouth.

"Judge, I would've come over to the courthouse."

"I needed some air after this morning."

"First sentencing day. Don't worry, you'll get used to it."

"That's what I'm afraid of. And, Grady, I'm still just Beck, except when I'm in the courtroom."

"And I'm still just Grady . . . except when I pull you over and conduct a body cavity search." He smiled. "Come on back."

Beck followed Grady into his office, placed Heidi's file on the desk, and sat. Grady plopped into his chair behind the desk and picked up a massive hot dog. "Mind if I finish my lunch? Kraut dog. You want Doreen to run get you one?"

Beck shook his head. Grady blew the toothpick into a trash can across the room like an aborigine firing a dart out of a blow-gun. He then bit down on the dog.

"First sentencing day and you get 'assault with a frozen burrito.'" Grady shook his head. "Don't know why the city cops arrested Jesus. He's a good man, works at the turkey plant, construction on weekends. Built my barn. And Macarena, she does have a mouth, that one. Was me, I'd've thrown a side of beef at her, something with some weight behind it. You did the right thing, sending Jesus home. Hell, living with her is hard time compared to six months in my jail."

"What about Ignacio Perez? I do the right thing with him?"

"Questionable."

"Why?"

Grady swallowed hard. "Ignacio, he's a two-bit user. I told Junior not to waste county money on him, but he wants to build his conviction record. I wanted to use Ignacio to get the suppliers."

"Is there a drug problem here?"

Grady drank from a can of root beer. "Meth and marijuana, some coke, kids huffing, puffing, and dusting."

"I don't know what any of that means."

"You will soon enough." Another bite of the dog. "Alcohol's still the biggest problem here, kids raised on Weissbier, drinking and driving." He grimaced. "Sorry. But drugs came to our town. What'd you have today, ten drug cases?"

"A dozen."

"Used to be none."

"Why so many Latinos? Anglos don't use?"

"'Course white kids use. Hell, last year couple cheerleaders got caught snorting coke in the restroom at the high school. Most of the softball team after that. Good German girls."

180

"What happened to them?"

"Nothing. City cops didn't even arrest them."

"Why not?"

"'Cause their daddies run this town."

"Twenty-four years and nothing's changed."

"You won the election. That's a change."

"I didn't win."

"No, you didn't. But you're the judge just the same."

"So Heidi could've gotten the cocaine here?"

Grady finished off the root beer, swiped his sleeve across his mouth, and wadded the wrapping into a ball. He tossed it at the waste basket like Shaq shooting a free throw. He missed.

"Yep. You can buy condoms at the H-E-B and cocaine at the high school."

Grady was now digging around in his desk drawer; he gave up and dug into his pants pocket instead. He pulled out the pocketknife and opened a small blade. He picked his teeth.

"Used to be, Mexicans wanting to come north for work could just walk across the border. After 9/11 the Feds clamped down hard, so now they gotta hire the *coyotes*—smugglers, they charge a thousand bucks a head. Migrants can't afford that, so the *coyotes* make them mules to pay the fare. Which means we got more people bringing more dope across the border. They pack marijuana, cocaine, ice—crystal meth—up to San Antonio, locals bring it back here. They're the ones I'm after. And I'm gonna find 'em before they start selling meth over at the middle school."

He shook his head.

"Wouldn't know it now, but Dee Dee Birck used to be a cute kid."

"Grady, it's more than a job for you."

He nodded. "I got kids, and a grandkid now. I don't want it to happen to mine like it happened to Dee Dee . . . and Heidi. You look at her file?"

Beck nodded. "What happened to her shoes and purse?"

"Never found them. We searched a hundred-yard radius from

181

where she was found and up and down Baron's Creek right there."

"New Year's Eve and she was barefooted?"

"She was stoned."

"And now she's dead."

"So, you find something I didn't?"

"No."

"Then do him a favor . . . Aubrey. Get him to let her go. She's never coming back, and we're never gonna find the guy."

"He's really fixed on finding him."

"Needs to find a woman."

"He wants Randi back."

"He's still pining for her after all these years?"

"Yeah. Said she lives in Austin."

"And he figures she's still available?"

"I guess."

"Doubtful. She was a good-looking gal, most likely married money."

"Aubrey figures winning state might land him a college job, maybe at UT. More money, he might be able to win her back."

Grady shook his head. "Men get a serious case of the stupids when it comes to women, don't we? 'Course, you take the stupid out of life, me and you wouldn't have jobs. So he's banking on winning state to get his life back together?"

"That seems to be the plan."

"That kind of puts you between a rock and a hard place, don't it, Beck?"

"What does?"

"You figuring on finding his daughter's killer, make amends for the past . . . now you hold his future in your hands."

"Grady, what are you talking about?"

"I'm talking about Slade."

"The quarterback? What about him?"

"His case."

"What case?"

"You don't know?"

"I must not."

"Three weeks ago, Slade beat the hell out of a Mexican boy over at the movie theater. Julio Espinoza. Good kid, stays out of trouble. Theater's outside the city limits, my jurisdiction. Time we got there, the boy was a mess . . . broken nose, broken jaw. We arrested Slade for aggravated assault. Second-degree felony plus hate crime enhancement, he's looking at five to ninety-nine years in the state pen."

"*Hate crime?*"

"He was calling Julio a wetback and a spic, while he was hitting him. Took four deputies to pull him off the boy. They would've just shot him, except the backup quarterback ain't no good."

"Four cops? Was he on drugs?"

"Toxicology came back clean for alcohol, coke, meth, PCP. Slade's a big boy, but he was wired on something."

Grady opened a side drawer and removed a file. He placed the file on his desk and pushed it across. Beck opened the file and recoiled at a color photo of a slight Latino boy. His face was badly bruised and cut in several places; his left eye was swollen shut; his lips were cut and puffy. His nose sat lopsided. Blood stained his white shirt.

"*Jesus.* What'd he hit him with?"

"His fists."

"*Why?*"

"Caught him talking to his girlfriend. Nikki Ernst, she's a cheerleader. That's what I'm talking about, why Mexicans don't even look at German girls. They don't want trouble."

"He did this just because the boy was talking to his girl?"

"Yep."

"No provocation?"

"Nope. Julio was working the snack bar, talking to the girl . . . witnesses say Slade stormed in, didn't say nothin', just grabbed Julio, dragged him over the counter, commenced to hitting him. Julio was in the hospital five days, signed his affidavit there. We got statements from Nikki and a few other kids."

"Slade played Friday, so he must've made bail."

"No bail. JP released him on his personal bond."

"For aggravated assault?"

"Walt's a big football fan. Walt Schmidt, he's the Justice of the Peace."

"So the star quarterback's case is on my docket?"

"Not your docket."

"What do you mean?"

Grady let out a deep sigh. "I knew this boy was trouble when they moved to town."

"Slade?"

"Yep. Now he beats up Julio, starts a time bomb ticking in my town. Got my men on alert in case that bomb goes off."

"*Time bomb?* What's going on, Grady?"

Grady shut the pocketknife, stuffed it back into his pants pocket, and said, "First off, we ain't having this conversation. This is between you, me, and that stuffed buck up there."

"Okay."

"Second, you need to know the lay of the land these days. How long you been gone?"

"Twenty-four years."

"Well, things have changed around here. Considerably. Before you left, this place was all German all the time. But we got what they call 'competing interests' these days."

"What kind of competing interests?"

Grady held up a finger.

"There's the Germans, of course, and since their great-granddaddies settled this town they figure they still own it and everyone else are just renters. They still hold every seat on the county commission, city council, school board—employee directory over at city hall reads like the Berlin phone book. And they'll fight to their last kolache to keep control over this town."

"Well, that hasn't changed."

184

"No, but their town has, and they don't like it."

Grady pointed at an old map on the wall.

"That's what this place looked like in 1846, when the Baron laid out the town. For the next hundred years, the Germans lived out here, surviving off the land, isolated from the outside world—Austin was a week away by horseback. Then LBJ gave them the mohair money back in the fifties. Next forty years, they were fat and happy, raising their goats and getting government checks every year. Hell, life don't get no better than that."

"That's the way it was when I left."

"It ain't that way no more. When Clinton cut the mohair money back in ninety-six, people 'round here figured it was the end of the world. Goat ranchers my age and older, they went their whole lives getting those government checks. Then one day they go out to the mailbox and it ain't there. It was like someone died. Killed off goat ranching and all the Main Street businesses with it."

"So what happened? Downtown's booming."

"Well, about that time, city folk had gotten real tired of the crime and congestion, gangs and drugs, wanted a simpler life, so they started moving out here—Austin's only an hour away by Volvo. Yuppies, hippies, artists, folks with tattoos and money, they all came out here. Bought land, fixed up old homes, rented the Main Street buildings, started all those businesses and wineries and restaurants—we got *two* French restaurants now. Land values shot through the roof, and all of a sudden, the old Germans are making more money selling their land and renting their buildings than they ever did off mohair."

"So why aren't they happy?"

"Because those newcomers brought the outside world here with them. And the old Germans, they don't like their town anymore—too many Democrats and Mexicans."

"Liberals and Latinos."

Grady nodded. "They want to go back to the days when Main Street businesses were owned by Germans talking German eating German and drinking German—and the government was sending them checks. They go over to the goat auction and talk German and pretend their world ain't changing. But it is. It already has."

"So why don't they just stop selling their land and renting their buildings to people they don't want here?"

"'Cause they want the money. I heard one old boy complaining about *Ausländers* in town so I says to him, 'Didn't you sell your land to a Californian?' And he says, 'Yep, but I was forced to sell—the bastard paid me five million. Cash!'"

Grady chuckled.

"Grady, you're German."

"Full-blooded, but I ain't like that. Guenthers, we never ran goats. Fact is, Beck, most Germans here ain't like that. Most are good people, just working hard to make a living, keep this a safe place for their kids, don't believe God made them better just 'cause they got white skin and a German name. But every town's got a few folks figure they're entitled to run the show. Ours just happen to be German."

"So what's all that got to do with Slade?"

"Hold your water, I'm getting there."

The second finger.

"Then there's those newcomers opened those tourist businesses—Spunky Monkey, Zertz, Dogologie. How you figure you can make a living on a store selling stuff just for dogs? And we got spas where they'll wrap your whole body in seaweed—what's that about?" He shook his head. "Anyway, the Main Street business owners, they're white but they don't *sprechen Deutsch*, if you know what I mean. They just wanted to get out of the big city, move to a better place to raise their kids, make a good living."

The third finger.

"And then there's the Mexicans. The old Germans figure the Main Street business owners for renters and Mexicans for trespassers. They're a third of the population now, not that you'd know it walking down Main Street. Some legal, more not, so

186

they stay out of sight over in the barrio, working at the turkey plant. But we got a few Mexicans looking for a cause. Heard they're trying to start up a *La Raza Unida* chapter."

"There's a barrio now?"

"Down on South Milam, across the creek. Migrants, they used to come up here, work a while, make some money and take it home. But like I said, the Feds clamped down on the border, so now once they get here, they stay. They just wire the money home."

"The law of unintended consequences."

"The law of dumb-asses in Washington don't got a clue."

Beck said, "That's three groups—Germans, Main Street business owners, and Latinos. What about African-Americans?"

Grady chuckled. "You only been gone twenty-four years, Beck, place ain't changed that much. Best I know, Gil's about the only black person living in the county."

"Grady, this is real interesting, but what's it got to do with Slade?"

"Competing interests, Beck. Like I said, the Main Street business owners, they just want to make a living. And they make most of their living between now and Christmas."

"Let me guess: white football player beats up a Latino, Main Street's worried those activists might make it a political cause, generate bad publicity, and that'll hurt the tourist trade?"

Grady nodded. "That's all this town's got now, Beck. A million tourists are gonna come here to shop in the next three months. Holiday shopping. You kill that, you kill this town. City hall protects this town's image like the old-timers protect their daughters' virginity." That amused him. "Y'all got homeless people in downtown Chicago?"

Beck shrugged. "Yeah."

"You see any homeless people on our Main Street?"

"No."

"They show up here, city cops pick them up, drive them down to San Antonio, and dump them out."

"You're joking?"

"Nope."

"How do they get away with that? If Chicago cops did that, the media would be all over it."

"No media here. See, Beck, city cops' number one job is to protect the tourist trade. City hall don't want nothing in the paper about cheerleaders snorting coke or homeless folks camping out in the Marktplatz or Mexicans marching down Main Street. They want nice news. They want white people to come here and be happy and shop. People in Dallas and Houston, they got homeless people and blacks and Mexicans up in arms about something all the time. They don't come here for that. They come here to live life the way it used to be—at least for a weekend."

"The perfect all-American, all-white, crime-free town."

"With a German festival." He chuckled. "Remember a year back, Mexicans marching in the cities over that immigration law? Not here they didn't. City cops keep a tight lid on this town."

"So the Main Street business owners wanted the D.A. to keep the Latinos happy—"

"At least until after Christmas."

"—by filing charges against Slade?"

"Yep."

"So did he?"

"Yep. But it took some convincing."

"What kind of convincing?"

"Well, Julio's folks are illegals. So Junior figured he could use that to get Julio to drop his complaint."

"What'd he do, threaten to deport them?"

"Way I hear it, that's exactly what he did. But the activists, they got Julio a lawyer out of San Antonio, used to be in Congress, name's Felix Delgado."

"I've heard of him."

"Anyway, Delgado came up here and jumped on Junior like

188

a *vaquero* giving the spurs to a bronc. Said he'd file a federal civil rights lawsuit, bring in the national media—white football star beats up a Mexican and walks, D.A. blackmails Mexican parents . . . *Sixty Minutes*, *Dateline*, they'd eat that up. Said he'd have our little town on national TV looking like Mississippi back in the sixties, except with Germans instead of the Klan as the bad guys. And he threatened street protests on Thanksgiving weekend."

"Why that weekend?"

"His wife comes up here to shop that weekend every year."

"So?"

"So he knows that's the biggest shopping weekend of the year, make-or-break for Main Street. Mexicans marching down Main Street, that'd kill the tourist trade, Californians would take their money somewhere else, property values would plummet, taxes would decrease . . . this place won't be another Santa Fe, it'll be another Odessa after oil prices crashed."

"So the D.A. backed off Julio's parents?"

"Yep."

"And took Slade to the grand jury?"

"Nope."

"Grady, you said he filed charges."

"Yep. See, when we arrested Slade, law requires we take him before a magistrate. Justice of the peace. Walt Schmidt. Walt read him his rights then released him. Until the grand jury hands down an indictment, the case stays in JP court."

"Is Schmidt a lawyer?"

Grady shook his head. "Goat rancher. Ran for JP when his mohair checks stopped coming, finally had to work for a living. If you call being JP working."

"So when is the D.A. taking the case to the grand jury?"

"He ain't."

"Why not?"

"'Cause if Slade's indicted, he's suspended from school, his football season is over and so is any chance of winning state, and he'll lose his scholarship at UT."

189

"So?"

"So his daddy don't want that to happen. He wants Slade at UT and then in the pros."

"Slade committed a crime. He's got to answer for that."

"Not if Quentin McQuade has anything to say about that. You heard about him, his big development out west?"

"Some."

"Well, whatever you heard, it's worse. Day after the arrest, he came out to the house. Tried to get me to drop the charges, wipe the arrest off the books. Quentin don't want his boy to lose his football career just for beating up a wetback. At least that's what he told me when he made me an offer."

"A bribe?"

"Couldn't prosecute on what he said, he's too smart for that, but that was the deal."

"What'd you tell him?"

"I told him I don't need his money. He laughed."

"Do you? Need his money?"

Grady shook his head. "Year ago, I sold a hundred acres of the homestead to a Californian with more money than sense. He paid two million. I'm what you call 'independently wealthy' now."

"A millionaire sheriff?"

"Yep."

"Why do you still do it, the job?"

"For Dee Dee Birck and Heidi and kids like them. That Californian made me immune to politics, but Quentin's got most of the politicians in the county—including Junior—in his pocket, one way or the other."

"So why are the old Germans siding with McQuade?"

"Well, that's another competing interest—two, actually. First one is, they want that state championship bad. Ain't had one since you played. That was a helluva game, Beck."

"Football can't be that important."

He chuckled. "You been in Chicago too long, Beck. You forgot the way it is here, football."

190

"What's the other competing interest?"

"What else—money."

"Where's the money?"

"Building those two hundred homes in Quentin's development. That's two, three hundred million in new construction, more than this town sees in twenty years. Old Germans stand to make a lot of money building those homes, but they gotta keep Quentin happy 'cause he decides who shares in that pot. That's why he thinks his balls clank when he walks down Main Street."

"So Quentin bought himself a German name?"

"So to speak."

"But how can the D.A. not take this case to the grand jury? Slade put Julio in the hospital, you've got witnesses."

"Well, Slade's lawyer, ol' Judge Stutz—"

"*Stutz?* I thought he had a heart problem?"

"Yep, problem is, he don't have a heart. Meanest bastard I've ever met. I figure it's 'cause he never got married, couldn't find a woman desperate enough, not even here." Grady sighed. "But he was the judge for almost fifty years, so he knows everyone's secrets. No one screws with Stutz."

"So he's representing Slade?"

Grady nodded. "Demanded an examining trial—magistrate determines if there's probable cause to send the case to the grand jury. I've never seen one in thirty years 'cause the D.A. always takes felony cases straight to the grand jury."

"So why isn't he doing that?"

"Because this ain't a criminal case . . . it's a political case. Quentin don't want Slade indicted, so Junior and Stutz cooked up this little end run to keep the case in a friendly JP court. JP don't find probable cause, the case don't ever get to the grand jury. No grand jury, no indictment."

"But how does that keep that time bomb from going off?"

"I'll tell you how, least the way they figure it: first, Junior filed charges against Slade to keep the Mexicans and Delgado

191

happy, at least for now. Second, he kept the case in JP court and set the examining trial for January, after the playoffs and the holiday shopping season when there ain't no tourists in town—that made the football fans and Main Street happy. And third, it keeps the lid on this thing long enough to buy some time, maybe let this ruckus die down."

"And what do you figure?"

"I don't figure Delgado for a fool. I figure he'll make good on his threat."

"A Thanksgiving weekend protest?"

"Yep."

"Well, that's their free speech right."

"No, Beck, that's a time bomb. City cops, they'll try to arrest the whole bunch of 'em. And that could turn Main Street into another Alamo, only with the Mexicans losing this time. All it would take is one trigger-happy cop . . . or deer hunter."

"Thanksgiving still the biggest hunting weekend?"

"Yep. We'll have more guns in town that weekend than they got in Baghdad. Every pickup and SUV in town'll be packing thirty-ought-six rifles and deer hunters, both loaded. One dumb-ass and we got dead Mexicans on Main Street."

"So that's what, eight weeks from now, before that time bomb goes off?"

"Yep."

"And all this happened three weeks ago?"

"Yep."

"One week before the election?"

"Yep."

"That's why the D.A. dropped out of the election?"

"Chicago lawyers, y'all are real smart. Yep, they needed Junior in the D.A.'s office to pull it off. If he's in your chair on the second floor of the courthouse, he can't control the case. Another D.A. might've sent Slade straight to the grand jury. Junior, he wasn't happy about it, but they promised him the judgeship would be his for life. Starting next year."

192

"And you told me all this because . . . ?"

"Because Slade walking on this don't sound like justice . . ."

There was that word again.

". . . And I don't like it when some people figure they're above the law. Figured you might not like it either."

"I don't. But I don't have jurisdiction until the grand jury indicts him. And the grand jury can't indict unless the JP finds probable cause and refers Slade over."

"Which ain't gonna happen . . . unless you do something about it."

"Such as?"

"You got original jurisdiction over all felony cases. You can order Slade's case transferred from the JP court to the district court. Then you preside over the examining trial. You decide if there's probable cause to send Slade to the grand jury."

"Will the grand jury indict Slade if his dad's connected?"

"Fifty-fifty. But there's three Mexicans on the grand jury, that's the law now, so there can't be a cover-up. I figure if Slade goes to the grand jury, he'll plead out."

"Only problem is, Grady, I've got to have good cause to transfer the case out of JP court or Stutz will just appeal my order and the appeals court will kick it back to the JP."

"Good cause, huh? Like the JP biased in favor of Slade?"

"That'd be good."

"Like the JP biased against Mexicans?"

"That'd be better. But, Grady, I've got to have evidence."

"Evidence, huh? Like a tape recording?"

Beck laughed. "Yeah, a tape recording of a judge exhibiting bias is pretty good evidence, Grady, but in my experience those recordings are kind of hard to get a hold of."

"Oh. Okay, I'll see what I can do about that."

"You do that."

"You'll be in the rest of the day?"

Beck nodded. "After the next court session." He picked up Heidi's file. "Mind if I keep this a while longer?"

193

Grady shook his head. "I know where you work." Beck stood and Grady said, "Funny, ain't it?"

"What's that?"

"Tourists. Every weekend they come to town, shop on Main Street, go to a festival at the Marktplatz, eat at a nice restaurant, think the place looks like a picture-postcard, figure living here must be damn near perfect." Grady shook his head. "But they don't have a clue what's really going on, right below the surface of this small town."

Chapter 15

One walk up and down Main Street had convinced Robert and Lisa Davenport that Fredericksburg, Texas, was just the kind of small town they wanted to retire to. They had grown tired of the crime and cold winters of Cleveland and wanted to spend their senior years in the crime-free country and warm climate of Texas. They bought a two-acre tract just outside the city limits and built their dream home. They moved in on the first Friday in November a year ago. They fell asleep—with their windows open, something they had never done in Cleveland—around 10:30 P.M. to the sounds of a quiet country night.

They awoke at 6:55 A.M. to the sound of gunfire.

Deer hunting season in Gillespie County had begun at sunrise that Saturday morning. Their neighbor, William Raymond Boenker, aka Billy Ray Boenker, enjoyed passing the time of day by sitting on his back porch popping off the tops on beer cans and rounds from his .30-06 Remington rifle at any deer that dared show its face on his property; from his rocking chair, he had an unobstructed view of his entire four acres. His back porch was only two hundred feet from the Davenport's back patio; at that distance, his .30-06 sounded like a six-inch cannon.

By Billy Ray's own estimation, he fired off three hundred rounds a day seven days a week through the first weekend in January, when deer hunting season officially ended.

Not being native Texans, the Davenports assumed that Billy Ray's hunting practices were illegal; they called the sheriff. The deputy dispatched to their home explained that in Gillespie County there was no minimum acreage requirement for deer hunting. City ordinances prohibited the discharge of firearms within the city limits, but since Billy Ray's property was outside the city limits, his actions, while stupid, were not criminal.

The Davenports then filed a civil suit seeking a permanent injunction against Billy Ray's hunting on such a small tract; they alleged nuisance, harassment, and intentional infliction of emotional distress. Both parties had filed various motions, culminating in Billy Ray's Motion for Summary Judgment, which had been pending when Judge Stutz abruptly retired.

Beck had inherited the case. He was sitting behind the bench facing the Davenports and their lawyer and Billy Ray Boenker and Lawyer Polk. Again with this guy.

"Mr. and Mrs. Davenport," Beck said, "Texas law is clear on this point. It's asinine, but it's clear. Mr. Boenker is entitled to hunt deer on his four-acre tract. Therefore, I must grant his motion and rule in his favor."

Beck turned to Billy Ray Boenker. "Billy Ray, how far can a .30-06 bullet fired at shoulder level travel?"

He shrugged. "Forty-five degree angle, maybe two miles."

"Two miles. Which means you could fire your rifle from your back porch and the bullet could travel across your land and the Davenport's land and a few other people's land?"

"I ain't aiming their way."

"It doesn't matter where you aim, you don't own enough land to keep the bullet on your property."

"I aim down."

"Don't you understand how dangerous it is for you to sit on your back porch and fire off a rifle?"

"I got my rights." He grinned at the Davenports. "And come November three, I'm gonna exercise my rights all day every day for two months."

The neighbor from hell.

"Billy Ray, if you ever shoot anything that's outside your property line, you're going straight to jail, you understand?"

Billy Ray gave him a hard look. Beck turned to the Davenports. "I'm sorry, but there's nothing I can do."

"Well, there's something we can do," Mrs. Davenport said.

"Now, Mrs. Davenport, I know you're disappointed, but you cannot take the law into your own hands."

She shook her head. "We're moving back to Cleveland. Texans are nuts."

"Yes, ma'am."

"You got a tape player?"

Sheriff Grady Guenther was waiting for Beck when he returned to his chambers. Beck shut the door and walked over to his desk.

"There's one around here somewhere."

Beck sat and rummaged through the bottom drawers. He found a tape player and placed it on the desk. Grady reached into his shirt pocket and pulled out a cassette tape. He snapped the cassette into the recorder.

"Not many folks know it, but the law requires the magistrate to record his communications with the suspect, so there's proof he gave him the Miranda warning and notified him of his rights. When my men took Slade before Walt that night, that was all recorded."

Grady hit the PLAY button. A gruff voice came across.

"Justice of the Peace Walt Schmidt presiding. It is ten-thirty P.M. on Saturday, September eighth. Appearing before me is Slade McQuade. Mr. McQuade, you have been arrested for aggravated assault, to wit, it is alleged that you did inflict serious bodily injury upon one Julio Espinoza."

197

There was the sound of paper being shuffled and then it was obvious Schmidt was reading.

"Slade McQuade, you are hereby advised that you have the right to remain silent, that anything you say can be used against you in a court of law, that you have the right to an attorney prior to questioning, and that you have the right to have an attorney present during questioning. You have the right to terminate the questioning at any time. If you cannot afford an attorney, you have the right to have one appointed for you prior to any questioning. You have the right to an examining trial at which this court will determine if probable cause exists to send your case to the grand jury. Mr. McQuade, do you understand your rights as I have explained them?"

Slade: "Yeah."

Schmidt: "Son, best you don't say nothing till your daddy gets here."

There were garbled sounds, something about "my football."

Schmidt: "Heckuva game last night. But why the hell did y'all punt on fourth-and-one?"

There was no response from Slade.

Schmidt: "Slade? Why'd y'all punt on fourth-and-one?"

Still no response.

Schmidt: "Son, are you gonna answer me?"

Slade: "You told me not to say nothing."

Schmidt: "I didn't mean about football. I meant about beating up the Mexican."

Slade: "Oh. Coach didn't want to run up the score."

Schmidt: "Why the hell not? Ah, here's the gal with my football. Can't wait to see you play for the Longhorns, Slade. State championship here, national championship there. Say, how about signing my football?"

Slade: "Yeah, okay."

Grady hit the STOP button.

"Walt's a big football fan."

He hit PLAY.

Schmidt: "Now, don't you worry, son. We ain't gonna let this keep you from playing football for us. We know how to handle Mexicans."

The sound stopped. Grady hit the STOP button, looked up at Beck, and said, "That one of those tape recordings?"

Beck was shaking his head. "Why would Schmidt say that knowing he's being recorded?"

"'Cause A, he don't do the recording. Clerk does, so half the time Walt forgets he's being taped—you wouldn't believe some of the stupid shit he says. B, law requires these tapes be preserved for four months, then they're destroyed, so he ain't never had one come back and bite him in the butt. Three, he—"

"C."

"See what?"

"No, you said A, B, three, instead of A, B, C."

"Oh. C, he didn't know he'd be presiding over Slade's examining trial. Stutz hadn't dreamed it up yet. And D, Walt ain't the smartest goat rancher in the county."

"How'd you get the tape?"

"Deputy that took Slade in that night, he told me what Walt said. So when you said you needed evidence, I just moseyed on over to his office and asked Ingrid for it. She's his clerk."

"Why'd she give it to you?"

"Like I said, Beck, most Germans here are good people."

"Grady, you got any advice on handling Schmidt?"

"Well now, I'm not telling you how to do your job, Beck, but was me I'd walk that order down the hall and hand it to Walt personally, then I'd step over to the shelf where he keeps that football and I'd pick it up and say, 'Why, is that Slade McQuade's autograph? When did you get him to sign your football, Walt?' Then I'd give him a look that says I know everything, see? And I'd whisper that if he objects to the transfer, that tape recording will be transcribed and printed on the front page of the newspaper. He won't want that. Unlike me, he needs his job."

199

"That's a good idea, Grady."

"Thought you might like it."

"Grady, how'd all this stay quiet for three weeks? Can't keep a secret for three hours in this town."

He nodded. "People in a small town do talk. But they also know when to keep their mouths shut. This was one of those times. Not many folks knew about it, but those that did knew it could be real bad for this town. So they kept it quiet." He looked at Beck. "But I figure that's about to change."

"Yeah, Grady, that's about to change."

Grady smiled and stood. "Well, good luck with that, Beck."

"Grady, you're not what I expected. I figured—"

"I was that sheriff from *In the Heat of the Night*?"

Beck felt his face flush. He lied. "Oh, no, Grady, I—"

He waved Beck off. "You know, that's my all-time favorite movie. 'Cause that old sheriff, he changed. Way I figured, I got my job because of my daddy, but I didn't have to be my daddy. I know what his reputation was, and I ain't particularly proud of it. I want my kids to be proud of their daddy."

Grady stepped over and opened the door, then said, "I've been holding that time bomb in my lap for three weeks . . . feels good to hand it off to you." He smiled. "Welcome home, Beck."

The Fredericksburg Athletic Club was not like Beck's downtown Chicago gym: there was no valet parking, no burled walnut lockers, no saunas or steam rooms, and no old naked men playing gin rummy in the plush locker room. This gym was located in a strip mall next to a taco joint and across from the Wal-Mart. Four-wheel-drive pickups were parked outside.

Inside, beyond a barbell archway, middle-aged men and women waged personal wars against gravity; they were running, pedaling, climbing, stepping, and striding on the treadmills, ellipticals, stair climbers, high steppers, and stationary bikes that faced two TVs tuned to Fox News and CNN. Young women got tans in a side room, and at the rear of the club young men pumped iron in the free-weight room and admired their muscles in the mirrored walls.

Beck was not in the free-weight room. He was in the circuit training room with the other forty-somethings, too old for barbells but too young to retire to a stationary bike. When he had arrived thirty minutes before, Judge Beck Hardin had been greeted like a local football legend. He was now on his last two reps on the lying leg press machine; his thighs burned from the one hundred fifty pounds of weight—*nineteen, twenty.*

He released the weight and sat up. He grabbed his towel and wiped sweat from his face and then from the vinyl seat. He walked over to the lying leg curl machine—and his eyes were instantly drawn to a beautiful butterfly. Its wings were bright blue with deep purple highlights and a four-inch span. In the center of each wing was an eye, a human eye staring back at Beck—and he was staring intently at the tattoo inked into the smooth white skin of a young woman's lower back.

The butterfly was visible because the woman's black Spandex shorts barely rose high enough in the back to cover her bottom, much less conceal her body art. It was a very nice bottom. Three weeks before at last harvest, seeing Jodie stomping grapes with her skirt hiked high, the steel door inside Beck that had been locked shut for over a year now had cracked open just the slightest; but the bottom he was now staring at blew the door open like a bomb had gone off. His body was suddenly flooded with hormones that magically washed away the years and pains of life.

He was a nineteen-year-old boy again.

The woman was lying face down; her legs were extended and her ankles tucked under pads. Her muscular hamstrings again contracted and her ankles raised the pads that engaged the pulley connected to the iron plates until the pads almost touched her firm glutes. She released the weight and sat up. Both butterfly and bottom disappeared from Beck's sight.

201

"Hi, Judge Hardin."

Beck's eyes shot up to the woman's face. She looked familiar. She was Meggie's kindergarten teacher.

Beck blushed. "Oh . . . uh . . . hi, Ms. Young. I was just, uh . . . admiring your tattoo."

She stood and Beck fought to maintain eye contact, but he lost the battle. She was wearing the shorts and a black tube top; between them was an open stretch of white skin and lean abs, a sheen of sweat glistening under the fluorescent lights.

"Ms. Young, you look different without your clothes . . . on . . . outside school . . ."

She smiled. "Judge, I'm just Gretchen."

"Beck."

"I'm glad you won."

"I didn't win."

She frowned. "But you're the judge."

"Yeah, I'm the judge."

It had been a long first day.

Gretchen stepped away from the machine, and Beck stepped over and sat down. He set the weight at eighty pounds; on his first circuit, he had struggled to lift sixty pounds, but Gretchen had just lifted seventy.

"Meggie's a sweetie," she said.

"I like her," Beck said. "How's it going at school?"

"Oh, it's a battlefield at the primary school." She shook her head. "In Austin, we had gangs fighting for turf in school. These people fight over a foreign language." She bent over and stretched her hamstrings. Beck's face felt hot. When she came back up, she said, "But that's just old people scared of change—and this place is like Grandparents Day that never ends."

"There are a lot of old people here."

"But you know what I don't get?"

"What?"

"The young Anglo parents. They say, 'Oh, we don't hate Latinos. But they hold our kids back, so we've got to separate

202

our kids so they get a good education.' They justify it by saying they're just doing right by their kids. But they can't do right for their kids by doing wrong to another kid."

"You really care about those children?"

"I'm a teacher, Beck. They're my children, at school. That's where you find out what kind of community you really live in."

"And?"

"Everyone here goes to church and talks about being Christian, but what they're doing to the Latino kids, that's not Christian."

"So why'd you move here?"

"For my horse. They tore down my stables in Austin for condos. It was either move or give her up."

"Well, your kids are lucky you came. Meggie, too."

"Thanks, Beck." She took a step away, then pulled back. "You know, Beck, the only single guys in this town are either goat ranchers or gay guys moved here from Austin to open another trendy restaurant for tourists. I haven't had a date in over a year. How about dinner, Saturday night?"

The nineteen-year-old boy inhaled sharply: *The teacher was asking him on a date!*

The forty-two-year-old man exhaled slowly: "Gretchen, how old are you?"

"Twenty-five."

"Well, I'm . . . a little old for you."

"Maybe. But you're a man, you're single, and you're reasonably handsome." She smiled. "Saturday night then?"

"But you're Meggie's teacher."

"I'm also a woman." She sighed. "Look, Beck, I fight for my kids at school every day. It's very tense, there's a lot of stress, people here are crazy. So I work out here every night. Then I feed my horse and I go home. I eat by myself, I watch TV by myself, and I go to bed by myself. I'm lonely, Beck. I have needs."

Needs? Beck was sure his heart had gone into tachycardia.

Gretchen put her hands on his shoulders and leaned into him and put her lips close enough to his ear that he could smell her sweaty scent and feel her soft breath on his skin when she whispered in his ear.

"Physical needs."

Beck's eyes darted around the room for a defibrillator.

Gretchen stood straight and said, "Saturday night."

"But we barely know each other."

"Beck, women my age, we don't wait for love."

She abruptly twirled around and walked across the room to another machine. Beck stared after her. After that bottom.

The nineteen-year-old boy was pumping his fist. *Yes!*

"Cute, aren't they?"

Jodie was standing next to him. Beck hadn't heard her walk up from behind. He had been in the zone.

"Who?"

Jodie nodded toward Gretchen.

"Children."

She walked off in her baggy sweat pants and tee shirt, her red ponytail bouncing behind her. And Beck Hardin was again a forty-two-year-old man with two children and a dead wife.

Dear J.B.,

Surgery is tomorrow. Modified radical mastectomy. I cried for my breasts, but now I just want the cancer out of my body. I want to be here for my children. I'm going to get fake breasts. Really big ones. Beck will love those.

Love, Annie.

A week later, Annie had written:

Home now. Very tired. Seeing the doctors again tomorrow. Pathology report on the lymph nodes. Love.

Another week passed. J.B. had sent an email every day asking about her. She finally responded.

Sorry for not writing back, J.B. I had my hopes built up, when we got the pathology results, I lost it. All lymph nodes were positive. The cancer has spread. Very bad. They call it metastatic. More tests tomorrow. Bone scan. CT scan. To see if it's in my bones, lungs, liver. They say I've had cancer for at least ten years and never knew it. I can't believe it.

Her next email:

It's everywhere, J.B. Stage IV. Crying now. Love.

"J.B., can I ask you something personal?"

"Boxers."

"Not that. Mom died a long time ago. Have you, uh . . . you know, been with . . . seen another . . . ?"

"Damn, Beck, we're two grown men. You can say it straight out: Have I had sex since Peggy died?"

"Well, have you?"

"Not even with a farm animal."

"Why not?"

"'Cause it never was like that between me and my goats."

"No. With a woman."

"Oh. Well, I didn't even think about it for the longest. Then the prostate acted up."

"You had problems?"

"Fifteen years ago. They cut it out. Things never worked since."

"They've got drugs now."

J.B. snorted. "What's the point if it requires chemicals?"

"You're only sixty-six. That's not too old."

"Too much trouble."

"Gretchen asked me out, today at the gym. She's, uh . . ."

"Young."

"That, too."

"You going?"

"She caught me by surprise, but after I started thinking . . ."

"About Annie?"

Beck nodded. "Doesn't seem right."

"Beck, Annie's been gone more than eight months now. She wouldn't want you to be alone all your life."

"I have the kids."

"They'll leave one day."

"I have you."

"I'll die one day."

"I'll have Butch."

"Butch don't belong to no one. Look, Beck, after your mother died, I didn't just withdraw from you, I withdrew from the world. From life. And then you left, and it was just me and the goats. I didn't see people or talk to people . . . until Jodie came to town. We started talking and I spilled nineteen years worth of thoughts on her. I loved your mother, but I should've let another woman in my life. Someone like Jodie."

"She's a lesbian."

"I'd still marry her. Not for sex, for conversation. That's what I miss most about your mother, sitting right here and talking at the end of each day. Not that I didn't like the sex."

"Gretchen said she has needs."

J.B. chuckled. "When was your last physical?"

"She's got a tattoo."

J.B. grunted. "Never figured her for a tattoo. She shaves her legs."

"What does shaving her legs have to do with her having a tat . . . never mind."

"What kind?"

"Blue butterfly, right above her bottom."

"I'll be damned. Girl's got a nice behind, too. I'd like to see that . . . her tattoo. Don't hurt to look at her behind neither, does it? Your mother had a nice behind."

206

"J.B.?"

"Yeah?"

"Let's don't go there."

J.B. chuckled, then pushed himself out of the chair, said good-night, and went inside. Beck forced himself to stop thinking about Annie and Gretchen and sex, and focus on Heidi's case file in his lap. He had been reading the Autopsy Report, looking for something, anything, that might take him somewhere other than the medical examiner's conclusions. Cause of death: "acute cocaine intoxication." Manner of death: "accidental overdose." Not homicide. Not manslaughter. Nothing to suggest foul play. Just a tragic accident. His old high school buddy couldn't accept the hard fact that his daughter's death had just been a tragic accident.

J.B. reappeared wearing Hawaiian print pajamas and said, "Was thinking in the shower. Why didn't Aubrey tell you about Slade, him getting arrested? He's the coach, he had to know."

Chapter 16

"What the hell are you doing?"

At 8:45 the next morning, the D.A. was standing in Beck's chambers looking like he wanted to come across the desk and strangle him. Beck had taken Grady's advice; after he raised the possibility of the tape recording being transcribed and printed in the newspaper, Justice of the Peace Walt Schmidt had not objected to his transferring the examining trial to the district court.

"Mr. Eichman, you'd better find your manners or you'll be sleeping in jail tonight for contempt of court."

The D.A. worked his jaws like he was grinding granite into dust. Beck didn't like the D.A. standing over him so he stood.

"Judge Hardin, *Your Honor*, you don't transfer a case or set a trial date without asking me."

"Where does the law say I need the D.A.'s permission to exercise this court's authority?"

"It's customary."

"Not anymore. Things are going to be different in my court."

The D.A. snorted. "*Your* court? If Slade hadn't beaten up that Mexican kid, I'd be sitting in that chair and you know it."

Beck wanted to say, Not if I had gone public with your half-

208

Hispanic child in Austin. Instead he said, "You gave up the judgeship for Slade McQuade?"

"No, for Quentin McQuade. But only for a year. This time next year, it'll be *my* court." He stepped to the window and gazed out. "You stir things up in the barrio, Judge, you're gonna get some dead Mexicans on Main Street."

"The best way to prevent that is to let justice prevail."

The D.A. turned to Beck with a bemused expression.

"'Let justice prevail'? This isn't moot court in law school, Judge. This is the real goddamn world. And your decisions have real consequences. For everyone."

"Friday morning, nine o'clock."

A finger pointed at Beck. "If this town explodes and Mexicans die, it's your doing. Remember that."

"Then take Slade to the grand jury. Let those twelve citizens determine probable cause."

"You know damn well the law requires grand juries to represent the county population."

"Meaning there are Latinos on the grand jury?"

"Three."

"That leaves nine Germans. Takes nine to indict."

"Which won't happen."

"But then you've got Latinos marching in the streets on Thanksgiving weekend, scaring off tourists. That won't be good for business."

"Won't be good for the Mexicans if a few of them get killed."

"Then do the right thing."

"'Do the right thing?'" The D.A. shook his head. "Is that what you told your corporate clients at your big Chicago firm? Look, Judge, I know the kind of lawyer you were. So don't come to my town and preach to me, okay? Besides, those Mexicans won't ever get to Main Street."

"Why not?"

"Trust me—it won't happen. And you don't want it to happen. So best thing is for you to find no probable cause."

"That's what the examining trial is for—to determine probable cause."

"No, Judge, it's to keep a lid on this town. We had this deal worked out for everyone—"

"Except Julio."

"Everyone that counts. But you stuck your nose where it doesn't belong, so now this town is in your hands. You're responsible now."

"I'm responsible for seeing that justice is done."

"*Justice?* You screw this up and you'll see what justice looks like."

"What do you mean?"

"Look, Judge, the Mexicans know you're not aligned with the Germans, so if you find no probable cause, they'll believe you." He smiled. "Heck, this could work out even better than we had planned. They trust you. Your word could end this."

"Why do they trust me?"

"They know J.B. partnered up with a Mexican. They figure like father, like son."

"They'll hear Julio's testimony and the deputies'. Grady won't let his men slant their testimony."

"No, Grady figures he's above it all now." The D.A. shook his head. "Worst thing that ever happened to this county, Grady getting rich. Now he can afford to be honest."

"I've read Julio's affidavit and the deputies' reports—there's probable cause. There's no way I could rule otherwise."

"There'll be a way."

"What do you mean?"

"You'll see Friday morning. Don't blow it."

Beck drove out the back parking lot of the courthouse and turned onto Main Street. Heading east, he crossed Adams, Llano, Lincoln, Washington, Elk, Lee, Columbus, Olive, Mesquite, and Eagle Streets, names selected and arranged by the city so the first letters would spell ALL WELCOME.

Just beyond the city limits sign where Heidi's body had been found, Beck turned south onto Old San Antonio Road. He drove over Meusebach Creek where it merged into the Pedernales River. Open land lay before him. He liked that about a small town: you could pull out of your parking space in downtown, drive five minutes in any direction, and be in the middle of nowhere. Drive five minutes from downtown Chicago and you're two blocks away.

He downshifted when the Navigator began the slow climb up Mt. Alamo, a hill ten miles southeast of town that stood twenty-three hundred feet above sea level. Aubrey lived in Alamo Springs, an old hippie community atop the hill. Beck turned east onto Alamo Drive and drove over the Bat Cave, an abandoned narrow-gauge railroad tunnel that was now home to three million Mexican free-tailed bats. Every evening at dusk the lot of them emerged to forage the countryside for insects. A distinct advantage of living in Alamo Springs was that there were few flies to contend with during the summer.

Beck continued past the Alamo Springs General Store & Cafe and turned south onto Apache Road, a dead-end. From that elevation, the view of the Texas Hill Country went on forever.

The view of the Geisel house was not as good. The paint on the small frame house seemed lifeless. The grass in the front yard was brown, as were the plants in the gardens. Weeds snaked a few feet up the side of the house. The shades were drawn. The house had died with the daughter.

Beck parked and got out, walked past an old Ford truck, and stepped up onto the porch. He knocked on the door. Aubrey answered without a second knock.

"Beck, come on in."

Beck stepped past Aubrey and inside the house. Aubrey was holding the cane in one hand and a beer in the other, and from the smell of his breath, it wasn't his first of the day.

"Don't you have practice today?"

"I can cuss drunk. Let's go out back."

Aubrey led Beck through a den with a decor straight out of a funeral home, through sliding glass doors, and out onto a wood deck. Beck went over to the rear railing to catch the breeze. It was dry without a hope of rain.

"Aubrey, you knew about Slade beating up that boy, getting arrested?"

"Sure."

"Why didn't you tell me?"

He shrugged. "Because it don't involve either one of us."

"It damn sure does. You're the coach and I'm the judge."

"Slade don't answer to me . . . or you."

"Oh, he's going to answer to me."

"I don't think so, Beck. Besides, I thought it was taken care of."

"By whom?"

"Quentin. The D.A."

"You figured Quentin's money had bought Slade out of this?"

Aubrey shrugged. "That's how things are done around here."

"Not anymore. Slade's examining trial is set for Friday morning, nine o'clock, in my court."

"Might be biting off more than you can chew, Beck. First week on the job, you gonna take on Quentin and the old Germans?"

"I'm gonna do my job. And that might affect your plans."

"What plans?"

"Winning state, trading up for a college job, getting Randi back. If Slade's indicted, you won't win state."

Aubrey limped over to the railing and stared out; after a moment, he exhaled heavily and without turning back said, "Hell, that ain't no plan, Beck. That's a pipe dream. My life ended the day Heidi died. She ain't coming back and Randi ain't either." He now turned back. "You do what you got to do with Slade. I'd rather put Heidi's killer in prison than win state. Now what do you know?"

It was now Beck's turn to stare at the distant hills. Looking south, he could see the path the train had once taken after emerging from the tunnel; it ran right past Hillingdon Ranch, Alfred Giles' old place. His grandson now ran the ranch. Beck looked up and gazed into the blue sky; he watched an eagle ride the currents for a bit, then he turned back to his friend.

"Aubrey, I know it's time to let her go. There's no chance of ever finding this guy, and even if we did, he was probably a college kid. It was just an accident, Aubrey."

Aubrey pointed the cane north toward town. "Giving cocaine to a sixteen-year-old girl, dumping her in a ditch—that ain't no goddamn accident! He killed her same as if he stuck a gun to her head and pulled the trigger!" Aubrey stared out into the distance again and calmed; then he said, "You're holding out on me, too, aren't you, Beck?"

Beck didn't answer. But he wondered if he was doing Aubrey a favor or himself a favor. Was he telling Aubrey to forget his daughter so he could forget her, too?

Aubrey said, "I want to show you something."

He limped back inside the house, and Beck followed. They walked through the den and down a hall. Aubrey stopped, opened a door, and hit the light. He entered the room like he was going into church. Beck stepped into a shrine.

The bed was neatly made with a pink comforter and fluffy pink pillows. Pink shag rugs dotted the wood floor. Framed photos of Heidi hung on the blue walls and played out her short life: a cute blonde toddler with her mother and father . . . a pretty girl about Meggie's age . . . a German *Fräulein* with braided pigtails . . . an all-American high school cheerleader . . . a beauty queen. She looked like Miss America. She did not look like the girl in the crime scene photos or a girl who would have had sex with two men in one night or a girl who would have snorted enough cocaine to kill a bull. She did not look like the dead girl in the ditch.

"She was my little princess," Aubrey said.

On a shelf next to the bed were trophies, crowns, and banners

213

from beauty pageants. Peach Blossom Queen. Peach Festival Queen. Peach Days Queen. Homecoming Queen. County Fair Queen. Rodeo Queen. Farm Bureau Queen.

"Won every pageant Randi put her in." He paused a moment to gather himself. "I tried to rehab the leg. Once I knew I'd never play again, it was like she lost interest in me . . . Randi. She knew I couldn't get her out of this town. From then on, it was like she put all her chips on Heidi."

Aubrey focused on a photo of Heidi and Randi and wiped his eyes; Beck averted his and opened the closet door. Inside were the clothes of a sixteen-year-old girl: cheerleader uniform, dresses, jeans, sneakers, and one pair of low heels.

"Any of her shoes missing?"

"Hell, Beck, I didn't keep track of her shoes."

"What about her purses?"

"Those either."

"Why didn't you let her have a cell phone?"

"Seemed like the kids with phones always got in trouble."

"Were you strict on her?"

"Not strict enough, I guess." Aubrey sat on the bed. "She was a great kid, Beck. Loved to go fishing and hunting, but she could never bring herself to pull the trigger on a live animal. I thought she'd always be that girl." He paused and his shoulders slumped. "When she turned fourteen and her body came in, men on the street started staring at her. It changed her."

"How?"

"Her world got bigger. She started thinking maybe her future was out there somewhere and not here in this small town. That she could have a better life than this." He pulled a handkerchief from his back pocket and blew his nose. "Other parents, they were always jealous 'cause she was prettier than their girls. Now I wish Heidi had been plain. I'd even take ugly. Because I'd still have her. I miss her, Beck."

Aubrey stood and limped around the room, removed photos from the wall, and used his shirttail to wipe dust from each.

And Beck thought of J.B.: had he walked into Beck's room every day for the last twenty-four years and dusted his trophies?

"I left her room just like it was, so I'd remember her like this. The way she was." He reached up and touched his daughter's image. "But I don't. I remember her lying on that slab at the morgue in Austin. That's how I remember my daughter, Beck."

Four years, nine months, and two days before, Aubrey's life had stopped, suspended in time as if the hands of all the clocks in the world had frozen in place, just as Beck's life had stopped the day Annie had died eight and a half months ago. Beck didn't keep a calendar because he had only life to blame for his wife's death. Aubrey had a human being—someone, somewhere out there.

"Aubrey, leaving her room like this, maybe that's not healthy."

"*Healthy?* Like eating vegetables?" He waved the cane around the room. "Look around, Beck. This is all I got left of her." He limped to the door, but stopped. "Beck, you don't owe me."

Beck's eyes fell to the cane and stayed there a moment. Then he looked up and pointed at a photo on the wall. Another girl was in it with Heidi.

"Who's the girl?"

"Kim Krause. They were best friends. She's Claude's daughter. He still owns the gas station on West Main. She works the desk."

The Gillespie County Courthouse marks the boundary between East and West Main Street. To the east are the "Three Magic Blocks." The 1.5 million tourists who visit Fredericksburg each year park their cars on East Main Street, shop at the stores on the Three Magic Blocks, then get back into their cars and drive home. Few tourists venture west of the courthouse. There was no magic on West Main Street.

The Krause Gas Station was located on West Main Street.

Beck drove west down Main Street past the courthouse. He

crossed Crockett, Orange, Milam, Edison, Bowie, Acorn, Cherry, and Kay Streets, the first letters of which spelled COME BACK. He drove past dilapidated homes and abandoned gas stations, the Zion Lutheran Church and the old Catholic convent, the Amish Market and the shuttered Knopp & Metzger Department Store where his mother had taken him shopping as a boy, a health food store and the Choo Choo Trolley Patio Shop.

The Krause station sat on the south side across from the Texas Pawn Shop just before the Y, where Main Street ended and split into Highway 290 West, the road to El Paso, and Highway 87 North, the road to Amarillo. Claude Krause repaired old cars in the old garage; Kim Krause watched the pumps from the desk inside and took the money. Krause's was not a pay-at-the-pump place.

But Claude Krause was sitting behind the desk and downing a Dinkel Acker beer when Beck walked in. It was 12:01 P.M. Claude said he never drank before noon. He also said that Kim had gone home to watch her favorite soap; home was an old frame house just behind the gas station. Beck now weaved around a dozen junk cars Claude was dismantling for the parts and a pile of tread-worn tires and walked across a dirt yard shaded by wide oak trees. He stepped up onto the creaky porch and knocked on the screen door.

Claude obviously liked repairing old cars more than his old home; white paint was peeling from the siding and black paint from the wood trim. The Krause house made Aubrey's look new. Beck could hear a TV through the screen door. A young woman smoking a cigarette appeared and spoke through the screen like an inmate conversing with her lawyer.

"Yeah?"

"Kim?"

"Who's asking?"

"I'm Judge Hardin." Beck hoped his official title might encourage Kim to cooperate. "I'd like to talk to you about Heidi."

216

If Kim was Heidi's age, she'd be twenty now; she looked thirty. She shrugged and pushed open the screen door.

"You scared me, wearing that suit looking like the undertaker. Come on in."

"Is your mother home?"

Kim exhaled smoke and said, "She left us a long time ago."

Beck didn't think it wise for a judge to be alone in the house with a twenty-year-old girl, so he said, "Let's sit out here on the porch."

"Suit yourself."

Kim came outside and plopped down on the top step. She was blonde and blue-eyed like Heidi, but she didn't look like Heidi. She was wearing a black tube top and cut-off jean shorts. She was a bit overweight, and she was barefoot. Beck took off his coat and sat next to her.

She said, "Why are you asking about Heidi?"

"A favor, for her father. We were like brothers back in high school."

She nodded. "Me and Heidi, we were like sisters."

"Tell me about her."

"She was beautiful."

"What did she want out of life?"

"To be a star."

"Why?"

"To get out of this town."

"Why? This is a nice place to live."

"Oh yeah, it's a real nice place to live . . . unless you're a girl or gay or Mexican or don't like football or George Bush. Then it sucks."

"How did she plan to become a star?"

"Send her pictures to Hollywood, get an audition."

"You have pictures of her?"

Kim smiled. "Do I have pictures of Heidi Fay?"

"Heidi *Fay*?"

"Heidi Fay Geisel, but Geisel didn't sound Hollywood so she

217

dropped it for her stage name." Kim took a drag on her cigarette and said, "Why do you want to see her pictures?"

"I'm trying to understand why she ended up in that ditch."

"You been to her house?"

"Yeah, just now."

"Seen her room?"

He nodded. "Aubrey's kept it just like it was."

"He would. Those pictures on the wall, those were for him."

"What do you mean?"

"I mean, that wasn't the real Heidi." Kim hesitated, then said, "I have her portfolio. Come on in, I'll show you. It's on my laptop."

"Can you bring it out here?"

"Suit yourself."

Kim disappeared inside and returned with a laptop. She sat, opened the laptop, took one last drag on her cigarette, then flicked it into the dirt yard. She tapped the keyboard several times until the wide screen was filled with a close-up shot of Heidi's face: her hair was blonde, her eyes as blue as the sky, her skin smooth and flawless, and her teeth a brilliant white.

"She never drank tea or coffee," Kim said. "To keep her teeth white. And she never had braces or caps."

Kim's face was now that of a kid opening Christmas presents. She tapped twice again and another photo appeared on the screen. This one was a full-body shot of Heidi wearing short-shorts, cowboy boots, and a pink halter top. Her thumbs were stuck in her front pockets, the snap was unbuttoned, and the zipper was halfway unzipped, revealing a lot of white skin below her navel. Her abs were lean and her legs muscular. She was not the German *Fräulein* or the all-American high school cheerleader in the photographs in her bedroom. She was a sexy twenty-five-year-old woman.

Kim said, "Her legs were incredible."

"How old was she in this one?"

218

"Sixteen. Couple months before she . . ." Kim shook her head. "She was so gorgeous."

There was no envy on Kim's face. There was pure admiration. She tapped again and Beck recoiled. In this photo, Heidi was still wearing the same clothes in the same pose, but her halter top was untied and her breasts were fully exposed.

"She had perfect tits," Kim said. "And those aren't implants. They're real."

Beck—State District Judge John Beck Hardin—felt uneasy looking at the bare breasts of a sixteen-year-old girl, even in a photo. So he said, "Next."

Kim tapped again. This one was worse.

"Look at that butt," Kim said. "Also perfect."

This photo showed Heidi with her back to the camera and twisting her upper body around. Her halter top was off, and her shorts were pulled down enough to show her bare bottom. She was wearing a black thong.

"She wore thongs?"

Kim shrugged. "Sure. Everyone does. You can buy them at the Wal-Mart."

Beck said, "Next," but when the next photo appeared, he wished he hadn't. Heidi was now completely nude, a full frontal. Her blonde hair framed her perfect face . . . bare breasts . . . a narrow waist . . . and a genital area without pubic hair.

"Brazilian wax job," Kim said.

Beck blew out a breath, stood, and walked a few steps into the yard. He needed to gather himself. Here he was, on the front porch of a little house in a small Texas town at the intersection of no place and nowhere and this girl was showing him nude photos of her dead best friend as casually as a new mother showing her baby pictures. Was this considered normal today? Had he been locked away in a Chicago law office for seventeen years while the outside world had taken a sudden sharp turn and didn't tell him? Is this what teenage girls did these days, take nude photos of each other and get Brazilian

219

wax jobs? When Beck returned to his spot next to Kim, she was grinning.

"We went to Austin to get our wax jobs. Now that was weird."

"Why?"

"How would you like some strange Korean woman messing with your privates, yanking your—"

"No. Why'd y'all do that?"

"Oh. All the Playmates do, and stars like Britney and Paris. The paparazzi caught them getting out of their limos without their panties on. Could you imagine how much fun that'd be?"

"Not wearing underwear?"

"No. Being so famous that photographers followed you everywhere."

"Why did she want to be famous?"

Kim looked at him like he was nuts. "Everyone wants to be famous."

"I don't."

"You're old." She got a faraway look in her eyes. "If you're famous, people recognize you . . . they're jealous of you . . . of your life. You got people to do your hair and put on your makeup and paint your nails and run get stuff for you. You can have anything you want anytime you want it. You're special. You're somebody. You're not a nobody in a hick town where goats and football are the biggest things in the whole world."

She threw a hand toward the gas station.

"My daddy's been fixin' people's cars in this no-count town his whole life and what's he got to show for it? That dump of a gas station and this dump of a house."

"Why don't you go to college?"

"And work all my life?"

"Do you have any friends? A boyfriend?"

"My friend died. And I don't want a boyfriend, not here."

"Why not?"

"*Why?* So I can get married, have a bunch of kids, and be

fat and bored all my life with a German guy starts drinking beer at noon and smacks me around at night? No thanks. I've already lived that life."

She lit another cigarette.

"I'm sorry, Kim."

"Ain't your fault."

"Where did you take these photos?"

"I didn't. Her mom did."

"Her *mom*?"

"Yeah, with a digital camera. I uploaded them. But I didn't touch them up, that's really her."

"Heidi's mother took nude photos of her?"

Kim shrugged. "You gotta do nudes for *Playboy*."

"Her mother wanted her to pose for *Playboy*?"

She nodded. "When she turned eighteen. Her mom figured if she could pose in *Playboy*, she'd get to live in the Mansion out in Hollywood—"

"What mansion?"

"The *Playboy* Mansion. Her mom figured she'd get discovered there. She was, like, obsessed with Heidi becoming a star."

"Her mother pushed her?"

"Heidi was her ride out of town . . . mine, too, I guess. She was gonna take me with her, to Hollywood, when she hit it big. I was gonna be her gofer."

"You were okay with that?"

Another shrug. "Sure. All the stars have an entourage. And I'd be in Hollywood. Better than living in a town that don't even have a Hooters."

"What do you want out of life, Kim?"

She blew out smoke and turned her big blue eyes up at Beck and said, "I want to be rich. I want to have everything. I want to live like those people on TV."

"Were you with Heidi the night she died?"

Kim's face changed, and Beck knew from his experience cross-examining reluctant witnesses that she was about to lie.

221

She shook her head. "Nunh-uh."

"You don't have any idea where Heidi went that night?"

She shook her head again. "Nunh-uh."

Kim wouldn't make eye contact with him now. She was lying. But why?

"Did Heidi drink?"

"Not even beer. She didn't want to gain weight."

"Drugs?"

"No way. You see how people look old when they do meth? Like Dee Dee? Heidi knew her looks were her ticket out of here."

"She died of a cocaine overdose, you know that?"

She nodded.

"But you never saw her use cocaine or other drugs?"

"No."

"Did she have a boyfriend?"

"Nope. She didn't want any ties to this place. She said she wanted Fred in her rearview mirror."

"Fred?"

"Fredericksburg."

"Did she hang out with Mexican boys?"

"In this town?"

"Any college boys?"

"What college guys would come here?"

"Kim, Heidi had sex with a man the night she died, did you know that?"

"I figured, with the sheriff wanting DNA samples from every guy in town. I saw that on *CSI Miami*. I like that show."

"She apparently wasn't raped."

Kim nodded.

"Which means, Kim, that Heidi met a man. Where would she meet a man in Fredericksburg?"

No eye contact again. She shrugged. Beck decided to gut-punch Kim.

"Kim, there's something else you should know. Heidi was with two men that night."

222

Now she made eye contact. "*Two* men?"

Beck nodded. "Apparently she gave oral sex to the first man earlier and then had unprotected intercourse with the second man, the man that dumped her in the ditch."

Kim's eyes dropped. She bit her lower lip and wiped a tear from her cheek. Now she looked thirteen. Without looking up she asked, "Does Coach know?"

"No."

She looked up. "Don't tell him, okay? He would die. He thought she was his little princess. He always called her that. I thought it was corny back then, but now I kind of like it, that he felt that way about her. My dad wanted me to be a mechanic."

"She wasn't? A princess?"

"She was on the pill. Her mom got them for her, right after—"

Kim caught herself. She tossed the cigarette into the dirt, slammed the laptop shut, stood, and walked into the house. The interview was apparently over.

When Beck walked back into his chambers, he found retired Judge Bruno Stutz leaned back in his chair with his feet kicked up on Beck's desk. His eyes were closed. He was a white-haired man in his seventies with sharp facial features.

Bruno Stutz was an old German.

Beck cleared his throat loudly. Stutz's eyes opened; he smiled. He slowly removed his feet from Beck's desk and stood. He was tall and lanky and dressed in a simple black suit—his suit *did* look like the undertaker's.

"Sorry, Judge," Stutz said. "Used to take a nap in that chair every day."

Stutz walked around the desk; they shook hands.

"Beck Hardin . . . Judge."

"Bruno Stutz . . . Judge." He shook his head. "After forty-six years, hard to call someone else judge. Look, instead of this judge-judge bit, how about I call you Beck and you call me Bruno?"

"That'll be fine . . . except in the courtroom. How's your heart?"

"Still ticking."

"Must have improved since you resigned the bench?"

"Oh, that just sounded better than the truth."

"Which was?"

"Quentin McQuade offered me a half-million-dollar salary to be his lawyer."

"His lawyer or Slade's?"

"All in the family. Mind if I sit?"

Beck shook his head. Stutz groaned as he settled into the chair. Beck walked around and sat behind the desk. His gut told him to keep some distance from Stutz. The old judge's next words proved his gut right.

"Beck, I don't want Slade in your courtroom. I want you to rescind your order. I want that examining trial in the JP court just like I had planned. Take care of that today, okay?"

Beck stared across his desk at the old man issuing orders to a district judge like he was ordering bratwurst and sauerkraut for dinner. *Who the hell does he think he is?*

"Bruno, that's not going to happen. Slade McQuade's examining trial will be held Friday morning upstairs in the district courtroom. And this is an *ex parte* communication between the court and one party to a case. I don't do that."

Stutz smiled. "Hell, son, nothing would ever get done in a courthouse without *ex parte* communications. That's why lawyers give campaign contributions, to buy the right to *ex parte* the judge."

"Not with me."

Stutz leaned down. He straightened up with a document in his hand. He tossed it on the desk: CONSENT TO EX PARTE COMMUNICATIONS. The D.A. had waived all objections to Stutz having private conversations with Beck regarding Slade McQuade.

"D.A. and I are on the same page. Look, Beck, we thought

224

we'd give Slade a break on this one, so he can get on with his football career."

"He beat the hell out of that kid. He doesn't deserve a break."

"Did you?"

"I never beat anyone up."

"Someone still got hurt."

"That was different . . . and twenty-four years ago."

"I have a long memory." Stutz sighed heavily. "Look, Beck, there's an easy way and a hard way to do this. That was the easy way. You won't like the hard way."

"Are you threatening a state district judge?"

"Did you threaten a justice of the peace?"

"Is that what Schmidt said?"

"Yes, that is what he said. You know, threatening Walt with that tape recording, that's something I would've done. Wouldn't have expected that from you."

"That tape recording is public record, Bruno. It's not a threat to disclose a public record."

"No, it's not. And, hell, it's Walt's fault anyway, saying that kind of stupid shit when he's being recorded. Said he forgot the tape was running." Stutz shook his head. "Walt's not the smartest goat rancher in the county."

Beck stood. "Anything else I can do for you, Bruno?"

Stutz did not stand. "How's J.B.?"

"He's fine."

"Goat rancher turned winemaker." He shook his head. "When Peggy died, God bless her, and then you left town, I didn't think he'd make it. But J.B.'s made of hard wood, that's a fact. But, you know, Beck, there's always a chisel sharp enough to split any wood."

"What's your point, Bruno?"

Stutz turned his blue eyes up to Beck, and Beck saw there the meanness Grady had spoken of, the same face Beck had seen that day when Stutz had sentenced Miguel Cervantes to prison.

"I first met your mother when she was only sixteen, living out there on that land with her folks running goats. That was nineteen sixty-three, November twenty-second. I remember that day well because that was the day they killed that Commie-loving bastard up in Dallas. She came into my courtroom that afternoon with her folks. Everyone else had gone home to watch TV about Kennedy. She was a pretty little gal, your mother. She had that glow about her that women get on two occasions in life: when they're getting married and when they're having a baby. Peggy wasn't getting married that day, Beck."

Beck fell back into his chair.

"She was giving that baby up for adoption. She came in to sign the papers. That was a Friday. She had the baby that Sunday out at the ranch with a Mexican midwife, and a nice couple from Odessa adopted the child. Girl, as I recall. Papers were sealed and no one ever knew. As I also recall, Peggy wore a white wedding dress when she and J.B. got married over at St. Mary's."

Beck had been blindsided many times in a court of law; clients always had secrets they didn't reveal to their lawyer. But those secrets always came out. Beck had tears in his eyes when he stood and stared at Bruno Stutz.

"I heard you were a mean old bastard, but you're way past mean. You're scary."

"You goddamn right I am. I've been scaring the people of this county for forty-six years, because I know everyone's secrets. That's why I'm valuable to McQuade. Time I'm through representing him, I'll know his secrets, too."

"The county's going to be a better place when you're dead."

"Don't hold your breath."

"Get out . . . before I throw you out."

Stutz slowly pushed himself out of the chair and walked to the door. He turned back.

"I've been holding on to that secret for forty-four years.

226

I'd hate for J.B. to learn the truth about Peggy this late in life. That's just the sort of thing that could spell the end of a man, learning something like that about his beloved dead wife."

"'Wedding dress. Size eight. Never worn. Paid six-fifty, sell for one-fifty.' Well, something surely went wrong there. Makes you feel for that gal, don't it?"

J.B. was reading the classifieds when Beck walked out onto the back porch and sat down hard in Peggy's rocking chair.

"Wonder was she just hoping or did she figure on getting married enough that she buys herself a dress? Now she's got to sell it. Makes me sad for her and I don't even know her. Any gal walking down the street might be the one carrying that burden."

J.B. shook his head. Then he looked at Beck.

"You look like you're carrying a heavy burden yourself."

Beck nodded.

"You got troubles?"

"We got troubles."

J.B. turned in his chair to face Beck. "Let's have it."

"Bruno Stutz came to see me today."

"Been wishing that old bastard would die for fifty years."

"I just met him and I want him dead."

"And?"

"He threatened me, if I don't drop Slade's case."

"What was his threat?"

"Said he'd reveal a secret he's been hanging on to for forty-four years."

"Forty-four years? Then it's not about you. So it must be about me."

Beck felt the tears come into his eyes again.

"Not you, either."

J.B. put the paper down. "Then that leaves Peggy."

Beck nodded.

"What is it?"

227

"J.B.—"

"Tell me."

Beck told it fast. "He said Mom got pregnant when she was sixteen, gave the baby up for adoption. Papers were sealed."

J.B. sucked in air. He blinked hard, then stood and walked to the screen. He stared out at the darkness a long moment and let out a long sigh, then turned back to Beck.

"I always wanted to punch Bruno in that sharp beak of his. Him being judge, didn't figure that would be a smart move. Figure I will now."

"I'm sorry, J.B."

"No, I'm sorry you had to learn about it from Bruno."

"You *knew*?"

"'Course, I knew. Peggy told me when I asked her to marry me. She said there'd never be secrets between us."

"Why didn't you tell me?"

"We ain't talked in twenty-four years, Beck, when was I supposed to tell you?"

"Before I left."

"You were an eighteen-year-old boy mad at the world 'cause your mama died—would you have understood? She made a mistake, Beck. She was a human being, just like you and better than me, and she made a mistake just like we have before and will again. But she was the best human being I've ever known."

"So I have a stepsister?"

J.B. nodded. "She lives up in Odessa. Married, got five kids now. Named Peggy. About twelve, thirteen years ago, she looked me up. Said the law allowed adopted kids to find their birth mothers. She wanted to know about her mama."

Beck was shaking his head.

"Beck, I hope this don't make you think less of your mama."

"No, it doesn't. She gave up her own child so the child could have a better life. That couldn't have been easy."

"It pained her considerably. But you eased her pain, Beck. She loved you enough for both her children."

228

J.B. sat back down.

"Bruno didn't tell you the whole story. He was a young man at the time and he fell hard for Peggy that day. But she wouldn't have nothing to do with him. When she married me two years later, he took it personal . . . and he got mad. Been mad ever since."

J.B picked up the newspaper, turned the page, and said, "Yep, next time I see Bruno, reckon I will punch him in the nose. Figure I won't go to jail seeing how I know the judge."

Chapter 17

Bruno Stutz was again sitting in Beck's chambers when he arrived the next morning.

"I've got to get better security," Beck said.

Stutz did not stand. He sat with the confidence of a man holding aces. "Well?"

"Peggy didn't keep secrets from J.B. He met her daughter twelve years ago."

Stutz sighed and shook his head. "That's the problem with secrets—people today just can't keep a secret."

"Any more threats, Bruno?"

Stutz's eyes narrowed. "Don't push me, Judge. You and the Mexicans will regret it."

"Oh, just so you know, Bruno, J.B. said next time he sees you he's going to punch you in the nose."

"J.B. making a threat?"

"More like a promise."

Stutz stood and walked out just as Mavis walked in. Behind Stutz's back, she held her hands up and formed a cross, as if to ward off the devil. He liked Mavis more each day. She was as wide as she was tall, she was a part-time goat rancher, and she had a crush on J.B. What wasn't to like?

"What do we have this morning, Mavis?"

"Divorces. I hate divorces."

Beck donned the black robe, and they again climbed the staircase—Beck went first—and entered the courtroom. Beck sat behind the bench. On his desk were eight gold file folders. Gold for divorce.

No county inmates sat shackled in the jury box and guarded by Deputy Clint, and no D.A. gave Beck suspicious glares. The same lawyers were present, but with a different set of clients. Criminal cases yesterday, divorce cases today—the life of a country lawyer. The spectator pews looked like a wedding: groom's family on one side, bride's on the other. Husbands to the left, wives to the right. Mavis called the first case.

"Danz versus Danz."

A rugged-looking middle-aged man wearing a firmly set jaw, jeans, boots, and a plaid shirt stood in the spectator section and walked to the bar; he looked like he could throw a bull to the ground. He held the gate open for an attractive but slightly chunky woman who might have been beautiful twenty years and several pounds before. Beck glanced at the file: *Lynnette Danz vs. Earl Danz*. They had been married for twenty-five years and had four children, ages twenty-three, nineteen, fourteen, and eleven. Two lawyers escorted them to the bench. One of the lawyers was familiar.

"Mr. Polk."

"Judge."

Beck opened the gold file, another case inherited from Judge Stutz. "Well, everything looks in order. All I need to do is sign the decree and your divorce will be final."

Beck searched the desktop for a pen, but couldn't find one. He turned to Mavis. She felt around her puffy hair a moment, then withdrew a pen and handed it to Beck. He put the pen to the order and started to sign, but looked up at Mr. and Mrs. Danz.

"Twenty-five years . . . y'all were high school sweethearts?"

Earl said, "Yep."

"Your kids live here?"

"Not the older ones. Kids these days, soon as they graduate high school they hightail it to the big city. Oldest boy, he's a real-estate broker up in Dallas, making money hand over fist. Girl, she's studying up at Tech. Straight As."

"You seem proud of them."

"Yep."

"Y'all must've been good parents."

"We tried."

"They upset about this, the kids?"

"Pretty much."

"How's it going to work with your young children?"

"Well, Mom here . . . I mean, Lynnette—"

Lynnette spoke up. "The boys are gonna live with me—Earl can't cook to save his life—but he'll still spend time with them. Boys need their father."

"Is he a good father?"

She nodded. "The boys are his life."

"I lost my wife. It's been tough, raising my kids alone."

"We're gonna work together, for the kids."

"Good."

Mavis was tugging at Beck's robe. He leaned her way. She whispered, "Don't go there."

"Where?"

"Playing Dr. Phil."

Beck ignored Mavis and turned back to the Danzes. "My wife and I, we argued some, but now that she's gone, all I remember are the good times. Y'all must have had some good times?"

"Well, sure we did, Judge, married twenty-five years."

Lynnette said, "Went to Hawaii one time, back between the second and third kids."

"My wife and I went once. We had a great time." Beck raised his eyebrows. "A romantic time."

Lynnette blushed and dropped her eyes. Earl glanced at her and said, "It was pretty romantic for us, too, Judge."

Lynnette turned her eyes up to Earl. They stared at each other like newlyweds. Beck gave them a moment and Mavis an "I told you so" look. She just shook her head.

"Y'all sure you want me to sign this order? Twenty-five years, that's a long time. Lot of history there. You know, I hear Hawaii's still out there in that Pacific Ocean. You could fly out there, see if that romance is still there, too."

Beck saw Lynnette's face soften; he thought, *Dr. Beck saves a marriage!* So without even realizing he was digging a hole for himself, he dug the hole even deeper.

"I mean, if you quit now, it's like . . . well, it's like you're cashing in a municipal bond before it matures."

Lawyer Polk had been sleepy-eyed throughout Beck's marital counseling; but his eyes suddenly got wide and he backed up a step and gave Beck a sharp slash sign across his throat, as if to say, "Cut!" Beck ignored him, too.

"Like you're selling an investment before its full value is realized."

Lynnette Danz abruptly turned to Beck and imbedded her fists into her hips like a Sumo wrestler facing off an opponent. Her face was no longer soft; her voice was firm.

"That's exactly what I said to Earl. I've invested twenty-five years of my life in this marriage and I want it to pay off!"

Earl stiffened and his square jaw clenched. "See, Judge, that's the deal: women look at marriage as some kind of goddamn investment. Men look at marriage as an adventure. I ain't nobody's municipal bond. I ain't her investment. I'm a goddamned man that wants an adventure! I want some excitement in my life before I die! Twenty-five years later, biggest excitement I got is looking at the underwear ads in

233

the Sunday paper!" He caught himself, then added, "The women's."

Lynnette said, "That's all he talks about, Judge, having an adventure. Excitement. He got cable and now all he does is watch the *Playboy* channel—that's an adventure? He wants me to buy a thong!" She turned and pointed at her bottom. "This butt in a thong—that's his idea of excitement?"

Beck glanced at Mavis for help; her face was now buried in her hands. But Earl's face was now bright red; his jaws were clamped so tight he could crack walnuts between his teeth. He reached over and banged a gnarly finger on the order.

"Sign the goddamned thing!"

Beck quickly signed the order dissolving the marriage of Earl and Lynnette Danz. They stormed out of the courtroom. Mavis looked after them; she shook her head and said, "Heck, I'd wear a thong to keep Earl in my bed."

Beck stared at Mavis and shuddered at the thought.

Kim Krause was lying. She knew where Heidi had gone that night. She might have even gone with her. But why would she lie about it? Did she know the man . . . the men . . . Heidi had been with that night? Was she protecting them? Or Heidi? Or herself?

Beck opened the case file to the interview statements and found Kim's. She said she had picked up Heidi about noon on New Year's Eve, and they had driven into town. Heidi had been wearing jeans, a tee shirt, and sneakers. Beck turned back to the Evidence Report: Heidi's body had been found clothed in a skirt and blouse, not jeans and a tee shirt. Back to Kim's statement: She said most of the stores had closed early for New Year's Eve, so they had window-shopped on Main Street and eaten at the Brewery. At approximately four P.M., Kim had gotten bored and returned home. Heidi wanted to remain in town. She said she'd call her mother to pick her

234

up. That was the last time Kim had talked to Heidi. She had stayed at home the rest of the night. Her father had vouched for her presence.

Claude Krause did not strike Beck as a liar.

But he was sure Kim was lying.

Beck exited the courthouse and cut across the lawn past the Eagle Tree. Brown oak leaves were floating through the air on a cool northerly breeze and falling on the courthouse grounds. Traffic on Main Street consisted of three cars backed up at the red light at the busiest intersection in town. Rush hour.

He walked east on Main Street two blocks and turned up the rock path leading to the bookstore. He needed a coffee and he needed to ask Jodie about Heidi; the sheriff said she had hung out here. Beck found Jodie at the checkout counter.

"Hi, Jodie. Small nonfat latte, please."

She looked up at him and said, "Figured you'd be over at the primary school, Judge."

She looked back down. *Judge?*

"Jodie, are you okay?"

"I'm fine."

"You don't seem fine." Beck Hardin didn't know women, but he knew a pissed-off woman. "Something you want to talk about?"

"Yes, there is." She called out, "Ella, I'll be in the court-yard!"

"Can I get my coffee first?"

"No."

She came around from behind the counter and walked outside; Beck followed her to the two-person bench. They sat quietly while she worked up to what she had to say.

"Beck, I've tried to help you with Meggie."

He nodded. "We're making progress."

"Then I don't want to see her regress."

"*Regress?* How?"

"Finding out her father is dating her teacher. It's all over town."

"How can it be all over town? We haven't even gone out yet."

"It's a small town." She faced him. "Beck, don't you think Gretchen's a little young for you?"

"That's what I told her."

"And what did she say?"

"She said she has needs."

Jodie gave a knowing nod. "She wants sex."

"She hasn't had a date in over a year."

"So what, this is like community service for you? You're just being neighborly to the teacher? Carrying her books to the car, cleaning the chalkboard, satisfying her needs . . ."

"She's twenty-five."

"And you're forty-two."

"I feel like I'm sixty-two."

"But she made you feel young?"

He nodded. "Just her asking made me feel like I was nineteen again. I didn't feel so tired."

"My husband said his secretary made him feel young."

"He was an idiot."

"I know that but how do you know that?"

"Because I know you." Almost a smile. "Jodie, can I ask you something?"

She nodded.

"Would it hurt Annie? I feel like I'd be cheating on her."

"Did you ever cheat on her?"

"No."

"Never?"

"No."

She gave him a suspicious look. "Not even a little touchy-feely with a secretary, maybe a few drinks and some grab-ass with a female associate after-hours?"

"No. Nothing. I loved her. I still do."

236

Jodie sighed. "Annie wouldn't mind then. It's cheating on us while we're alive that pisses us off."

"She wasn't happy."

"Annie?"

"She told J.B., in her emails. Because I worked long hours, was out of town a lot. She said she learned to sleep without me."

"Ouch. It's hard to be married to a lawyer."

"Were you ever happy, with your husband?"

"Maybe at the beginning. It didn't last long."

"You seem happy now."

"Not living with a lawyer will do that."

She straightened herself, and Beck noticed that instead of jeans, she was wearing a skirt and a short denim jacket over a black tee shirt. She was still wearing the red cowboy boots.

"That's a nice outfit. Makes you look young."

"Hey, I'm only—" She caught herself. "Nice try."

"Thanks. Are we okay?"

She smiled reluctantly and nodded.

"Good. Do you know Kim Krause?"

"Yeah. She tagged along with Heidi. No one ever saw her. Heidi got all the attention."

"Was she jealous of Heidi?"

"More like in awe of her."

"She has nude photos of Heidi. Her mother took them."

"Heidi's mom?"

Beck nodded. "Her mom wanted her to pose for *Playboy*."

"*Playboy* came to Austin one time. UT girls lined up. They were interviewed on TV, said their parents thought posing nude was a great opportunity. I remember thinking, an opportunity for what? Harvard Law School? Med school?"

"I thought women wanted an equal right to be doctors and lawyers . . . and bookstore owners."

"Girls don't want to be regular people anymore. They want to be Paris Hilton."

"Why?"

"Because she's rich and famous."

"Kim said she doesn't wear any underwear."

"Kim?"

"Paris. She said all the girls here wear thongs, said you can buy them at the Wal-Mart."

Jodie nodded. "I thought we had left all that behind in Austin, but it's here now. Only difference is, girls in Austin can afford to buy their thongs at Victoria's Secret."

"In Chicago, at Luke's soccer games, all the mothers wore thongs. You could see them right through their shorts."

"Soccer moms in thongs." She shook her head. "I thought feminism was about financial freedom. Turns out, it was just about sex. The thong won out over feminism."

"So how do I protect Meggie from all that? Not let her wear a thong?"

"Not at five anyway." She smiled. "You can't protect them, Beck. You just try to teach them to protect themselves, to think for themselves, to make good decisions. And when they make bad decisions, and they will, you talk to them and maybe you punish them, and then you hug them. You always love them."

"'Is your mama a llama? I asked my friend Dave. No, she is not, is the answer Dave gave.'"

Beck was reading Meggie's favorite book, *Is Your Mama a Llama?* by Deborah Guarino. He had read it five times that night and had just started over.

Meggie said, "J.B. has a llama named Sue."

"He sure does."

"Can I have a pony?"

"You've got a goat."

"I can't ride Frank."

"When you're a little older."

"When did you learn to ride?"

"Oh, about your age, but I was raised here, in the country."

"Other kids at school, they're riding horses."

"They're country kids."

"What am I?"

"You're my kid."

Beck found an email from March of last year:

Dear J.B.,

First chemo treatment. Beck went with me, but halfway through he had to leave the room. I think he was crying. I'm going to beat this disease, J.B., even if it kills me. (That's a joke.) Just threw up in the sink.

And one three weeks later, from April:

Hair started falling out. I think I'm going to shave it all off, I'll look like a football player. Second treatment today. Makes me so tired. Beck's in trial, billions at stake. I told him I could do it alone. I wish now I had told him the truth.

A month later, from May:

I'm bald as a baby's butt now. Bought a wig. Hate it. Too hot, makes my head sweat. I look like an old guy with a bad toup. So I went to a biker shop and bought doo-rags. They had a biker tee shirt, on the back it said, "If you can read this my bitch fell off." I started laughing so hard I had to sit down on the floor and then I started crying. The shop owner is this big hairy guy with tattoos. He came over and asked if he should call the ambulance. I yanked off my wig and screamed, "They can't help me!" I shouldn't have done that. He sat down on the floor with me, said he lost his wife three years ago. Breast cancer. We cried together, the bald and the beast. He wouldn't let me pay for the doo-rags. Meggie wants to shave her head and wear doo-rags to school. She doesn't understand. Luke is getting scared. Beck is afraid to touch me now.

239

Chapter 18

Beck was wearing latex gloves.

It was 8:30 the next morning, and he was in the sheriff's office. Grady was showing him the physical evidence from the crime scene box labeled GEISEL, HEIDI FAY. Grady removed a large zip-lock plastic bag from the box. He unzipped the bag and removed a white blouse; he held it up with his gloved hands. The light shone through the material.

"Nothing left to the imagination there," Grady said.

"Where was the DNA sample located?"

Grady pointed to a spot just below the collar on the right side. "Right there."

While he folded the shirt in mid-air and replaced it in the bag, Grady said, "I hear you're dating Gretchen."

"You know her?"

"Beck, I'm the sheriff of a small rural county—I know every-one."

"You know Kim Krause?"

"Her and Heidi were friends. Said she wasn't with Heidi that night, didn't know where Heidi went."

"She's lying."

"How do you know?"

"I've cross-examined enough lying witnesses to know."

"Why would she lie?"

"That's what I don't know. Did you polygraph her?"

"No reason to. Claude said she was home all night. But if you want, I'll bring her in, give her a little scare."

"No. I need to figure some things out first."

The next bag contained a black miniskirt that seemed too small for a sixteen-year-old girl. Grady pulled on the material, then released it; it snapped back.

"Spandex."

Grady removed another black item from the next bag: a tiny black thong with a red sequined star on the front.

"I never showed her clothes to Aubrey."

"Why not?"

"Would you want to know if your girl was wearing this stuff?" He shrugged. "And he never asked. Maybe he knew the way she was, didn't want to face it."

"That's all she was wearing?"

"That's all we recovered."

"Kim's statement said Heidi was wearing jeans that day."

Grady nodded. "Aubrey and Randi said the same thing. I figured she changed clothes. Girls do that. They get past the folks wearing jeans, then change to go partying in Austin."

"No shoes? No purse?"

"Nope and nope."

"Your wife ever leave home barefoot or without her purse?"

"Nope."

"Doesn't seem right, does it?"

"Beck, there ain't nothing right about this case. Or Slade's."

241

Chapter 19

The local paper that week made no mention of Slade McQuade's assault of Julio Espinoza or his upcoming examining trial. So when Beck climbed the spiral staircase to the second floor of the Gillespie County Courthouse at nine that Friday morning, he entered a nearly vacant courtroom.

It was his fifth day on the job.

He sat behind the bench. The D.A. was sitting at the prosecution table, and Bruno Stutz was at the defense table. Slade sat next to him; he looked like an action-figure in a suit. Quentin McQuade was directly behind them in the spectator pews; next to him sat a teenage girl.

Only a handful of people occupied the spectator pews. On the front row across the aisle from Quentin McQuade was a young woman with a small notebook in one hand and a pen in the other, no doubt a reporter. About halfway back was a Latino boy whom Beck recognized as Julio Espinoza; sitting next to him was an older white-haired Latino man dressed in a suit, former Congressman Felix Delgado. In the pew directly behind them sat three Latinos whose body language said "La Raza Unida." Leaning against the back wall by the entrance doors was Sheriff Grady Guenther.

Beck turned to his left: the jury box was empty—an examining trial was before a judge, not a jury—but the court reporter's chair was also empty. He turned to his right.

"Mavis, where's the court reporter?"

The D.A. stood. "Your Honor, I informed Bernice that her services would not be required today."

"*You* informed her?"

"Yes, sir. As you know, Judge, this is an informal proceeding, so Judge Stutz and I agreed that there was no need for a transcript of the proceedings."

Beck turned to Mavis: "Call Bernice and get her over here."

"Well, Judge," the D.A. said, "she's out of town today. Said she was taking a long weekend in San Antonio."

Beck again turned to Mavis: "Call Bernice and tell her she's fired. Hire a new court reporter who understands that she works for the judge, not the D.A."

"Judge, if you'd prefer, we can postpone this proceeding until such time as a court reporter is available."

"No, we'll proceed. The code allows me to summarize each witness's testimony."

"Very well, Your Honor."

Beck caught the D.A. winking at Stutz.

"And we'll tape record the proceeding. Mavis, go downstairs and get a tape recorder."

Mavis stood and disappeared behind Beck. The D.A. wasn't winking now.

"Your Honor, the Code of Criminal Procedure doesn't authorize tape recording this proceeding."

"It doesn't prohibit it either. Might be good to have so my summary is accurate."

The D.A. stepped over to the defense table; he, Stutz, Slade, and Quentin McQuade huddled like a football team calling an audible. When Mavis returned, she placed the recorder on the witness stand and hit the RECORD button. When she sat down, Beck nodded at her. Mavis called out: "Cause number

243

forty-three sixty-one, State of Texas versus Slade McQuade. Aggravated assault with hate crime enhancement. Examining trial."

Beck said, "Gentlemen, please make your appearances."

The D.A. stood and said, "Niels Eichman, Jr., Gillespie County District Attorney, representing the state."

Stutz stood and said, "Judge Bruno Stutz, for the defense."

Beck said, "This is an examining trial to determine if probable cause exists to refer this matter to the grand jury. We are not here to determine guilt or innocence. Slade McQuade, you have the right to make a statement regarding the charges filed against you, but you cannot be compelled to make any statement. Any statement you do make can be used in evidence against you. Do you understand that?"

Stutz nodded at Slade, who said, "Yes, sir."

"But you must make any such statement prior to the testimony of any witness. Do you want to make a statement?"

"No, sir."

"Very well. Mr. Eichman, present the state's case."

"Your Honor, the state calls Julio Espinoza."

The Latino boy stood and came forward through the gate in the bar. Walking into the well of the courtroom, he looked like a sacrificial lamb. His brown skin contrasted sharply against his white shirt. He was a slender, handsome boy. Except for the boxer's nose and several freshly-healed scars on his face, he did not exhibit any physical evidence that he had been severely beaten just four weeks before. Mavis swore him in.

"Do you swear to tell the truth, the whole truth, and nothing but the truth, so help you God?"

Julio answered: "Es."

Beck said, "Mr. Espinoza, would you please speak up?"

"Es!"

Beck leaned toward Julio and looked at him closely.

"Mr. Espinoza, are your jaws still wired shut?"

244

"Es!"

Julio opened his lips wide like he was trying to grin; Beck could see wires holding little hooks on each jaw and tiny rubber bands secured to the upper and lower hooks to hold his jaws tightly together. Beck turned to the D.A.

"How is he going to testify with his jaws wired shut?"

The D.A. shrugged. "That's why I set the hearing for January, Your Honor. So his jaws would have time to heal."

The D.A. gave Beck a look that said, *Now what are you going to do, Judge?* Julio reached to his back pocket and pulled out a little notepad and pen; he acted as if he were writing.

"You'll write your testimony?"

"Es."

Mavis tugged on Beck's robe then tapped on the document on his desk. Julio's affidavit. Beck nodded then addressed the court. "Since the sole purpose of this proceeding is to determine probable cause to refer this case to the grand jury and not to determine guilt or innocence, I will admit Mr. Espinoza's sworn affidavit he signed the night of the alleged assault."

Stutz stood and said, "I object. That would deny my client's right to confront the witness."

"He's sitting right there. Confront. Objection is overruled." Beck turned to Mavis. "Mavis, please read Mr. Espinoza's affidavit into the record."

Stutz said, "Defense withdraws the objection, Your Honor."

Stutz did not want the affidavit read in open court. Beck was about to have Mavis read it anyway, but Grady caught Beck's eye. He tapped his wristwatch and nodded toward the Latino activists. The ticking time bomb. Beck turned to Julio.

"Mr. Espinoza, is your affidavit a true and correct account of what happened that night?"

"Es."

"That's a yes?"

Julio nodded.

"Mr. Espinoza answered in the affirmative. The affidavit of

245

Julio Espinoza is admitted into evidence." He turned to the D.A. "Any questions, Mr. Eichman?"

"No, Your Honor, you handled my case quite well."

"Thank you. Judge Stutz, your witness."

"No questions, Your Honor."

The D.A. called the four deputies who had arrested Slade that night. Each testified that when they had arrived at the theater, Slade had been beating Julio and calling him a wetback and a spic. Stutz did not question the deputies. When the D.A. rested for the state, Stutz stood and called his first and only witness.

"Defense calls Nikki Ernst."

The teenage girl sitting next to Quentin McQuade stood, walked up to the witness stand, and was sworn in by Mavis. She was blonde and blue-eyed and looked every bit the German girl she was. Stutz approached the witness stand.

"Miss Ernst," Stutz said, "how old are you?"

"Eighteen."

"And you're a senior at the high school?"

"Yes, sir."

"Miss Ernst, were you at the Stagecoach Theater on the night of Saturday, September the eighth?"

"Yes, sir."

"And did you have occasion to speak with Julio Espinoza?"

"Yes, sir, at the snack bar."

"And were you previously acquainted with Mr. Espinoza?"

"Yes, sir, we're both seniors. We have several AP courses together. I thought he was a nice guy."

"And have you changed your mind about that?"

"Yes, sir."

"And when did you change your mind?"

"That night."

"Would you please tell the court what Julio Espinoza did to change your mind?"

She ducked her head as if she were embarrassed. "He made inappropriate remarks to me . . . of a sexual nature."

246

Stutz now had the expression of a grandfather talking to his granddaughter. "I know this is difficult, Miss Ernst, but please tell the court exactly what Mr. Espinoza said."

"Well, I went up to the counter to get my popcorn and when he handed it to me, he said I looked sexy."

"Sexy. Well, now, Miss Ernst, some girls your age might consider that a compliment, isn't that true?"

"Yes, sir. But there was more."

"More? Please go on, Miss Ernst."

"He said he wanted to, um, have sex with me."

"Are those the words he used?"

"Well, no, sir."

"What words did he use, exactly?"

"He used the f-word."

"The f-word?"

"Yes, sir."

"Please tell the judge exactly what Julio said, in his words."

Nikki took a deep breath, as if saying the f-word went against every fiber in her being.

"Julio said, 'I want to fuck you.'"

There was a loud grunt from the audience. Julio was standing in the spectator section, his arms spread and a distressed look on his face. Nikki's eyes dropped to her lap.

"Please sit, Mr. Espinoza."

Felix Delgado pulled Julio to his seat, and Stutz continued with Nikki. "And did Slade McQuade hear him say that?"

"Yes, sir. Slade had just walked up when Julio said that. I guess Julio didn't see him."

"And Slade got mad?"

"Yes, sir. Very."

"So Mr. Espinoza's statement provoked Slade's actions?"

"Yes, sir."

"No further questions, Your Honor."

Nikki glanced at Slade; he gave her a wink. Beck had listened to thousands of hours of testimony under oath; he

247

knew when a witness had rehearsed. Nikki Ernst had rehearsed.

"Mr. Eichman."

"No questions, Your Honor."

Beck stared at the D.A. "The state is not going to question the defense's only witness?"

"No, Your Honor. Miss Ernst seems credible enough to cast real doubt as to whether probable cause exists here."

The D.A. gave Beck a look that said, *Get it? This is the way out.* Beck turned to the witness.

"Ms. Ernst, why didn't you mention any of this to the deputies that night?"

"Your Honor," the D.A. said, "may counsel approach?"

Beck waved him up; Stutz followed. The D.A. arrived and whispered, "Judge, this is the way out for everyone."

"Not for Julio."

"For the town."

Beck waved them off. Bruno Stutz glared at him.

"Mark my words, Judge, you proceed with this witness and that Mexican boy is going to regret it."

"Sit down." He turned to Nikki: "Ms. Ernst, why didn't you mention this to the deputies that night?"

"I guess I was just so upset."

"Ms. Ernst, have you previously discussed your testimony with Mr. McQuade or Judge Stutz?"

"Slade's dad?"

"Or Slade? Or his lawyer?"

She glanced over at Slade and Stutz.

"Ms. Ernst, don't look at the defendant or his lawyer for an answer."

"Well . . . we maybe talked some . . . a little."

"Did anyone suggest to you to testify that Mr. Espinoza provoked Slade?"

"*Suggest?* Well, I don't know . . ."

"Ms. Ernst, will you graduate this year?"

"Yes, sir."

"And what are your plans? College?"

"Yes, sir, UT."

"You've been accepted?"

"Yes, sir. Top ten percent."

"You're in the top ten percent of your class?"

"Yes, sir."

"So you're a smart girl?"

"I guess so."

"What are your career plans?"

"I want to be a doctor."

"A doctor?"

"Yes, sir."

"College then medical school?"

"Yes, sir."

Beck grabbed the Penal Code and thumbed through the pages.

"Ms. Ernst, you're eighteen, correct?"

"Yes, sir."

"So you understand that even though you're still in high school, the law regards you as an adult?"

"Uh . . . yes, sir."

"Ms. Ernst, do you know what perjury is?"

"Not exactly."

"It's lying under oath in a court proceeding. Like today."

"Oh."

She bit her fingernail.

"Ms. Ernst, the Penal Code states that a person commits perjury if he or she makes a false statement under oath. And it's aggravated perjury if that false statement is material, which means the testimony will determine the result of the proceeding. Aggravated perjury is a third-degree felony punishable by a prison term of two to ten years. Do you understand that if it is subsequently discovered that you lied about Julio's statements to you that night, you could be charged with perjury?"

"Uh . . . no, sir . . . I mean, yes, sir."

She now had both hands in front of her mouth; her teeth

were nibbling on her nails so hard Beck could hear the sound.

"And if convicted, you could be sentenced to prison for two to ten years?"

She stopped nibbling.

"*Prison?*"

"Yes, Ms. Ernst. The women's prison in Huntsville."

Her face went ashen. "No one said anything about prison."

"Ms. Ernst, this isn't a game. This isn't about doing what Slade wants you to do. This is about your future. You're a smart girl. Think before you throw your future away by lying to this court. A person convicted of perjury doesn't go to college and medical school. She goes to prison."

Nikki was now staring at Slade. When she turned back to Beck, she had tears in her eyes. And he had her.

"Ms. Ernst, do you know what the word 'retract' means?"

"Yes, sir. To take something back."

"Exactly. The code also states that if the witness who made a false statement retracts it and tells the truth before completion of his or her testimony, he or she does not commit the crime of perjury. Do you understand what that means?"

Almost a whisper from Nikki: "If I tell the truth right now, I won't go to prison?"

"Yes, that's exactly what it means. Now, Ms. Ernst, before I dismiss you, is there anything about your testimony that you would like to correct?"

Nikki had gone back to biting her nails. Her hands were in front of her mouth and her head was down, almost as if she were praying. Perhaps she was.

"Ms. Ernst?"

She finally raised her head and glanced at Slade. She shook her head. Then she turned to Beck.

"Yes, sir, I would like to correct something."

"And what is that?"

"Julio, he didn't say any of that stuff to me. He's a good guy. We're friends." She looked at Julio in the audience. "Or were.

But Slade, he's insanely jealous. At first I liked that, but then it became . . . kinda scary, you know?"

"You bitch!"

Nikki recoiled in the witness chair; her hands flew up as if to block a blow. Slade was standing at the defendant's table.

"Mr. McQuade, sit down!"

Slade glared at Beck, but when Grady stepped to the defendant's table, Slade sat down. Beck turned back to Nikki.

"Ms. Ernst, what do you mean, Slade's jealousy became scary?"

"Uh, nothing."

"Look at me, Ms. Ernst."

The girl turned in the witness chair until she was directly facing Beck. He rolled his chair as close to her as the bench would allow; he leaned over. They were no more than three feet apart. He wanted her to focus only on him.

"How long have you and Slade been dating?"

"Almost a year."

"Has he ever hit you?"

"Oh, no, sir. He would never hit me."

"Did you ever see him hit anyone else, other students?"

"He hits walls."

"Walls?"

"Unh-huh. He punches holes in walls, when he's in a bad mood."

"Does Slade have bad moods often?"

"Oh . . . you know . . . sometimes."

"Did Slade beat up Julio because he's Latino?"

"Oh, no, Judge, Slade's not like that. His heroes are black athletes."

"Did you hear Slade call Julio a wetback and a spic that night?"

"Yes, sir, but that's what everyone calls them."

"At school?"

"In town."

"So Slade beat up Julio for no reason at all?"

251

"It wasn't his fault."

"Julio's?"

"Slade's."

"Ms. Ernst, Julio suffered a broken nose, a concussion, two teeth were knocked out, three broken ribs, and a broken jaw— his jaws are still wired shut. He couldn't even testify today. Whose fault would that be then?"

"Well, I meant . . ."

"You meant what?"

She shrugged.

"Ms. Ernst, did Slade beat up Julio?"

"Yes, sir."

"So it was his fault?"

"Well, yes, but . . ."

"But what?"

"He . . ."

"What, Ms. Ernst? I need to know or I'm going to revoke bond and put Slade in jail—today!"

She suddenly appeared panicked. "*Jail?* You can't do that! He's got a game tonight! A district game!"

"Football games don't matter in a court of law, Ms. Ernst."

"But, Judge, it wasn't his fault! He can't control himself when he's cycling!"

"'*Cycling?*'"

The D.A. was on his feet: "Judge, I, uh, I think Ms. Ernst is becoming frazzled. Perhaps she needs a break."

"Hush." Back to Nikki: "Ms. Ernst, what do you mean 'cycling'?"

Nikki's face was stricken; her eyes were pleading to Slade for help and her teeth were chewing on her nails again; half her fingers appeared to be in her mouth. Quentin McQuade was jabbing at Stutz from his seat on the first row. Stutz stood.

"Your Honor, you're harassing my witness. Certainly you've gotten the testimony you need for the purpose of this proceeding."

252

Beck ignored Stutz. "Ms. Ernst, look at me."

She turned back to Beck; she was crying.

"Ms. Ernst, what do you mean by 'cycling'?"

Her head was down; she whispered: "When he's juiced."

"Juiced? You mean steroids?"

She nodded.

"Was Slade on steroids that night?"

She nodded again.

"Please answer aloud."

"Yes."

"How do you know?"

"Because I stuck him."

"You injected him?"

She nodded. "He's afraid of needles. He used to get other guys at those Austin gyms to inject him, but since I'm going to be a doctor—"

"Where did you inject him?"

"At his house."

"No, where on his body?"

"His butt."

"So he was in a steroid cycle that night?"

She nodded. "He cycles every month . . . like a girl's period, I tell him. That way his body doesn't become dependent on the steroids, otherwise his testicles will shrink up to the size of a pea. At least that's what he said."

"How long has Slade been using steroids?"

"As long as we've dated."

"And when he injects, he becomes aggressive?"

"Totally, especially when he's stacking."

"Stacking?"

"When he does several kinds of juice at the same time. It's supposed to work better that way. See, he pyramids—"

"Pyramids?"

"Yeah, he starts a cycle with a low dose then increases the dose until he peaks. Then he backs off. When he's at the peak, that's when he has bad moods. Mad moods. He calls it 'roid rage. I stay away from him, for like, two or three days, that's why I went to the movie that night without him. He gets real mean . . . and punches walls. And he gets insanely jealous. He usually pumps iron really hard those days, he says that's when he can add bulk. But when the stuff wears off, he gets real down."

"Down as in depressed?"

"Yes, sir. Once he evens out, he's okay, but the peak days are always a rollercoaster for him."

"And that was a peak day?"

"Yes, sir. A really big dose."

"All right, Ms. Ernst, so you injected steroids into Slade that Saturday morning. Did you see Slade again that day?"

"Not until at the theater. Like I said, I stay away from him on those days."

"At the theater that night, you were talking to Julio at the counter and Slade just grabbed Julio and yanked him over the counter and started beating him?"

"He was raging."

"Ms. Ernst, where does Slade get his steroids?"

"At gyms in Austin where the freaks hang out."

"Freaks?"

"Those bodybuilders. Slade says they're freaks."

"Knew the girl was the weak link."

An hour later, Quentin McQuade was standing in Beck's doorway with a rolled-up magazine in his hand like he was looking for a dog to smack.

"Mind if I come in, Judge?"

He walked in without waiting for an answer. Quentin McQuade looked every bit the rich real-estate developer, oozing confidence and money. He stood over six feet tall in his expensive suit, but he didn't have his son's body mass. Being in real estate, chances were he wasn't on steroids.

254

"Didn't want an official record, thought getting rid of the court reporter would fix that. Nice move, the tape recorder."

He said it as if complimenting an opposing coach on a play call. Beck said, "I could have you charged with subornation of perjury."

McQuade chuckled. "Good luck with that. Like you never coached a witness?"

He had.

"I didn't tell them to lie."

"Coaching, lying . . ." He shrugged. "Semantics."

"Mr. McQuade—"

"Quentin. It's Beck, right?"

"No, it's Judge Hardin."

"Judge Hardin, then. Can we talk?"

"Why not? *Ex parte* doesn't seem to mean much around here."

"*Ex parte*? Is that like an ex-wife?" McQuade chuckled as he sat in the visitor's chair. "So, when will you rule?"

"Law requires me to rule within forty-eight hours. So first thing Monday morning, since Slade's not in custody."

"Any way to postpone your ruling?"

"If the defendant requests a postponement."

"He does."

"Mr. McQuade, I don't see any reason to delay my ruling. There's clearly probable cause to send Slade to the grand jury."

McQuade sighed like Beck had just told a corporate client his deal wouldn't close.

"Yeah, problem with that is, grand jury is twelve people. Nine Germans, so an indictment isn't likely, but still a possibility. The more people that get involved, the harder this thing is to control, see? Never know when someone might grow a conscience. Nope, I just don't like those odds."

"Those are the odds every American citizen faces when they commit a crime."

McQuade smiled slightly. "I'm not every American citizen, Judge. And Slade is my son."

"Mr. McQuade, even if Slade is indicted, what are the odds of his being convicted by a trial jury packed with Germans?"

"Slim to none."

"Because you came here and bought influence with the locals."

"Can't buy something that's not for sale." He smiled. "Most of the public officials and businessmen in this county benefit from my development, Judge, that's true. But that's just good business, same way business is done in Dallas or Houston or anywhere else in this state or this country. Only problem with buying public officials is, sometimes they don't stay bought."

"I wouldn't know."

"Sure you would. Lawyers know all about buying judges. When one of my companies gets sued, first thing my lawyer in Austin does is find out who the judge is and what lawyer was his last campaign treasurer—then he hires that lawyer. Doesn't matter if the guy writes wills, he wants that lawyer sitting at our table in front of that judge at trial. Now, I didn't dream up that little scheme. My lawyer did. And he used to be president of the bar association. No doubt your Chicago law firm did the same thing."

It did.

"So what's your point, Mr. McQuade?"

"My point is this: I can't let the grand jury indict Slade because an indictment kills his football career. Cable sports channels will be all over it like stink on shit—live from the front steps of this courthouse. UT'll drop him like a fresh cow patty. No UT, no NFL first-round draft pick, no fifty-million-dollar contract, no endorsements. That makes for a bad investment."

"A bad investment?"

"Last ten years, I've invested a half-million bucks in the boy's career."

"His *career*? He's a high school player."

"Who'll be playing pro ball in two years."

"So he's your investment?"

"One of them. And he's going to pay off. Our agent's already got him in a Gatorade commercial—"

"He's got an agent?"

"Sure. He can't get paid and still play college ball, so that commercial's a freebie, just prepping the market, getting his pretty face out there. We're negotiating a Nike deal that'll take effect the day he turns pro. He'll be a gold mine."

McQuade tossed the magazine he had been holding onto the desk: *Sports Illustrated*. Slade was on the cover, bare-chested and holding a football; the byline was THE NATURAL.

"That's a lot of pressure to put on a boy, Mr. McQuade."

"Pressure is part of the game. He can handle it."

"You've been prepping him for the pros since he was nine?"

"Crazy, isn't it? But that's the way it is now. Personal trainers, passing, running, and strength coaches, nutritionists—all that doesn't come cheap. I've had the best quarterback coach in the country working with him since he was twelve, forty hours a week in the off-season, learning how to read defenses, call audibles, footwork, watching film . . ."

"What about being a boy?"

"Doesn't pay. With the kind of money in sports today, there's no time to be a boy. Sports are for the young and strong, so you've got to grab it while you can."

"Did you ever grab it, Mr. McQuade? Did you ever play?"

He shook his head. "I wasn't good enough."

"So you're living out your dream through Slade?"

"Damn right I am. He's my son. But it's his dream, too."

"Maybe he's not good enough, if he has to use steroids." Beck gestured at the magazine. "He's not natural. He's juiced."

"We're off the record, right, Judge?" He again didn't wait for an answer. "Slade had the same arm when he weighed one-ninety. But he can't play pro at one-ninety because he wouldn't survive the punishment today. That's what's changed in the game: quarterbacks have to be big, real big, just to survive the hits. Because the guys hitting them are bigger. Hell, Namath

257

and Staubach, they could throw the ball with anyone today. But they wouldn't last a full game, getting mauled by those three-hundred-pound guys. Namath played at one-ninety, Staubach at one-ninety-five. What did you play at?"

"One eighty-five."

"College water boys weigh more than that. What did your offensive line average at Notre Dame?"

"Two-fifty."

"NFL quarterbacks weigh that today. Football is played by giants. Did the human race just suddenly experience a growth spurt? And only among athletes?"

"Mr. McQuade, twenty years ago at Notre Dame we had seminars about steroids. They work, but the side effects can be very dangerous—'roid rage is real. Right after injection, your testosterone level shoots up to that of a gorilla—and your personality turns into that of a gorilla. And when you come down, you often go into depression. It's a cycle of rage and depression, just like Nikki said. Some users have even committed suicide. And even if they don't suffer side effects, they're still damaging their bodies long term."

McQuade laughed. "Hell, getting slammed to the turf by those big sons a bitches damages their bodies long term, too. But that's the deal you make with football, you sacrifice your body for glory and money. Time Slade's thirty, with his contract and endorsements, he'll be worth a hundred million. Took me till I was fifty."

"You're worth a hundred million dollars?"

"Two. I'm fifty-five now."

"Mr. McQuade, you're his father. You should be telling him not to use steroids."

"Judge, tell a high school boy there's a magic potion that'll make all his dreams come true, what do you think he's going to do? Steroids are the American way—using science to make your body better. No different than men taking drugs to make their dicks hard or women getting breast implants."

258

"I've never heard of a woman with breast implants going into a rage and beating the hell out of someone."

"You never met my first wife." He smiled; Beck didn't. "Look, Judge, that was regrettable. But it's also fixable. I paid the boy's medical bills, and Stutz is talking to Delgado and the boy's family right now about a settlement."

"How much?"

"I've authorized Stutz to offer a million."

"A million dollars?"

McQuade shrugged. "A business expense."

"Civil cases are settled, Mr. McQuade, and you don't need my approval to settle a civil case. This is a criminal case."

"D.A.'s already signed off on the deal. He'll dismiss the charges if Julio accepts the settlement."

"The D.A. can't dismiss without the court's approval."

"That's why I'm here."

"Be careful—bribery of a public official is a felony."

McQuade smiled. "At the capitol in Austin we call it lobbying. But I'm not offering you anything, Judge. I'm offering to settle with the Mexican boy so my boy can get on with his football career."

"How? After this morning, the whole world is going to know Slade's on steroids."

"No, it won't. That's not gonna leave that courtroom."

"Nikki testified under oath in open court. The Austin and San Antonio papers—"

"Weren't in the courtroom."

"But the local paper was and they—"

"Won't do a damn thing."

"Why not?"

"Because Stutz already threatened to sue them for libel if they print anything about steroids and Slade."

"You can't win that case."

"You and I and Stutz know that, Judge, but they don't. And they can't afford to take a chance. Small-town paper, they'd go broke just defending the case. So they caved."

259

"Your money buys just about anything you want, doesn't it?"

Quentin McQuade smiled. "Pretty much. Imagine what a million bucks can buy for the Mexican boy and his family."

"Well, Mr. McQuade, like I said, that's civil. It has nothing to do with Slade's criminal case."

"Judge, if the criminal case isn't dismissed, there won't be a civil settlement."

"Julio can still sue."

"He can sue Slade, not me. Slade owns a Hummer, and a Hummer won't pay the Mexican boy's college tuition."

McQuade stood and walked to the door; he turned back.

"Judge, you don't want to find out what else my money can buy."

Beck entered the athletic club for the second time that week. He didn't notice that no one smiled at him or waved at him or greeted him with a hearty "Hi, Judge Hardin" because his mind was focused on one thing, the same thing most nineteen-year-old boys' minds are focused on 24/7.

His eyes were searching the circuit training room for the blue butterfly. He found it. He walked toward it. The butterfly was floating up and down and up and down in a slow rhythmic motion, its wings seeming to move gracefully above . . . that bottom. Gretchen Young was doing standing squats on a rack fronting a wall mirror. Each time she squatted, the black shorts stretched almost to the breaking point. He broke a sweat.

"Hi, Gretchen."

Their eyes met in the mirror in front of her; she didn't smile at him. She was holding a barbell balanced on her shoulders behind her neck; a fifty-pound iron plate was locked on each end of the barbell. She hefted the barbell onto the rack and ducked under the bar. She adjusted the weights and whispered to him without looking at him.

"Beck, go away. I can't be seen talking to you."

"Why not?"

She jabbed her head toward the cardio room. "See those two old men on the ellipticals? They're on the school board. They see me talking to you, I'll get fired. They fired the principal for saying the Pledge in Spanish—they'll probably arrest me!"

"They fired Ms. Rodriguez?"

"Yes! Now go away before you get me fired!"

"Why would I get you fired?"

"Because they say you're going to ruin their football season. One of the teachers, her husband works at the courthouse. I told her we were going out Saturday—she said to stay away from you."

"They won't fire you. You're dating the judge."

"No, I'm not. Beck, I'm sorry, but I need my job."

"But you have needs."

Her face softened and she sighed. "Tell me about it."

Then she, her butterfly, and her bottom walked away. Beck stood there, staring and stunned.

"Fickle, aren't they?"

Jodie again.

"Who?"

She nodded toward Gretchen. "Children."

Chapter 20

The sounds of Oma & The Oompahs filled the Marktplatz in downtown Fredericksburg. The town was celebrating Oktoberfest, the granddaddy of all German festivals. The grounds were crowded with white tents and tourists. Authentic German beer, food, music, crafts, and costumes harked back to the old country. The autumn air was crisp and cool, the tourists were drinking and buying, and the locals were speaking German and making money. All was well in Fredericksburg, Texas, that Saturday morning.

But not with Beck.

Luke said, "What'd you do?"

Beck had brought Luke and Meggie to Oktoberfest. They were now eating lunch at a picnic table in the open-air Adelsverein Halle surrounded by unfriendly locals. Beck felt like Custer at Little Bighorn—but with dark German glares instead of sharp Sioux arrows being shot his way.

"What do you mean?"

"No one's talking to you. And I heard people say you're ruining the football season. You did something. What?"

"Slade beat up a boy. I might have to put him in jail."

Luke dropped his Kraut dog onto his paper plate and looked up at Beck in disbelief. "Great. You move me here and put me in school with a bunch of cowboys and now you do this."

"I'm trying to do the right thing, Luke."

"I'm trying to survive fifth grade."

"Luke, I . . ."

"I wish we had stayed in Chicago. I wish Mom was here. I wish you had died instead."

Luke's words cut him, but Beck didn't take what his son said to heart; he had said the same words to his father when his own mother had died. Meggie said, "Mommy's coming back."

Beck patted her and said in a low voice to his son, "Me, too, Luke. It would have been better that way, for all of us. But she died, and I'm all you've got."

"I've got J.B."

Beck turned away from his son and saw Aubrey limping toward their table. He was obviously drunk. He was working the cane with his right hand and carrying three cans of beer in his left hand. When he arrived, he placed the cans of beer on the table and sat down next to Beck. He leaned his cane against the table, popped the top on one can, and drank from it. He didn't notice that Luke had tears in his eyes.

He said, "You ain't exactly the most popular judge in town."

"Yeah, but I'm the only judge in town."

"Didn't see you in the stands last night."

"Figured I might not be welcome."

"We won. Slade threw for seven touchdowns, ran for two."

"I heard."

"Did Kim know anything about Heidi?"

"Did you know Slade was using steroids?"

Aubrey turned to the bandstand at the other end of the pavilion and stared at the dancers wearing traditional German costumes and dancing a polka like pros. When he turned back, he said, "Can we talk about Heidi instead?"

"After we talk about Slade. Did you know?"

Aubrey took a long drink, then said, "Figured."

"You didn't ask him?"

"Like I said, he don't answer to me."

"What about other players? Are they using?"

"Possibly . . . probably."

"The school district doesn't test?"

"Yeah, we've had a random drug testing program for a few years now. But we've never had a positive for steroids."

"Has Slade ever been tested?"

"Nope."

"What about the other football players?"

"Nope."

"Why not?"

"'Cause the same boys are picked for every test. Mexican boys that play soccer."

"Doesn't sound random."

"It ain't. Hundred-thirty-pound Mexican boy sure as hell ain't juicing, so he gets tested. We tell the parents our boys tested clean, they're happy. That's what they want to hear. It's like the Army's 'don't ask, don't tell' except it's 'don't test, don't know.' Long as they don't know the truth, they can still believe it's all good here."

"Who picks the kids that get tested?"

Aubrey looked away. "I do."

Beck stared at his old friend. Aubrey drank from his beer. He finally said, "Look, Beck, I test a football player, I'm fired that day. Their daddies, they run this town."

"You should stand up to them."

"Did you stand up to your corporate clients in Chicago? Beck, no one wants to go there. Easier to look the other way."

"Aubrey, looking the other way, that's the same as telling them it's okay to cheat."

"Beck, they don't need me to tell them that. They see the pros getting paid real good for cheating. Why shouldn't they?"

"Because it'll harm their long-term health."

"Long-term is next week for these boys."

"Then because it's wrong."

"It's only wrong if they get caught."

"That's a hell of a thing to tell your players, Aubrey."

"I'm not telling them that, Beck, the world's telling them that. They got TVs, they can read the paper . . . well, most of them. They see businessmen, politicians, athletes cheating, breaking the law and getting rich. Why can't they? That's what the world's telling them to do—get rich. Do whatever it takes, but get rich." He exhaled. "The state put in a no-pass, no-play law so kids gotta pass their classes before they can play. So the school board just exempts a bunch of classes so the kids can fail and still play. What's that but cheating? Cheating to win. That's the real world, and these kids ain't stupid. They get it."

"Did you look the other way so you could win state, get a college job, and get Randi back?"

"Maybe. Not that I could've stopped them."

"You should've kicked Slade off the team."

"Tell you what, Beck—I'll kick Slade off the team the day you put him in jail for beating up that Mexican boy."

"That might happen."

"Not in this life, Beck. And not in this town."

"I'm not going to roll over for Quentin McQuade . . . or the Germans."

"Nope. They're gonna roll over you."

"How?"

"I don't know, Beck. But they will. That's how they do things around here. That's how they get their way . . . with football coaches and judges."

Aubrey pushed himself up and finished off a beer and threw the can into a trash bin. He said, "Hell, Beck, I don't know why you're worried about a bunch of boys taking steroids. Worry about finding Heidi's killer. We only got eighty-six days left!"

265

Beck was mad at his old friend, he was mad at himself, and he was mad at Kim Krause. He said, "Why would Kim lie to me?"

When Beck drove up to the house, he found Grady Guenther leaning against the side of his Gillespie County Sheriff's Department SUV and chewing on a toothpick. The kids got out and went running down the caliche road toward the winery; Frank the goat ran to catch up with Meggie. Beck walked over to the sheriff. Grady said, "I hear Chicago's nice this time of year."

Beck smiled. "Yeah, it is."

Grady nodded toward the front gate. "J.B. really got pit bulls?"

Beck shook his head. "He put up that sign to run off the real-estate brokers."

Grady chuckled. "J.B.'s a piece of work, those shirts he wears, buying a bulldozer."

"What bulldozer?"

The loud roar of a diesel engine sounded like a tornado rising from back of the house. Grady yelled over the noise: "That bulldozer! The hell's he gonna do with a dozer?"

Beck yelled back: "Beats me."

They walked down the caliche road so they didn't have to yell. Grady took in the land and said, "Nice place. Never been out here. What's J.B. got, a thousand acres?"

"Eight hundred. They combined the Hardin and Dechert places when he married my mom. Peggy Dechert. Did you know her?"

"Sure. Knew her old man, too. Surprised he let her marry an outsider. That didn't happen much back then."

"Why not?"

"The land. Germans came to Texas 'cause they could own land here. So the land became the family jewels. The old-timers, they fought like hell to keep the land in the family."

"You mean, in Germans?"

"I mean, in the family. There was a lot of intermarrying here,

266

cousins marrying cousins—I'm talking first cousins—to keep the land in the family."

"I never heard about that."

"It's our little secret no one talks about. It was pretty much the deal right until my time. Still happens some. Joke is, nobody can afford to have a family reunion 'cause you'd have to invite the whole town." He chuckled. "Hell, my mama and daddy were cousins and so were their folks. Guess that's why I try hard not to act like an idiot, afraid I might actually be one."

"I think you escaped that fate."

"Crazy, ain't it?"

"What's that?"

"It was all about the land for our folks and their folks, keeping it in German hands. Now we're selling out to Californians." He chuckled. "The Baron's turning over in his grave." He shook his head, then said, "You were pretty good yesterday, with Nikki."

"She's a kid."

"You're a pro."

"I've crossed pros—politicians and corporate executives."

"You figure out why Kim's lying?"

"No."

"You figure out what you're gonna do with Slade?"

"He's going to the grand jury."

"That final?"

"Will be Monday morning when I sign the order."

"Quentin know that . . . the Monday morning?"

"Yeah."

Grady kicked dirt. The white dust covered his boot.

"Makes sense then."

"What?"

"One of my deputies driving by Quentin's place this morning, said it looked like a big powwow going on. Recognized Stutz's truck and the D.A.'s SUV. That's how they do things."

"Who?"

267

"The old Germans. City hall, that's where they announce in public what they already decided in private."

"Grady, I've been gone a long time, but even Texas has an open meetings law."

"Maybe so, Beck, but no one complains 'cause if they did, they'd be treated like an Amish slut come home for the holidays. No one would do business with them, their boys wouldn't make any sports team at school, their girls wouldn't make cheerleader—that's how things work in a small town."

"So what do you think they're up to?"

Grady shook his head. "Don't know. But they're up to something . . . something to stop you from signing that order Monday morning."

"Well, there's nothing they can do to stop me."

"Beck, don't bet the ranch on it."

Grady drove off, and Beck walked around back. Fifty yards south of the house, his father was driving a bulldozer like he knew how. Beck waved at his father. J.B. shut down the dozer.

Beck said, "What are you doing?"

J.B. flashed a big grin. "She's a peach, ain't she?"

"What are you gonna do with it?"

"I'm building a baseball field."

"For Luke?"

"Build it and he will come. I saw that in a movie a while back, on cable. Guy builds a baseball field so his dad'll come back. Worked for him, figure it might work with Luke."

"That was a movie, J.B."

"Good one."

J.B. fired up the dozer again, and Beck walked down to the winery to collect the children and Frank. Luke was working with Hector, and Meggie and Frank were playing with Josefina, so Beck went upstairs to J.B.'s office. He sat at the computer, but this time he did not read Annie's emails. Instead, he searched for information on steroids. He found eighteen million web hits. For the next hour, he read.

Anabolic steroids . . . injection . . . carried to muscle cells . . . receptors transport the steroids to the cell nucleus . . . react with DNA to stimulate the cell's protein production . . . protein plus exercise results in increased muscle mass. Bulk.

But you're messing with your DNA.

Mega-dosing . . . one hundred times normal testosterone level . . . cycling . . . stacking . . . pyramiding . . . one million high school athletes use steroids in the U.S. Side effects: acne, baldness, high cholesterol, high blood pressure, heart damage, cancer, mood swings, depression . . . homicidal rage.

Beck sat back and stared at the last two words on the screen: homicidal rage.

Five hours later, J.B. was driving his rocker on the back porch. Beck said, "You still take your truck to Claude Krause?"

"Yep."

"Would Claude lie for Kim?"

"Claude wouldn't lie for himself. That's why he's the poorest mechanic in town."

J.B. looked up from the newspaper. "Never asked—how'd it go with Gretchen?"

"It didn't."

"You had second thoughts?"

"She did."

"Oh."

"She was worried she'd get fired, if she was seen with me. After yesterday."

J.B. nodded. "What are you gonna do?"

Beck shrugged. "Nothing. If she doesn't want to—"

"No. About Slade."

"Oh. I'm sending Slade to the grand jury."

Chapter 21

"Judge, if you send Slade to the grand jury, you're sending those Mexicans back to Mexico."

Beck had been wrong: there was something they could do to stop him. He had arrived that Monday morning to find Bruno Stutz, Quentin McQuade, and the D.A. in his chambers.

Stutz said, "Those Mexicans will never get to Main Street. ICE will raid the turkey plant before Thanksgiving weekend."

"ICE?"

"Immigration and Customs Enforcement," the D.A. said. "They changed the name from INS when Homeland Security took over."

"You're going to call in the Feds to deport those people?"

Stutz said, "Creates a nice little diversion, the Mexicans getting arrested and deported. Puts Julio on the back-burner."

"Delgado can still stage his protest."

Stutz laughed. "There won't be five Mexicans left in town . . . and the city cops can handle them if they step onto Main Street. Hell, I figure Julio won't even be here. He'll take his brothers and sisters and follow his folks to Mexico. The Julio problem goes away—literally."

"You'd have those poor people deported just to keep Slade's football career on track?"

"*Just?*" Quentin McQuade said. "Slade's gonna make more money his first year in the NFL than all the Mexicans in this town will make in their entire lives combined."

"You deport the Mexicans, that'll close the turkey plant. A lot of turkey farms will close, too. German turkey farms."

Stutz shrugged. "Collateral damage."

McQuade said, "Here's the deal, Judge. My offer to the boy still stands. One million dollars to settle all civil claims against Slade, and you and the D.A. here dismiss the criminal charges. That's a good deal. Let's get it done."

The D.A. was nodding like a puppet on a string.

"That's civil. This is criminal."

"Well, Judge, if the criminal case isn't dismissed, there won't be a civil settlement. But there will be an ICE raid. My money can buy that, too."

Stutz said, "I'll come back with a written request to postpone your order, right after I give Delgado the good news."

The three men stood.

McQuade said, "Once we make the call to ICE, Judge, there's no stopping that train. The Feds are coming to town, and those Mexicans are going home."

"Julio gets beaten up, but his parents get deported. That's his justice?"

Quentin McQuade shrugged and said, "Life ain't fair."

"Son of a bitch!"

Beck had just ruined Sheriff Grady Guenther's hot dog lunch.

"That's Stutz's doing. He's been wanting a raid more than George W. wanted Saddam."

Beck was sitting in the visitor's chair in the sheriff's office. Grady was shaking his head.

"Sorry I got you into this, Beck. Should've just let things go like they've gone around here for a hundred and sixty years.

271

You figure just once something ought to go the right way."

Grady stuck a toothpick in his mouth.

"Grady, the Mexicans do all the manual labor in this town. Without them, the Germans will have to pay higher wages."

"Yep. White people won't work for the Mexican wage."

"You really think they'll deport those people if it costs them money?"

"Money is what's been keeping them from doing it before now. But like I said, it wouldn't be the first time the Germans pulled the trigger without drawing first. And you know how it is, Beck, when it's Anglos versus Mexicans in Texas, common sense ain't part of the equation."

"You think maybe Stutz and Quentin are bluffing?"

"Don't know about Quentin, but Bruno ain't. He's a scary bastard 'cause he never bluffs. He'll make that call to ICE, and when he does, it's a done deal. Those Mexicans will be bused to Mexico."

"Only way to stop that is to dismiss the criminal charges."

Beck could only think of two words: homicidal rage.

"What if Slade hurts someone else?"

"I swear to God, Beck, I'll arrest him and break his throwing arm myself." Grady spit the toothpick into the trash can. "Look at it this way, Beck. Two months from now Slade'll be enrolled at UT. He'll be their problem then. He beats up someone in Austin, even Quentin don't have enough money to buy off those crazy liberals. They'll crucify him."

"He beats the hell out of Julio, and now he's going to walk because his daddy's worth two hundred million dollars."

"Quentin's a goddamn fool to pay a dime to that Mexican boy," Bruno Stutz said. "Was me, I'd call in ICE and be done with the bunch of them. But Quentin's a businessman. He likes settlement agreements with confidentiality clauses."

Stutz had returned with the postponement request.

Beck said, "What did Delgado say?"

272

Stutz chuckled. "He wasn't a happy Mexican."

"He threatens protests, you and McQuade threaten ICE raids."

"You shouldn't make threats the other side can trump."

"Bruno, an ICE raid would destroy this town."

"Good. I don't like this town anymore."

"Then leave."

"No! I want the *Ausländers* to leave, the Mexicans and Californians and those Main Street folks from Austin. They're nothing but a bunch of goddamned liberals, bringing their politics and tattoos to my town. And good Germans are selling out to them so they can buy a goddamn Lexus."

Stutz stood.

"Hell, I've been wanting to get rid of the Mexicans for thirty years, but everyone else just wanted to let things be—because we're addicted to the Mexicans' cheap labor. Man my age, I don't give a damn what everyone else wants. I want the Mexicans gone. The tourists, too. I want this to be a German town again."

"Bruno, you like Mexican food?"

He shrugged. "Enchiladas. And those little rolled-up things, fried with chicken inside . . ."

"*Flautas?*"

"Yeah, those. And *sopapillas*. I like their food, Beck, but I hate them. I hate what they've done to my town."

"What? Roofing German houses? Processing German turkeys? Picking German peaches?"

"Killing German girls. I guarantee you, it was a Mexican that raped and killed her."

"Heidi? She wasn't raped. Sex was consensual."

"He drugged her, and that's not consent. Kids here, they used to drink beer . . . I don't need to tell you that. Then the Mexicans came to town and now kids use marijuana, cocaine, meth—that's why I sent every Mexican I could to prison."

"Like Miguel Cervantes?"

Stutz laughed. "Oh, yeah, I remember you in the courtroom

that day, the star quarterback crying for his spic buddy. You know where he ended up? Dead in Dallas. Drug deal gone bad."

"Maybe being sent to prison for smoking a joint when he was eighteen put him on that path."

"Being born Mexican put him on that path."

"And what did you do to German kids?"

"I sent them back home to daddy. Believe me, once their old man got through with them out in the goat shed, they wished I had sent them to prison. Like Merle Fuchs. He's our local Congressman."

"So you figure it's okay for Slade to beat the hell out of that boy?"

"Not in public." A grin. "We always took them out to the country." A pointed finger. "That boy, he was romancing little Nikki, they call it *machismo*. You seen all those barrio bastards they sired? Born sucking off the government's tit."

"German goat ranchers sucked off the government's tit for forty years."

"That was different. We're citizens."

"Those Mexican kids are citizens, too. Born in the USA."

Stutz snorted. "Just like your daddy, a man of principle."

"Thanks."

"It wasn't a compliment."

"Does your boss really want a raid?"

"He wants his boy in the NFL." He shook his head. "Never met a man got football on the brain like him. But truth be known, Beck, I don't like McQuade either, coming in here with his money and buying everything in town."

"He bought you."

"Nope. He's renting me."

"You're a mean man, Bruno."

"You don't how mean I am. But you push me, Beck, and you'll find out. And so will those wetbacks."

★   ★   ★

274

After court closed for the day, Beck drove straight to the winery to pick up the kids. He walked through the tasting room and into the tank room. Luke was working with Hector.

"Luke, where's Meggie?"

"In the vineyards with Josefina and Butch."

"J.B. upstairs?"

Hector said, "He is up at the house, riding the bulldozer. J.B., he likes to build things. Beck, may I have a word?"

Hector led Beck to the open barn doors. From there they looked out upon the fifty acres of vines. He saw the girls playing under Butch's watchful eye.

"Beck, word of the Espinoza boy has traveled throughout the Mexican community. The Mexicans, they have faith in you, that you will do the right thing."

"Problem is, Hector, I don't know what the right thing is."

"There are rumors of a raid. People are nervous."

"I'm not going to let that happen, Hector. I'll find a way. I'll figure out justice in this case."

"You are the judge, Beck, so you decide what is the law. But only God decides what is justice."

"Well, Hector, you might be right about that, but if ICE raids our town, those Mexicans will be deported. Not even God can stop the Federal government."

The children were asleep, and the Hardin men were in their rockers on the back porch. J.B. said, "What are you gonna do?"

"I don't know. A settlement would help Julio and his family and keep ICE out of our town. But if Slade hurts someone else, that'd be on my watch."

Homicidal rage.

"It'd be a damn shame to see those Mexicans deported."

"What about Hector?"

"He's legal. We got his green card, then his citizenship."

"How?"

"If a Mexican's got a half-million bucks to invest in a business, government puts him on the fast track."

"Hector had a half-million dollars?"

"Nope. But I did. From selling the goats. So I loaned him some and folks from his hometown put together the rest. Hector sends half his share of the profits down to Matamoros."

"A Mexican with money can buy his way in, but a Mexican who just wants to work has to sneak in. You'd think politicians could see how stupid that is."

J.B. snorted. "That'll be the day."

Chapter 22

Felix Delgado was seventy-five years old, he was an American citizen born of Mexican immigrants, he had served sixteen terms in Congress from his San Antonio district, and he had one year to live.

"Brain tumor," he said.

Delgado had been waiting for Beck at the courthouse that Tuesday morning. He had driven up from San Antonio.

"It is a beautiful drive," he said. "I used to drive very fast. Now I drive very slow."

"The tumor?"

"The time. When you do not know the date of your death, you race ahead. When death may be around the next curve, you do not hurry."

Beck started to express his sympathy, but Delgado waved him off. "Do not feel sorry for me. I have lived a long life."

"Felix, you understand that if this is not resolved soon, they will call in an ICE raid. I don't think they're bluffing."

Delgado sighed. "The D.A. threatens to deport Julio's parents, so I threaten protests on Main Street, so Stutz threatens an ICE raid—it is like the Cold War, escalating threats until we arrive at nu–cu . . . nu–clu . . . nuclear war." He shook his head. "Every time I hear George W. say 'nu–cu–lar bomb' on TV, it is three weeks before I can again say the word correctly."

"That bomb is ticking, Felix. And the barrio will be ground zero."

"When a man like McQuade has the money to wield the Federal government like a club, it is not a fair fight."

"He'll win that fight. And Julio and his parents will lose."

"Yes, he will and they will."

"Do you want me to approve the settlement and dismiss the charges against Slade? Is that the justice you want for Julio?"

Delgado exhaled. "What kind of name is that anyway, Slade?"

"It's a football name."

"Ah. Football. Is he good?"

"Very."

"So he will go to college for free?"

"Yes, he will."

"But Julio must pay. Seems odd, does it not? Julio wants to build rockets at NASA, but he must pay tuition. Slade wants to play football, so he need not pay."

"Julio's a smart kid. Can't he get a minority scholarship?"

"He says he does not want to be in the debt of Anglos."

"So he won't take a free education? That's false pride."

"No, it is not. I know. I went to the Congress ready to fight for my people, but I compromised my principles to curry favor and power. I incurred political debts and became an indentured servant. I enjoyed the power, and I did not want to lose it. So I could not say what I truly believed. I could not just do the right thing. As you are now trying to do."

"I just can't figure out what that is."

"When I left the Congress, I freed myself of those debts. I again sought justice for all Latinos in Texas. I fought against this immigration hysteria that is sweeping the country, I fought against racial profiling, I fought against the border fence. I failed. So I

278

have lowered my sights. Now I seek justice one Latino at a time."

"And what is justice for Julio Espinoza?"

"I am, as they say on television, conflicted."

"But I'm the judge, Felix. I've got to decide this conflict."

"Julio wants the settlement."

"That's civil, Felix. This is criminal. If I let Slade walk, he's not being punished or prevented from hurting someone else. That's not justice."

"Is it justice that Latinos must live in the barrio? That they must work in the turkey plant for the Mexican wage? Have you been to the barrio? Have you seen where Julio's family lives?"

"No."

"Then go to Julio's home and sit on his couch as I have and tell him his family must live in the barrio always. Tell him his parents must always work in the turkey plant. Tell him he cannot go to college. Tell him he will not work at NASA. Tell him he will work at the turkey plant all his life. Tell him that is his justice." Delgado sighed. "He said to me, 'Señor Delgado, I want to be the visible Julio.'"

"Visible? What does that mean?"

"It means that here he is not recognizable as a human being because his skin is brown. It is as if the Anglos cannot see him. He says if he does not soon leave this town, he will explode."

Beck nodded. "I felt the same way when I was his age, but for a different reason."

"And did you leave?"

"Yes."

"How?"

"Football scholarship to Notre Dame."

"Ah, yes, the Fighting Irish. Good Catholics. And you were good?"

"Not a very good Catholic, but a good player."

"But you returned to your hometown?"

Beck nodded. "Three months ago."

"And what brought you back?"

"My wife died."

"*No.*"

"Yes."

"How old?"

"Thirty-seven."

Delgado shook his head. "Life is not fair. You are a young man, too young to be without a wife. I have told my wife, 'When I am gone, find another husband. Life is too short to live alone.'"

"You wouldn't feel betrayed?"

Delgado laughed. "I will feel nothing. I will be deceased. She will be alive. Life is for the living, Beck. I love her, so I want only for her to be happy. We are not meant to be alone."

"Felix, do you mind if I ask you a personal question?"

"Ask."

"How much of McQuade's money will go into your pocket?"

"None."

"You're not being paid?"

"What does money mean to a dying man? I have money, Beck. It is time I do not have. If I take my final breath knowing that I have helped to get Julio into college and his family out of the barrio, I will die a happy man. I will not have failed them."

"But what if Slade hurts someone else? That would be on my tab."

"What if ICE raids the turkey plant and the barrio? That will also be on your tab."

He was the judge in a small rural Texas county; it was supposed to be an easy job. It wasn't.

Beck was sitting in a lawn chair on the balcony outside the second-floor courtroom. His feet were propped up on the low railing. His thoughts were of Julio Espinoza and Heidi Geisel: Could he give them justice?

280

He now turned to Heidi's case. He was sure Kim Krause had lied to him, but Claude Krause had sworn that she had been home that night. So she hadn't been with Heidi. She hadn't lied about that, but she might have lied about knowing where Heidi had gone that night and whom she was with.

Heidi's case file was in his lap. He flipped to Aubrey's statement. Aubrey said he had watched football all day New Year's Eve. Heidi had left with Kim during halftime of the Cotton Bowl, about noon. She was wearing a shirt, jeans, and sneakers. Randi Geisel confirmed the time Heidi had left home and her clothes. She said she had not grown worried when Heidi had not returned home by ten when she had gone to bed. She assumed Heidi was staying over with Kim, as she often did.

That seemed odd to Beck. When he had worked late in the city, if he hadn't called Annie by eight she'd call him, even though he worked late every night. He had been a forty-year-old lawyer, but she had still checked on him. She had still worried about him. Heidi had been a sixteen-year-old teenager—wouldn't her mother have checked on her? Wouldn't her mother have worried about her?

He needed to talk to Randi.

He went downstairs to Mavis' office. She was gone, but he found an Austin phone book. He checked the white pages for "Geisel, Randi." There was no listing. He went into his chambers and turned to his computer. He logged on to the Travis County appraisal district website, which had tax records for every parcel of real property located in Travis County. Austin was the county seat.

He clicked on *owner search* and typed in *Geisel, Randi*. No properties came up in her name. He thought for moment, then tried *Barnes, Randi*. One property came up: a single-family residence located on Lakeshore Drive in Austin with an appraised value of $3.25 million. He wrote down the street address. Was this the same Randi Barnes?

★   ★   ★

281

"She's a bitch."

Beck had heard the gunshot and run outside. From his rocking chair on the back porch, J.B. had spotted the coyote stalking Frank the goat in the last light of day. He loaded his rifle and put a bullet in the coyote from fifty yards. J.B. now kicked the dead coyote over.

"Yep, she's a bitch all right."

In hunting parlance, a young coyote is a whelp, a male is a dog, and a female is a bitch. This one was a female.

"Big one, too," J.B. said. "Maybe fifty pounds."

The coyote looked like a big dog with a bushy tail. Her coat was thick and gray, with red around her ears and a pale underbelly. Coyotes weren't big like wolves, but they were strong for their size and vicious carnivores.

"You seeing them up here?"

"River peters out downstream 'cause of the drought," J.B. said, "so they're coming upstream, looking for water. This one had a drink in the river, smelled Frank, figured she'd do for dinner. There'd be hell to pay if this coyote had killed Frank. Maybe I should've let the little gal keep Frank in her room."

"Meggie had Frank in her room?"

"Yep. Said she kept her goldfish in her room."

"What'd you tell her?"

"I told her goldfish don't crap on the carpet." J.B. smiled. "I told her Frank preferred to live outside. Wasn't right to pen her up. She's a free-range goat. She was damn near a dead goat."

J.B. scanned the land a moment, then he said, "Keep an eye out, Beck, with the kids."

Chapter 23

STATE CHAMPIONSHIP IN JUDGE'S HANDS
Judge Hardin to Decide Fate of Slade and Season

The next day, the local paper carried a front-page story about Slade McQuade. Details of his "alleged" assault on Julio Espinoza and Nikki Ernst's conflicting testimony were included, but there was no mention of steroids.

"Funny how a small town works, isn't it?"

Beck looked up from the newspaper to the D.A. standing in the door. He said, "Are you going to investigate steroid use by Slade?"

The D.A. shook his head. "Nope."

"He's using, some of the other players are probably using, and you're not going to do anything?"

"Nope. I'm not going there, Judge, and you can't make me. If no charges are filed, you've got no jurisdiction."

"Nikki testified under oath that she injected steroids into Slade. You should take it to the grand jury."

"You want me to have the grand jury investigate high school football players using steroids?"

"Yes."

"Judge, those boys' fathers *are* the grand jury."

The D.A. walked over to the window and gazed out. "Let it go, Judge. Approve the settlement, dismiss the case, and get on with your Heidi Geisel wild-goose chase. This one's over."

"Not until I dismiss the case, it isn't. And I haven't talked to Julio or his parents yet."

"I just talked to Delgado. They're on board." He now turned to Beck. "Look, Judge, I grew up here and I don't want to see this place destroyed. Quentin, he's here to rape and pillage. Once he sells out the homes around his golf course, he'll pull up stakes and move on to his next big deal. And Stutz, he's an old man mad at the world because the world's changing. But he's like that guy down in Waco—he'll set fire to his own home just to prove a point. He'll do it. He'll call ICE."

"And what if Slade hurts someone else?"

Homicidal rage. Beck could not shake the thought.

"He'll stay out of trouble for two months. He'll win state and go to Austin. He'll be out of our lives then."

"He committed a crime. And I'm the judge. I'm supposed to see that justice is done."

"Yeah, well, you can tell the Mexicans all about justice when they're boarding those ICE buses for the border." He shook his head. "Look, Judge, in case you don't know it, the shit has hit the fan!" The D.A. pointed at the newspaper. "Everyone's talking about that story—even in the barrio. The police chief called me first thing this morning. Said his cops drove through the barrio and the Mexicans threw rocks at their cruisers. That's never happened here. Said he's getting ready for a goddamn riot on Main Street—right in the middle of holiday shopping and hunting season. Mix the Mexicans with a bunch of drunk deer hunters named Bubba and we got blood on Main Street. Is that what you want, Judge? 'Cause that's what you're gonna get!"

Beck stood. "I want to see Slade."

★   ★   ★

284

Slade McQuade arrived at noon with his father and his lawyer. He was wearing black athletic shorts and a black Under Armour shirt that was so tight against his muscular upper body it looked like black skin. But he was not the cocky stud football player Beck had met that day at practice. He was subdued and repentant.

Bruno Stutz said, "Judge Hardin, this conversation is off the record. Nothing Slade says may be used against him, agreed?"

Beck nodded and they sat down. Slade said, "Judge, I apologized to Julio. I'm not like that."

"Except when you inject steroids?"

Stutz said, "I advise my client not to answer that question."

"We're off the record, Bruno."

"Still, Judge, you're asking him to confess to a crime."

"I want to know about steroids on the team."

"Well, he might be willing to discuss that . . . hypothetically."

"Hypothetically?"

"Yes. For the purposes of this discussion, we shall assume that steroids have or are being used . . ."

"I know what hypothetically means, Bruno. So, Slade, when you inject steroids do you often experience 'roid rage?"

Slade glanced at Stutz, then said, "Hypothetically, if I did use steroids, I would hypothetically experience 'roid rage. But if I did, and if that caused me to hurt someone, I would adjust the dosage, hypothetically speaking, of course."

Beck, Quentin McQuade, and Bruno Stutz were now staring at Slade. Stutz said, "Very good, Slade. You managed to use 'hypothetically' three times in two sentences."

Slade seemed pleased with himself. "Thanks."

Beck said, "Are other players using steroids?"

"Hypothetically, yes."

"And what are they using?"

"Hypothetically, Deca-D . . . Deca-Durabolin, Norbolethone, Winstrol, Dianabol, Andro, HgH."

"You sound like a pharmacist. What's HgH?"

Slade seemed amused now. "Where have you been the last twenty years, Judge?"

"In a law firm."

"Human growth hormone. Makes muscles tighter. Tighter muscles are faster muscles. The pros use it 'cause it's harder to detect. Hypothetically."

"Slade, steroids, human growth hormone—it's illegal."

"It's required. Judge, the NFL's minimum size for a quarterback today is six-three, two-twenty. I was one-ninety, now I'm two-thirty-five. Being a pro quarterback is my dream, and the stuff will help get me there. Just like it's helping lots of other players. I've met guys on college teams all over the country, and they all say the same thing—they get to school and first thing the coaches tell them is, 'You gotta bulk up.' They don't say 'You gotta go on steroids,' but everyone knows what 'bulking up' means. And how you do it. Why do you think they redshirt most freshmen? So they can adjust to college life, make good grades, meet new friends? They need that year to bulk up."

"And where do you get it from?"

"Gyms in Austin."

"Give me names."

Slade shrugged. "Look in the yellow pages, that's what I did."

"No. Names of the people selling the stuff."

He had amused Slade again. "Judge, you don't get names."

"So you just go to any gym in Austin and buy steroids?"

"The hard-core body-building places. We'd inject the stuff right in the locker room."

"It's that easy?"

"No, it hurts. I can't do that to myself, so I got the other guys to stick me, and then Nikki—"

"No. I mean buying it."

"Oh. Yeah, it's that easy. Heck, Judge, it's harder to get cold medicine these days. Dopers used it to make meth."

"You're doping."

"Steroids aren't dope, not like cocaine or heroin. I would never put that stuff in my body. I eat a low-fat, complex-carb, high-protein diet. Four percent body fat."

"You eat right, but you use steroids. It's cheating."

"It's competing. Judge, the game's changed. Bigger, stronger, faster. By any means necessary. That's the deal."

Beck sighed. He knew in his heart that the boy was right.

"Slade, you're endangering your long-term health for short-term success."

"Judge, I saw a deal on TV about supermodels. They smoke five packs of cigarettes a day to stay skinny. Why isn't that illegal? Cigarettes kill people. Steroids just make you bigger. But tobacco companies got lobbyists."

Quentin McQuade smiled and said, "That's my boy."

"Slade, steroids are dangerous."

"Not if they're used properly."

"But you have 'roid rages."

"Only at the peak of the pyramid. It levels out real fast."

"You could go bald."

"Why do you think so many athletes shave their heads?"

"Steroids can make you sterile."

"I don't want kids."

"You can become impotent, steroid dependent, your body won't produce its own testosterone."

He nodded. "That's why I take Clomid after every cycle."

"Clomid? What's that?"

"Fertility drug. Stimulates natural testosterone production. Keeps my body doing what it's supposed to do."

"You have an answer for everything, don't you, Slade? Then answer this: What if you hurt someone else?"

"It'll never happen again, Judge. I swear."

"If it does, Slade, your dad won't be able to buy your way out. You'll go to prison. You understand that?"

"Yes, sir."

"Nikki said you suffered depression. Is that true?"

287

"Sometimes. When I'm off the stuff. But when I'm on it, I love the way it makes me feel."

"How does it make you feel?"

"Better than sex."

Beck looked at Quentin McQuade and turned his palms up. Quentin just shrugged. "Hell, Judge, makes me want to juice."

Beck turned back to Slade. "When you're depressed, have you ever thought about suicide?"

"*Suicide?* With my future? No way." Slade smiled; it was the bright smile of a future NFL star quarterback. "Judge, I like me way too much to hurt myself."

"Slade, if I agree to this settlement, will you promise to stop using steroids?"

Stutz said, "Yes, Judge, he promises."

"I asked Slade."

Slade looked at his lawyer and then at his father; both were trying to nod a yes out of him. Slade turned back to Beck.

"No, Judge, I won't make that promise because I won't keep it."

Quentin McQuade exhaled loudly and threw his hands up. "Good thing the boy can play football because he'd never make it in the business world. If I've told him once, I've told him a thousand times: a successful businessman has got to be able to look a man directly in the eye and lie convincingly."

Beck needed a coffee, so he was walking to the bookstore. He hadn't made it one block down Main Street when he was stopped by a business owner wielding the newspaper.

"Judge Hardin, I've heard the Mexicans are planning marches and street protests—on Thanksgiving weekend!"

"I'm working on it," he said. He kept walking, but the owner shouted after him.

"When they marched in Houston over that immigration law, they shut down the businesses! That's not supposed to happen here!"

288

He got halfway down the block before he was again stopped.

"Judge Hardin, Main Street voted for you. We wanted change, but we don't want our businesses destroyed. The old Germans, they wouldn't let this happen. They know how to keep order!"

"You want order or civil rights?"

"I want to make a living!"

He kept walking; the key was to not slow down. Two more blocks and four more business owners later, Beck turned down the stone path leading to the bookstore. At least this would be a friendly business owner.

"I can't believe you would do such a thing!"

Jodie jumped him before the door had shut behind him. She pulled him back outside—

"Can I get my coffee first?"

"No!"

—and over to their bench.

"What thing?"

"Let Quentin McQuade buy you off."

"Jodie, McQuade isn't buying me off. He's—"

"Buying Slade off."

"No. He's—"

"What? What is Quentin doing?"

"He's *trying* to buy Slade off."

"So you haven't agreed to it?"

"No."

"And you're not going to agree to it?"

"I didn't say that."

"Beck!"

"Jodie, you need to know all the facts first."

She folded her arms. Her face was flushed almost as red as her hair. By the time Beck had finished laying out the case, her hands were in her lap and her face was pale.

"A raid at the turkey plant? Can you stop it?"

"They're federal, Jodie. They don't answer to a state court judge."

289

"Beck, you can't let that happen."

"What if Slade hurts someone else?"

"What are you going to do?"

Beck checked his watch: 4:30.

"School's out. I'm going to talk to Julio."

"When will they unwire your jaws?" the judge asked.

Julio Espinoza held up four fingers.

"Four more weeks?"

Julio nodded. They were in the living room. Julio was sitting in the chair, a soccer ball in his lap; Judge Hardin sat on the couch next to Julio's *madre*, who was cradling the baby. His mother's black hair was wet. She always bathed immediately upon coming home from the turkey plant. She wanted to get the smell of turkeys off her as quickly as possible. Maria Espinoza was thirty-six years old, but sitting there in her thick pink bathrobe with her face scrubbed clean, she appeared almost like a girl. She was singing a quiet Mexican lullaby to Juan.

Rosita, the two-year-old, had climbed onto the judge's lap, but he seemed unconcerned that she might throw up on his nice suit. The judge now looked around at Julio's small home— the sparse furnishings; the few toys; the bare walls except for the framed image of the Virgin Mary and the crucifix; Margarita, the four-year-old, and Gilberto, the six-year-old, sitting cross-legged in front of the little television and watching *Sesame Street*; Jorge, the ten-year-old, picking his nose—and Julio saw in the judge's eyes the pity of Anglos.

Julio pulled out his small notebook and pen and wrote: *I do not want your pity, Judge. I want McQuade's money. I want my mother and my father out of the turkey plant and out of the barrio. I want to go to college. I want to be visible.*

He tore out the page and handed it to Judge Hardin. The judge read it. "Visible." He turned to Julio's mother and asked, "Mrs. Espinoza, do you and Mr. Espinoza want the settlement?"

290

Julio's mother stopped singing and first looked to the judge and then to Julio. She spoke to Julio in Spanish.

He wrote: *Mi madre, she is embarrassed to speak to you, the judge. Her English is not good. But she wants what I want.*

The judge read the note and said, "Julio, Slade hurt you badly. He should be punished."

Julio wrote: *My jaw will heal. Slade in jail will not give my family a better life. His father's money will. That is what I want.*

He tore the page out and handed it to the judge then again he wrote: *Señor Delgado said they have threatened a raid if I do not make this settlement. My parents are fearful. Everyone in the barrio is afraid. If there is a raid, we will be punished, not Slade. Do not let that happen.*

The judge read the note then pointed at the soccer ball. "You play?"

Julio nodded.

The judge said, "Have you ever been tested for steroids?"

Julio laughed then wrote: *Yes, 5 times last year, twice so far this year. Only Latino soccer players are tested.*

Julio was embarrassed each time the coach came to his class and pointed at him and he had to walk out past the Anglos while the hulking football jocks laughed because they knew they would never be tested.

The judge read the note and sighed. "Eight people live here? Where does everyone . . ."

Julio wrote: *Sleep?* He tore out that page and handed it to the judge, who read it and nodded. He wrote again: *My father works nights at the turkey plant and sleeps during the day. My mother works days at the plant, so she sleeps in the bedroom with the niños. The others sleep in here.*

"And where do you sleep?"

Julio stood and motioned for the judge to follow. They walked out of the living room, through the kitchen, and then into the small bathroom. Julio pointed at the bathtub.

"You sleep in the bathtub?"

"Es."

When they returned to the living room, Julio's mother was breast-feeding Juan; his eyes were closed and his mouth was tight around the nipple of her plump brown breast. The judge turned away. "Julio, let's go outside."

They stepped outside and into the small yard. There was no driveway, so Beck had parked the Navigator on the grass not ten feet from the front door of Julio's tiny house.

"Let's take a walk."

They walked down the narrow asphalt street past small houses, nothing more than shacks, sheds, and shanties. Several houses were clustered on lots intended for a single residence. Some weren't even houses in the structural sense. Some had once been on wheels, others tilted at precarious angles, and still others were actually travel trailers with wheels sunken into the ground, as if relatives had come to visit and refused to leave. Some were small outbuildings or one-car garages that had been converted into residences of a kind. Some were brightly painted, most were dull and unpainted. One had a full Nativity scene out front; Mary, Joseph, and Baby Jesus were fake, but the goats, turkeys, and chickens were real. In the yards young children were playing and speaking in Spanish. A girl who appeared no older than Julio stood watch; she was very pregnant. She waved at Julio.

"Are the children citizens?"

Julio wrote on his pad and handed a note to Beck: *Yes. Born in the USA. Isabel, she is 15 and Mexican. The young girls, they want to have the babies as soon as they get here. They think the government will let them stay if they have American babies.*

"Do most people rent these homes?"

Julio wrote again: *Most own. The law says they cannot work here, but they can own homes here. Who makes these laws?*

Beck nodded. "Doesn't make much sense."

Julio wrote: *The trailers are rented. Maybe 15 men live in each one. They work in the plant, send their money home to Mexico.*

292

"How can fifteen men live in each trailer?"

Julio wrote: *The trailers, they are just for the sleeping. Each man pays $400 per month for a pad on the floor. To the Anglo landlord. He owns many such trailers in the barrio.*

"Four hundred each? That's six thousand a month. They could rent the fanciest house in town for that."

Julio wrote: *No, they could not. The city would not allow 15 men to live in one home north of the creek, but looks the other way here, so there are workers for the plant.*

Old cars were parked in the yards or jacked up on cement blocks. Chickens and goats were in pens like backyard pets; a Hereford bull grazed in one yard. Junk was piled everywhere. Neat rows of tall green cornstalks grew in one vacant lot, agave plants in another. Julio wrote: *Pedro makes homemade tequila, from the agave.*

Appliances sat on porches, and furniture—couches, recliners, rocking chairs—sat in small yards, arranged as if they were in a family room but the walls had blown away. Clothes hung from lines and blew in the breeze. The people here lived outside, except apparently when they watched TV: many houses had a satellite dish attached to the roof.

They were only five blocks south of the glitz and glamour of Main Street, but they were no longer in Fredericksburg. They were in Mexico. Beck's senior class trip had been to Nuevo Laredo. He had seen the same living conditions there. Looking around now, it was as if an entire neighborhood from Nuevo Laredo had been set down whole in the middle of Fredericksburg: Mexicans living in the same third-world conditions, albeit with more TV channels.

They walked the streets of the barrio: Buena Vista, Santa Rosa, St. Mary's, St. Gerelda. Just down the road stood the turkey plant, a gray windowless building with white steam rising into the blue sky above it and a tall chain-link fence with barbed wire on top surrounding it. The plant looked like a prison.

Julio pointed at a trailer. And he wrote: *At that trailer, you*

293

may obtain the fake ID cards, social security numbers, driver's licenses, so you can work at the plant.

"It's done out in the open?"

Julio wrote: *Sure. The plant managers, they send new workers to that trailer, so they can tell the government that they did not know they were hiring illegals. It is a game.*

The new Milam Road extension provided a shortcut around downtown and cut right through the barrio, like the interstates in urban areas always cut through the poorest parts of town. Milam was a wide roadway with the only curbs and gutters in the barrio.

Julio wrote: *When it rains, the water runs to the creek, but not fast enough. The houses and trailers are often flooded.*

Beck had never been in the barrio. He wasn't sure there had even been a barrio twenty-four years ago. But maybe they had always been here, these people who lived and worked just a few blocks from Main Street but don't come onto Main Street or eat at the restaurants on Main Street or shop in the stores on Main Street. Walking down Main Street, you would never know this place or these people existed. Julio was right: they were invisible.

And the boy sleeps in a bathtub.

"Two million to the Mexican boy," Quentin McQuade said. "And curbs, gutters, and paved roads for the barrio? What do I look like, the public works department? Curbs and gutters don't come cheap, Judge. You're talking two, three million. I offered one million, you counter with five. That's not fair negotiation."

"Like you said, Quentin, life's not fair."

Quentin shook his head and chuckled. "And for that Slade's case is dismissed?"

"Yes. And ICE stays out of our town."

Quentin smiled. "You've got a lot of hard-ass in you, Judge. I like that. When the Germans vote you out of office next year, maybe you'll come work for me."

"Maybe not. Besides, you've already got the biggest hard-ass in the county working for you."

"Yeah, but Bruno's got the loyalty of a pit bull. He'll turn on me if it suits his purposes."

"How do you know I wouldn't?"

"Because you're one of those rare creatures, Judge—an honorable man burdened with the need to do the right thing. My secrets would be safe with you."

"Do we have a deal?"

Quentin McQuade stood, looked Beck directly in the eye, and said, "Yep, we sure do."

Quentin stuck his hand across Beck's desk. Beck started to reach out, but hesitated. He felt as if he were making a deal with the devil. Maybe he was. But that's what lawyers do. He just wasn't sure a judge should. They shook on it.

Quentin said, "Oh, I'll need that tape recording, Judge, from the examining trial. Can't have that played on national TV."

Chapter 24

The time bomb was defused on Monday morning.

Julio Espinoza signed a settlement agreement that included a release of all claims against Slade McQuade and a confidentiality clause. Quentin McQuade wired $2 million to Julio's new account at Chase Bank and signed an agreement to construct roads, curbs, and gutters in the barrio. Judge John Beck Hardin signed an order dismissing all criminal charges against Slade McQuade and turned over the only copy of the tape recording from the examining trial to Quentin McQuade. Everyone was happy: the victim and his parents, the offender and his father, the D.A. and the Germans, Main Street and the Latinos. Everyone except the judge.

"Hi, Judge Hardin."

Beck nodded at the woman. Julio's parents could now afford a few acres and a nice house. Julio and his siblings would go to college. Main Street would have a booming holiday shopping season. The old Germans would get their state championship and their money from building homes on Quentin's golf course. The Mexicans would not be deported; the barrio would not flood again.

"Judge."

Beck nodded at the man. But had he done the right thing? Had he misused the law? Had he abused his power? Was the black robe the only difference between Quentin McQuade and Beck Hardin?

"You did a good thing, Beck," Jodie said.

Beck was running on the treadmill next to Jodie at the gym. "Hi, Beck."

Gretchen was suddenly standing between Beck and Jodie and casting those blue eyes up toward him.

"You sure you should be seen talking to me?"

"Oh, you're safe . . . for now. No telling about tomorrow in this town."

"How are y'all doing without Ms. Rodriguez?"

"No one's speaking Spanish at the primary school. But I'm still fighting for my kids." She shook it off, then smiled at him. "So, Beck, how about that dinner, Saturday night?" Gretchen leaned in close to Beck—and Jodie leaned over so far he thought she might fall off her treadmill—and whispered, "I still have needs."

Jodie cleared her throat loudly enough to get the attention of a walker three treadmills away. Beck looked at her over Gretchen's head. She was giving him the look. He sighed.

"Gretchen, I'm too old for you."

She looked him up and down. "You're in pretty good shape for an old guy."

"Oh, thanks. I've been working out again and . . ."

Another loud throat-clearing from Jodie. He looked at her and then at Gretchen. He sighed.

"But I'm still too old for you."

Gretchen shook her head. "Call me if you change your mind."

She walked off. That butterfly. That bottom.

Jodie cleared her throat again. He turned to her. Again the look. "You're staring at her butt."

297

"I was just thinking of her . . . needs."

"Yeah."

She increased the speed on her treadmill.

J.B. said, "Took Luke fishing down at the river after school."

"He wouldn't go with me."

"I'm safe. He knows I didn't kill his mama. He figured you could save her. You were his hero and that's what heroes do. His mother dying for no better reason than she had the bad luck to get cancer, that's a hard thing for a boy to get his mind around."

Beck nodded. "Did he talk?"

"Yep."

"About what?"

"Matters of the heart. His heart's broken, Beck."

"I don't know what to do for him."

"He needs a woman in his life."

"He's too young to date, J.B."

"I'm thinking Jodie."

"You want him to date a lesbian?"

"She's a woman, she's smart, and she's a mother. Figure maybe he should spend a little time at the bookstore, seeing how this is the slow season down at the winery."

"You think Jodie would be up for that?"

"She said yes."

Beck scanned through Annie's emails over the summer months when she had had a chemo treatment every three weeks and then six weeks of radiation, every day. He found an email from September:

Dear J.B.,

I'm still fighting. Trying another kind of chemo. My bones hurt. And I'm gaining weight. I can't eat but I gain weight because I'm on steroids for the nausea now. How stupid is that? This is the dumbest disease I've ever had. And the only disease I've ever had.

The kids are back in school, Beck goes to work, and only my hard-core friends come around now. The others, it's like when they look at me, it scares them.

And one from October:

J.B., they can't stop this shit! It's pissing me off!

Sorry. I scream and curse now, when I'm alone. I've been reading about treatments in Mexico. Coffee enemas. (Never thought about doing that with my espresso!)

Beck can't raise my children. He doesn't have a clue.

Chapter 25

By the next morning, Beck had put the Slade McQuade case out of his mind. The papers had been signed, the money paid, the case closed. Justice had been done for Julio Espinoza, or as close to justice as the law can come. Heidi Fay Geisel now occupied his thoughts. There were only seventy-six days to find her justice.

She haunted him now.

Maybe because of the debt he owed her father . . . maybe because of his fear that his own daughter might die in a ditch . . . or maybe because there had been no justice in life for his mother or his wife. Whatever the reason, Heidi Fay Geisel was part of his life now.

So Beck was driving to Austin to see Randi Barnes. He drove down a Main Street still vacant at eight-thirty and accelerated to fifty-five when Main became Highway 290 East and crossed over Baron's Creek—but he abruptly braked and pulled over onto the grass shoulder at the city limits sign. Aubrey had already been out with fresh flowers for the white cross.

Beck got out.

He walked down into the low ditch where Heidi's body had

been found. He squatted and ran his hand over the grass. Four years, nine months, and sixteen days ago, a girl had died here. But the grass beneath her body had not. The grass had continued to grow, the sun to rise and set, the world to turn. Life had gone on without her. Just as life had gone on without Annie. But he knew how Annie's life had ended. How had Heidi's life ended?

Beck ran through the likely scenario of that night again: Kim and Heidi go to the Brewery. (Grady had interviewed the wait staff, but no one recalled seeing them.) Kim leaves and Heidi has an encounter with the first guy, then she meets the second guy, maybe a college kid from Austin here for a New Year's Eve party. They drink, snort cocaine, and have sex in his car. She passes out. He tries to wake her, but discovers that she's dead. He panics. He wants out of town fast, so he drives out 290 toward Austin. He's got a dead girl in his car, and he wants her out. It's late and raining hard now. When he comes to the first desolate stretch of highway, he pulls over. He runs around to her side. He checks for traffic, then pulls her from the car. He rolls her down into the ditch. Then he jumps back into his car.

Beck got back into the Navigator, started the engine, and drove east again.

Just as the guy had that night, trying to think clearly: Could the cops tie her to him? Would anyone at the Brewery remember seeing him with her? It was crowded, and he had paid with cash, so they couldn't trace him through his credit card. No, they would never connect her to him. He's home free. He smiles and reaches over to turn up the radio and . . . he sees her purse and shoes there on the floorboard. Evidence that puts her in his car and him in prison—that connects her to him.

He panics again.

Seventy miles lay between him and Austin; state troopers are out patrolling for drunk drivers on New Year's Eve. What if he's stopped? They'll give him a breathalyzer; he'll fail miserably.

301

They'll arrest him and search his car. They'll find her purse and shoes. They'll find her. He'll be charged with her murder. He pulls over again.

Beck pulled over again.

Directly in front of him was the bridge over the Pedernales River, two miles east of the ditch where Heidi had been found and Baron's Creek, where Grady's men had searched and found nothing—because there was nothing to find. The guy hadn't thrown Heidi's shoes and purse into Baron's Creek; he had thrown them into the Pedernales River. He was an outsider, so he wouldn't have known about the drought. It was raining, so he probably assumed the river ran deep and the current strong. But in a drought, it would have taken more than one rainy night to fill the Pedernales.

Beck cut the engine and got out. He walked down to the embankment. Except for a sliver of water flowing twenty feet below the bridge and down the center of the riverbed, both bed and bank were dry and rock hard, baked like a desert by the drought.

He was now glad he had opted for jeans and boots instead of a suit and tie. The bank was steep, and he slipped and fell twice as he worked his way down to the riverbed. He slapped the dirt off his jeans and got his bearings with the bridge; he figured how far the guy might have thrown a purse and shoes. He walked south to that point and turned around. He slowly walked back toward the bridge down the west bank, searching.

He found nothing.

He repeated the search on the east side. Nothing. He walked under the bridge to the north side. The purse and shoes might have been carried downriver; the river must have run stronger at some time since that night. He followed the river on the west bank two hundred yards. Nothing. He crossed the narrow river and worked his way back toward the bridge on the east bank. He stopped.

Lodged in a clump of debris was a black shoe.

He cleared the debris away. It was a high-heeled shoe. Black leather. Dirty. He used his pen to pick the shoe up. He carried the shoe out in front of him like he had carried Meggie's wet clothes to the washer that morning. He arrived at the bridge and climbed up the bank. He placed the shoe on the hood of the car and found a plastic trash bag in the console. He put the shoe into the trash bag and tightened the draw string. He got back into the car and put the bag on the passenger's seat. He started the engine and pulled onto the highway heading east toward Austin. He glanced at the trash bag. Was that Heidi's shoe?

The pink granite state capitol at Congress Avenue and 11th Street marks the northern boundary of downtown Austin. Ten blocks due south, the Colorado River forms the southern boundary; in town, the river is called Lake Austin. Seven blocks to the east, Interstate 35 runs north-south through town. People without money live east of the interstate; people with money live west. People with a lot of money live on large lots fronting Lake Austin.

Randi Barnes lived on one such waterfront lot on Lakeshore Drive. Was she the former Randi Barnes Geisel? Beck turned into the circular driveway. He parked behind a late-model silver Mercedes-Benz coupe under a porte-cochere. He got out with the black trash bag. It was eleven A.M. His appointment with the Travis County medical examiner wasn't until one, so he had decided to try Randi first. He had not called ahead. He wasn't sure why.

The house was a Mediterranean-style villa with a white stucco exterior, a red-tiled roof, and palm trees and lush tropical plants lining both sides of the slate walkway to the front door. Beck rang the bell. The door opened on a short middle-aged Hispanic woman dressed in a black uniform and a white apron.

"Hi. Is Randi home?"

"Señora, she is still in bed. Maybe you come back later?"

She started to shut the door, but Beck said, "Would you tell her Beck Hardin is here?"

"Señora does not like to be wakened."

From inside, a familiar voice: "Who is it, Lupe?"

Lupe pushed the door almost shut, but Beck heard her say, "Beck Hardin."

The door suddenly swung wide. Standing there on a white marble floor in a thick white bathrobe was Randi Barnes—the same Randi Barnes, although she had aged since Beck had last seen her. But it was obvious where Heidi had gotten her looks; Randi had her daughter's blonde hair and blue eyes, but the wear of forty years showed on her face. She had put on some weight, but she appeared as solid as the goat rancher's daughter she had been twenty-four years before. She had always created quite a stir at the goat auction. She held her arms out to him. "Beck!"

He stepped into her arms, and they hugged.

"Come on in." She looked down at the black bag. "Trash?"

Lupe closed the door behind them, and they walked into an expansive sun-drenched living room with white walls, a white vaulted ceiling, and white furniture. A bank of windows looked out onto a pool shimmering in the morning light and the blue water of Lake Austin beyond. Randi led him to a fluffy couch by the windows. They sat at opposite ends.

"It's been a long time, Beck."

"Twenty-four years."

"You visiting or staying?"

"Staying. In Fredericksburg."

"Thought you were never coming back?"

"My wife died."

"Oh, Beck, I'm sorry."

"I've got two kids, five and ten. I needed help."

"From J.B.? Is he still alive?"

Beck nodded. "He's changed."

"You and him talking again?"

304

"He wouldn't talk back then, now he won't stop."

"That's good. How's Aubrey?"

"Not so good."

"I haven't seen him since the divorce, but I still check the paper to see if he won. Not sure why."

"They're favored to win state."

Randi picked up a pack of cigarettes, pulled one out, tapped it against the back of her hand several times, then lit it. She took a long drag, exhaled a cloud of smoke, and said, "I guess you're here about Heidi?"

Beck nodded. "Aubrey asked me to look into it."

"Paying off an old debt?"

"Maybe. I'm the judge now."

She smiled. "Did Stutz finally die?"

"Unfortunately, no. He found a better-paying job."

"He needs to find dirt six feet down. How'd you get elected out there?"

"By default."

She gestured at Beck's jeans. "Speaking of dirt . . ."

Beck had carried the dirt from the river onto Randi's white sofa. He jumped up and dusted the dirt off the sofa. Randi said, "Don't worry about it, Beck. You been playing in the dirt?"

"The river. Where I found this."

Beck placed the trash bag on the couch and opened the top to expose the shoe. "Randi, is this Heidi's shoe?"

"*What?*"

Randi leaned over and held her hand out as if to touch it. Beck said, "Don't. Might have fingerprints."

Randi examined the shoe closely. "Where'd you find it?"

"The river, where it crosses 290. Her shoes were never recovered, so I figured the guy might've tossed them. River seemed like a good place."

"And it was still there?"

"Downstream about a hundred yards. Is it hers?"

"I think so."

Randi stood and walked to the windows. She was quiet for a while. Then she said, "She was so beautiful, Beck." She turned back to him. "Did Aubrey show you her pictures, at the house?"

Beck nodded. "Yeah."

"She could've been a star, Beck."

"Then how did she end up in that ditch?"

Randi stepped over to a potted plant and stuck the cigarette butt into the soil. She motioned for Beck to follow. He stood and followed her up a marble spiral staircase with a wrought-iron railing and into an all-white bedroom. The walls were covered with glamour shots of Heidi: Heidi's face; Heidi bent over to show off her cleavage; Heidi looking twenty-five and sexy; Heidi the sexpot; Heidi the semi-nude Playmate wanna-be.

"Kim showed me her portfolio."

Randi didn't flinch. "I took those. She had a perfect body. She could've been Playmate of the Year."

"You wanted her to pose in *Playboy*?"

"Don't look so shocked, Beck. It's a straight shot to Hollywood. We were going together." Her eyes glistened. She turned away and went over and sat on the bed. "I died with her."

Randi put her face in her hands and sobbed. Beck wasn't sure what he should do, so he went to her and sat beside her. He put his arm around her shoulders, and she leaned into him.

Randi and Aubrey had double-dated with Beck and Mary Jo. But Randi had always touched Beck or brushed against him or looked at him in a way that had made him uncomfortable. She now turned her face up to him and looked at him that way. Then she stood before him and dropped her robe. She was naked. She sat on his lap and kissed him hard. He smelled her perfume and tasted her last cigarette. She leaned into him, and they fell back onto the bed. He rolled her off him and got off the bed.

"Randi, I can't."

"Can't or won't?"

"Either way. I'll be downstairs."

Beck walked out and went downstairs and out onto the covered patio fronting the pool. Beck stood at the edge of the patio and inhaled the cool breeze off the lake. Rowing teams were gliding downstream out in the center and several small sailboats tacked in the distance, their white sails capturing the wind and the sun.

"I'm sorry, Beck."

Randi was now wearing a tee shirt and jeans.

"Heidi never called you that night?"

"No. I figured she was at Kim's."

"Why didn't you call to check?"

She sighed. "It was New Year's Eve, Beck. I was drinking and fell asleep on the couch. Didn't wake up until the call."

"Your statement said she was wearing jeans. But she was found wearing a skirt."

"She changed."

"You knew?"

"I figured. I did the same thing when I was her age. So did Mary Jo, remember?"

Beck nodded. "Aubrey wants to find this guy."

"He needs to find a life."

"He wants you back."

"I'm never going back there."

"He'll come here."

She laughed. "Aubrey in Austin? I don't think so."

Beck had seen no sign of a man of the house, so he went fishing. "What are you doing these days?"

But his real question was, *How can you afford this place?*

Randi didn't answer.

The Travis County Forensic Center is located at 12th and Sabine a few blocks east of the capitol; the three-story white limestone building abuts the interstate that divides Austin into crime-free and crime-ridden.

"Closer to our customer base," Travis County Deputy Medical Examiner Dr. Leonard Janofsky said, apparently a morgue joke. He was a board certified forensic pathologist, and he was wearing Longhorn burnt orange scrubs and New Balance sneakers. His hair was gray, and he had the gaunt look of a runner. "Never had a judge come in. Must do things differently in the country."

Beck said, "It's different all right."

"You ever find the guy?"

"Not yet."

"How long you got?"

"Seventy-six days."

"That's right. New Year's Eve. Well, we preserved tissue and blood from the victim in case you do."

"Why?"

"DNA testing gets more sophisticated every year. We've solved a lot of cold cases with old DNA and new tests."

"Tell me about Heidi."

They were in the deputy ME's office. Beck was sitting in the visitor's chair, Dr. Janofsky behind his desk. He was looking at his autopsy report. "Let's see, the body arrived on January 1, 2003, at 1:17 P.M., and was positively identified by Aubrey Geisel, father of the deceased, and Randi Geisel, mother of the deceased."

Beck had seen his wife's dead body, but he couldn't imagine walking into a morgue to identify his daughter's body.

"External examination . . . Deceased is clothed in a white blouse, black skirt, black undergarment. Hands and feet are bagged. Jewelry . . . silver loop earrings, ankle bracelet. Body is that of a normally developed female. Height, 68 inches. Weight, 110 pounds. No wounds, scratches, or bruising evident. No defensive marks on her hands. Genitalia . . . no evidence of bruising or injury. Pubic hair has been shaved."

"Did you find any pubic hairs from the guy?"

"No. I found a few threads, cotton, from a towel. She wiped herself or he wiped her."

"Was he trying to remove evidence?"

"Why bother? He left a lot of himself inside her." Back to the report. "Internal examination . . . No injury to any organ. No perforation of the nasal septum."

Beck said, "What does that mean?"

"It means she wasn't a user, or at least not a regular user. She had no damage to her nasal passages, which is a sign of repetitive cocaine insufflating."

"Insufflating?"

"Snorting. It might've been her first time."

"Why do you say that?"

"Cocaine particles were evident in and around her nostrils and on her breasts and on the inside of the blouse."

"Which means?"

"She sneezed. Regulars don't sneeze when they snort cocaine. Wasteful. But no dirt particles were found in her nasal passages."

"And that means?"

"She didn't inhale dirt. She was dead before she was dumped into the ditch."

"Could she have walked to where she was found?"

"No dirt on her feet. No shoes arrived with the body."

"Cause of death?"

"Cardiovascular failure caused by acute cocaine intoxication. Her heart stopped. She insufflated a significant amount of cocaine, enough to cause sudden death."

"How do you determine that?"

"We analyze the liver. See, the liver's function is to clear the body of toxins, so it tells us what was in the body just prior to death. We found very high levels of benzoylecgonine."

"Which is?"

"Which is what cocaine breaks down into once it enters the liver."

"So if the level of this benzo . . . stuff is high, that means she had snorted a lot of cocaine?"

"Exactly. The liver was trying to clear it when she died."

"How does that work, a person dying from cocaine?"

"When a human being snorts cocaine, the onset of the effects occurs within five minutes and peaks at about thirty minutes. The cocaine acts to block the catecholamine reuptake and that causes sympathomimetic syndrome. So the central nervous system and cardiovascular systems become highly agitated. Tachycardia. A heart attack. And investigators found diet pills in her room. Stimulants. Would have exacerbated the effect."

"Did she suffer?"

The doctor shook his head. "There's a very rapid progression from inhalation to death. She passed out before she suffered respiratory arrest. She just went to sleep."

"When?"

"Time of death was between ten and midnight."

"And your official opinion as to manner of death?"

"Accidental overdose."

Beck blew out a breath. "Damn."

"I see these cases all the time," the doctor said. "Cocaine, heroin, now methamphetamines."

"Anything else?"

Dr. Janofsky looked over his report. "Samples thought to be semen taken from her blouse and hair. Genital system showed evidence of recent sexual intercourse. Vaginal fluid samples were saved for analysis. Evidence of prior D&C and—"

"D&C?"

"Dilation and curettage."

"What's that?"

"She had an abortion."

In Fredericksburg, Texas, you can buy guns and rifles of every kind and caliber, but you can't buy an iced caramel macchiato at a Starbucks.

You can buy hand-embroidered Levi's 501 jeans for $300, an authentic handcrafted Zuni turquoise-and-silver Squash Blossom necklace for $5,000, a hand-carved life-sized statue

310

of the Virgin Mary and Baby Jesus for $14,129, a handmade mesquite pool table with a burnt orange UT Longhorn playing surface for $22,000, and twenty-five homes for over $1 million, but you can't buy a foreign-made automobile for any price.

You can find twenty-eight churches—Southern Baptist, Bible, Catholic, Charismatic, Church of Christ, Mormon, Evangelical, Lutheran, Methodist, Pentecostal, Presbyterian, Seventh-Day Adventist, and even a New Wine Church—but you can't find a synagogue.

You can get a horse shoed, a cow serviced, and a deer processed into sausage and its head mounted on your wall, but you can't get your body pierced or tattooed.

You can get microdermabrasion, botox, spider vein reduction, liposuction, a facelift, and breast implants, but you can't get an abortion. You have to go to Austin for that. Which is what Heidi Fay Geisel had done when she was sixteen.

"Her mom took her," Kim said. "She said she wasn't going to let Heidi ruin her life like she ruined hers."

Kim was sitting behind the desk at the gas station writing out checks to pay the monthly bills. She forged her father's signature, with his permission.

"After that, she went on the pill. Her mom took her to Austin to get them. Doctors here, they won't give you the pill until you're eighteen. Praise the Lord and keep our girls virgins."

"Was Heidi promiscuous?"

Kim looked up from the checkbook and laughed. "*Promiscuous?* How old are you?"

"Is that a yes?"

"We had sex . . . not with each other, with guys."

"A lot?"

She shrugged. "Hooking up, it's no big deal."

"Since when?"

"Since we've been alive."

"Did you and Heidi practice safe sex?"

311

"Guys hate wearing rubbers."

"Haven't you heard of AIDS?"

She shook her head as if to say again, *God, you are so old.*

"So who was the father of her baby?"

"I don't know."

He looked at her and she looked away. She was lying again.

"Your statement said she was wearing jeans and sneakers. But she was found wearing a skirt."

"She probably changed."

"Did she do that often?"

"All the time. Coach wouldn't let her out of the house in what she really wore out."

"Did she wear this shoe?"

Beck pulled out the shoe, but Kim couldn't identify it. She said, "Maybe it'll be in one of her videos."

"What videos?"

"Her audition videos."

She reached down below the desk and came back up with her laptop. She opened the top and tapped several times and Heidi's face filled the screen over the words "Heidi Fay."

Kim said, "This is her music video."

Heidi was singing, and not that badly. Her voice was sharp and the music had a throbbing beat. She was wearing a bustier and miniskirt; she was thrusting her hips as if simulating sex. The video was intercut with other images of a sexy Heidi. It looked professional, except—

"You caught yourself in the mirror."

For a brief moment, a face had been visible in the mirror on the wall behind Heidi.

"You wanna see her striptease act?"

"No." Beck pointed at the screen. "She's wearing high heels."

When the heels were in view, Kim froze the frame. They looked just like the shoe in the trash bag.

"Kim, you're pretty good with computers, making videos. You ever thought about working at that?"

312

"They've got some courses over at the community college."

"Might be a job in Austin for someone with those skills."

"You think?"

Beck drove back down Main Street and caught the red light at Crockett Street. A female jogger ran past on the sidewalk in front of city hall. Her legs were muscular and her bottom firm. Lately his mind kept switching back and forth between thoughts of law and sex like he was channel surfing, and he felt guilty every time: how does a man remain faithful to his dead wife? When the light changed, he accelerated and glanced her way— *Jesus, it was Jodie.* She saw him and waved; he waved back.

He shook his head: *looking like that at a lesbian.*

Beck parked behind the courthouse and took the trash bag with the shoe into the Law Enforcement Center. It was after hours now; Grady was gone, but a deputy was on duty. Beck wrote a note to Grady. The deputy signed for the shoe. Beck then walked over to the courthouse. He found the cleaning lady in his chambers.

"I come back," she said. "Is okay, I am here all night."

"No, no, Carlotta, go ahead."

Carlotta was Hispanic and middle-aged. Beck sat in his chair, removed Heidi's case file from a drawer, and placed it on his desk. He opened the file and wrote his notes of that day. He stared at the crime scene photos of her body lying in the ditch.

"*Muy bonita.*"

Beck looked up. Carlotta was pointing at the photos.

"The *señorita* from the ditch. She was very pretty."

"You remember her?"

"*Sí.* The old judge, he was *muy enojado.* Mad. He say a Mexican killed her. But I don't think so."

"Why not?"

"Because of the long black car."

Beck sat up. "What long black car?"

"In the street. I was cleaning this office that night, it was very

313

late. Outside, there was the rain, and much lightning. A long black car, it stopped in the street, right there."

She pointed out the window. Beck stood and went to the window that faced north. Main Street was not more than thirty yards from where they were now standing.

"The driver, a big *hombre* with the bald head, he ran to the back and climbed in. But the door, it was still open. The light inside and the Christmas lights and the lightning, I see him."

"See him what?"

"Like on the TV. Kneeling and pushing."

"Pushing?"

"*Sí.*"

She held her hands together and moved them up and down as if she were bouncing a ball.

"Kneeling over someone and pushing . . . He was doing CPR!"

"Then he got out and ran to the front. He turned the long car right there, he make the, uh . . . what you say?"

"U-turn?"

"*Sí.* Then the car drove that way."

She was pointing east. Toward Austin.

"Do you remember what time it was?"

"*Sí*, the clock. *Uno.*"

"One A.M.?"

"*Sí.*"

"Why didn't you tell anyone about this back then?"

"I am illegal. The old judge, he would deport me."

"Why are you telling me now?"

"Because you are not like the old judge. You do not hate the Mexicans. You are the good judge."

Chapter 26

The black limo Carlotta had seen that night had made a U-turn on Main Street and headed east toward Austin. So a week later, Beck was again driving to Austin. There were no limousines to be had in Fredericksburg, Texas.

An hour later he exited Highway 290 and turned north on South Congress Avenue. South Congress, or SoCo, as the residents called this stretch of Austin's main avenue, is south of Town Lake, downtown, and the capitol; it's also the last holdout for the way Austin used to be. SoCo's motto is emblazoned in neon on the Austin Motel sign: *Keep Austin Weird.*

Limos To Go was tucked between two tattoo shops on South Congress. It was a renovated gas station with tall palm trees where the gas pumps had been; two black limos were parked out front. Beck parked next to the limos, went inside, and introduced himself to the receptionist. A short stocky middle-aged man soon appeared; either his cologne was Pennzoil 30-weight or he had spilled motor oil on himself. He said, "You're a judge?"

Beck had again skipped the suit in favor of jeans and boots. "Beck Hardin."

"Shorty. What can I do for you?"

Beck said, "On New Year's Day, 2003, a sixteen-year-old girl was found dead on the side of Highway 290 just outside Fredericksburg. She died of a cocaine overdose."

Shorty shook his head. "Dope is the devil."

"It's a cold case. All we have is the suspect's DNA."

"Like on those *CSI* shows."

"Exactly. We're trying to find this guy before the statute of limitations runs out."

"When's that?"

"Midnight, New Year's Eve."

"Not much time."

"Sixty-nine days."

"So where do I come in?"

"The night she died, a black stretch limo was seen on Main Street in Fredericksburg. That's unusual. Closest place to get a limo is here or San Antonio. I started here because the girl was dumped on the highway heading toward Austin."

Beck showed Heidi's photo to Shorty.

"Pretty girl. I got a daughter her age." He gave the photo back to Beck. "I've never rented a limo to go out to Fredericksburg, but I've had people take my limos to Dallas then call me to pick 'em up. Come on, I'll check my records."

Beck followed Shorty back to his office, which sported a NASCAR decor. Shorty sat behind a computer perched on a desk, put on reading glasses, and tapped on the keyboard with two fingers like a kid playing the piano. He leaned back in his chair and pointed at the computer screen.

"Hell, I wasn't thinking. That's the year they held the film festival over the last weekend of the year, finished up on New Year's Eve. Sixth Street was a real zoo. After that, they moved the festival to October. It was two weeks ago."

"What film festival?"

"Austin Film Festival. It's a big deal now. We get movie stars, directors, producers. I rent out a lot of limos."

"You supply the drivers?"

Shorty nodded. "For the B-list and even some of your name directors. The big stars, they bring their own, bodyguards too."

"Who did you rent to that night?"

Shorty eyed the computer screen through the reading glasses. "No names you'd recognize. Movie people, they got lawyers, so they put everything in corporate names."

"They pay with credit cards?"

"Oh, yeah. I don't take checks from those bastards." Shorty snorted. "Those people, they're animals."

"How so?"

"What they do to my limos. One weekend with a movie star in it and we gotta clean the car like a goddamn OR. Carpets soaked with whiskey and beer, leather seats got burn marks from their joints, inside looks like someone blew up a baby powder factory. We find used rubbers, bottles, drugs, clothes—they're drinking, doping, and screwing in my limos. What is it about screwing in a limo? They got fancy hotel rooms, but they get into a limo and all of a sudden they're dogs in heat." He shook his head. "Hell, I collect more DNA from my limos after one weekend with a movie star in it than they do in a whole season on *CSI*."

He had amused himself.

"Where do they get the drugs from?"

"Not from me, Judge. My limos are stocked with liquor and beer. They want drugs, they gotta find it on their own. 'Course, most of them bring their dope with them. There ain't no carry-on restrictions on private jets."

"The movie stars using your limos, they pick up girls?"

Shorty smiled. "Oh, yeah. Sixth Street looks like a goddamn hooker convention, college girls hoping to get discovered, like that *American Idol* show. Except they ain't singing."

"Did you drive anyone on New Year's Eve that year?"

Shorty checked his records and nodded. "Director, B-list, maybe sixty. Pathetic. He couldn't pick up a gal at a nursing home, but he was begging girls to get into the limo. No go. Those girls, they ain't stupid. They do their homework, they know who can open doors in Hollywood and who can't. They ain't gonna waste their pussy on nobodies. They're only screwing stars."

Austin had always been hip and cool and a bit weird, especially for Texas, the kind of place where politicians from the city wore cowboy boots and cowboys from the country smoked dope and everyone regardless of political persuasion got drunk and danced to Willie Nelson at the Armadillo World Headquarters. And next to SoCo, the hippest, coolest, and weirdest part of Austin was Sixth Street in downtown. East of the Driskill Hotel, restaurants, bars, tattoo parlors, and nightclubs featuring live music lined the street. The Armadillo had put Austin on the music map, but Sixth Street had made Austin the "Live Music Capital of the World."

Beck had shown Heidi's photo to every bartender on the north side of the street. He was now on the south side. He walked into the Coyote Ugly bar. It was midday and the music was loud. The bartender was a big bald guy with tattoos and nose rings; he was wearing a black *Coyote Ugly* tee shirt. He didn't recognize Heidi from the photo.

"You should've been here two weeks ago for the film festival. A thousand girls just like her were lined up outside, hoping to get discovered on Sixth Street." He shook his head. "I think those girls never got over watching *Cinderella* when they were kids. They all want Prince Charming to pluck them out of obscurity and make their lives perfect, like Tom Cruise did for Renée Zellweger. He picked her out of a face book for *Jerry Maguire*. Look at her now."

"Difference is, he didn't pick her up in a cheap bar for a one-night stand."

The bartender said, "Hey, our drinks ain't cheap."

★   ★   ★

Heidi wanted to be a star. That was her dream. But only a star can make that dream come true. So Heidi Fay Geisel would have gone to the film festival. She would have gone to Austin to meet a movie star, someone who could make her dream come true. She would have gone to Sixth Street and lined up for the stars, wearing a see-through shirt and a tight miniskirt and stiletto heels. She would have stood out among the other girls. She would have been picked up. She would have gotten into the star's long black limo. She would have drunk alcohol and snorted cocaine and had sex with him. She would have done anything to be a star.

Instead, she died.

Beck tried to think it through. Why would a star who picked Heidi up in Austin have driven her back to Fredericksburg and then dumped her in that ditch? What could have happened that night?

Maybe Heidi had passed out in the limo. Maybe he discovered that she was underage. He couldn't just throw her out, someone might have seen her with him or gotten the limo's plates. Maybe he decided to take her home. Maybe they drove to Fredericksburg, and when he tried to wake her, she wouldn't wake. Maybe the driver pulled the limo over in front of the courthouse and tried to revive her with CPR, just as Carlotta had seen that night.

But maybe it was too late.

Maybe they turned the limo around and headed toward Austin on Highway 290 East. Maybe they pulled over and dumped her in the ditch. Maybe they drove on but discovered her shoes and purse were still in the limo. Maybe they pulled over at the bridge and threw her shoes and purse into the Pedernales River.

Maybe Kim was lying.

Kim was crying.

"I picked her up at her house and we went back to mine and changed. She kept all her sexy clothes at my house."

319

"What was she wearing that night?"

She got up and went inside. She returned with the laptop. They were sitting on the front porch of the little house behind the gas station. She tossed her cigarette into the yard then tapped on the keyboard and opened a photo of Heidi dressed in a white see-through blouse with the tail tied under her breasts, black miniskirt, and black stiletto heels. Hanging over her shoulder was a little black purse.

"That was her that night."

She tapped again. "Here's me that night."

She was wearing a similar outfit.

"I know, we looked like hookers. Curb appeal."

"So what did y'all do?"

"We drove over to Austin, to Sixth Street. Stalking stars, we called it. Whenever we saw a limo, we'd pose on the sidewalk with the other girls. The guys inside the limos, they always tried to pick up Heidi. But when they rolled the window down, they'd be old guys, directors and producers and even writers— like any girl is gonna screw a writer."

"What big stars were there?"

"Eddie Steele, Joe Raines, Teddy Bodeman, Chase Connelly, Zeke Adams."

"And Heidi knew they were there?"

"That's why we went—she figured on hooking up with one of them, to get an audition."

"So she was specifically looking for one of these stars?"

"Yeah. We went into some bar 'cause everyone was saying Teddy Bodeman was in there. He was, but he was with his wife and some other people. But Heidi sat down next to him in a booth."

"Nobody checked your ID?"

That "old guy" look again. "Not girls who looked like us."

"What happened in the bar?"

She shrugged. "I was talking to some guy at the bar, next thing I know Heidi says Teddy Bodeman's an asshole. We left."

"Did she give Teddy oral sex in the bar?"

"She didn't say anything."

"And then what did y'all do?"

"Stalked stars, like I said. About ten, ten-thirty, this limo stops right where we're at, so we give it our best pose. The window rolls down just a bit and a finger sticks out and points at Heidi. So she walks over real sexy-like and peeks in. The door opens and she jumps in. But she gave me a look like she'd hit it big."

"You didn't see who was in the limo?"

She shook her head. "The windows were all blacked out. But it had to be a big star, or she wouldn't have gotten in. No way."

"And you never saw Heidi again?"

Another shake of her head. "I tried to call her—"

"On a cell phone?"

She nodded. "My other phone."

"You had two phones?"

"Coach wouldn't let her have a phone, so I got two and gave her one. Family plan."

"How'd you get cell phones when you were only sixteen?"

"Through the gas station. I sign all the checks for my dad, he never knew."

"Okay, you tried to call her and . . .?"

"She didn't answer."

"So what did you do that night?"

"I stayed with some guy in Austin."

"A star?"

"A guy. The next morning, I got up and called Heidi again. She still didn't answer, so I drove home. When I got into town and saw the police by the highway and the body on the ground and the blonde hair, I knew it was Heidi."

"Your father's statement said you were home all night."

"He starts drinking beer at noon, drinks himself to sleep by seven. I told him I was home, so that's what he said. He trusts me."

321

"Why did you lie back then?"

"Because it would've been in the paper. Everyone would've said she was just a slut. I didn't want that for her."

"But maybe they could've found the guy who killed her."

"How?"

"I don't know. Maybe track down that limo."

"We saw more limos than you could count."

"Christ, Kim. Who was in that limo? And what happened to her purse? And that cell phone?"

Rudy Jaramillo was holding the girl's purse and cell phone. Sixty-nine days from now, he would be a very rich man.

His criminal career had begun at twelve, when he and some *amigos* robbed a convenience store. He quickly graduated to narcotics. On his third arrest, he went up for two years. But he was big and he knew how to fight, so he had survived in one piece. When he got out, he went right back to the life and right back to prison. Two strikes. When he got out, he decided to make money a different way: extortion.

So he got his chauffeur's license. He hired out to limo services in L.A., worked short stints for various movie stars, then lucked into the little man. Theodore Biederman. What a name. Hell, he would have changed it, too.

First night driving Theodore around, Rudy knew he had hit pay dirt. He was just too reckless with his dick. Hundreds of girls got into the back seat of the limo, and then that night in Austin when the blonde girl got in, Rudy's retirement plan was funded. Theodore gave her alcohol and he gave her cocaine and she died right there in the limo. They dumped her, and Rudy tossed her shoes into the river. They drove back to Austin, and he dropped Theodore off at the hotel. He parked the limo and checked the back for incriminating evidence.

He found some.

The girl's purse on the floor and down in the folds of the seat, her cell phone; and on the cell phone, Theodore's picture

322

with the girl. What an idiot, letting the girl take their photo together. Proof that they were together that night. And he didn't even wear a rubber; he left his DNA inside the girl. Conclusive evidence that Theodore Biederman had had sex with a minor. That he was guilty of stat rape and maybe murder.

Only problem was, Rudy Jaramillo was an accomplice-after-the-fact.

So he had to wait until the statute of limitations ran for both of them. If the law caught up with Theodore and sent him to prison, his $50-million-a-year income would be history; there would be no money to extort and no leverage against Theodore. The world would know. And Rudy might be in an adjacent cell. So he had to wait until midnight on New Year's Eve.

On January first, Rudy would make his move. He would show the cell phone photo to Theodore and give him a choice: he could either pay Rudy a million a year for the rest of his life or Rudy would go public with the cell phone photo, the girl's family would sue him for wrongful death, get his DNA, and prove to the world that he had given cocaine to a minor, had sex with a minor, and murdered a minor. The studios don't pay $20 million per film to murderers and molesters. Come New Year's Day, Rudy Jaramillo would own Theodore Biederman like a pimp owned a two-bit street hooker.

He opened the phone and looked at the photo of Theodore and the girl again. That photo had become Rudy Jaramillo's most prized possession in life. He treasured it, he protected it, he cradled it to his bosom like a mother holding her newborn; and he had never shared it with anyone.

But the girl had.

She had sent the photo to someone that night, to another cell phone. To someone called "Sis," according to the cell phone's log. But Rudy had gotten the girl's obituary; she had been survived only by her mother and father. She had no sister. And Sis's phone number had already gone out of service a few weeks after that night when he had called it from a pay phone in L.A.

323

So he had been diligent in eavesdropping on Theodore's phone calls in the limo, sure the photo would eventually surface and charges and lawsuits would be filed. But nothing happened. Theodore's life had only gotten better: more fame, more fortune, more girls in the limo. And Rudy had made his retirement plans.

But that one question still nagged at him always: who else had that photo?

Chapter 27

Beck snapped a photo of the kids.

Meggie and Josefina were dressed as Munchkins, Luke as the Scarecrow, Danny as the Tin Man, and Libby as Dorothy down to the Ruby Slippers. Jodie was Glinda the Good Witch and Janelle the Wicked Witch of the West. The bookstore was decorated to look like the Emerald City.

It was the Hardin family's first Halloween without Annie.

Jodie was sitting on the floor surrounded by kids; she was reading scary stories. Janelle was painting the children's faces like Munchkins. *The Wizard of Oz* was playing on a big-screen TV. Jodie had asked J.B. to dress up as the Wizard, but he had said, "That'll be the day." So instead he was handing out candy and wearing another loud Hawaiian print shirt, which was scary enough for the kids. Beck was the official photographer.

This was a kid-safe Halloween. The candy was safe, the place was safe, and the kids were safe. Jodie took a break and walked over to Beck. He snapped her picture and said over the noise of the movie and the kids, "You're a sexy witch."

Her mouth fell open and she said, "What did you call me?"

"I said, you're a sexy witch."

"Oh. I thought you said I was a sexy bitch." She smiled and said, "Thanks."

"How's Luke doing, working here?"

"We're talking."

"He'll talk to everyone but me."

"He'll come back to you, Beck. Be patient. But when he does, be there for him. Hug him. That's what he needs. Is J.B. really building him a baseball field?"

Beck nodded. "With bleachers, like in that movie."

"I love J.B."

Dear J.B.,

Beck's taking the children trick-or-treating in the neighborhood. His first time. He's trying to be a father now, but he's got a lot to learn. He thinks plaintiffs' lawyers are hard cases, wait till he meets the mothers in the PTA. (Hurts when I laugh.) Taking care of children 24/7 makes 3000 billable hours seem like a vacation. I have a pain specialist now.

Beck refuses to talk about my dying.

326

Chapter 28

Maria Espinoza coughed against the stench of turkey shit.

She reached her hand inside the next cold turkey and stuck her finger into the hole and pushed out any shit remaining in the dead bird's bowels. She had pushed shit out of almost fifteen thousand dead turkeys that day—but more birds kept coming down the line. She did not count. She knew that was the plant's daily quota during the months before Thanksgiving. If the quota was not met today, the line would run even faster tomorrow.

Her hands ached as they always ached after twelve hours on the line, from the work and the cold. They had reduced the temperature on the line to fifty degrees; the colder temperature slowed the growth of bacteria so they no longer needed to stop the line at mid-shift and wash the shit off the floor. Now, the line never stopped, more turkeys could be processed each shift, and Maria was standing in a twelve-hour pile of turkey shit. She looked at the clock on the wall: 2:47. Her shift ended at 3:00.

This would be Maria's final day at the turkey plant.

Maria had moved with Rafael to Fredericksburg to work in the turkey plant nineteen years ago, when she was only seventeen.

Representatives from the plant had come to Piedras Negras to recruit workers; they said the Americans had given illegals amnesty a few years before and surely would again. They had promised them jobs and good pay and housing. They showed them pictures of nice little houses and a clean new plant with smiling employees; it was not their house or this plant or these employees. Their house was not nice. This plant was not new. The employees did not smile.

But Maria was smiling this day.

With the money Señor McQuade had paid to Julio, she would no longer have to work the turkey line. But she had to finish out the month or she would not be paid for a month of pushing the shit out of turkeys. She wanted her last paycheck. She had earned it.

Beginning tomorrow, she would be a stay-at-home mom. They would move out of the barrio and into the country. Rafael would build a little house with a yard for the children to play in instead of Rose Street where they now played. Two new families from Mexico had already joined together to rent their house from their Anglo landlord when they moved out.

She again looked at the clock on the wall: 2:52.

For nineteen years, she had lived with the smell of turkey on her; she could never escape the disgusting odor. She wanted the last eight minutes to hurry past because she wanted to get the smell of turkeys off her forever.

And because she needed to pee very badly.

The mid-shift washdown, when the line was stopped for a short time, had been the workers' only break. They had hurried to the bathroom and to eat lunch; they had to be back when the washdown was done and the line again started. But when the mid-shift washdown had been eliminated, so had their only break.

Now, once the line started, she could not leave her place to eat or to go to the bathroom. She could not allow the turkeys to go past with the shit still in their bowels. She drank no water before her shift so she would not have to pee during her twelve hours on the line. She did not like to squat at her place on the line and pee into the pile of turkey shit on the concrete floor, even though all of the workers on the day shift line were also Mexican women and they also squatted to pee.

But she would not make it until end of shift.

She did not want to pee in her clothes because she would then be cold *and* wet. So she quickly yanked her pants and underwear down below her bottom, grabbed hold of the rail, and squatted. She peed into turkey shit, being careful not to pee into her rubber boots. When she finished, she stood and pulled her underwear and pants back up and glanced around. She had peed on the floor many times, but still she was embarrassed by such a public act; but none of the other workers had even noticed. Their eyes had never left the turkeys.

Today, they were processing free-range turkeys.

She had missed five turkeys while she peed. Perhaps quality control would push the shit out of those birds; perhaps not. They came down the line so fast; she had less than three seconds to push the shit from each bird because the next bird was already upon her. Working the line was all about the speed: *¡Más rápido! ¡Más rápido! ¡Más rápido!* And injuries. Many workers suffered the injuries. But no one ever complained or missed a day of work; to complain or miss work was to get fired.

Maria did not like pushing shit out of turkeys, but it was much better than working on the kill line or the evisceration line, standing in turkey blood or guts all day, or cutting the heads and paws off the turkeys. There were many injuries on those lines, and Maria often threw up. She only threw up sometimes pushing the shit out, usually when she was pregnant.

She wanted to have another baby.

Rafael said they now could. Tonight would also be his last shift at the plant. He was right now in the changing room putting on his white suit and rubber boots and gloves; he worked on the night cleanup shift. For the next twelve hours he would scrub and clean and wash down the line. She would kiss Rafael on her way out. But when he returned home tomorrow morning, they would be free of the turkey line. They would be free of the barrio. They would be free-range Mexicans, Rafael had said.

The day-shift line started at exactly 3:00 A.M. each day and did not stop until the clock on the wall again showed 3:00. It had never stopped before end of shift in her nineteen years. But now, suddenly, the turkeys stopped. They swayed gently there for a moment, hanging by their necks on the line, then fell still. The entire plant had fallen still. The workers stood frozen in place, as if life had stopped.

The line had stopped.

Maria looked at the clock: 2:56.

Seven blocks north of the turkey plant, Beck checked his watch: 2:57. Chicago was in the same time zone as Texas. He picked up the phone and dialed. When the receptionist at his old law firm answered, he asked for Ruth Moore and was put on hold.

Heidi Geisel had not been murdered by a local from Fredericksburg, an illegal from Mexico, or a college boy from Austin. She had been murdered by a movie star from Hollywood. A movie star who had given her a lethal dose of cocaine and then had sex with her, a man who was more than three years older than Heidi. Which made him guilty of murder and statutory rape. A murder conviction was unlikely, but his DNA made a statutory rape conviction a certainty. A movie star was going to prison—if Beck found him in the next fifty-nine days, obtained a DNA sample, had it tested and matched to the DNA from Heidi's body, and got the grand jury to indict him.

He needed DNA samples from five of the biggest movie stars in Hollywood. But how does one go about getting a movie star's DNA? Do you walk up to him at the Academy Awards with a DNA Saliva Collection Kit and ask him to open wide, stick a swab inside his mouth and obtain a sample of his saliva,

330

and then place the swab in an evidence bag and say "thank you"?

Do you push the buzzer on the intercom outside the entrance gates to his Hollywood mansion and request a urine sample?

Do you call his Hollywood agent and ask for a publicity photo and a vial of blood?

Beck didn't think so.

And issuing a subpoena for a DNA sample was out of the question. First, Beck was a judge, not a cop; he wasn't supposed to be investigating the murder of his buddy's daughter. So while he would officially have jurisdiction over the case once a suspect was indicted, he was not officially on the case.

Second, there was the Fourth Amendment to the U.S. Constitution: "No Warrants shall issue, but upon probable cause . . ." And there was no probable cause for a search warrant to obtain a DNA sample from any of those movie stars. The mere fact that Heidi and those five stars had all been in Austin on the night Heidi had died did not add up to anything resembling probable cause. He had no evidence placing Heidi in the company of any of those stars, other than Kim's statement that Heidi had sat down at Teddy Bodeman's table in a Sixth Street bar.

And third, even if a Texas judge issued a subpoena, a California judge would have to enforce it; and no California judge would enforce it against a movie star with high-powered California lawyers who put that judge in office and could take him out.

Beck could not go through the normal legal channels.

He needed DNA samples from five stars: Teddy Bodeman, Joe Raines, Eddie Steele, Zeke Adams, and Chase Connelly. Heidi had been with one of them that night, he was sure of it. One of their DNA matched the DNA found inside Heidi. He had researched them on the Internet. They all ranged in age from twenty-nine through thirty-eight. They all had been big stars five years ago. They all were married and had suffered rumors of drug use. They all had been in Austin that night. They all had DNA.

One was shooting a film in Chicago.

Unlike polygamists in Utah, lawyers in the U.S. may legally have two wives: the one at home and the one at the office; the latter is called a secretary. Most lawyers only have sex with the one at home. Ruth Moore had been Beck's wife at work. She had taken care of every aspect of his professional life. She had typed documents, filed pleadings, arranged conferences (office and phone), scheduled lunches, meetings, and travel, ran errands, and shopped for presents for his children and his other wife at home. For seventeen years, any activity that wasn't worth $800 an hour had been delegated to Ruth Moore. She answered.

"Beck, my God! How are you?"

"We're doing better. How are you, Ruth?"

"I'm fine. How are the children?"

"Luke's still pretty quiet and Meggie . . ."

"The doll?"

"Yeah."

"Are you practicing?"

"No. I'm judging."

"You're a judge?"

"It was that or work at the Wal-Mart."

"Close call. Must be pretty boring, a small-town judge."

"Not as boring as you might think. Which is why I'm calling you. I need your help."

"Sure, Beck, anything."

"It's a long story, but bottom line I'm trying to get someone's DNA sample."

"Someone here at the firm?"

"No. Zeke Adams."

"*Zeke Adams?* Are you serious? Why?"

"I am serious, and Ruth, you don't want to know why."

"You want me to get his DNA?"

"He's filming a movie in Chicago."

"In downtown. All the girls go over at lunch and watch."

"Are you going today?"

"Yes."

"Can you get close to him?"

"They put up barricades, but he comes over and signs autographs and takes pictures. He's real nice."

"Good. Take a plastic bag and tweezers—you still got some in your desk?"

"Of course."

"Okay, take those and watch Zeke. Look for anything that might have his DNA on it."

"Like what?"

"Chewing gum, hair, cigarette butt, saliva, blood . . ."

"Blood?"

"Well, don't cut him. Just watch him closely. If he spits out gum, use the tweezers, pick it up, put it in the bag, and overnight the bag to me at the Gillespie County Courthouse, 101 West Main, Fredericksburg, Texas. Can you do that?"

"I can do that. When will you tell me what this is about?"

"One day, Ruth. And thanks."

"Beck . . . take care of yourself."

Beck hung up, then dialed again. One movie star down, four to go. They all lived in L.A. And Beck knew a guy in L.A., a private investigator he had used in a corporate espionage case. The guy had gone dumpster diving to get the evidence Beck needed to win the case. He answered on the first ring.

"Wes, Beck Hardin."

"Beck, how long's it been?"

Wes was yelling. No doubt he was driving the L.A. freeways in his Mustang convertible.

"Five, six years!"

Now Beck was yelling.

"You don't gotta yell!"

"Sorry. Wes, I need your services."

"You got 'em, buddy. What do you need?"

"DNA."

"My specialty. From who?"

333

"Eddie Steele, Joe Raines, Teddy Bodeman, and Chase Connelly."

"I hear you right? You want me to get DNA from four of the biggest stars in Hollywood?"

"And I need it yesterday. When you get a sample—and I know you will—put it in a plastic bag and overnight it to me."

Beck gave Wes the courthouse address.

Wes said, "Texas? The hell you doing in Texas?"

"It's a long story."

"Same rules apply?"

The rules: Wes wouldn't ask Beck why he wanted their DNA, and Beck wouldn't ask Wes how he got their DNA.

"Yeah."

Wes yelled, "I'll get it!"

And Wes would.

Julio Espinoza looked at the time: 3:29.

He sat invisible in the back corner of the classroom with the other Latinos while the old German teacher taught the Anglo students sitting up front. The only time she came to the back and talked to Julio was right before the state achievement tests. "We need you, Julio!" she would say. Yes, they needed his perfect score to bring up the Latinos' average and to make the Anglos look good with the state: "See, we are teaching our Mexicans!" Two million dollars in the bank did not alter the fact that to the Anglos, he was still just a Mexican.

The bell rang. Everyone rushed to the door as if the fire alarm had gone off. Julio was the last student to exit the room.

"Hi, Julio."

He turned and stared into the blue eyes of Nikki Ernst. He said hi as well as he could through his wired jaws. Nikki appeared very beautiful in her cheerleader outfit; there was a football game that night. Julio breathed her in and felt faint.

She said, "When will you get the wires off?"

Julio held up one finger.

"One week? That's great! Just in time for homecoming."

Not that Julio was going to homecoming. Not that any of the Latinos were going to homecoming. Nikki stepped closer; Julio stepped back until he was pressed against the metal lockers that lined the hall. She touched his arm; he felt his body come alive.

"Julio, I never said how sorry I am for saying what I did about you that day in court. But I really am. Sorry. Slade's dad and that mean old Stutz, they scared me, said it was up to me to save Slade's football career and our football season. But I still shouldn't have done it. Can you ever forgive me?"

Julio nodded.

"Julio, have you asked anyone to the homecoming dance?"

Julio shook his head.

"Well, no one's asked me."

Julio said, "Ade!"

"*Ade?* Oh, you mean Slade?"

Julio nodded.

"I'm not going with him to the dance or anywhere else. We broke up. So, Julio, you want to take me to the homecoming dance?"

Julio's heart fluttered. But his mind worked. He pulled out his notepad and wrote: *What about your friends?* Nikki was reading as he wrote.

"Well, if they don't accept you, they're not my friends, are they? You know what, Julio, I'm ready to get out of this town."

Julio wrote again: *What about your parents?* Nikki again read as he wrote.

"Yeah, my parents will go apeshit. But I'm eighteen years old and I'm an adult, just like Judge Hardin said. I'm making my own decisions now. So they'll just have to get over it. I like you and I want to go to homecoming with you."

Julio was suddenly struck with fear. Nikki saw it in his face. She said, "Now don't be afraid. You don't have to come to my house. I'll pick you up, okay?"

But Julio's fear at that precise moment was not of Nikki's German parents. His fear was more immediate. His fear was of Slade McQuade's massive body coming down the hall at a quick pace and directly toward Julio Espinoza. He pointed. Nikki spun around just as Slade arrived almost at a run. She stuck her hand out like the crossing guard to the cars outside the school. Her hand hit Slade stomach high.

"Stop, Slade! You leave Julio alone! I mean it!"

Slade ignored her and said, "Julio, I heard my dad and Stutz talking last night. They're gonna raid the turkey plant today. And the barrio. That ICE."

Julio scratched on his notepad: *When?* He showed the pad to Slade.

"They said at shift change."

Julio sucked in air too quickly, and he began choking and then coughing. It became worse, more violent coughing. He couldn't breathe. He tried desperately to open his mouth for air, but he could not. His body was making a high-pitched wheezing noise as he fought to breathe. Nikki cried out, "Julio, do you have asthma?"

He fell into the lockers and started to slide down the slick metal locker faces. Slade grabbed him under his arms and held him up. Nikki grabbed his face with her soft hands.

"Julio, what is it? What's wrong?"

Julio's head was now jerking back and forth as he tried to breathe. He was going to pass out or throw up. He had to save himself. Nikki had to save him. He reached to his back pocket and grabbed the little scissors the doctor had given him and told him to carry always in case he should ever choke or vomit; he was to use the scissors to cut the rubber bands holding his jaws together. He held the scissors out to Nikki.

"What, Julio? What do you want me to do?"

He opened his lips and tapped the bands with his finger.

"You want me to cut the rubber bands?"

He nodded. Nikki came very close to his face and peered

into his mouth. With the fingers of her left hand she spread his lips; with her right hand she put the scissors against his teeth and cut the bands. He fell to the floor.

He opened his mouth for the first time in almost eight weeks and sucked air like a man saved from drowning. After a few minutes, his breathing calmed. Nikki was patting his back; Slade was squatting next to them. Other students had stopped and were now staring at them as if a car wreck had happened in the main hall of the high school.

Julio turned his eyes up to Nikki and said, "You will be a good doctor." He now turned to Slade. "The ICE raid will be at shift change?"

"Yeah. When's that?"

"That is now. I must go!"

Slade said, "Come on, I'll drive you."

Nikki said, "I'm coming, too."

Slade pulled Julio up as easily as if lifting an infant and they ran out of the school and to the parking lot where Slade's big black Hummer was parked. Nikki jumped into the passenger seat and Julio into the back; Slade started the engine. Rather than circling around the parking lot to the exit, he drove over the curb nearest the road and tore up the grassy incline. They bounced hard over the street curb. Slade accelerated toward the turkey plant. Nikki said, "What are we going to do?"

Julio said, "Slade, take me to the judge. He will know what to do."

Beck glanced at the clock on the wall as he exited the back door of the courthouse: 3:43. He spotted Grady getting out of his SUV in the parking lot between the courthouse and the Law Enforcement Center. He called out to him, then walked over. They leaned against the SUV.

"Nothing on the shoe," Grady said. He shook his head. "Can't believe you found it. The river's two miles east of where she was dumped. That's good thinking, Beck." He smiled. "When the Germans vote you out of office next year, maybe you'll come to work for me."

"I'm going to find this guy."

"Figure that'll pay your debt in full?"

"Maybe. Maybe it'll give me some answers I'm looking for."

"So maybe you don't make the same mistakes with your girl?"

Beck nodded. "I've learned a few things, about Heidi. She was with a movie star that night. Kim said she got into a black limo in Austin about ten or ten-thirty and a black limo was seen on Main Street about one that night."

"A movie star? Why the hell did Kim hold back on that?"

Beck shook his head. "Why would a girl want out of this town so badly she'd have sex with a stranger?"

"Kids want excitement. They're bored here."

"This is the next Santa Fe."

Grady laughed. "Folks saying that, they drank the Kool-Aid."

"You don't buy it?"

"I don't figure rich folks are gonna flock here just to be run off the farm-to-markets by some bubba driving a jacked-up pickup with a pit bull in the back 'cause they're slowing him down. This is a nice little country town, Beck. Nothing more. But that's not enough for kids. They want more. Like you did. Who saw the limo here?"

Beck nodded toward the courthouse. "Carlotta."

"*Carlotta?* Why didn't she tell me?"

"She was afraid Stutz would've deported her."

"I told the Mexicans I didn't give a shit about their immigration status. But I can't blame them, with Stutz—"

The sound of tires squealing interrupted Grady. A black Hummer turned sharply off San Antonio Street and into the parking lot then accelerated over to them and skidded to a stop.

"What the hell?" Grady said.

Slade McQuade was driving; Nikki Ernst was in the passenger's seat. Julio Espinoza jumped out of the back door of the Hummer and ran over to them. His face was frantic. He could talk.

"Judge Hardin, they are raiding the turkey plant!"

"Who?"

"ICE."

"When?"

"Now!"

Beck turned to Grady. "You didn't know?"

"Hell, no! Come on!"

Grady ran around to the driver's side of his SUV; Beck yelled to Slade, "Follow us!" then got in the passenger's side. Grady hit the lights and siren and sped out of the parking lot.

The turkey plant was located seven blocks south of Main Street. Grady turned down Milam, cut through the barrio, and drove fast down the road leading to the plant. At the plant entrance, he hit the brakes hard, and the vehicle skidded to a stop in a cloud of gravel dust in front of a Department of Homeland Security barricade.

Black SUVs blockaded the front gates to the plant. At least a hundred federal agents in black jackets with POLICE and ICE in white letters across the back and ICE down each sleeve were swarming the plant. Every agent was armed; some were wearing flak jackets and cammo pants and carrying assault rifles. It had the look of a military coup. Five buses were lined up at the plant entrance doors inside the tall fence.

They got out. The Hummer with Slade, Julio, and Nikki pulled up behind them. Beck and Grady went over to the agent manning the barricade. Grady said, "What the hell do you think you're doing?"

The agent looked Grady over. "And who are you?"

"I'm the goddamn Gillespie County Sheriff, that's who. And you're in my jurisdiction. And he's the district judge."

The agent stepped away and said something into a handheld radio. Moments later, another agent jogged over to them from what appeared to be the command post. He was wearing a flak jacket and packing a big nine-millimeter weapon at his waist. He addressed Grady. "I'm Agent Lucas, Homeland

Security. Immigration and Customs Enforcement. And you are?"

"Pissed off." Grady pointed at the plant. "A hundred agents with assault rifles and body armor? Don't you think that's overkill for a bunch of Mexicans armed with dead turkeys?"

Agent Lucas ignored Grady's sarcasm. "You're the county sheriff?"

"Yeah, I am."

Agent Lucas turned to Beck and looked him up and down. Beck was again wearing jeans and boots. "You're a judge?"

"Judge Beck Hardin."

"Federal?"

"State."

"Oh. So what can I do for you gentlemen?"

Grady said, "You can explain what the hell you're doing conducting a raid in my jurisdiction without informing me."

Agent Lucas offered that smile unique to federal employees. "Well, first of all, Sheriff, the entire U.S. of A. is our jurisdiction. And second, in accordance with federal law—which preempts state law—we're conducting a workplace raid. Operation Return to Sender."

Beck said, "*Return to Sender?* That's real cute. These are human beings, not mail."

Agent Lucas ignored Beck as well. "And third, we did notify local law enforcement. The chief of police. Isn't this plant within the city limits?"

"Yeah. But it's customary—"

"Not anymore. After 9/11, it's need-to-know basis."

Beck pointed at the plant. "Those people aren't terrorists. They're just Mexicans processing turkeys. They're just working."

Agent Lucas said, "And they're working in this country illegally. We're executing a federal civil warrant, Judge. That supersedes your authority."

"I understand the law, Agent."

"Good. Then let us take care of national security."

340

Beck laughed. "What, you think these Mexicans are plotting terrorism while pulling the guts out of turkeys?"

Agent Lucas's face turned red. "Back off, Judge! Go back to your little courtroom and handle traffic tickets or grant divorces or whatever it is you do in this thriving metropolis. But don't interfere with my operation or I'll arrest your ass and take you before a real judge!"

Beck stepped toward Agent Lucas, but Grady stepped between them. "These people been working in that plant for thirty years. Why now?"

"We waited until shift change so we could apprehend all illegal workers. Both shifts."

"Why today?"

"We got a tip that these workers engaged in identity theft, stealing IDs and social security numbers to get their papers."

"A tip? From who?"

Agent Lucas said, "A confidential source."

Slade stepped past Beck and said, "My father. And Stutz."

Beck said, "They did this?"

Slade nodded. "I heard them talking last night."

Grady spat. "They double-crossed you, Beck."

Agent Lucas said, "If you gentlemen will excuse me, I've got work to do."

Beck said, "What's going to happen to these people?"

"They'll be bused to a detention center in San Antonio, processed, and then deported. They'll be in Nuevo Laredo tomorrow morning."

Julio stepped forward. "*Nuevo Laredo?* My parents, they are in there. What will we do without them?"

Agent Lucas said, "We who?"

"We, their children."

Agent Lucas eyed Julio and stepped toward him. Beck and Grady blocked his path. "He's legal, Agent. He's an American citizen. So are his brothers and sisters."

"If you say so, Judge. My agents are in the barrio looking

341

for runners, and Child Protective Services has been called in. They'll be going door to door in the barrio." Agent Lucas looked at Julio like a sport fisherman who had just lost a big catch. "Born in the USA." He threw a thumb back at the plant. "Fifty-seven of the women in there are pregnant. They have those babies here, they're U.S. citizens same as me and you" —he nodded at Julio—"and him. They have them in Nuevo Laredo, they're Mexicans just like their mamas. That's reason enough for this raid."

Beck said, "Those people have a right to counsel, even if they are here illegally."

"They're signing documents as we speak waiving their right to counsel and agreeing to immediate voluntary departure."

"You're pointing guns at them! That's not voluntary. And they can't waive their right to counsel if they don't even know they have a right to counsel."

Agent Lucas turned his hands up, shrugged, and walked off.

Grady said, "If they fight deportation, they'll sit in jail for a year, then get deported. Better to get bused to Mexico tonight and let go. They can be back in a few weeks."

Julio shouted, "Look!"

The workers were exiting the plant single file. They were wearing white uniforms and hard hats and black rubber boots and shuffling through a gauntlet of ICE agents toward the buses; chains were wrapped around the workers' waists and their hands and feet were shackled to the chains, as if the Feds were apprehending Hannibal Lecter instead of Rafael and Maria Espinoza.

"¡Madre! ¡Padre!"

Julio's parents had just walked out of the plant.

"¡Madre! ¡Padre!"

They did not hear him or see him. They disappeared onto a bus. Julio began sobbing. Beck put his arm around the boy. Nikki hugged him from the other side.

"It's my fault."

Beck turned to Slade.

"It's all my fault," Slade said again.

He wasn't speaking to anyone in particular. He walked over and kicked the side of his Hummer; he leaned over and buried his face in his hands and the hood.

A black diesel pickup with blacked-out windows drove up and stopped. The driver's side window lowered slowly. Bruno Stutz. Beck released Julio and walked over. Beck had never punched a senior citizen, but he was seriously considering it at that moment.

"You did this?"

"Goddamn right I did."

Beck wanted desperately to hit the man. Instead he said, "I hope you die soon."

Stutz just laughed, shifted the truck into gear, and drove down the road. The diesel made for slow acceleration; before Beck even realized what he was doing, he reached down, picked up a baseball-sized rock, and threw it at Stutz's truck. It fell short.

"Damnit!"

Slade was now beside Beck. He picked up a similar-sized rock, tossed it in his massive right hand a few times, and eyed Stutz's truck, now fifty yards away and moving farther and faster away.

"He's out of range," Beck said.

Slade gripped the rock, stepped forward, and threw the rock. It rose high into the sky on a true path and fell directly at the rear window of Stutz's truck. Beck heard the crack of breaking glass. The taillights on the truck flashed red. A long arm extended out the driver's window; Stutz shook a raised finger at them, then drove on. Beck turned to Slade, "You've got a hell of an arm, son."

"When I hit Julio, I set all this in motion. It's all my fault."

Slade turned to Julio and said, "I'm sorry, Julio." He then walked over to his Hummer, got in, and drove off down the gravel road. Grady walked over; he was shaking his head.

"Our judge is throwing rocks at cars?"

"That a problem, Grady?"

He shook his head. "Gives me hope for our judicial system."

The black ICE SUVs backed away from the gates, and the five buses drove out of the plant and past them. Julio searched for his parents' faces, but did not see them.

Beck said, "Julio, I'm gonna get your parents back."

"How?"

"I know people." He turned to Grady. "You feel like driving to San Antonio?"

Grady checked his watch. "We'll have to eat dinner there?"

"Yeah."

"I'm in. Anything to avoid my wife's cooking."

They walked over to Grady's SUV. Julio started walking down the street toward the barrio. Beck said, "Are you going to be okay, Julio?"

Julio wiped his face and said, "I must find the children."

Nikki ran after him and said, "I'll help you."

Beck got into the SUV and pulled out his cell phone.

"You really know people?" Grady asked.

Beck nodded. "One of my partners in Chicago was a former Assistant AG at the Justice Department. He's political. Lots of important people owe him favors—and he owes me a few. If anyone can get Julio's folks freed, he can."

"You know, Beck, I'm really starting to like you."

Beck pointed. "Follow those buses."

When Beck arrived back home that night after he and Grady had dropped Rafael and Maria Espinoza off at their house in the barrio, the children were already in bed and asleep. He found J.B. on the back porch reading the paper.

"You get 'em?" J.B. asked.

Beck fell into his rocker. "Yeah, we got them. They're back home. Friday night, and the barrio looked like a ghost town."

"Raid made the TV—San Antonio news. Felix Delgado was

interviewed. He was pretty upset. Said it was a tragic miscarriage of justice."

There was that word again.

"Grady's a good man," J.B. said. "You're a good man, too, Beck. I'm proud you're my son. I wish I could take the credit, but you raised yourself."

Beck looked at his father looking at him.

"You get more credit than you know, J.B."

Beck saw his father's eyes well up. J.B. looked down and said softly, "That means a lot, Beck."

Beck leaned back. "You know, J.B., I don't want to be the judge. I don't like this town anymore."

"It ain't the town, Beck. It's a few people in the town. A few old farts like Stutz can't abide the fact the world's changing—they're still wearing plaid and the rest of the world's wearing Hawaiian prints. But those old farts are gonna die off soon and young folks like you and Jodie are gonna take over and lead this town in a better direction for kids like Meggie and Luke and Libby." His father looked at him. "If you quit on this town, Beck, you're quitting on them."

"Did they have a good day, the kids?"

"Yep . . . oh, Gretchen said hi . . . for me to say hi . . . for her to . . . aw, hell, you know what I mean. Fixed the kids buffalo burgers, then took them to the ballgame. Goats won, forty-two to nothing. Slade ran for six touchdowns."

"He *ran* for six touchdowns?"

"Yep. Didn't throw the ball once the whole night. Kind of odd, too. He'd take the ball and just run, even when he was supposed to pass. And he didn't run away from the other team. He ran right at them, like he wanted to hit them. Like he wanted to kill them."

Homicidal rage.

345

Chapter 29

TURKEY PLANT RAIDED
Part of Nationwide Immigration Crackdown
By Mary Alice Mueller
Staff Writer

U.S. Immigration and Customs Enforcement agents raided the turkey plant Friday. ICE stated that Operation Return to Sender netted 839 illegal Mexican nationals. The detainees were processed in San Antonio and bused to Laredo for "voluntary departure."

Child Protective Services was attempting to locate all the children of the detainees, thought to number 2,000. Minors will be offered transportation to the border to be reunited with their parents. At least six hundred children had not been accounted for at press time.

Local residents Jodie Lee and Janelle Jones went door to door in the barrio Friday night, Saturday, and Sunday to check on the children and to provide food. Ms. Lee said, "It's shameful. Taking parents away and leaving no one to care for the

346

children—that's America? How can the government just come in and take all those people away without warning?"

Other residents voiced support for the raid. "It's about time," a local goat rancher said at Tuesday's auction. "They should've raided the plant twenty years ago. Those Mexicans were here illegally, they were getting free food stamps and medical care at our hospital, their kids were getting free education at our schools. We work for a living. They had their hands out to the government. I sure as hell won't miss them."

An official with the Houston-based owner of the plant, Fredericksburg Turkeys LLC, said they were "shocked" to learn that the workers were in the country illegally. The official had no further comment except to say that the plant, a Fredericksburg fixture for over thirty years, would likely be closed and the property sold to an undisclosed buyer. Asked if the workers' final paychecks would be paid to their children, the official declined comment. ICE said that at this time no criminal prosecutions against the owner were planned.

U.S. Rep. Merle Fuchs, R-Fredericksburg, talking by cell phone from Washington on his way to a fundraiser, said, "Our laws must be enforced and those individuals that violate our laws must face the consequences. And the illegals are certainly a drain on public resources." Rep. Fuchs added that he was working "diligently" to restore the mohair incentive in the next USDA budget.

The economic impact of the raid on Fredericksburg is unclear. Two Mexican restaurants were forced to close because their entire staffs had been deported. Local home builders are expected to raise their prices since they'll have to pay higher wages to legal workers.

The only bright spot is that ICE raided the plant the day before deer hunting season opened, so there was expected to be no adverse economic impact on hunters.

Ed Huber, with the Turkey Growers Association, said the

plant closing would likely put a dozen local turkey farmers out of business. And prices for Thanksgiving turkeys would surely increase.

At the primary school, the usual chattering in Spanish was not heard in the halls. "Most of my students just disappeared," bilingual kindergarten teacher Gretchen Young said. "I fought for them every day, but how do you fight the Federal government?"

It was five days later when Beck looked up from the newspaper to Quentin McQuade standing in his doorway. He had come to gloat.

"Morning, Judge."

"You looked me right in the eye and lied."

"I didn't have my hand on the Bible." He chuckled. "Judge, did you really think you could blackmail me into spending three million dollars to fix up the barrio for a bunch of Mexicans?"

"You signed a settlement agreement that expressly requires you to pave, curb, and gutter specific streets in the barrio. McQuade, if you don't comply with that agreement, I will haul your ass into court and hold you in contempt."

"Whoa, Judge—those curbs and gutters are gonna be built."

"But you just said—"

"I said I wasn't going to spend three million dollars on the barrio for a bunch of Mexicans." He smiled. "See, Judge, the barrio is the very definition of urban blight. Dilapidated homes and trailers and shacks—have you seen how those people lived? Goats and chickens wandering the streets, and you can't even count all the code violations. My Austin lawyer says the law allows a city to condemn land that constitutes urban blight and sell it to a developer who's going to build something new on that land."

"A developer like you?"

"Exactly like me. In fact, me."

"So your money for the barrio will be spent on—"

"My development. The barrio will be condemned, bulldozed, and sold to me. Those streets—Buena Vista, Santa Rosa, St. Mary's, St. Gerelda—they will be paved with curbs and gutters, just as the agreement requires. It just won't be the barrio anymore. It'll be second homes owned by rich people from Houston and Dallas. I'm thinking hacienda-style—what do you think?"

He was enjoying himself.

"Who's going to pay a lot of money to live next to the turkey plant?"

"Oh, that plant's history. It'll never reopen. Too many safety violations, outdated equipment, pollution . . . I'm negotiating to buy it. It'll be bulldozed, too."

"There'll be court fights over the condemnation."

"No, there won't. Most of those shacks are owned by the Mexicans that just got deported. They won't be around to fight. Besides, my lawyer also told me there's not a damn thing a state court judge like yourself can do about it because the United States Supreme Court said it was perfectly legal."

He smiled.

"Funny how the law works, isn't it, Judge? You used your legal and political influence to free the boy's parents, Mexicans here illegally. I used mine to condemn their home, legally." McQuade shook his head. "Is America a great country or what?"

"That's why you called in the raid, to steal those people's homes?"

"Yep. And it's all because of you."

"Because of me?"

He nodded. "I would've never thought of it if you hadn't tried to blackmail me. Hell, I never even knew where the Mexicans lived. When you put the curbs and gutters in the settlement, I decided to drive through the barrio and when I did, I saw an opportunity—a great piece of land just blocks from Main Street shopping. So I owe you a big thanks, Judge."

McQuade walked to the door then turned back.

"See, Judge, this is all your doing. You got the turkey plant

349

raided, you put the Mexicans on those buses, you got them deported and their homes condemned. You did all that—when you tried to use your judicial power to make their lives better. You thought you could, but you can't." He sighed. "If you had just let me pay the million to the boy and be done, none of this would've ever happened."

"McQuade . . . your day will come."

Quentin McQuade shook his head. "I don't think so, Judge. There's two hundred million dollars standing between me and that day."

When Felix Delgado had sat across from Beck in his chambers that day exactly one month before, he thought he had one year to live. He did not. He had one month.

After McQuade had left, Beck took a walk to gather himself. He bought a San Antonio paper and he was now sitting on a bench at the Main and Llano intersection. It was sunny and seventy in November. Fat men in camouflage hunting outfits walked down Main Street, and a pickup with a dead deer strapped across the hood drove down Main Street, no doubt en route to The Butcher Haus, a local deer processor whose motto was *The Buck Stops Here*.

Felix Delgado had died two days ago. His wife told the news-paper reporter that the ICE raid in Fredericksburg had so upset her husband that he had lost all will to live. His last words to her had been, "I have failed them."

Beck had failed them, too.

"You okay, Judge?"

Mavis was standing in front of his desk.

Beck nodded. "What's on the docket this afternoon?"

"Bail hearings and motions. Criminal and civil."

They climbed the narrow stairway to the courtroom above. Beck sat behind the bench. Standing in front of the bench was Billy Ray Boenker. Beck read the few pages in the red file.

350

"First day of deer hunting season, and you killed a cow?"

Billy Ray had mistaken a cow for a deer and had put a .30-06 round right in the bovine's head. The cow belonged to his neighbor.

"Looked like a deer," Billy Ray said.

"Were you drinking?"

"I was awake."

"Shooting while intoxicated."

Lawyer Polk—again—said, "Judge, if we jailed every drunk deer hunter in the county, we'd have to add on to the jail."

"Bail is denied. You're a danger to the community. You can sit in jail until your case comes to trial or you plead out."

Deputy Clint led Billy Ray away. Mavis said, "Bail hearing," and handed Beck another red folder: *The State of Texas vs. Ignacio Perez*. Lawyer Polk maintained his position in front of the bench and was joined by the D.A. and a shackled Latino. The D.A. said, "Told you, Judge. They all come back."

Ignacio Perez had come back, charged with possession of a controlled substance with intent to distribute. He had been arrested with ten pounds of ice—crystal meth—on his person.

Beck said to Lawyer Polk, "Have you mastered Spanish yet?"

"Uh, no, Judge."

"Then how do we converse with Mr. Perez?"

"Not so good?"

Mavis said, "I can call Inez, the librarian from next door. She's bilingual."

"Do it."

Five minutes later, Inez Quintanilla was standing in front of the bench next to Ignacio Perez. Beck said, "Ask him why?"

Inez spoke in Spanish to Ignacio. He spoke back; one word caught Beck's attention: *coyote*. Inez said, "He was arrested in the ICE raid and deported to Nuevo Laredo. He was very afraid there due to the *narco-traficantes*. So he tried to come north several times, but was stopped at the border crossing. Then he hired a *coyote* to get him across. But the *coyote* charged him one thousand dollars, which he did not have. The *coyote* allowed him to earn his way by carrying the meth up here."

"And what was he supposed to do with it when he got here?"

Inez and Ignacio conversed in Spanish again. Then she said, "Someone was to find him in the barrio and take the meth."

"Who?"

Again they conversed.

"He does not know who."

Beck looked at Ignacio Perez and felt his heart turn hard. To Inez, he said, "Tell him this: I gave him a break, but he made me look like a fool. I can live with that, but I can't live with his bringing meth into our town. No more breaks."

Inez repeated his words in Spanish to Ignacio. He started to cry. But today Beck had no sympathy.

"Bail is denied. Flight risk."

The deputy led Ignacio Perez away. The D.A. started to turn away, but Beck said, "What happened to Jesus Ramirez, the 'assault with a burrito' guy?"

The D.A. stared at his shoes a moment then said, "Deported."

"His wife and kids?"

"Macarena was deported, too. The Catholic church, the old one that says Mass in Spanish for the illegals, they took in their kids. Plus about two hundred others."

"Jesus Christ."

"Exactly." The D.A. turned away, then turned back. "I didn't want that . . . the raid."

He walked out of the courtroom.

Beck put his elbows on the bench and his face in his hands. He had failed all those children. He felt like crying and he felt like hitting something at the same time. The anger won out; his blood pressure built until he thought he would explode. He needed fresh air. He raised his head and found himself looking at Mary Jo and Stanley Jobst.

"Mary Jo . . . Stanley . . . What's up?"

They looked down and shuffled in place. Two lawyers bookended them. Mavis tapped Beck on the arm with a case file. A gold case file. A divorce file. *Mary Jo Jobst vs. Stanley Jobst.*

"What is this? *Divorce?*"

Their heads turned up. Mary Jo was crying. Stanley was fighting not to cry; he said, "She went on a diet."

"You're getting divorced because she went on a diet?"

"'Cause of you."

"You're getting divorced because of me?"

"She went on a diet because of you."

"What have I got to do with how much Mary Jo eats?"

"She wants . . . she wants to be slim again. For you."

"*For me?*"

That did it. Beck stood.

"No! This is *not* happening! I won't do it!"

He threw the gold case file over their heads and almost to the spectator section. He pointed a finger at Mary Jo Jobst.

"Mary Jo, I don't love you. I love a dead woman. You've got four children who need you and a man right there who loves you. Go home and take care of them. Get over your problems, get over yourself, get counseling. But get out of my courtroom!" They stood there frozen. Beck pointed the way. "Get out!"

Beck walked off the bench, ducked through the window, and sat in his lawn chair on the back balcony. He sat there until the sun dropped behind him and the courthouse shadows stretched out in front of him to the Eagle Tree and then until the shadows reached Main Street. He sat there until he had worked through his five weeks as judge of this small Texas county and each of his failures. He sat there until Jodie ducked through the window and sat next to him.

"Mavis called me. You okay, Beck?"

"No."

They sat quietly until Beck said, "We were eighteen. It was just a few days before I was to leave for Notre Dame and he was to leave for UT. We both had football scholarships. But I was mad at the world and drinking beer, and . . . driving my old truck. I didn't make a curve on Ranch Road 16, went off the road, hit a tree. On his side. I walked away. Aubrey almost lost his leg. He could never play again. I took all his dreams away—college, maybe the pros. He was good enough. But I took all that away from him."

"Did they charge you?"

Beck shook his head. "They gave me a break."

"And you figure on making things right by finding the guy that killed Heidi?"

"I figured on coming back and making a lot of things right. But all I've done is make things worse, for my kids and those Latino kids. I don't belong here anymore."

"What are you going to do?"

"I'm going to find this guy, for Aubrey. I'm going to find him in the next fifty-four days and bring him to justice. Then I'm going to take my children back to Chicago. That's where I belong."

"Annie wanted y'all here."

"She's dead."

Chapter 30

A week later, a FedEx package arrived for Judge Beck Hardin. Inside was a plastic baggie with a cigarette butt and a note that read: *Beck, we went to the film shoot every day, but Zeke didn't show for a week. When he finally did, we screamed for him to come over. He was smoking. When he tossed his cigarette on the ground, I picked it up (with the tweezers). That's Zeke's butt! I could probably sell it for $1000 on eBay, so you owe me. Ruth.*

Ruth had been a great office wife.

Beck walked the baggie with the butt over to Grady's office. Doreen waved Beck back. "He's eating brunch."

"*Brunch?*"

Beck walked down the hall and into Grady's office; he stopped short. Gillespie County Sheriff Grady Guenther was eating all right, but he wasn't eating a messy Kraut dog with his hands. He was dining with a silver fork off white china on a cloth setting. A white cloth napkin was tucked under his chin.

"Grady, are you eating quiche?"

Grady nodded. "I don't know who Lorraine is, but she eats good."

"Where did you get quiche from?"

"The chef."

"The jail's got a chef now?"

Grady nodded again. "For thirty days." He called out: "Doreen, tell Lester to bring over another plate of this Lorraine stuff for the judge!" To Beck: "Brings his own dishes and silverware. Pots and pans, too."

Soon standing in the doorway was a chubby young man wearing a black-and-white striped GILLESPIE COUNTY INMATE uniform, black clogs, and a white chef's hat. He was holding a plate of quiche.

"*Oui, monsieur?*"

Grady pointed his fork and made introductions through a mouthful of quiche: "Beck, this here's Lester Fritz. Lester, meet Judge Hardin."

Lester gave Beck a little nod of his head, then handed the quiche to him. Beck put the plastic baggie on the desk.

"Thanks, Lester."

Grady said, "What's for dinner, Lester?"

"Chicken *cordon bleu*, risotto, *et soufflé au chocolat.*"

"Damn, that sounds good. Can we have some of them beignets tomorrow?"

"*Oui, monsieur.*"

Lester bowed then left. Grady said, "He ain't French, but he is a little light in his loafers. Owns that French restaurant— Lester's on Llano. His daddy's a goat rancher, but Lester didn't exactly fit in with the old Germans over at the auction house, so his daddy used his mohair money to send Lester to cooking school in New York. He come back five years ago and opened his place. Packs 'em in, cost you a hundred bucks to eat there. Lester's kind of gone whole hog, talking French and all, but the boy can cook. I let him out at night so he don't have to close his restaurant. Don't tell his parole officer."

"Why's he in jail?"

"Blue warrant."

"What's that?"

356

"Parole revocation warrant. We call 'em 'blue warrants' 'cause they used to be in blue jackets. Deal is, if the parole officer charges a parolee with a parole violation, law says we got to arrest and hold him in the county jail. No bond pending the parole board's determination whether to revoke parole."

"What did Lester do?"

"Nothing. He's on parole for a drug offense, but he's in my jail 'cause his parole officer gives him jail therapy twice a year."

"Jail therapy?"

"Little jail time just to make sure he's staying straight."

"Is he?"

"I figure so, now that he's got the restaurant. But if his parole officer jacks him, there ain't nothing I can do. Parole board won't revoke 'cause he ain't done nothin', but the law says he's got to spend thirty days in my jail no matter. Upside is, he cooks for everyone, guards and inmates. He's good about it, gives me a grocery list, I send one of the deputies over to the H-E-B. We use our Homeland Security fund."

Doreen stuck her head in. "Sheriff, Maurice Lackey's on the line, wants to know can he come in and serve his blue warrant. He heard Lester's in."

"Yeah, tell Maurice to come on in."

Doreen disappeared and Beck said, "You got guys with outstanding warrants calling to surrender?"

Grady nodded. "Happens every time Lester's in."

"No one surrenders in Chicago, I don't care how good the food is."

"Eating Lester's food three times a day for free, watching the soaps, it don't get any better than that for Maurice. Soon as word gets out that Lester's in, I'll have a waiting list."

"Surrendering for jail food?"

"Hell, Beck, I'd serve thirty days to eat Lester's cooking. Damn sight better than my wife's. You ought to come over tomorrow for his beignets, those suckers are good." Grady pointed his fork at the baggie. "What you got there?"

357

"Zeke Adam's butt. Cigarette."

"And?"

"I want a DNA test on the saliva on that butt to see if it matches up with the DNA samples from Heidi."

"You're serious about tracking this guy down."

"Yeah, I'm serious."

"Okay. You're the judge." Then: "Lester'll be back in a minute with fresh coffee. French roast."

Wes was drinking a Starbucks on a Malibu beach.

Wes Wagner was the dirt man. His specialty was digging for dirt. He would dive into dumpsters and sift through trash bags. He would wait outside hotel rooms and cheap rent houses with a camera. He would pose as a repairman or a telephone lineman or the dogcatcher searching for a stray. He would follow cheap hookers all night, and he would catch a husband or CEO with his pecker in the wrong place. He would do whatever it took, but he would always get his dirt.

He knew his job.

He also knew his DNA: you can get DNA from blood (liquid or dried), skin, saliva (spit, licked envelopes, cigarette and cigar butts), semen (liquid or dried), hair (with follicle attached), fingernails, bone, teeth, urine, and anal swabs (Wes didn't go there); you cannot get DNA from hair without follicle attached, blood without white blood cells, or dried urine.

He would get Joe Raines' DNA that morning.

He was standing behind a rope stretched between barricades. They were shooting a big-budget motion picture, so Wes wasn't alone. Standing there with him were a hundred barely-dressed groupies hoping to catch Joe's eye as he walked from the set to his air-conditioned trailer after the shoot wrapped. Gorgeous girls hoping to become Joe's latest lay. All he had to do was wink or point or send his personal bodyguard after a girl.

The girls' voices rose above his thoughts: "Joe! Joe!"

Joe Raines was walking their way. He was dressed only in

358

swim trunks. Best Wes could tell, he was playing a lifeguard in the movie. He was only thirty and his body was tanned and had been shaped by a personal trainer. He slowed as he approached the groupie gauntlet. His eyes scanned the crowd; the girls pushed to the front where they could be seen and their bodies appreciated. Wes noticed Joe's eyes pause on a redhead. Funny, but there could be a hundred gorgeous blondes and one redhead, and the stars would always go for the redhead. Why is that?

Joe walked to the trailer and climbed the few steps and entered. His bodyguard followed him in, but didn't shut the door. The bodyguard backed down the steps and came over to the chorus line. He walked straight to the redhead.

Wes shook his head: told you.

The redhead ducked under the rope and followed the bodyguard to the trailer. She was an incredible specimen: long lean legs, a miniskirt, and a tank top; a perfect body; and that mane of red hair. Wes once had a one-night stand with a girl who looked like her; she had cost a thousand dollars.

The redhead disappeared into the trailer, and the groupie gauntlet sighed as one. They had struck out today. Even Joe Raines couldn't keep that up after every take.

The other girls slowly scattered, muttering about trying again tomorrow. Wes waited. If he knew his movie-making business, and he did, Joe had only a thirty-minute break before the next take. Once the director and crew had set the scene with a double for camera distance and angle, Joe would be called back to the set to say his lines. Which lines he was supposed to be studying at that moment instead of some red-haired pussy. But Joe Raines was a star. He could do whatever he wanted to do.

Sure enough, thirty minutes later the bodyguard reappeared and knocked on the trailer door. Joe soon appeared; he walked down the steps and over to the set. The bodyguard held the door open. Wes heard him say, "Hurry up."

Some thanks.

The redhead appeared in the doorway; her hair was a mess and she was adjusting her top. The bodyguard locked the trailer door behind her. She walked toward the barricades. Wes stepped over and lifted the rope for her. He said, "I'll give you a hundred dollars for your panties."

She stopped and stared at him like he was a pervert.

"You're sick. Besides, I'm wearing a thong."

"I'll give you a hundred dollars for your thong."

She started to walk on.

"Two hundred."

She stopped.

"Cash?"

Wes reached into his pocket and pulled out two crisp hundred-dollar bills. "Did Joe wear a rubber?"

She laughed. "Stars never wear rubbers."

"Jump up and down," Wes said.

"*What?*"

Wes motioned with his hand. "Jump up and down. So gravity can do its work. I want those little Joes."

"You really are sick."

"Three hundred."

She jumped up and down.

He timed her for fifteen seconds, then said, "That'll do."

He pulled out another hundred and held the three bills out to her. She snatched them out of his hands. He reached to his back pocket and removed the zip-lock plastic baggie. Freezer-sized. He didn't want to touch that thing. Thong.

"Give it up."

She reached under her skirt and pulled down her thong, then stepped out of it. Wes held out the baggie.

"In the bag."

She dropped the thong into the bag like she was making a donation to the Salvation Army Santa at Christmas, then she walked away. He sealed the baggie and went over to his Mustang up on the street. He placed the baggie in the FedEx overnight box with Beck Hardin's address on it, wrote *Joe Raines* and $500 on the back of his business card, and dropped the card into the box. He then drove to the nearest FedEx drop-off and sent Joe's DNA to Texas.

Only two weeks before, the Immigration and Customs Enforcement Division of the United States Department of Homeland Security had come into Fredericksburg and conducted a raid, arrested eight hundred thirty-nine Mexican nationals residing in town, and deported them to Mexico. Families had been torn apart, lives disrupted, and businesses shuttered. But high school football in Texas went on.

When they walked into the Gallopin' Goats Stadium for the final game of the season against arch-rival Kerrville, Beck knew this game was going to be different. A big banner announced the "Nike High School Football Game of the Week." Television cameras were perched on portable towers positioned around the field. The field was lit up like high noon.

High school football on national TV.

From the conversations he overheard on the way to their seats, the national exposure the game would give Fredericksburg was viewed as a major stroke of luck: more shoppers for Thanksgiving weekend. No one spoke of the deported Mexicans.

They took their seats. Judge Hardin was again an accepted member of the community, so he was greeted with smiles and handshakes from nearby spectators. Jodie and Libby swapped seats with a coach's wife and joined them.

The Goats took the opening kickoff. On the first play on offense, Slade ran around right end and didn't stop running until he crossed the goal line seventy-six yards away. He walked over to the sideline and kicked over the Gatorade cooler, then stood alone ten yards away from the rest of his team. Aubrey turned toward Slade; before he turned back to the field, he looked up to where Beck was sitting. He turned his palms up.

With every touchdown Slade scored, four in the first half,

his anger escalated and two words haunted Beck: homicidal rage. When Slade scored again in the second half to put the Goats up 35–0, he stood in the end zone and pounded his chest like Tarzan. He was flagged for unsportsmanlike conduct. The game was a rout, so Aubrey tried to remove Slade from the game, but Slade refused to be taken out. He scored again; this time he threw the ball at an opponent. He was ejected from the game. He walked to the sideline and kicked the team bench over. On national TV.

Beck found Quentin McQuade a few rows over. His son had scored five touchdowns, but the look on his face wasn't that of a proud father. Quentin looked like an investor watching the stock market plunge.

Chapter 31

Eddie Steele was thirty-five years old and married with three children. The young blonde sitting at the table next to him, whose lovely right hand was rubbing Eddie's left leg, wasn't his wife or daughter. She was his girlfriend. Eddie lived with his wife in L.A., but he screwed around on her in La Jolla.

A week after collecting Joe Raines' DNA, Wes had followed Eddie Steele down the Pacific Coast highway. Eddie had gone to his girlfriend's condo and taken care of his base desires, so semen would not be the source of his DNA. Wes went to Plan B. Blood.

The restaurant had open-air seating on the deck overlooking the ocean. It was a small private place where you could dine with your mistress without being mugged by photographers. Wes had taken a table across the deck from Eddie and the girl. He now pulled out a large bill and stood. He walked toward Eddie and the girl and just as he was next to their table he dropped the hundred. It floated to the ground. The girl spotted it and instinctively dove for it. Wes squatted quickly so his face was almost touching hers when they simultaneously grabbed the bill.

"Oh, I'm sorry," he said. "Is this yours?"

"Yes."

Wes waited. The girl waited. Finally Eddie leaned over them, and when his shadow blocked out the light, Wes abruptly rose, driving the top of his head directly into Eddie's surgically perfected nose. Which, combined with his regular cocaine habit, made for a nasty nosebleed.

Eddie cried out—"Shit!"—and cupped his nose. Blood appeared on his fingers. Wes was quick with the new white cotton handkerchief; it was out of his pocket and onto Eddie's nose before Eddie could say "shit" again.

"Man, I'm sorry. Are you okay?"

Eddie pushed him away. "Get off me!"

Everyone was looking now, and waiters were hurrying their way. Wes walked away with a blood sample and the hundred-dollar bill. He glanced back. The girl was searching both sides of her chair for the bill.

Chapter 32

"Look at these pictures of little kids with big guns and dead animals," Jodie said.

She held the paper up for Beck to see. During hunting season, the local paper printed a special section with photos of kids and the deer they had killed.

Jodie said, "There's actually a program called 'Take a Child Hunting'? Is it just me, or is that kind of creepy?"

Aubrey said, "It's just you."

"That's supposed to teach a kid character? Why don't they call it 'Teach a Kid to Kill'? Maybe they should have 'Take a Child Bar Hopping' or 'Take a Child to a Crack House'. I've seen this every year for ten years and it's still disgusting."

"Jodie," Aubrey said, "Hunting's a tradition in the country."

"Praise the Lord and pass the ammo. All those fat guys in camouflage outfits—Main Street looks like an NRA convention. And why do the schools let out for the stock show but not for Martin Luther King Day—it's a national holiday, for Pete's sake."

Aubrey said, "Maybe 'cause there's thousands of livestock in the county but no black people . . . except for Gil."

"Yeah, they're afraid of being deported back to Africa." She shook her head. "I still can't believe all those people are gone, kids still without their parents." Back to the paper: "Oh, look, they printed the bag limits on deer, wild boar, Mexicans . . ."

Aubrey shook his head. "Girl, you are fired up today."

J.B. called from the kitchen: "All right, boys and girls. Let's eat our Thanksgiving chicken."

The Hardins had always eaten turkey on Thanksgiving. But not that Thanksgiving. Beck had stood in the frozen food department at the grocery store staring at the birds, but he couldn't bring himself to buy one. So J.B. had barbecued chicken instead. Thanksgiving chicken. J.B. said, "Well, it don't make much sense, but it eats good."

Jodie, Janelle, and their kids had brought sweet potato casserole, fruit salad, and pumpkin pie. Aubrey had brought beer.

After lunch, they found spots around the big-screen TV and watched the Cowboys play the Colts. Fredericksburg was geographically closer to Houston than Dallas, but the Cowboys were the overwhelming team of choice among the locals, even though the Cowboys had a Mexican quarterback. Of course, he didn't call the plays in Spanish.

No Spanish was spoken in the Cowboys' huddle or on Main Street in Fredericksburg, Texas, that Thanksgiving weekend. No Mexicans marched in the street or on the sidewalks. Those who had not been deported remained invisible. Only white shoppers from the city crowded Main Street. Sales were booming. All was well in Fredericksburg, Texas. But not with Aubrey.

"Don't hold back on me, Beck. Tell me what you know."

The sun was orange and low in the sky. They were sitting on the front porch watching the llama named Sue chase the pot-bellied pig down the caliche road. Aubrey turned his head and spat a stream of brown tobacco juice straight through the white porch spindles five feet away.

"I'll tell you one thing I know, Aubrey. If you miss and spit on J.B.'s porch, he's going to take that cane of yours and beat you stupid."

366

"He'd do that, wouldn't he?"

"You damn right he would."

Aubrey pushed himself up and limped to the railing. He spat out the wad of chewing tobacco then returned to his chair.

"Tell me what you know, Beck."

What did he owe his old friend? Did he owe him the truth about his daughter? Or just his leg? The life he could have had or the life he had had? Beck didn't know.

So he told Aubrey about Heidi's dream of being a star (but not about her nude photos or her abortion); he told him about Heidi going to the Austin Film Festival and the black limo in Austin and the black limo in Fredericksburg that same night (but not about Heidi's clothes or that she had sex with two men); he told him about the shoe he had found but that no fingerprints had been found (but not about the two different DNA samples that had been found on her body); and he told him that Heidi had been with a movie star that night.

"A movie star killed her?"

Beck nodded.

"Which one?"

"I'm getting DNA samples."

"How?"

"Don't ask."

"We've only got thirty-nine days to find him."

"I know."

And he told Aubrey about Randi's house. "How could she afford that kind of house?"

Aubrey said, "I don't know. Hell, she didn't want a dime in the divorce. She just wanted out. But she's a good-looking woman. I didn't figure on her waiting tables." He paused, then said, "Did she ask about me?"

The pig was now chasing the llama named Sue back up the caliche road. Jodie stuck her head out the door. Beck winked at Aubrey and said, "Jodie, did you vote for Reagan in eighty-four?"

"Eighty-four? No, I was only . . ." She shook her head. Beck laughed. She said, "Almost. Where's Luke?"

Beck said, "Down at the winery."

"J.B. just came up from the winery, said he wasn't there."

"Maybe he's on the baseball field."

"He's not. I checked."

Beck stood.

"He's not inside?"

"No."

Aubrey stood.

"Jodie, did J.B. drive the Gator up here?"

"Yeah."

"Aubrey, take the Gator and go down to the west pasture. I'll go down to the river. We're losing light."

"Yep."

Aubrey limped across the porch. Beck jumped the rail and ran in the opposite direction. He ran around the house and past the baseball field and down the sloping land, picking up speed. His cowboy boots thudded loudly on the wood planks of the bridge across Snake Creek. Once across the creek, he ran full out down to the river. He broke through the cypress and willow trees at the river's edge, and he saw Luke. He was standing on the rock bridge on the far side of the river, pinned against the limestone bluff by three coyotes.

Beck saw the fear on his son's face.

And he felt that familiar surge of adrenaline hit him, the human body's fight-or-flight response. He was fighting. His boots would give him no traction on the rocks, so he ran into the shallow river without slowing. The coyotes heard him and turned on him. He waved his arms and screamed at the animals; one cut and ran. The others didn't. They were hungry. They turned and bared their teeth at him; they lunged at Beck and he at them.

He drove his fist into the first coyote's head, but the second one hit him hard and they went down into the water. The

368

coyote went for Beck's neck, but he threw him off and got to his feet just as the other one came at him. Beck grabbed the coyote by the neck as it kicked at him with its rear legs; he stared into those yellow eyes and felt the claws dig into his skin and bring blood and all the anger that had burned inside Beck Hardin for the last twenty-nine years to the surface. He grabbed the coyote with both hands and screamed as he swung it around and slammed its head onto the flat rock that Luke was standing on.

The animal's skull cracked like a pecan.

Beck heard the other coyote's growl and spun around just as it lunged for him. He reached out to grab the animal but heard an explosion and the coyote was knocked out of the air and into the river. It didn't move. Beck looked to the riverbank: J.B. lowered a rifle from his shoulder; Jodie was standing next to him and Aubrey was sitting in the Gator. Beck turned to his son. Luke took a frightened step toward him, then dove into his arms. Beck slumped down onto the rock, suddenly spent. He hugged his son hard. The boy was sobbing and his body was shaking.

"Are you okay, Luke?"

He nodded through tears. "Are they dead?"

"Yeah. They're dead."

"They came up the river, behind me. I never heard them. I turned and they were there. I didn't know what to do."

"You did good."

His son cried and said, "Why couldn't you save Mom, too?"

"Cancer's not like coyotes, Luke. I couldn't fight it for your mother. I couldn't get my hands on it. I wanted to. I wanted to kill it before it killed her. But I couldn't."

"I blamed you."

"I know."

J.B. and Jodie came splashing through the river to them. Aubrey limped behind. J.B. kicked the two dead coyotes.

"Bitches."

"Beck," Jodie said, "you're bleeding."

Beck now looked at himself. His shirt was shredded and wet with water from the river and blood from his chest and arms. He released his son and removed his shirt. He dipped the shirt into the river and wiped the blood from his body. He then pulled his boots off and dumped the water out.

"Well, these boots are shot."

Aubrey gave him a hand up and said, "Jodie, that's why kids in the country learn to shoot."

Dear J.B.,

I've seen the future. This is my last Thanksgiving and your last one alone. They will be with you next year, Beck and the children.

Love, Annie

Chapter 33

The Monday after Thanksgiving, Wes Wagner was on another movie set, this time at a winery in Napa Valley. Teddy Bodeman was playing the son of a winery patriarch who falls in love with the daughter of his father's bitter rival who owns the neighboring winery. *Romeo and Juliet* meets *Sideways*. Who thinks up this shit?

It was supposed to be a romantic comedy, but what was funny was the fact that Teddy Bodeman had to pee in a cup whenever the studio rep told him to. Teddy had been in and out of drug rehab since his first hit when he was twenty-three. He was thirty-seven now. His movie contracts now contained the "pee in a cup" clause: to prove he was staying clean throughout the entire filming, Teddy had to pee in a cup several times a day. A grown man pissing on command. But Wes figured, for $20 million, he'd pee on himself in public. Which he had done on more than one occasion for free.

Wes spotted the studio rep, the only guy wearing a suit. What a job, waiting around for some random opportunity to collect urine from another man. The shoot wrapped, and Teddy walked off the set. The studio rep intercepted him. No doubt he told

Teddy he wanted a cupful of pee because Teddy now appeared annoyed. The rep followed Teddy over to his trailer and climbed in after him. A few minutes later, the rep appeared with a little white sack. He carried it like he was carrying a feminine hygiene product.

Wes followed the rep to the parking lot. He was driving a Beemer convertible. Wes liked it when the target made his job easy. The rep got into the car and checked his hair. Wes walked around the other side and quickly jammed a roofing nail into the rear tire. He then said, "Hey, you got a flat tire back here."

"What?"

The rep got out and came around to that side.

"Yeah, you must've run over this nail."

"Shit."

Wes walked over to his Mustang. The rep stood there a few minutes, then went inside the winery, apparently looking for someone to change his tire. Wes went over to the Beemer. He leaned over, opened the white sack sitting on the passenger's seat, removed the urine specimen, and substituted another specimen. His specimen. When the test results on that urine came back, Teddy Bodeman was going to have some explaining to do.

Chapter 34

"Judge, it says here results on the first sample went out yesterday. But I've got staff taking off for the holidays. We'll get to the others next year."

"Next year will be too late. We've only got twenty-one days before the statute of limitations runs. I've got to have those test results by New Year's Eve!"

Two weeks later and the DPS Crime Lab was still so back-logged that Beck had not yet received results on the DNA samples from Zeke Adams, Joe Raines, Eddie Steele, and Teddy Bodeman. Wes was still searching for Chase Connelly.

"Judge," the DPS Crime Lab director said, "if it were a murder case, we'd expedite. But stat rape . . . come on."

"You know who's DNA you're testing?"

"No."

"Movie stars'."

"Like who?"

"When you get a match, I'll tell you."

The director laughed. "Okay, Judge, I'll push 'em."

Beck hung up. The lab was on board; now he had to get the D.A. on board. The D.A. said, "Our little beauty queen got picked up in Austin by one of the biggest movie stars in the world?"

"Yep."

"And he gave her the cocaine that killed her?"

"Yep."

"And he had sex with a minor?"

"Yep."

"Even if you're right, Judge—"

"Niels, it's time you called me Beck."

"Even if you're right, Beck, a DNA match from those samples isn't enough to convict. There's no chain of evidence. God knows where you got those samples from."

"A reliable source."

"Oh, yeah, I'll go to trial with that."

"It's enough to indict. All we need is probable cause. We can indict the guy that matches, then I'll sign a search warrant to get an official sample to confirm."

"Beck, I get the grand jury to indict one of those stars and it turns out he's the wrong guy, I'm gonna look dumber than that Duke D.A. And hell, this is all moot anyway. No way the crime lab is gonna have DNA results in time."

The D.A. stared past Beck as if in deep thought. He finally said, "You've got company," and nodded at the window. Beck turned. Jodie was standing at the window in her running outfit. She smiled and held up a cup of coffee. Beck opened the window.

Jodie said, "Small nonfat latte. I was coming this way, thought our coyote-killing judge might need one."

Beck thanked her and took the coffee. She jogged off, and Beck couldn't help but look after her a moment. When he turned from the window, the D.A. was frowning.

"You're not . . . you know"—he made a little punching motion with his fist—"with the lesbian?"

"No, I'm not. And her name's Jodie."

Beck needed the D.A., so he decided to play the ego card.

"Niels, that Duke D.A. didn't have DNA evidence. You will. Conclusive DNA evidence proving that a movie star had sex with a sixteen-year-old girl who died of a cocaine overdose in his limo. Imagine the media attention that case will bring, a Hollywood movie star on trial right here in Gillespie County, Texas. Hundreds of TV cameras camped out front, thousands of reporters . . . and you'll be the star of the show. You'll be on national TV every day."

The D.A.'s expression changed; Beck could see his mind working through the possibilities.

"National TV, huh?"

"Network."

"Could we televise the trial?"

He asked like a child asking if he could have an ice cream cone. Beck shrugged. "Sure, why not?"

"That'd be better than O.J. All these guys are white, so I wouldn't have to include minorities on the jury. I could stack it with my people—twelve angry Germans doing the Lord's work!"

"Hallelujah, brother."

The D.A.'s eyes got glassy. "This kind of case, I could skip right over being a judge, move straight up to the big house."

"The mansion."

"The Governor's Mansion. I'd be the D.A. who convicted a movie star, whoever this guy is. My name recognition would be off the friggin' charts all over the state."

"The nation."

The D.A. pointed a finger at Beck. "Let's find this guy! I'll have the grand jury on standby. We'll indict that son of a bitch on a Sunday if we have to!"

The D.A. was officially on board. Just then Sheriff Grady Guenther walked into the room and placed a plate of crepes covered in plastic wrap and a document on Beck's desk.

"From Lester. Strawberry. And this just came in. No match on the cigarette butt. Zeke Adams ain't the guy."

375

"Damn."

The D.A. said, "Lester got anymore of those?"

Grady said, "Yep," then turned to Beck and winked. "You know, killing a coyote barehanded, that's the kind of thing could make you unbeatable in next year's election."

The D.A. stood and walked to the door. "Things go right, you can have that chair the rest of your life because I'll be running for governor next election. Call me when you get a match."

Three days later, Grady walked into Beck's chambers and placed another plate and another document on Beck's desk.

"Beignets. No match on the semen from the thong. Joe Raines ain't the guy."

"Damn."

The next day, Grady walked into Beck's chambers and placed another plate and another document on Beck's desk.

"Cream puffs. No match on the blood. Eddie Steele ain't the guy."

"Damn."

Four days after that, Grady Guenther walked into Beck's chambers and placed another plate and another document on Beck's desk. Beck looked up at him.

"Strawberry crepes?"

"Cream cheese. Enjoy 'em, 'cause it's Lester's last day."

Beck held up the document. "No match?"

Grady smiled. "Match."

"*What?* We got him? Teddy Bodeman had sex with Heidi?"

"Oral. His DNA matches the sample from her blouse."

Beck slumped back in his chair. "Damn."

"Yeah. And we don't have jurisdiction to charge him—that blowjob occurred in Austin and that's Travis County."

"There might be something I can do."

★   ★   ★

"Judge Hardin, my client does not consent to this phone conversation being recorded. If you record it, you're violating the federal wiretapping law, and we will have you prosecuted."

"I'm not recording this conversation."

Beck had found Teddy Bodeman's agent's name and phone number on the Internet. He had called the agent, who refused to pass on Beck's request that Teddy call him back, until Beck told him it was in reference to a "blowjob Teddy got in Austin five years ago from a sixteen-year-old girl who died of a cocaine overdose in a movie star's limo that same night." An hour later, Teddy's lawyer had put through this conference call. Teddy Bodeman was on the line, but his lawyer was doing all the talking.

"Good. Now, Teddy has an airtight alibi for that night. From nine P.M. until eleven P.M., he attended a dinner at the Governor's Mansion in Austin with the governor of Texas, the governor's wife, the mayor of Austin and his wife, and two hundred other people. After the dinner, he went to a screening at the Paramount Theatre with the governor and the mayor and their wives. That lasted until one A.M. After that, Teddy gave the governor a ride home—in Teddy's limo. The governor of Texas was in Teddy's limo that night, Judge, not a sixteen-year-old girl."

That was a pretty good alibi, not that Beck thought Teddy had killed Heidi.

"I emailed the girl's photo. Do you recognize her, Mr. Bodeman?"

"No."

"Then why does your DNA match the semen sample obtained from her blouse?"

Teddy's lawyer: "How did you obtain Teddy's DNA?"

"None of your business."

Not that Beck knew how Wes had obtained Teddy's urine sample.

"We could sue and find out."

"But you won't. Answer my question, Mr. Bodeman."

"Look, there were lots of willing girls at that festival, there always are. Some blonde gave me a hummer in a booth in a bar. No big deal."

"Does that happen often?"

"All the time."

He sounded truthful.

"But you don't recognize Heidi?"

"No. They all look the same when their head's in my lap." Teddy chuckled; Beck didn't.

"After she gave you oral sex, what happened?"

"She asked if I could get her an audition."

"And what did you say?"

"I said that *was* her audition."

"Nice. And then what happened?"

"She left. A while later, we went to the dinner."

"Who's we?"

"My manager and my wife."

"Your wife was in the booth with you while a girl gave you oral sex?"

"Judge, we're a little less uptight about sex out here in Hollywood than you people in Texas."

"And you never saw the girl again?"

"No."

"Well, Teddy, your DNA proves that you had sex with a minor."

"She was in a bar, how would I know she was a minor?"

"Doesn't matter whether you knew or not."

"That's dumb."

"That's the law."

Teddy's lawyer jumped in: "Judge, his DNA doesn't prove anything. Teddy admits a blonde girl gave him oral sex that night. But that doesn't mean it was this girl. There were hundreds of blonde girls that night. Maybe some of Teddy's semen was left on the seat of the booth or on the edge of the table, and maybe this girl sat down in that booth when Teddy left and got his semen on her shirt that way. Or maybe the girl who gave him oral sex was walking out of the bar and sneezed on your girl and his semen was deposited in that manner on her shirt. Or maybe the girl wiped her mouth and had some on her hand and then wiped her hand on your girl's shirt. Or maybe . . ."

"I get your point."

"Good. So don't even think about going public with this, Judge, because I will sue your ass in a California court for defamation. And you don't have judicial immunity out here."

"Teddy, let me ask you something?"

"What's that?"

"You got kids?"

"Three."

"You think they'd be proud of you if they knew all this?"

"I think they're proud to be living in a mansion with servants."

"How old are you?"

"Thirty-seven."

"Grow up."

Teddy laughed. "Oh, and what would you do if a gorgeous young girl offered you sex, Judge? Would you turn it down?"

Gretchen was helping the children into their cars. Beck saw her from his spot deep in the carpool line. And he thought about what Teddy Bodeman had said. Was his law degree and lesser income the only difference between Beck Hardin and Teddy Bodeman?

He inched the Navigator forward in the carpool pickup lane outside the primary school until he was at the door. He spotted Meggie waiting there with her backpack strapped on; the thing was so big she looked like a little mountain climber.

Gretchen opened the back door for Meggie. "Hi, Beck."

"Hi, Gretchen."

She helped Meggie into her booster seat and strapped her in. "How's it going?"

"Scores came back, from the state achievement tests the kids took before the raid. Latinos didn't do well but no-one cares now—all the Latinos are gone." She shook her head. "Haven't seen you at the gym lately."

"It's been busy at the courthouse."

"I've still got Saturday nights open."

"I'm still forty-two."

"I've still got needs."

She winked at him, then shut the door.

Chapter 35

Wes could not find Chase Connelly.

Beck had called Wes twice a day; Chase Connelly had disappeared. Until J.B. found him that night. He called out to Beck from inside. "Here's your boy!"

"What?"

"I was looking for *The Beverly Hillbillies* and there he was."

"Who?"

"Chase Connelly. He's on TV."

Beck jumped out of the rocker and ran inside and over to the TV. On the screen was Jay Leno behind his desk. Sitting next to him was a young blond man wearing a black tee shirt under a leather jacket, jeans, and cowboy boots. He had a long cigar in his mouth. Beck turned up the volume.

Chase was saying, "Aw, heck, Jay, I ain't nuthin' but a country boy likes to swim nekkid in the creek down on the ranch."

That brought shrieks from the females in the audience.

"You can take the boy out of Texas, Jay, but you can't take Texas out of the boy." *Cain't.*

"You have a big ranch down in Texas?" Leno asked.

"Outside Austin, but it's not a big ranch. Just seven thousand acres."

Leno laughed. "That's not a big ranch?"

"Not in Texas. Golly, Jay, Texas is a big state."

"*Giant.*"

"Bigger than giant."

"No, the movie."

"What movie?"

"*Giant.*"

"It's big."

Beck pulled out his cell phone and hit the speed dial for Wes. It was two hours earlier in L.A. Wes answered on the second ring.

"Wes, it's Beck. Get over to the studio where they do the Leno show. Chase Connelly is over there right now!"

"It's a rerun, Beck. I checked. Chase is in Africa, some kind of celebrity we-are-the-world AIDS tour."

They hung up. Beck watched the rest of Chase's appearance on Leno. He was thirty-four years old and earned $20 million for each film plus a percentage of gross. He was married with a four-year-old daughter he adored. His playboy days, he assured Leno, were a thing of the past.

Which brought groans from the females in the audience.

Dear J.B.,

I have to get you ready for them, and we don't have much time. I'll email everything you need to know about the kids, what they eat, school, immunizations, etc. Can you build bedrooms for them? I'll send photos and I'll order everything and have it shipped to you. I want it just like home for them.

Meggie won't understand for a while that I'm really gone. Be patient and let her little mind work through it.

382

Luke will understand and he'll get angry. He'll go inside himself, he's just like Beck. Get him busy. And playing sports. Get him on a baseball field, that's where he's the happiest. I was thinking, can you build a baseball field? Eight hundred acres, there should be enough space. If you can build a winery, you can build a baseball field. Luke's good.

Beck is in denial.

Love, Annie

Chapter 36

Every Texas county has an appraisal district. And every appraisal district has a website. And on those websites are searchable listings of all real property in the county. The next morning, Beck had searched the Travis County website for *Connelly, Chase,* and found no properties recorded under his name. But Chase had said that he owned a ranch outside Austin.

So Beck had searched the counties adjacent to Travis County and the counties adjacent to those counties and the counties adjacent to those. He found no listings for Chase Connelly. Either Chase was lying about owning a ranch outside Austin or the ranch was listed in the name of an entity owned by Chase or . . . Chase Connelly wasn't his real name.

How would you find a movie star's real name?

But another thought occurred to Beck. A terrible thought. One he didn't want to even entertain. But he had to.

He logged back on to the Travis County appraisal district website. He typed in *Barnes, Randi,* Randi's property listing came up. He scrolled down. Total land and improvement value was $3,250,000. Total annual property taxes for Travis County, the

Travis County Hospital District, and the school district were $56,000. The deed date was 03152003.

He went to Mavis' office and asked her to pull the *Geisel vs. Geisel* divorce file. He took the gold file back to his chambers. He wrote out a timeline.

Heidi had died on December 31, 2002.

She was found on January 1, 2003.

She was buried on January 5, 2003.

Randi filed for divorce on January 10, 2003.

The divorce decree was signed by Stutz on March 12, 2003, the sixtieth day after filing, the statutory minimum waiting period. Randi waived all community property rights; she didn't want her share of the house valued at $157,000, or the checking account of $952, or the savings account of $4,231, or Aubrey's state teachers' retirement fund of $47,850. She just wanted out. She packed her clothes into her 1991 Volkswagen and left. The Austin house had been conveyed to Randi Barnes on March 15, 2003, three days after the divorce.

Beck walked out and told Mavis he was driving to Austin. She said, "You got a girlfriend over there?"

When Randi opened her front door, Beck said, "You blackmailed Chase Connelly."

Randi exhaled a stream of cigarette smoke, then said, "I settled with Chase Connelly."

She turned and walked into the living room. Beck shut the door and followed Randi outside onto the deck. She was dressed in a sweater, jeans, and high heels.

"When he killed her, he took all I had in life. We were more like sisters, Heidi and me, than mother and daughter. She even called me 'Sis.'"

"How did you know Heidi was with Chase?"

"She sent me a photo of them from inside the limo. Cell phone camera. My lawyer said that photo was enough to get a search warrant for Chase's DNA sample and once that sample matched what they found in Heidi, he'd be an inmate, not a movie star."

"Where's the photo?"

"In a safe place. And I won't give it up, Beck."

"That photo is enough to indict Chase."

"And mess up my deal."

"How much did he pay you?"

"Twenty-five."

"*Million?*"

She nodded.

"You sold out Heidi for twenty-five million dollars?"

"I settled a wrongful death claim for twenty-five million dollars."

"Why didn't you go public with that photo, after he paid you?"

"Confidentiality agreement."

"Where's that document at?"

"Also in a safe place."

"Chase Connelly isn't his real name?"

She shook his head.

"What is it?"

"I don't know."

"But you signed a settlement agreement with him."

"It was all done through an L.A. law firm. They wouldn't let me see his real name. I signed and they wired the money to my lawyer. He wired it to me . . . after deducting his share."

"Didn't you get a copy of the agreement?"

"My copy is held by a trustee who can give it to me only if Chase fails to pay. He paid five million upfront then one million a year for twenty years. If I talk, the money stops." She waved her hand at the house. "All this goes away. If I ruin Chase's career, he ruins my life. My lawyer said that's what they call a Mexican standoff."

"Randi, I can't believe you let Heidi's murderer go free."

"What was I supposed to do, Beck?"

"Go to the sheriff. Give him the photo so Chase could be charged with murder."

"Oh, yeah, like a jury's gonna convict Chase Connelly."

"Those hard-asses out there would."

"Not once the national media descended on that small town. They'd get stars in their eyes like everyone else."

"He could've been convicted for stat rape."

"Maybe. Maybe not. But the whole world would've said Heidi was just a slut. I didn't want that."

"No, you wanted money."

"Beck, she was gone. My dream was gone."

"So he still owes you, what?"

"Sixteen million."

"Has he already paid you for this year?"

"Yeah."

"It'd be cheaper for him just to kill you, too."

"He's not a killer, Beck. He's just a movie star. Besides, that cell phone, the photo, and a complete statement is in a safety deposit box. My lawyer will go public if anything happens to me and Chase doesn't pay—my lawyer wants his third. I'm not stupid, Beck. If I die, the money goes to Aubrey."

"He won't want it."

"Then he can give it away."

"You knew about her abortion?"

"I took her to get it."

"Who's the father?"

"I don't know."

"I think you do."

Beck gazed out on Lake Austin. The white sails of a dozen sailboats glowed in the sunlight.

"Randi, if Chase isn't indicted by midnight on New Year's Eve, he goes free. We've got twelve days to get justice for Heidi."

"Justice." She shook her head. "You're gonna mess up my deal, aren't you?"

"I always advised my clients to take lump sum settlements."

★　★　★

Beck returned to Fredericksburg and to his chambers. An hour of searching the Internet under *Chase Connelly* yielded names of two managers. One was Chase's former manager. His name was Billy Gray. Beck found a listing in L.A. Beck's experience had been that former employees often nursed grudges and could be sources of damaging information. Billy answered his own phone.

"Mr. Gray, my name is Judge Beck Hardin. From Texas."

Billy sighed heavily. "Who is it?"

"Who is what?"

"Which of my clients did something stupid in Texas?"

"Chase Connelly."

Billy laughed. "Good."

"Why is that good?"

"Because he's not my client anymore."

"When did you quit him?"

"I didn't. He fired me four years ago. I made him what he is today, a star worth twenty million per film, but I'm not getting my ten percent."

"Why'd he fire you?"

"Because Clooney won 'Sexiest Man Alive' instead of him. Five films since then, he owes me ten million."

"I doubt he'll voluntarily pay up."

"No, he's got lots of high-priced lawyers, Theodore does."

"Do you have his home—who's Theodore?"

Billy laughed. "His name's not Chase Connelly. I made that name up. His real name is . . . oh, I signed a confidentiality agreement . . . but he owes me money . . . so why can't I tell what I know? His real name is Theodore Biederman. He's a rich boy from Houston. His father's a doctor."

"Billy, do you have Chase's . . . Theodore's phone numbers?"

"These might not be current."

Billy gave Beck two numbers.

"Does he have a regular driver?"

388

"Rudy Jaramillo."

"You got his number?"

The numbers Billy Gray gave Beck were all disconnected, and there were no new numbers listed. So Beck called information for the Houston area code and asked for a home phone number for "Doctor Biederman." He dialed that number; a woman answered.

"Hello."

"Mrs. Biederman?"

"Yes."

"I'm Judge Hardin, from out in Fredericksburg."

"Oh, Fredericksburg. We loved to shop there, the doctor and I. Until he died."

"I'm sorry to hear that."

"Cancer. Six months ago."

"Mrs. Biederman, I'm trying to find Chase . . . Theodore."

"You'll have to go to Hollywood. He came home for the funeral, but he hates Texas. I don't know why."

"Do you have his phone number in L.A.?"

"You're a judge?"

"Yes, ma'am."

"Because he gets mad when I give his private number out."

"Oh, he'll be happy to hear from me."

Beck dialed Theodore's private home number in L.A. A woman picked up. "Hello."

"May I speak with Chase, please."

"He's out of town. May I take a message?"

"Is Mrs. Connelly home?"

"I'm Helen Connelly. Who is this?"

"I'm Judge Hardin in Texas. I need to speak with Chase."

"He's out of the country. What is this about?"

"Well, it's of a personal nature."

389

"Is it of a female nature?"

"Why do you ask?"

She sighed. "Because I know my husband."

Chapter 37

He had taken his wife for granted. She had always been there, and he had just assumed she always would be. Then one day she wasn't there. She wasn't there to kiss him goodbye when he left in the morning or kiss him hello when he returned that night. She didn't answer when he absentmindedly pulled out his cell phone and hit the speed dial for her cell phone, to tell her he'd be late. She wasn't there when he turned over in bed and reached out for her and . . .

Beck sat up in bed. Where's Meggie? He hurried down the hall to her room. She was sitting in bed talking to the doll.

"Hi, Daddy."

"You didn't have an accident last night?"

"Nope. We decided not to have accidents anymore. Mommy says you and J.B. are here to take care of me and I don't have to be afraid just because she's not."

December 22, and still no Chase Connelly. Nine days left, and Wes wasn't going to Africa to get Chase's DNA sample.

"Speed limit's sixty," J.B. said.

Beck was driving the Navigator. Riding in the third seat were

391

Libby (reading the newspaper), Danny (listening to an iPod), and Luke (playing the Gameboy); in the second seat were Jodie, Janelle, and Meggie in the middle (holding the doll). J.B. was wearing another Hawaiian print shirt (goat-crap yellow) and riding shotgun (giving instructions to Beck); he didn't like to back-seat drive, so he had sat up front.

"I know the speed limit," Beck said.

"Car must not. It's running sixty-five."

"J.B., you and that shirt can ride in the third seat on the way home. Jodie can ride shotgun."

Janelle said, "She's worse than J.B."

They were driving to San Antonio along with most of the residents of Fredericksburg for the state football championship game. Slade McQuade and the Gallopin' Goats were overwhelming favorites over the team from Houston. The caravan of SUVs and trucks stretched down Interstate 10 for miles. From the back, Libby said, "Mom, can we go to Austin next Saturday?"

"Why?" Jodie said.

"To go to a golf course."

"You want to play golf?"

"I want to watch Chase Connelly play golf."

Beck steered the Navigator to the shoulder and braked to a stop. He turned in his seat and said to Libby: "Chase Connelly is going to be in Austin next Saturday?"

"That's what it says here."

"May I see it please?"

Libby held out the paper. Jodie handed it forward to Beck. He read. Chase Connelly was scheduled to appear in a celebrity golf tournament next weekend at the Barton Creek Resort in Austin to promote AIDS awareness. Chase was an avid golfer and planned to arrive a few days early to practice. He would fly into Austin directly from Africa. His manager said, "Chase loves Texas. He can't wait to get home." He was also the newly crowned "Sexiest Man Alive."

★   ★   ★

392

Before dawn on March 6, 1836, eighteen hundred Mexican soldiers led by Santa Anna attacked one hundred eighty-nine men defending the *Misión San Antonio de Valero*, commonly known as the Alamo. By first light, the defenders were dead, including James Bowie, Davy Crockett, William B. Travis, a dozen Englishmen, eight Irishmen, four Scotsmen, one Welsh-man, and nine *Tejanos*. "Remember the Alamo" became the Texas battle cry, and the word "Alamo" came to symbolize all that was great about Texas. One hundred seventy-one years later, it was the name of a football stadium.

The Alamodome was built by the City of San Antonio in 1993 for $186 million as a state-of-the-art 65,000-seat football stadium for the specific purpose of attracting a pro football team to town. Build it and they will come.

They didn't come.

Today the Alamodome hosts home and garden shows, boat shows, dog shows, motocross and monster truck rallies, *American Idol* auditions, evangelical crusades, the Dallas Cowboys summer training camp, the Alamo Bowl, and the high school championship football game.

Few of the 65,000 seats were empty that day. The stands on the far side of the field were solid gold, the color of the Houston team; the Goats side of the field was solid plaid. The Goat band in their black-and-white uniforms was out on the field performing as part of the pre-game festivities. The Goat cheerleaders were performing stunts on the sideline, and the Goat Gals were doing dance routines. Television cameras surrounded the field; the game would be televised live across the State of Texas. Colorful advertisements for cars, trucks, soft drinks, and sneakers decorated the arena. It was the super bowl of Texas.

The two best high school teams in Texas were playing, but everyone had come to see the best high school football player in the country. Everyone had come to see Slade McQuade.

Quentin McQuade was standing before a TV camera and giving an interview. Slade was warming up on the sideline. He had single-handedly won all five playoff games by lopsided scores; and with each game his on-the-field behavior had become more bizarre. Taunting, fighting, cursing, spitting—he was a football player coming undone. Each time he ran the ball, he wasn't just trying to score; he was trying to hurt someone.

Homicidal rage.

When Slade took the field for the first time, the sea of plaid seemed to hold its collective breath, as if waiting for him to explode. They didn't have to wait long. Slade's first play was a thirty-five yard run; he got up and pushed the defender who had tackled him. He scored on the next play. He threw the ball in the tackler's face. The referee threw a yellow flag.

Slade scored four more times in the first half. He taunted the other players, he started fights, he cursed, and he got four more unsportsmanlike penalties. He came off the field and pushed one of his teammates, kicked over the Gatorade table, and threw his helmet at the mascot. Aubrey came over to calm him, but Slade pushed him away and walked twenty yards down the sideline. He stood there by himself until the half ended.

Slade's game ended with the first play of the second half. He ran the ball around end for sixty-seven yards and another touchdown. Then he stood over the last defender lying on the ground and taunted him; then he kicked him. The Houston players on the sideline ran onto the field en masse; Slade attacked the bunch of them. He punched players who weren't wearing helmets, he grabbed the facemasks of those who were and flung them to the ground, and he picked up one boy and threw him to the ground. He looked like something from a Schwarzenegger movie.

Police and security staff ran onto the field and separated Slade and the Houston team. The referees ejected Slade from the game. He walked toward the locker room, undressing along the way. He removed his helmet and flung it onto the field. His jersey and shoulder pads were next. Then came his tee shirt and wrist bands. Finally his doo-rag. His massive muscular body disappeared under the stands. Quentin McQuade jogged after his son. He didn't look like a man worth two hundred million dollars.

The drive home was quiet. Jodie rode shotgun. She said, "You okay?"

"Slade's out of control. He's going to hurt somebody."

When they arrived back in town, Beck cut over from Highway 87 to Ranch Road 6 and turned north to take Jodie and Janelle and their kids home. He drove a few blocks then abruptly turned west on Milam. He had gotten into the habit of driving through the barrio at least once a day. He stopped.

The barrio was gone.

The shacks, sheds, shanties, trailers, cars, furniture, trash, and even the Nativity scene were now just a huge pile of junk. The barrio had been scraped clean down to the dirt. Six massive bulldozers were scooping up the barrio and loading it onto dump trucks lined up and waiting to cart it all away to the city landfill east of town.

J.B. said, "I'll be damned."

Beck got out. He walked to where Julio's home had been. The Espinoza family had bought five acres outside of town and a trailer to live in until Rafael could build a house; they had moved out of the barrio two weeks ago. They had been the last to leave. They were gone and the barrio was gone. And it was Beck's fault. He felt someone next to him.

Jodie said, "I'm sorry, Beck."

"I wanted to get justice for these people. I wanted to punish Quentin for his son's sins. But I punished these people instead."

Judge John Beck Hardin had forgotten the law of unintended consequences.

Chapter 38

Christmas was different that year.

Three days after the game, Meggie and the doll woke Beck at six. Santa had found them at their new home, which had been a big concern for her. Beck acted happy for the kids. Jodie had helped him buy clothes and toys for Meggie, and he had bought Luke new baseball equipment and a bucket of batting practice balls. He smiled when he saw his presents. The baseball field was waiting. Then Meggie asked, "Will Mommy be back by next Christmas?"

And Luke's smile was gone.

Beck gave J.B. a belt with "J.B. Hardin" etched along the backside; J.B. gave Beck a pair of cowboy boots to replace the ones he had ruined in the river. J.B. then handed another wrapped present to Beck and said, "From Jodie."

"She gave me a present?"

On the box was a note card that read: *You're in a rut. Jodie.* Inside the box was a loud Hawaiian print shirt. Beck was still in his pajamas and robe when there was a knock on the front door. Meggie was showing J.B. her gifts and he was acting interested, so Beck stood and walked to the door.

"That's probably Aubrey."

It wasn't. Sheriff Grady Guenther was standing on the porch.

"Grady. Merry Christmas. Come on in."

Grady's face was somber. "You'd better come out, Beck."

Beck stepped out onto the front porch and shut the door behind him. "Something wrong, Grady?"

Grady stared into the distance and exhaled. "It's Slade."

Beck's heart jumped. "He hurt someone."

Grady shook his head. "He's dead."

"*Slade's dead?*" How?"

"Suicide. City cop patrolling about four this morning saw his Hummer outside the football stadium, so he stopped to check. Couldn't find him, so he turned on the stadium lights. There he was, spread-eagled on the fifty-yard line, with the championship trophy next to him. Self-inflicted gunshot to the head."

"He killed himself?"

"Yep. Gun belonged to Quentin."

The strength seemed to drain from Beck's legs. He dropped into a chair. He ran his hands over his face; the temperature was in the fifties, but he had broken a sweat.

"Quentin know?"

Grady nodded. "Drove out there myself. He said they had a big yelling fight the night before, about him bulldozing the barrio. Slade was pretty upset, crying and all. I searched his room—no note, but the place looked like a drugstore. Needles, vials, pills . . . and holes in the sheetrock, where Slade had punched. Quentin broke down and cried, said he was just trying to be a good father, pushing the boy to be better."

"I was worried he would hurt someone else. But not himself."

"Don't beat yourself up, Beck. Nothing you could've done."

"I could've put him in jail. I could've gotten him off steroids."

"Beck, you ain't his daddy. Quentin is."

"And Quentin isn't the judge. I am. Slade was my responsibility, too."

"You're just a judge, Beck. You can't make the world right."

★   ★   ★

At sunset, J.B. drove them into town for the Santa Run. He parked on Main Street at the finish line across from the courthouse and in front of the Marktplatz. He lowered the tailgate, and the four Hardins sat and waited for the Santas.

Christmas lights were strung over Main Street and wound up light poles and outlined every building, even the courthouse; the grounds were lit and the Eagle Tree spotlighted. The Marktplatz had Christmas trees and decorations and lights; every tree in the square was strung with lights. There was even a Nativity scene.

Hundreds of people had come into town for the run. The Santas had gathered at the starting line down Main Street at the Nimitz. They abruptly broke ranks and raced toward them, a herd of red-suited, white-bearded Santas stampeding their way. They cheered when Jodie crossed the finish line; she was the first woman. She won a prize. She came over and Meggie hugged her, and Luke gave her a high-five. J.B. congratulated her, and then she looked at Beck.

"What's wrong?"

"Slade's dead."

Dear J.B.,

Merry Christmas. Did you get the photo? That's Beck's favorite one of me. That's how I want him to remember me, young and alive. Put it where he'll see it always.

Oh, you'll have to remind Beck about birthday and Christmas presents because I've always shopped for the kids and his secretary always shopped for me. He doesn't know I know. Ruth always called and asked what I wanted.

I gave Meggie a doll for Christmas. She said it looked like me. I gave Luke a practice hitting trainer. I had a dream, J.B. Luke was batting, you were pitching, and Beck was catching the balls in the outfield. Meggie was sitting in the bleachers. J.B., build that baseball field. Do that for me.

I have a hospice nurse now. Her name is Julie.

Love, Annie

Chapter 39

Beck had failed as a husband and father. He had failed as the judge of a small rural Texas county. He had failed Felix Delgado and Julio Espinoza and 839 Mexicans and their children. He had failed Slade.

"It's my fault," Aubrey said.

"No, it's my fault." ·

"I knew he was on steroids."

"So did I. And I could've stopped him."

"But I helped him."

It was the next afternoon. Beck had driven into town past the high school where a satellite van for cable sports TV was parked. Aubrey was now sitting on the other side of the desk in his chambers.

"You helped him do what?"

Aubrey exhaled. "Slade introduced the other boys to the wonders of science. I knew something was up when half the team gained twenty pounds of muscle over the summer. I threatened to kick them off the team, but they knew I was bluffing—their daddies run this place and everything in it. And they liked what the stuff did to them. Bigger, stronger, faster. Steroids work."

"So what, you became the team doctor?"

"I tried to educate them so they didn't hurt themselves. Some guy at a body-building gym in Austin would tell Slade what to do, he'd tell the others, and the whole team's overdosing on the stuff. I had a bunch of goddamn psychos on the practice field. That's when I decided to help them."

"What'd you do?"

"Explained how to cycle, not to overdo it. Checked the stuff to make sure it wasn't made in Mexico from bull testicles."

"Did you supply the steroids?"

"No. Slade did. He bought the stuff in Austin."

"Jesus, Aubrey. I don't think you committed a crime, just giving them information, but you should've stopped them."

"Beck, they were gonna juice whether I liked it or not. These boys want out, and a football scholarship is a ticket out."

Beck sat back. "What am I supposed to do now, Aubrey? Look the other way? Aubrey, both of us should've done the right thing. Only two people in a small town with the power to stand up and do the right thing—the football coach and the judge."

Aubrey left, and Beck picked up the local paper. An entire section was devoted to Slade McQuade: his football career from seventh grade when he moved to town through his senior season that had just ended with a state championship. Slade's photos filled the pages; at nineteen his face was that of an action-hero chiseled from stone; at fifteen his face was still boyish and thin and . . . familiar. Where had Beck seen that face?

He remembered.

Kim Krause answered Beck's knock on her front door. He said, "May I see that video of Heidi again?"

She shrugged, went inside, and returned with the laptop. They sat on the steps, and she played Heidi's music video again. Beck watched closely.

"Stop. Right there. The face in the mirror. That's not you. That's Slade."

She nodded.

Beck said, "Slade was the father of Heidi's child."

Kim stared past him. "They were the two most beautiful kids in town." She shrugged. "They had to hook up."

"Did Slade know about the baby?"

She nodded. "His dad paid for the abortion."

Beck felt so tired. "Was she ever happy?"

"*Happy?* Who's happy?" Kim tapped on the computer. "Here's her *Oprah* interview."

"She was on *Oprah?*"

"We just pretended. She was practicing."

The video began playing. Heidi's image appeared on the screen. She was in her pink and blue room and wearing jeans, high heels, and a sweater. She sat in a chair next to her bed and faced the camera.

Kim said, "I was Oprah."

Kim's voice came across: "My special guest today is Heidi Fay, the nineteen-year-old star of the hit movie, *Once Upon A Time*. Heidi, this must be a dream come true."

Heidi, with a movie-star smile: "Oh, Oprah, it is. It really really is." She stopped abruptly. "I shouldn't say really twice. Sounds like a hick." She recaptured the moment and said, "Oh, Oprah, it is. It really is."

Kim as Oprah: "Tell us about your childhood back in Texas."

Heidi: "Oh, it was wonderful, Oprah. I grew up in a small Texas town, very quaint and beautiful, the perfect all-American town. My childhood was just wonderful. My parents are the greatest. They've been so supportive of my dreams and . . ."

The smile dropped off her face. Her shoulders slumped. She suddenly appeared sad. She said, "My father's a fucking prison warden, my mother's a fucking stage mother, and my hometown is a bunch of fucking goat ranchers scared of the outside world. Other than that, it's been a fucking great childhood, Oprah."

She looked at the camera—at Kim. She shook her head. "God, Kim, I'd do anything to get out of this town. And when

I go to Hollywood, it's just gonna be me and you. My mother is not coming."

She just sat there. Finally, Kim's voice came across: "I don't think you can say 'fuck' on *Oprah*."

Heidi looked at the camera, broke into a big smile, grabbed a pillow off the bed, and flung it at the camera. She jumped forward and knocked the camera over; it captured them rolling on the floor and giggling like little girls.

Beck now looked at Kim. Tears were rolling down her face. She said, "They both wanted to be stars. Now they're both dead."

Texas law requires that the medical examiner investigate all suicides, and if necessary to determine the cause of death, conduct an autopsy. Slade's body lay on a steel table in the Travis County Medical Examiner's office in Austin. Beck went back to his chambers and called Dr. Janofsky; the ME said he would complete the autopsy and have results from blood tests back the next day.

Chapter 40

On November 22, 1963, Texas Governor John Connally sat directly in front of President Kennedy in the presidential limousine in the motorcade through downtown Dallas. According to the Warren Commission, Lee Harvey Oswald's first or second shot struck Kennedy in the back of his neck, exited his throat, then struck Connally in his back, exited his chest, then struck his wrist, and finally lodged in his thigh. A pristine bullet was found on Connally's gurney at Parkland Memorial Hospital. This so-called "magic bullet" made Lee Harvey Oswald the lone gunman and John Connally a Texas legend.

Real estate made him bankrupt.

In 1985, Connally borrowed $93 million to develop Barton Creek Estates and Resort on the western outskirts of Austin and above the environmentally sensitive Barton Creek watershed that fed the Barton Creek pool where for hundreds of years everyone from the Comanche Indians to Robert Redford had swum. But where the Indians and Redford had seen untouched land and cool spring-fed waters, Connally saw million-dollar homes, a European spa, and a world-class golf course. The environmental group Save Our Springs opposed the development, but they were not Texas legends. John Connally built his Barton Creek Resort.

Two years later, it bankrupted him.

Now Beck was watching another Texas legend named Connelly whacking golf balls wildly on the driving range at the Barton Creek Golf Club. Chase Connelly was smaller than he seemed on television, no more than five-ten and perhaps one-fifty. He appeared almost gaunt. But he seemed congenial. He stopped when interrupted by fans seeking autographs; he signed, he smiled, and he allowed photos.

Beck sighed.

Chase Connelly had a wife and a four-year-old daughter. Would it be justice to put his wife's husband and his daughter's father in prison? Heidi had looked twenty-five and sexy. She had stalked him. She had voluntarily gotten into his limo and drank alcohol, snorted cocaine, and had sex. She had intentionally used her body to get an audition in Hollywood. Heidi had used Chase as much as he had used her. They were two of a kind.

Except she had been sixteen, and he had been twenty-nine.

That was almost five years ago. Chase was thirty-four now. Maybe he had grown up. Maybe he had been a boy back then and was a man now. Maybe he was a loving father and a faithful husband.

Maybe not.

A stunning girl wearing a tight blue sweat suit walked over to Chase and gave him a full-body hug and a strong kiss on the lips. She was too young to be Chase's wife and too old to be his daughter. Beck thought Chase's wife and daughter would be better off without him.

Unlike in Chicago, golf courses in Texas remained open for play every day except Christmas. It was December 27 and sixty-eight degrees. Beck had walked into the clubhouse and found the golf pro on duty that day. He was middle-aged and a Notre Dame football fan; he remembered Beck Hardin. Beck gave him an autograph and he gave Beck the tee time just before Chase's. For a $300 green fee.

Beck drove his cart over to the first tee on the Foothills Course. It was a 460-yard par four from the pro tees. Beck figured Chase's ego for the pro tees. Beck wanted to catch Chase on the course, so he hit his tee shot and drove the cart to the ball sitting in the fairway. He hit his second shot to the green and putted out in two. He waited for Chase on the second tee box.

When Chase arrived, he was smoking a cigar and drinking beer. He walked over to Beck. He coughed into his hand, so Beck did not offer to shake hands. Instead Beck said, "I hate to play alone because I can't bet against myself. You a betting man?"

Chase said, "Hundred a hole with carryovers?"

"Works for me."

Beck nodded toward the girl in the cart and said, "Your wife?"

"A perk."

"Perk?"

"Perks of the trade—girls, limos, jets."

"You must have a good trade."

Chase gave him a funny look and said, "I'm Chase Connelly . . . the movie star."

"A movie star? No kidding? What brings you to Austin?"

"Celebrity golf tournament Saturday. Something about AIDS."

"Then back to L.A. Sunday?"

"Oh, yeah."

The second hole was a 381-yard par four. Beck stepped up on the tee box and drilled his drive down the center cut of the fairway. Chase drove his ball into the rough.

"Shit!"

Chase threw his cigar down, stormed to his cart, and drove off. Beck bent down, stabbed the cigar with a tee, and carried it over to his cart. He pulled out one of the baggies from his golf bag, placed the cigar inside, and zipped it shut. Chase's saliva on the cigar would make a nice DNA sample.

By the time they made the turn, Beck had collected Chase's cigar and beer can, and, from the way he was carrying on with the girl, Beck might soon have a semen sample. He thought about calling Wes in L.A. and asking how he had obtained the thong with Joe Raines' DNA, but decided against it.

Eight holes and Chase was in the hole $800. On the tenth tee box, he said, "Let's double the bet."

By the time they reached the eighteenth, a 560-yard par five, Chase owed Beck $2,500. Beck said, "Tell you what, Chase, what do you say we go double or nothing on this hole? You win, we're even. You lose, you owe me five grand."

He coughed and said, "Let's do it."

Chase swung like Babe Ruth swinging for the fences. The ball rocketed off the tee and soared into the blue sky—turning hard left all the way. A massive hook into the lake. Chase's face turned bright red. He raised his driver over his head and slammed the clubface down onto the rock tee marker with great force. The metal shaft split in two. Chase held onto the top half of the shaft, but the lower half ricocheted up and the driver head struck him solidly on the mouth. He yelped. And he bled.

"Shit!"

Chase coughed and spit blood. He cupped his mouth and blood dripped through his fingers. The girl came running with a small white towel. Chase grabbed the towel and covered his mouth. He stopped the bleeding, threw the towel down, and went over to his cart. He got in, guzzled his beer, then drove off.

Beck went to his cart, got the biggest baggie, and grabbed the scorecard pencil. He returned, squatted, and used the pencil to lift the towel from the ground and place it in the baggie. He flung the pencil into the brush next to the tee box and zipped the baggie locked.

He had Chase Connelly's blood. But he wouldn't have DNA

407

results before Chase left town. So Beck decided to ratchet up the pressure. Beck scored a par on the hole; Chase had a ten. They walked off the green and Beck said, "Five grand, Chase."

"Give me your card, I'll send you a check."

Beck pulled his card out of his wallet and handed it to Chase. He stared at it, then looked back at Beck.

"You're a judge?"

"Yep."

"Where's Gillespie County?"

"Out west of here."

"Never been there."

"Sure you have. Fredericksburg."

Chase's face changed. It was the same change Beck had seen in Luke's face when Beck told him his mother had died. Beck saw in his son's eyes the knowledge that his life had just changed for the worse. Beck saw the same knowledge in Chase's eyes.

"You called my wife."

Beck said, "New Year's Eve, 2002, you were here for the film festival. You picked up a blonde girl named Heidi Geisel on Sixth Street. She probably called herself Heidi Fay. You gave her alcohol and cocaine and you had sex with her. And then she died in your limo. She was a sixteen-year-old minor, you were a twenty-nine-year-old man. That's statutory rape. You're also guilty of murder or at least manslaughter, but your lawyer—the same one you had settle with Heidi's mother for twenty-five million—he'll tell you we won't be able to convict you on murder or manslaughter, and he's probably right. But we can convict you of stat rape. So don't make plans for the Oscars."

"You can't prove nothing."

"Sure I can. We've got your DNA from Heidi." Beck shook his head. "Haven't you heard about safe sex?"

Chase coughed and said, "You can't match that to me."

"Bet I can."

"I'm not giving you my DNA sample."

408

"You already have. Your cigar, your beer can, and your blood. I have that bloody towel, Chase. And I'm heading over to the DPS crime lab right now for DNA testing."

"You can't use those tests against me."

"What, you're a lawyer now? No, you're right, we can't use those tests to convict you, but we can use them to indict you. And then I'll issue a warrant for your arrest. I'll send it out to California, and the next day the L.A. cops will come to your house and handcuff you in front of your wife and daughter. They'll hand you over to the Gillespie County sheriff, and he'll fly you back here and drive you out to Gillespie County and throw you in his jail. You'll be convicted and sentenced to the maximum prison term. You ended Heidi's life. Now I'm fixing to end yours—at least your celebrity life."

Chase coughed and stumbled over to his cart. When he drove past, Beck said, "Enjoy your final days of freedom, Chase."

Beck hoped he wasn't bluffing. He had to get the bloody towel to the DPS crime lab, the lab had to complete the tests, and the Gillespie County grand jury had to indict Chase Connelly—all before midnight on New Year's Eve. Beck had four days.

He drove the cart to his car in the parking lot. He stowed his clubs and changed his shoes. He returned the cart to the clubhouse and noticed a black limo parked in the fire lane. A large Latino man was leaning against the limo and smoking a cigarette. He was bald, like the limo driver Carlotta had seen that night in Fredericksburg. The Gillespie County grand jury could indict Chase on eyewitness testimony even without a DNA match. Beck walked over.

"Rudy?"

The Hispanic man said, "I know you?"

Beck said, "I know you."

Rudy flicked his cigarette aside. "How's that?"

"I just played golf with Chase. He's a piece of work."

Rudy smiled. "If he was twice the actor he thinks he is, he wouldn't be worth a shit. But he's got the looks, and that's all it takes in Hollywood."

"He gets a lot of girls?"

Rudy chuckled. "You'd need a calculator to keep count." He shook his bald head. "He's got the world on a leash."

"Bet you could write a book."

Rudy shook his head again. "Confidentiality agreement."

"He pay you well for your confidentiality?"

"You offering me a job?"

"A chance."

Rudy frowned. "For what?"

"To stay out of prison."

Rudy went pale. "What are you talking about?"

"I'm talking about New Year's Eve five years ago, right here in Austin, you were driving when he picked up a blonde girl on Sixth Street. She died in your limo, Rudy."

"It was a rental."

"It was a hearse. You dumped her in that ditch, Rudy. And then you threw her black high heels into the river."

Beck had Rudy now.

"I found one of those shoes, Rudy. Thing is, Texas has been in a drought for seven years. So that river never flowed fast enough to wash those shoes downriver. I found one and the crime lab found your fingerprints on it. You've been in the system."

Beck was bluffing, but Rudy was nodding.

"Two strikes?"

Another nod.

"Three strikes and you're out. Rudy, once we match Chase's DNA to the sample from Heidi, we're going to indict him, try him, and send him to prison. Only question is, are you going to share a cell with him? Or are you going to play it smart, get immunity, and testify against him? You didn't give her the cocaine and you didn't have sex with her, but you're

410

an accomplice. And I'm the judge of Gillespie County, where you dumped her. I can give you immunity in exchange for your testimony."

"What would I have to do?"

"Testify before the grand jury. Tomorrow. Or Saturday."

"I'll think about it."

"You do that."

Beck handed his business card to Rudy. He walked over to the Navigator, then turned back. Rudy was staring at him. Beck pointed at Rudy then at himself and held his hand to his ear with his thumb and pinky pointed out like a telephone.

Beck dropped the bloody towel at the DPS crime lab and begged for expedited tests. He then drove over to the medical examiner's office. Dr. Janofsky met him at the front desk and led him back to the autopsy room. Beck had never witnessed an autopsy. Seeing Slade's massive body stretched out on the table and sliced open like a field-dressed deer, Beck got nauseous.

Dr. Janofsky said, "You don't look so good, Judge. Maybe we'd better step outside."

They did, and Beck splashed water from a fountain on his face. He followed the doctor to his office. Dr. Janofsky sat behind his desk and picked up two documents. He looked from one to the other.

"What is it, Doctor?"

"Test results."

"Slade's?"

He nodded. "And Heidi's."

"You ran more tests on her?"

"Just one. On the blood we saved from her. Judge, you said yesterday that Slade was the father of the baby she aborted?"

"Yeah."

"Are you sure about that?"

"Pretty sure. Why?"

Dr. Janofsky frowned. He placed both documents on the desk, pushed them across to Beck, and pointed.

It was after five when Beck drove through the black iron gate at the Hardin homestead. He drove up the caliche road toward the house, steering hard left then right then left. He hit the brakes. From that spot in the road, he could see the baseball field. Luke was batting, J.B. was pitching, and Libby and Jodie were shagging balls in the outfield. Meggie and the doll and Frank the goat were sitting in the bleachers behind the batting cage. Annie's dream had come true.

Chapter 41

The next morning, Grady said, "You really think the limo driver will call?"

"Yes, I do."

The D.A. said, "I'll convene the grand jury Saturday."

Mavis stuck her head in the door. "Judge, there's a call for you on line one. Someone named Rudy."

Beck said, "Bingo," then hit the speakerphone. "Rudy."

"Judge, I'm coming to see you. Tomorrow, while Chase is in the tournament. I'll be there about noon. I'll testify, but I want complete immunity. You get that done today and fax it to my lawyer in L.A."

Grady shook his head and whispered, "A goddamn limo driver's got a lawyer."

Rudy said, "And I've got evidence."

Beck said, "What kind of evidence?"

"The girl's cell phone. With a photo of her and Chase in the limo that night."

"Bring it. And give me your cell phone number, Rudy."

He did and they hung up. Beck said, "We got him. Chase Connelly killed Heidi. And now we can prove it."

The D.A. was all smiles.

Chapter 42

Noon came and went on Saturday, December 29, but Rudy Jaramillo didn't show. "He stood you up, Beck," Grady said.

"I've had the grand jury upstairs for three hours," the D.A. said. "I've got to let them go."

"Let me try his number again."

Beck used the speakerphone and dialed Rudy's cell phone number. He answered.

"Rudy?"

"No, Judge, it's Chase. Rudy's unavailable."

"You killed him."

Chase laughed. "*Killed him?* Judge, you've been watching too many of my movies. I gave him a paid vacation to Acapulco. He took my jet. It was a retirement gift. He won't be testifying before your grand jury."

"He has evidence, Chase."

"You mean the girl's cell phone that I bought from him for a million dollars?" Chase laughed. "Sorry, Judge, you lose."

"I haven't lost yet, Chase. I've still got your blood."

"Yeah, but you don't have the results yet or we wouldn't be talking. And my lawyer says you've got no shot at murder or manslaughter, or even delivery of drugs to a minor. Like you said, your only shot is stat rape, and for that to work, you've got to get the DNA results, they've got to match, and the grand jury's got to indict me by midnight on New Year's Eve or you can't touch me. You've got two days, Judge, and tomorrow's Sunday."

"You're rolling the dice, Chase."

"I'm a betting man, I told you that."

"I hope your luck is better than your golf game."

"I shot an eight-four today. See you at the movies, Judge."

Chase coughed and hung up.

Grady said, "That boy is one country-sized prick."

The D.A. said, "Beck, if you don't get those test results in the next, what? . . . fifty-seven hours? . . . then I don't get to try a movie star for stat rape, I don't get national publicity, and I don't get into the Governor's Mansion. And you don't get to be judge after next election. I do."

He walked out and Grady said, " 'Course, Chase has got stiff competition for prick of the year."

Beck went home and spent the day with the children. At ten that night, after everyone else was asleep, he walked down to the winery. He turned on the computer and read Annie's words again. The tears came and he closed his eyes. He opened them when he heard a noise. Rudy Jaramillo was standing in the door. He was holding a gun. Beck's adrenaline kicked in and his heartbeat kicked up, but he tried to act calm.

"Rudy, you're not going to get immunity if you kill the judge."

"I'd rather have the money."

"I thought Chase sent you to Mexico?"

"He thinks that, too."

"You're freelancing?"

"I make my own career decisions."

"Well, Rudy, this is not a smart career move."

415

"Way I figure, if you're out of the way, I can go forward with my retirement plan."

"What retirement plan?"

"That photo's gonna pay me a million a year for life."

"Blackmailing Chase?"

Rudy nodded his big bald head.

"He said he bought that photo."

"I kept a copy. Chase, he ain't so bright."

"So you kill me and extort Chase?"

"That has a nice ring to it, don't it?"

"Getting rid of me won't fix the problem, Rudy. That DNA sample over in Austin at the DPS lab, that's the problem. And that doesn't go away with me."

"I think it will."

"Thinking can be a dangerous thing for a man like you."

"We'll see."

Beck said, "Aubrey, don't hit him too hard. That bung hammer weighs five pounds."

Rudy laughed. "What, I'm supposed to look behind me, so you can jump me, like in the movies?"

"No, you're supposed to stand real still while Aubrey whacks you in the head."

Which is exactly what Aubrey did. The five-pound cast-iron head of the bung hammer impacted Rudy just above his right ear and produced a sickening thud. Rudy's big body crumpled and dropped to the floor. Beck stood and kicked the gun away.

Aubrey was holding the bung hammer in one hand and a beer in the other. He said, "Dang near spilled my beer." He stepped over Rudy. "Heard you talking. Saw this hammer hanging on the wall. Figured it'd do. I hit him pretty hard, Beck."

"Yeah."

Rudy's big body lay motionless. Blood was flowing from his right ear. Beck squatted over Rudy and checked his pulse; he found none. He called Grady at home and told him that Rudy

416

had shown up after all and that he was dead. Grady said he was on his way. Beck and Aubrey sat on the couch. Aubrey said, "Am I in trouble?"

"Not for this. Defense of a third-party. But you've got to quit."

"Hitting people with a bung hammer?"

"Coaching."

Aubrey stared at his beer. "Coaching's all I know, Beck." He gestured with the bung hammer at Rudy. "Don't this count for something?"

"Yes, it does. Thanks for saving my life, Aubrey."

It was after midnight by the time Grady had come and gone with Rudy's body. Beck sat at the desk and dialed the number of Rudy's cell phone. Chase answered.

"Hello, Judge."

"Rudy's dead."

"In Mexico?"

"In my father's office."

"He knew your father?"

"No. He tracked me to my father's winery."

"Your father's got a winery?"

"Yes. He tried to kill me."

"Your father?"

"No. Rudy. Rudy tried to kill me."

"Why?"

"So he could use the photo to blackmail you."

"But I bought the photo from him."

"He kept a copy."

A sigh on the phone. "You can't trust anyone these days."

"Chase?"

"Yeah?"

"I'm gonna get you."

Chase Connelly hung up.

Chapter 43

"I've got to have those test results by midnight!"

Beck had called the DPS crime lab every hour on the hour all day and night Sunday, December 30. No one answered. He made his first call on Monday, New Year's Eve, at eight A.M. He left a message. He left another message at nine, ten, and eleven. It was now noon. He had exactly twelve hours to indict Chase Connelly.

Sitting across his desk were Grady and the D.A. Niels Eichman said, "Beck, I have the grand jury on standby, but I'm not calling them in until those test results come in. They're going to fax them over?"

Beck nodded. "They said expedited was four weeks. I gave them four days."

"So we don't know if they'll have results today or a month from today?" the D.A. said.

"They're working on it. Last time I talked to them, they said they were having problems testing Chase's sample, said they had to use more sophisticated testing."

Grady said, "That don't sound good."

The D.A.: "Why?"

Beck shook his head. "They said they can run DNA tests only on white blood cells."

"So?"

"So I don't know. That's all they said."

Grady said, "That don't sound good."

The cleaning lady arrived at six P.M. She was a stocky white woman named Gertie. Carlotta had been deported in the ICE raid.

Aubrey arrived at seven P.M. He just walked in and sat in the chair in the corner. For the next four and half hours, they waited for the fax machine to ring. Ten times Aubrey walked over to the fax to check that it was plugged in and operational. But the fax never rang. At 11:35 P.M., Beck called the lab again. There was no answer. Beck looked at Aubrey in the corner.

"It's not going to happen, Aubrey. I'm sorry."

"We've still got twenty-five minutes."

"We've got twenty-five minutes to get the results and indict."

"The grand jury still upstairs?"

Beck nodded. The D.A. had convened the grand jury at nine on New Year's Eve. The twelve citizens were growing restless, but they had come in because Heidi had been the coach's daughter.

Aubrey said, "I need to know the truth about Heidi."

"Aubrey, the truth is that Heidi was your daughter and you loved her."

"Tell me what you know, Beck. Everything."

"I've told you all I'm going to tell you."

"I'm entitled, Beck."

"No, you're not. You asked me to do this, and I did it for you because of what I did to you—"

"And to get some answers, for Meggie."

"Yeah, that too. Aubrey, you asked me to get justice for her, and I tried. I know things about you and Randi and Heidi I don't want to know. But I'm the judge and you came

419

to me for justice. So I know. And I have to live with it. You don't."

"I can handle it."

"No, you can't."

"Please, Beck."

Aubrey appeared on the verge of crying.

"I'll tell you one thing: forget about Randi. You don't want her back."

"Why not?"

"Just trust me. You don't want her back. And Aubrey, don't ever ask me again about this case. If that fax doesn't ring, this case ends at midnight."

It ended at midnight.

The grand jury left, the D.A. left, and then the sheriff left. Aubrey did not leave, so Beck said, "Go home, Aubrey. Or go to church. But this is a courthouse, I'm the judge, and the law has done all it can do."

Aubrey stood to leave.

Beck said, "What are you going to do?"

"Go home. I don't go to church no more."

"No. About coaching."

"I don't know."

"Aubrey, let's not see each other again until you decide."

"But, Beck . . . you and J.B. and the kids, y'all are the only family I got now."

"I know."

Aubrey walked out, and Beck leaned his head back. He closed his eyes. Grady was right: he had learned more about the people in this town than he wanted to know.

The fax machine rang.

Beck opened his eyes and glanced at the clock: 12:57 A.M. He had fallen asleep. The fax spat out two sheets of paper. Beck stood and stepped over to the machine. He picked up the pages and read the test results: Chase Connelly's DNA matched the DNA taken from Heidi's body. He was the guy.

He read the entire report and felt depressed. Fax in hand, he walked out of his chambers and climbed the spiral staircase to the second-floor courtroom. The Christmas lights at the Markt-platz across Main Street lit the room sufficiently, so he didn't turn the lights on. He sat behind the bench. He felt tired. There would be no justice for Heidi Fay Geisel.

"You must really like your job."

Beck jumped. Standing at the entrance to the courtroom was Chase Connelly.

Chase coughed and said, "Working this late on New Year's Eve, you must like being a judge." Chase walked slowly up the center aisle and glanced around at the courtroom. "You know, I'm reading a script right now, a legal thriller. The hero's a lawyer in a big law firm who uncovers a secret, the law firm hiding some kind of environmental disaster their rich client caused. He decides to go public, so the bad guys chase him. He's running, fighting, shooting —'Rambo Goes to Law School' or something like that."

"There's not a lot of gunfire in a corporate law firm."

"Except in the movies." He glanced around. "So where does the accused sit? Up here?"

Chase climbed into the jury box and sat.

"That's for the jurors. What do you want, Chase?"

"I want to know if I should take that role."

"How would I know if you should star in some movie?"

"Because you get to decide my next role: Rambo lawyer or prison inmate. Which is it, Judge?"

"Neither."

"I didn't finish college, Judge. You'll have to explain that. Am I going to prison?"

"No, Chase, you're not going to prison. You did it and we know it, but the DNA results came in too late. The statute of limitations ran at midnight."

"So there's nothing you can do to me?"

"There's nothing the law can do to you."

"Guess I'll take that role then." He coughed.

"Why'd you come out here, Chase?"

"Because I didn't want my daughter to see me getting arrested. I figured if it was going to happen, might as well happen here. Guess I made the trip for nothing." The weight of the world seemed to lift from Chase Connelly. "Hey, Judge, how about some free legal advice?"

"What's that?"

"Do I still have to pay the mother? I mean, twenty-five million, that's a pretty steep price for a perk."

"Chase, the price you paid was a lot higher than that. The law can't touch you now, but life can. It already has."

Chase stood and smiled like a movie star. "I like my life, Judge. A lot more now. Damn, I feel like a new man."

"Don't take that role, Chase, you won't finish it."

"Why not?"

"Because you're not a new man, Chase. You're a dead man." The smile left Chase's face.

"Is that a threat, Judge?"

"No, Chase, it's a medical fact. You've got AIDS."

"Bullshit."

"Your blood samples, Chase. DNA tests on blood are run on white blood cells—red blood cells don't contain DNA. That's why your tests took so long—the lab had to run extra DNA tests because you've got almost no white blood cells. Then they ran an AIDS test. The lab tech wrote on the report, 'If this guy catches a cold, he's a dead man.' How long have you had that cough?"

"A month."

"Have you lost weight?"

"Fifteen pounds."

Beck sighed. "You killed her and she killed you."

"What do you mean?"

"Heidi was HIV positive. You gave her cocaine, she gave you AIDS."

"That bitch!"

Chase fell into the juror's chair and put his hands on the railing and his face in his hands.

"Oh, God."

Dr. Janofsky's tests on Heidi's and Slade's blood had revealed that both were HIV positive. Beck figured that Slade had contracted the disease from shooting steroids with dirty needles at those Austin gyms. Then he had infected Heidi. And she had infected Chase Connelly.

Chase's face turned up to Beck. He was crying.

"What am I supposed to do now, Judge?"

"Go home, Chase. Go home to your wife and daughter."

Beck went home to his wife. He read her last emails.

My dearest J.B.,

Julie is with me. She gives me morphine. It feels so good. Better than a bottle of wine. Beck is with me, too. All the time now. I try to act brave for him, but I'm not. I'm so afraid.

One last favor, J.B. Please don't let Beck make your mistake. Encourage him to let another woman in his life when the time is right, someone who loves him and my children. He will think he can't fall in love again, but he can, he will, and he should. He kept his vows to me, and now I release him from those vows. I want him to love and be loved again.

Love, Annie

A final secret: Annie had appeared so brave in the face of death, but she had been afraid. Beck turned off the computer. He finally knew his wife, thirteen years after he had married her and a year after she had died. She had been right on so many things about him, but she had been wrong on one thing: Beck Hardin would always love only a dead woman.

Chapter 44

"Hi, Judge Hardin!"

Beck waved at the Main Street business owner. Downtown was quiet. January was the slowest month of the year; all the credit cards from Christmas shopping came due in January.

"Judge!"

Beck waved. Everyone knew the judge in a small town, and the judge knew them. He knew too much. Beck didn't want to be their judge anymore. This town wasn't good enough for its judge and he wasn't a good enough judge for this town.

"Judge Hardin!"

Beck waved absentmindedly but then spotted Kim Krause waving at him from across the street. He waited while she darted across Main Street. She had an armload of books.

"Hi, Kim."

"Hi, Judge. I like your shirt. Scary, but not as scary as those suits."

Beck was wearing the Hawaiian print shirt Jodie had given him for Christmas, jeans, and his new cowboy boots.

"Judge, I just wanted you to know, I'm taking those computer courses, over at the community college."

"Good."

"And I deleted our nude photos, mine and Heidi's."

"Better."

She grabbed his sleeve and pulled him down and kissed him on the cheek. When she pulled back, she had tears in her eyes.

"I miss her. Heidi."

"I know you do."

"Thanks, Judge."

"Good luck, Kim."

She walked east and Beck walked west. He had left this town without a mother and had returned without a wife. He had changed and his hometown had changed. He was a different man living a different life. It wasn't the life he had dreamed of, but it was the life he had. And he had his children.

"Judge Hardin!"

He again snapped out of his thoughts and saw Julio Espinoza and Nikki Ernst walking toward him. When they arrived, he said, "Julio, Nikki. How are you kids doing?"

Nikki said, "Great."

"How's it going at school?"

Julio said, "It is quiet. The Latinos are gone. And I will be gone soon, too."

"You going to UT?"

"No. To Rice. I am paying my own way."

Nikki said, "Me, too."

"Are you guys . . ."

"Dating? Yes, Judge, we are."

"What'd your parents say, Nikki?"

"About Julio or Rice?"

"Both."

"They had a cow. Or I should say, a goat. But they'll get over it—in twenty or thirty years."

"Nikki, can I talk to you . . . privately?"

Beck stepped away from Julio a few paces. Nikki followed.

"We'll be just a minute, Julio."

Nikki said, "What is it, Judge?"

Beck whispered, "Nikki, Slade's autopsy showed he was HIV positive."

She said nothing.

"Nikki?"

She sat down on a bench. Beck sat next to her. She stared at the sidewalk.

"You should get tested, Nikki."

She shook her head slowly. "We never had sex. Of any kind."

"You knew?"

"I thought. When he told me those other guys at the gyms had injected him, I knew that wasn't good. I told him to get an AIDS test, but he wouldn't. So I wouldn't." She sighed. "You know, underneath all that football star façade, he was a good guy. But his father pushed him so hard, and the steroids changed him." She was crying now. She leaned her face into his chest.

"Stay on your track in life, Nikki."

When she sat up, she wiped her face and said, "Judge, thanks for keeping me on track, that day in court."

They stood and returned to Julio. Beck said, "How are your folks doing?"

Julio smiled. "They are doing well. My father, he is building rock full-time with Señor Gil. He is very happy."

Beck had introduced Rafael Espinoza to Gil Johnson. Rafael had invested $500,000 in a new rock works venture with Gil, which entitled him and Maria to a green card. The Feds call it "Green Card Through Investment." Everyone else calls it "Citizenship for Sale." Thanks to Quentin McQuade's money, Rafael and Maria Espinoza were able to buy their way back into America.

"Good. How's your mother?"

"She is pregnant, so she is happy also. *Mi madre*, she says it is all because of you. She says you are the good judge."

★   ★   ★

427

The law is found in statutes and codes and rules and regulations. But wisdom can't be found in a law book. Wisdom is found in life. In death. And every day in between. And justice isn't found in a courtroom; it's found in the human heart.

"Judge, you got a minute?"

Standing in the door to his chambers were Earl Danz and his ex-wife, Lynnette. They were holding hands. Beck stood.

"Earl, Lynnette . . . come in."

"Judge," Earl said, "we'd appreciate it if you'd marry us up again."

"*Marry you?*"

Lynnette said, "We made a mistake, Judge, getting divorced. We'd like for you to fix that. Before we fly to Hawaii."

Fifteen minutes later, with Mavis as the witness, Judge Beck Hardin had performed his first marriage. When Mr. and Mrs. Danz turned and walked out the door, Beck could have sworn Lynnette was wearing a thong under her slacks. Mavis was wiping her eyes. Beck gave her an "I told you so" look.

She said, "Don't get cocky with me."

An hour later, Beck was sitting in his lawn chair on the balcony outside his courtroom; his new black cowboy boots were resting on the railing. The oak trees were bare, but the temperature was almost seventy, an Indian summer day in January in the Texas Hill Country. He was reading the first newspaper of the new year. On the front page was a photo of the first new baby of the year. Her name was Esperanza Peña.

"Mavis said you were up here."

Sheriff Grady Guenther ducked through the window. He pulled out the other lawn chair and sat.

"Nice day."

"Yep."

"You ain't figuring on quittin', are you, Beck?"

"Thought about it."

428

"Hope you don't. I like working with you."

"Same here, Grady."

"So, did you hear the news?"

"What news?"

"Quentin shut down his development and left town. Moved back to Austin. Put everything he has here up for sale."

"No kidding? So all those mansions around his golf course won't be built?"

"Nope."

"What's going to happen with the golf course?"

"He closed it down. I drove out there this morning. Goats were grazing on the eighteenth fairway."

"Well, at least things will quiet down now."

"Don't bet the ranch on it. Word is, Quentin's gonna sell all that land to some Muslims. They want to build a mosque." Grady stood and started to climb back through the window but stopped and said, "Oh, J.B.'s in my jail."

"*What?*"

"He punched Bruno."

"Where?"

"In the nose."

"No. Where did he punch him?"

"Oh. Downstairs."

"What was he doing here?"

"He followed Bruno in."

"What was Bruno doing here?"

"Mavis said he was filing suit against Quentin. Said Quentin stiffed him out of six months' pay. Bet he's gonna have a tough time winning that case."

"You think?"

"Yep, I think."

"What did Bruno do when J.B. punched him?"

"Went down like a sack of potatoes, way I heard. Said he was gonna get up and kick J.B.'s ass."

"What'd J.B. say?"

429

"Said, 'That'll be the day.'"

Beck laughed. "Tell J.B. I'll come over and bail him out . . . in an hour or two. Guess I'll have to sentence him to community service."

"Punching Bruno, that was a community service."

Grady had left but Beck hadn't moved from the lawn chair when Jodie poked her head out ten minutes later.

"Mavis said you were up here." She sat and said, "Nice boots . . . and shirt."

"Thanks, for the shirt and for helping me with the kids the last six months. I wouldn't have made it without you."

"Y'all are doing better?"

"Meggie hasn't wet the bed in two weeks. And Luke and I, we talk now."

"Good."

They sat silently for a while, then Jodie said, "Are you moving back to Chicago?"

"I've thought about it. But the kids seem happy here . . . and they've bonded with J.B. And he's bonded with them. I'm just not sure I belong here anymore."

"Beck, most people spend their lives searching for where they belong. I know I belong here. It's not a perfect town, but no town is. But it's a good town and it's my town. I'm here and I'm staying and I'm going to fight to make my town better. You belong here, too. In this town and in this courthouse. It's a better town with you as our judge."

Beck thought about her words.

"J.B. said it's not the town, it's just a few old-timers in the town who are afraid of change. He's right. He's right about most things. Yeah, Jodie Lee, I'm staying." Beck checked his watch. "That reminds me, I've got to bail J.B. out of jail."

"J.B.'s in jail?"

"He punched Stutz in the nose."

She smiled. "I love J.B."

"He loves you. Says he wishes he were younger, says he'd marry you even if you are a lesbian."

"That's sweet . . . I think."

"Annie knew my secretary bought all her presents."

"You mean like, birthday and Christmas? From you?"

Beck nodded.

"Not good."

"I thought I was too busy to do it myself. I wish I could go back and do it all over again. I'd do it right this time."

They sat silently, and Beck thought of his dead wife and his new life that she had known he would have before he did. He had to leave J.B. to know the father he had been, and his wife had to die for him to know the woman she had been.

"Gretchen came into the store," Jodie said. "She asked about you."

"Did she mention her needs?"

That look. "No."

Beck chuckled. "Well, I don't think it would've worked with Gretchen. But I'm glad she's Meggie's teacher."

"Annie wouldn't have wanted you to be alone."

"You want me to date Gretchen?"

"No. But I don't want you to be alone. Beck, you need a woman."

Beck reached over and patted her knee. "Well, Janelle's already got the best woman in town."

Jodie slapped her hands on her knees and abruptly stood as if he had said something wrong. He looked up at her; she was looking down at him with a funny expression.

"No, she doesn't. She's dating a widower down in Comfort."

"She's cheating on you? With a man?"

Jodie rolled her eyes. "Oh, for God's sake, for a smart man you can really be dense sometimes."

"What?"

She took a deep breath and exhaled like an athlete about to perform her event. Then in one quick movement she bent

431

down, grabbed his face, and kissed him full on the lips. She stood straight and said, "I'm forty years old, I'm a crazy liberal, and I love you, Beck Hardin."

She ducked through the window and was down the spiral staircase before he could recover: he had never been kissed by a lesbian.

He stood and went to the railing. When Jodie appeared on the sidewalk below, he called out to her.

"Jodie!"

She stopped, paused a second, then turned to face him.

"But you're a lesbian!"

Several passersby stopped dead in their tracks and looked up at Beck, then at Jodie. They shook their heads and walked on.

"That's what *they* said, Beck. I never said that."

Now that he thought about it, she never had said that.

"Why?"

"Why what?"

"Why'd you let everyone think you're a lesbian?"

"So every lonely goat rancher in the county wouldn't come into my bookstore looking for a wife."

She had a point.

"Why didn't you tell me?"

"I wanted us to be friends first."

They now stared at each other; it was an awkward moment, so she turned away and walked fast down the sidewalk—but she stopped at the Eagle Tree. She stood there a long moment like she was admiring the sculpture. Then she whirled around and marched back toward Beck. She stood directly below the balcony and looked up at him. The breeze blew her red hair across her face.

"I have needs too, Beck. I'm going back to the bookstore. I'm closing at five. If you want to tend to my needs, come on down. If you don't, we'll always be friends."

She turned and walked away and didn't stop this time. Beck

watched her all the way down Main Street until she disappeared around the corner. Beck plopped down into the lawn chair.

Tending to needs. With the town lesbian. Who wasn't.

I'll be damned.

Epilogue

On the first anniversary of her death, Beck reburied his wife in the Hardin family cemetery next to his mother. They would have enjoyed each other's company.

It was just the Hardins in attendance—J.B., Beck, Luke, Meggie, her doll, and Frank the goat. After J.B. and Beck lowered Annie's coffin into the natural limestone vault, J.B. said what a fine woman Annie had been and that he had been proud to know her, such as he did. He promised to help her children until he joined her and Peggy. Beck then said, "Annie, I should have brought you here before, but I've brought you here now. In a few months, these fields will be covered in bluebonnets as blue as your eyes. I think you'll like them. I think you'll like the Hill Country. Happy birthday."

He wiped his face and turned away, but stopped when Luke stepped forward and said, "It's not fair."

Beck said, "No, son, it's not. It's not fair at all."

Beck put his arm around his son. Tears were sliding down the boy's face when he said, "Mom, I'm going to make you cheer again."

Beck put his other arm around Meggie. She said in the tiniest voice, "Mommy's not coming back, is she?"

"No, honey, she's not."

Meggie stepped forward, kissed the doll, and placed it on top of her mother's coffin. Beck glanced over at J.B., who was trying not to cry but failing. He nodded at his father: Frank the goat had done the trick after all. Beck turned and saw Aubrey standing just outside the white picket fence. He said, "I quit today."

Beck nodded at his old friend. J.B. said, "Kids, let's walk up to the house, give your daddy a few minutes alone." J.B. stepped through the gate, Meggie under one arm and Luke under the other, and Frank following behind. J.B. slapped Aubrey on the shoulder and said, "Aubrey, you know anything about wine?"

The four of them walked up to the house. Beck sat alone on the bench and talked to Annie until the shadows grew long. He promised her that he would raise the children like she would have. He promised to fight for their children every day so neither of them ended up in a ditch. And he promised to love her until the day he died.

Then he went down to the river and sat on his rock.

Twenty-four years before, he had run away from his life here, and now he had come back. Beck Hardin was home. He had come home hoping to find justice in this life. To live where life followed a code of right and wrong. It didn't. Not here, not in Chicago, not anywhere. Good people die young and bad people live long. Life isn't fair, and justice isn't found in this life; in this life we only have the law. And the law has judges.

He stood and walked over to the natural rock bridge and stepped from rock to rock until he was at the midpoint of the river. The last light of day glistened on the water. He found a small flat rock and threw it low and watched it skip across the glassy surface of the river then disappear from sight. He watched the ripples spread out and die.

Ripples in the river.